Praise for *The Refusal*, Book 1 in the Te

D1581397

—

"Have you ever found yourself reading a really exceptional book and you find that you're forcing yourself to slow down on your reading because you simply don't want the book to end? That's exactly how I felt with Eve's debut novel." - **Shannon Kuhn, Writer and ARC Reviewer**

"I loved, loved, loved it! Jo and Janus have captured my heart. Definitely in my top 5 romance novels! I can't wait to see what comes next in the series. Eve M. Riley may be a debut author but she's right up there with the great romance authors. This book is a definite must read!" - **Clare Murphy, Romance Author**

"Let's all take a moment of silence now that I've finished this book and it's truly over until book two is released." - **Beauty and The Book, Book Blogger**

"I loved this book. I finished it in one day because I couldn't put it down." - **All the Romance, Book Blog.**

"I have to say, first of all, DAMN! This book was sensational!" - **Pride Prejudice and Pups, Goodreads Reviewer**

"Reading this book is like watching a really great romance film, with substance. The author writes with such energy and heart, the story ends way too soon . . . If you read one romance novel this year, make it The Refusal by Eve M. Riley." - **Readers Views, Book Awards**

"Run, do not walk, to your nearest retailer/ computer and get this book. Yes, it's that good. I'm not sure what else to say other than "devoured," "book hang-over," "amazing," and "need more." Did you get it yet? What? Not into tech heroes? Don't usually do modern romance? Listen, great writing is great writing--trust me, you'll be swept away." - **Nicole Wells, Romance Author**

"I barely even know how to send an email (lol). BUT-I loved ALL of it: the slow burn, the characters, the way the relationships developed." - **Bookish in Town, Book Blog**

THE REFUSAL

EVE M. RILEY

THE **TECHBOYS** *SERIES*

1

EVEMRILEY.COM

For Rob, my very own Techboy.

CHAPTER 1

Jo

I smooth my hands over the bun pulled tight on the top of my head and examine my shirt for bits of breakfast. The atrium of this downtown building is beautiful: drooping palms, huge windows, and sun slanting across the pale marble floor. Looking up, I watch the numbers tick down on the elevator board above my head and shift the band of my suit around my waist, curling my toes to ease the tightness of my heels. Why would anyone wear clothes like this normally? I glance over at the receptionist's steel-gray two-piece and sharp green glasses. *Imagine dressing like this every day.*

Hmmm. Maybe crazy hipster would have been a better choice than "cool executive" for this meeting? They'll probably all be rocking some techy vibe: ripped jeans and rock-band T-shirts. This is Janus Industries, after all. I straighten my spine. Why give them what they expect? I've stood out all my life—no point in switching tracks now, no matter how big the company. And with that thought, I can almost taste my father's exasperation.

Janus Industries. I still can't believe they called me. Why in the world would one of the best-known tech companies in New York give a security contract to a fish out of water like me? It's not like we're well known in the security industry.

I stare at my reflection in the glass doors of the elevator, chewing on a nail. Then movement catches the corner of my eye, and as I glance across the polished floor to my right, my whole body locks tight.

Oh.

My.

God.

Turning back, I open my mouth, bending forward a little to try and suck in air. A reflection appears alongside mine, and just like that I'm a foot away from Janus Phillips, tapping his hand against his leg in some fast rhythm, staring up at the board, fidgeting with a leather strap on his wrist. Slowly, I turn around to find he's already watching me, and a huge smile breaks across his face as two dimples pop out.

And, *my God*, he looks better than his pictures: messy dark hair in a crazy tousle on his head, thick eyelashes around deep brown eyes, and a grin that is so lopsided that one side of his mouth is much higher than the other. How is it even possible that someone's mouth could do that?

My lips are stuck together, breath still stuck in my nose. His jaw has this shadow that … He coughs, raising an eyebrow.

Shit.

Caught.

Staring.

Heat climbs up my neck as my eyes dart back to the elevator. My damn skin will be covering itself in blotchy red patches. Ugh. I try and unobtrusively expand my chest. *Calm, Jo.* Why can't I just say "Hi!" like a normal person? Would that be too challenging? I peek at him out of the corner of my eye. Would this meeting be worrying enough to go right up to the top? To *him*? My God, this huge company and it's *his.* He's thirty-one and looking after the data of some of the biggest organizations in the world.

Some cool designer jeans hang so low on his hips that the waistband of his boxers is visible, and I almost laugh when I catch a glimpse of a faded rock band logo on the front of his T-shirt. At least he's not wearing one of those 'OMG The Element of Surprise' T-shirts: I am so done with software guys who think *that's* funny. He's cute, but he *must* know that, *surely*?

And if the gossip columns are anything to go by, his type isn't nerdy tech girls like me, just lots and lots of blonde models—he's always out and about on the arm of some gorgeous girl or other. I'm sure he's got an ego the size of a planet. Given how tiny and flat-chested I am, I can guarantee I will be of no interest to someone like him.

As I glance back at the status board over our heads, my right arm feels like it's on fire. Thank God, the elevator is only two floors away. The silence is crushing until, without warning, the elevator gives a loud ping, and I jerk forward; almost colliding with the doors as they open. Dear God, how blotchy must I be *now*? I'm probably matching my hair color.

"Easy now."

The slightly condescending tilt to his tone lights a fire in me. He's *patronizing* me? He's right on my heels as I move inside and press the button for my floor.

"I'm sorry, but I'm not sure I've seen you around before—do you work in marketing?" he says.

His voice is all friendly, warm and deep. And, as I turn to face him, the monkey on my shoulder decides to wake up and have some fun. No one patronizes me and gets away with it. This desire to poke the bear drove my dad round the bend: he was forever being called into school to "talk about his daughter."

"Oh no." I purse my lips. "I'm here for a meeting."

He nods at me in that way people do when they're waiting for you to say more. I'll bet he expects me to know who he is. I'll bet women normally fawn all over him. Smiling, I turn away, desperately hoping the floor will come before I'm obliged to tell him anything else. A ticking silence sits over us, and he clears his throat.

"What company are you from?"

Bingo. Curiosity killed the cat, Mr. Phillips. Turning right around to grin at him, I have to stop myself from doing a little victory dance at the somewhat bemused expression on his face.

"Oh, I'm a freelance contractor." I'm not directly lying here, right? "What are *you* here for?" My smile is like saccharin.

Janus's eyes widen slightly, and he runs a distracted hand through his unruly brown mop, making it stick up at crazy angles. I stare at it in fascination. Is there *gel* in it? His hand drifts down his chest in the ensuing silence, and I track his long slim fingers, the square-trimmed nails.

"Oh, yeah, um, I work here?"

Oh, *very* interesting. *Not* the response I'd expect from someone whose ego has to be as big as a planet. I thought he'd say he was Janus Phillips and give me a knowing smirk. *Where's all the arrogance?*

"Oh, nice." I bob my head like a nodding dog. "It must be terrific to have a job here." I lean forward and lower my voice. "I've heard that Janus Phillips is so cool to work for. A friend of mine knows him and told me he was a peach." I tilt my head, trying not to laugh. What is coming out of my *mouth*? Janus's jaw drops and redness starts at the bottom of his neck; it makes me want to turn the screw a little more. "Have you *met* him?" I breathe.

He examines the floor for a while, and when his gaze comes back to mine, I'm taken aback by the crinkles around the corners of his eyes, the conspiratorial gleam.

"I've had a few meetings with him," he murmurs, and his eyes sweep over my hair and cheeks, coming to rest on my lips.

My heart gives a funny little stutter as I stare at him. What am I *doing*? He's … He's … Well, I'm not sure what his game is actually, but I am messing with him, and he probably chases anything in a skirt. The heat in my face feels like a furnace. He'll think I am some airhead who doesn't realize who he is, and, despite everything, I want this contract; doing Janus Industries security would put my little tech consultancy on the map. I wouldn't come to a meeting and not suss out the Chief Executive, now, would I? And here I am with my daft sense of humor about to completely screw it all up by playing some crazy game with the guy who is probably going to make the decision about whether to use my company or not. Ugh. *Idiot, Jo.* I'm opening my mouth to say God knows what—but I'm hoping an apology will leak out somewhere—when we judder to a halt, and, before either of us can say anything, the doors separate with a loud ping.

Janus shifts around me, giving me a half smile, which only makes everything worse, before he steps out of the elevator.

"Great to meet you, um … I didn't get your name …?" he says.

"Look I'm sorry—" I start as the doors begin to close. I search frantically for the stop button, but before my hand can get to it, I'm being whisked up to the twentieth floor and my meeting.

*

The small reception desk on the twentieth floor is all illuminated glass in bright triangles, and I chew the side of my nail, sweat trickling down my spine. The office stretches out before me like an aircraft hangar, giving an unrestricted view right across the partitions to the other side of the building. Colored glass walls cut through the space interspersed with gray steel pillars, bright carpets marking out the walkways between the workspaces. You'd need sunglasses to look at the lime-colored sofa in the reception area. *Wow.* The vibe up here couldn't be more different from the atrium downstairs, and I would give my right arm for an office like this.

But all this overt trendiness is not helping. Did I really just try to wind up the CEO of *this* place in his own elevator? What is it with me and winding people up? I need to find him and apologize.

My phone buzzes in my hand. Nora. Why is my finance person calling me now?

"Nora?"

"Hey, Jo, I'm sorry to call but, um, we've got a cashflow problem."

What? "How much is in the account?"

"About ten thousand dollars." Her hollow voice echoes through my phone.

My God. Payroll is way beyond that.

"I'm sorry but the rent had to go out on Friday. Payroll this month is *forty* thousand, Jo."

I don't say I know this. I don't say anything. The bright colors of the office blare out at me, success oozing from every pore. I feel like an ant. A very poor ant.

"What's the situation with the Caltech money?"

"I'm chasing it, but they said three weeks at the *earliest.*"

Oh, *God.* The bank won't lend me a cent—I've been down that road before.

I lower my voice to a whisper and pace a few steps away from the reception desk. "Look into credit cards, Nora, see if we can borrow anything," I say.

She makes a noise like she's been crushed under someone's heel, and I don't blame her. Cards are a terrible idea, but what options do I have? I'm hanging on by my fingernails here.

"Sorry, I know that's a rubbish idea, but it's all I have right now. I've got to go and do this presentation."

"Sorry, Jo, and good luck! Fingers crossed. It could sort all our problems."

Yeah. Right. I hang up and slide my phone into my pocket. Do unicorns work with ants? Or do they just trample them underfoot?

I scan the receptionist's oversized plaid shirt, lip piercing, the knitted cap that bobs as she types.

"Is Janus Phillips coming to this meeting?" I blurt out, and her gaze swings over me, coming to rest on where my hands are now white-knuckling my laptop case. Dammit.

"I'm sorry, Miss Williams, I don't know." She gives me a placating smile. "Here's Bob Sugar now," she says, gesturing to the red carpet that runs in a straight line through the desks from one end of the office to the other. "I'm sure he can answer any questions you have."

I groan inwardly as a tall man with peppered hair makes his way toward me. I'm damp under my arms, there's a burning warmth in my body—right before one of the biggest meetings of my life. *Great.*

Be professional.

Be professional.

Be professional.

If I repeat it enough in my head, maybe it will happen. Then Bob is in front of me offering a welcoming hand and jerking me back to reality.

"Jo Williams!" His earnest face is all wide smiles. "Good to see you again! I hear your company is doing well. You come highly recommended."

Doing well? My whole body tightens. He wouldn't say that if he could see the emptiness of our bank account. But never mind that, someone *recommended* me to Bob? After the fiasco that I'm now going to call *the elevator incident*, the very idea that I've somehow been selected ... I feel queasy. Can't I find some better behavior from somewhere? I paste on my best professional smile and hold out my hand.

"Me?" God, even my voice sounds false. "That's nice to hear. It's lovely to see you too, Bob. You were a legend when I was at college."

Janus poached Bob from one of the top tech colleges in the country, and he's got a reputation as a genius at managing both people and projects. He's close friends with my former professor at NYU, so we've crossed paths once or twice before. He's the kind of guy that hums as he walks down a corridor, tilts his head while he listens. A safe pair of hands. Lucky Janus. I have Des and James running my small team, and I love them to bits, but I also know that we're all young and inexperienced.

His eyes drop down to the floor like the reception carpet holds hidden secrets, and then he shifts, giving me a broad dismissing wave.

"Okay, okay, enough with the mutual back-slapping stuff. Has anyone offered you a cup of coffee?"

"I'm okay thanks," I say, and we set off through the desks and the walls, passing a large kitchen area where two guys are rapping balls over a Ping-Pong table. "Um, is Janus Phillips joining this meeting?"

Bob grins at me. "That man is a law unto himself. It's in his calendar and he should be there. Whether he will be is another matter. Have you met him?"

Damn. "Uh, not officially. Actually ..." I should say something about the elevator problem, right? If Janus arrives at the meeting and—

Bob gives a short snort. "He's got a bit of a reputation, which is not undeserved I might add, but he's an outstanding entrepreneur and boss. I like him enormously."

Oh God, really? That's high praise coming from him. I replay the smirking amusement from earlier, the bowed head, the knowing look in Janus's eyes as he scanned over my body: Bob *admires* someone like that? I'm probably not keeping the surprise off my face because Bob frowns, waving his hand again.

"The media print a lot of nonsense. The gossip about him is terrible." He grins. "Oh! To be thirty and single again."

This makes me laugh.

"Bob, I'm sure you don't really think that. You and Mandy are the stuff of legend."

Mandy is his wife, and the story of how they supported each other through the early days of their careers is tech industry folklore. They're totally dedicated to each other. No one has ever tolerated my quirks like that. Bob's eyes twinkle at me.

"Good to know I've got a bit of a reputation myself, albeit a different one. But to answer your earlier question, Janus did *say* he was intending to join us, to meet you."

His last sentence makes my stomach curl in on itself. I just met him, I think, and it didn't exactly go well.

Bob's smile fades and a small frown appears. "We're worried about the security breach, Jo. We need to get to the bottom of it and fast. We've got global clients relying on us."

We stop by the open door of a meeting room, sunlight spilling across the light-gray carpet. As I walk over the threshold to three pairs of curious eyes, I breathe a massive sigh of relief when Janus's aren't among them.

CHAPTER 2

Jo

Bob sits up straight and taps his pen on the polished table. "Okay, guys. Let me introduce Jo from Williams Security." He slides me a half smile. "She's going to take us through a short presentation about her company, and then we'll chat about how she might be able to help us. Jo, we talked a bit on the phone about the people here. This is Matt, our Head of Internal Security."

I take in the mop of blond hair, the ubiquitous band T-shirt and ripped jeans, and he winks at me as he leans back in his chair clasping his hands behind his head. I do an internal eye roll.

"And this is Delia, Head of Systems Management."

"Hi, Delia."

I give her a small wave, then hastily drop my hand to the wood of the conference table. Ugh. I am not making this better. Delia has a messy blonde babe hipster thing going on. As she does a top-to-toe sweep of the clothes I am wearing, it's clear she thinks I don't bear any of the hallmarks of someone who works in tech, never mind having the ability to understand complicated security issues. The way her mouth twists makes me think she's decided to put me in the trivial idiot box—one I am starting to think I deserve. Great. What with her and Janus, that will be two votes against me. At least Bob will be in my favor, and possibly mop-headed Matt. I turn to look at the third person at the table, a stunning dark-haired woman.

"This is Amanda, who runs our legal department."

"Hi, Amanda. Good to meet you." I smile enthusiastically. She smiles back in that tight-lipped way that some uptight people have and slides a document over to me. Jesus.

"I need you to sign the nondisclosure agreement before we start."

"No problem." I bob my head. This is standard fare for security issues that nobody can deal with and they're running scared. No one wants the media to get wind of it. Silence settles over the room as I skim through the document checking for unusual clauses—like harassing the CEO, I think to myself as my stomach drops—before signing with a flourish.

"Great," I say, smiling while trying to draw my plummeting confidence up from the floor. "Shall I start?"

A loud voice starts outside the door, and silence falls as everyone's eyes swing toward it.

"Yes, Pete, *I know*, it's a fucking disaster. I want everybody working round the clock on it." This is followed by a loud "Goddamn it!", and the door swings back heavily on its hinges, wood banging against the wall with a bounce, and a clearly agitated Janus Phillips strides in.

"Sorry, everyone." His eyes sweep the table, raking his hand through his hair. "This is such a fucked-up situation …"

His words tail off as his eyes come to rest on me. A small frown appears between his brows, and I'm sucked into his unsmiling face and the straight line of his lips. I'm hanging on the edge of a cliff waiting for the earth to crumble under my hands, breath cemented in my chest, trying to tamp down the heated flush that wants to climb into my face. He opens his mouth, closes it, opens it again.

"Um …" And then his expression starts to be replaced with something that looks a lot like amusement.

"Hi," he says, as his face transforms to that heart-stopping lopsided grin, and he stretches out his hand toward me. "You must be Jo Williams?"

"Great to meet you," I say, catching an easing breath and struggling awkwardly out of my seat to extend my hand over the table. His eyes dance at me, and the way they twinkle and crinkle at the sides catches me deep inside. My God, he's gorgeous.

"*The* Jo Williams, huh?" he says, nodding. "Nice to meet you properly." His lips curl slightly as he shifts his attention to the room. "Where have you got to?" And in a heartbeat, his amusement and joviality morph into sharp drive.

"Jo was going to take us through some background about her, and then we were going to talk about the issue at hand," Bob says slowly, his warm calm clearly the salt to the pepper of Janus's high spirits.

"Yeah, yeah." Janus runs his hand through his already unruly mop of hair. "We get what a goddamn genius she is—we've all seen her resume and know what she did to sort out Caltech. Bunch of jackasses. Let's cut to the sorting us out part, shall we?"

Someone coughs into the quiet. Everyone studies their laptops while I stare at him wide-eyed. *What resume?* The one where I scraped into college by the skin of my teeth? And *Caltech. Oof.* Six months ago, they called us in to look at the security problems all over their badly designed network. We sorted it out, but it was a huge headache.

And he doesn't appear to be in the least bit pissed with me—just highly amused and terribly impatient. Like things can't move fast enough for him. I snort inwardly. I'm not sure how he's going to deal with me, I'm the most methodical person on the planet.

"Okay," Bob says, breaking the silence. "Matt, do you want to kick off telling Jo a bit of history about our systems and how that's developed into the current architecture?"

And we are off. I pull out my pad and colored pens and, as they are answering my questions, arguing about the structure every now and then, I sketch a diagram of their system. The network starts to take shape as I draw in connections, highlighting in red and green where things strike me as being okay, what things are weak, and what's worthy of further investigation. After three hours, my little map is pretty detailed. The time has flown by.

"Do we know how they got into the system?" I ask.

Matt clears his throat. "Still unknown. We're running through all that data now. Could be a particular piece of hardware, software, or something that's got through our defenses like malware or a phishing email."

As Matt runs through what data he's got and what he's examining, Janus gets up to glance out of the window and then comes to stand behind me, leaning over my shoulder slightly and watching as I add notes to the map. He's been glancing at what I'm doing all the way through the meeting, and my writing falters as he shifts forward to put his hand on the table by my wrist. I glance sideways at the strong muscles roping down to long expressive fingers, the curl of dark hair on his arms. I chance a look up at him, and heat starts to build in my chest. He stares down at the pad, face serious as his eyes dart around the paper. Then his unsmiling gaze zeroes in on mine and I'm treated to his hot brown eyes roaming my face, dipping to the flush on my neck, and my tongue sneaks out to wet my lower lip as his eyes flick to it. What will everyone think if they catch him doing that? I swing my eyes back to my map. Maybe he does it all the time. Maybe he doesn't even realize he does it. Maybe I am unintentionally flirting too.

"I've heard a lot about this security technique of yours," he says suddenly, a long finger stretching to tap the side of my pad. And his tone holds a hint of sarcasm.

I survey my diagram and suddenly I'm hot all over. This is a billion-dollar company that operates around the world, and all I've got for a global network like this is a piece of paper and colored pens? And messing around in the elevator? *Really*? What am I *thinking*? Janus Phillips is … is … like THE person in tech right now. Janus Industries could cement our reputation in the security space. My flush climbs higher, and I blink once, twice, then suck in a deep breath. *He's a client*. He's entitled to question.

"I make notes this way," I say, but I can't shake off the stiffness in my voice.

As I turn to look up at his face, I realize two things: first, he hasn't missed

12

my mortification, and second, I am completely misreading his comment. He isn't judging me. His face is open and relaxed; he's genuinely interested. I groan inwardly. They're a professional outfit. Presumably Bob briefed him about me before the meeting and he just wants to understand how I work. A small frown appears between his brows, cool distance washing over his face, and I curse the terrible chip on my shoulder that is doing me no favors at all. He probably thinks I'm a real idiot now. I search desperately for something to rescue the situation.

"You know what they say, it's never that remarkable to the person who does it." I screw my face up at him, widening my eyes. I hope he gets it.

His eyes zoom in on my wrinkled nose and go a little unfocused, and then he smiles, nodding thoughtfully, and, although the smile doesn't quite reach his eyes, the frown has disappeared.

"What do the little squiggles mean?" His hand goes to the back of my chair, and he leans farther over me, gesturing at the notepad as the warmth of his body radiates through my shirt.

This feels far too like a teacher peering over my shoulder, when I would draw diagrams rather than do English assignments. I failed every inspection. I resist the urge to rip the paper from the pad and throw it across the room, and instead smooth my hand over the map.

"Well, some determine types of protection at each node and every network layer, based on a grading system that we developed. The colors denote certain security levels too …" I trail off.

"It's good," he says.

Is he being sarcastic? My head snaps back around to meet his eyes, but his gaze roams warm over mine. The grip of his fingers on my chair tilts it slightly toward him. Janus Phillips thinks my diagram is good? *Be still, my heart.*

"Thanks." I swallow hard, light-headed. This is officially the most surreal conversation of my life. "I can't get my head around stuff unless I have a map. I don't go anywhere without my colored markers." I try to smile as I tap the pens sitting at my elbow. "Definitely a bit low tech but … "

"I'm a great fan of paper." He gives me the full-wattage grin again, the one that makes my insides churn like I'm on a roller coaster. I take in his even white teeth, lashes thick around dancing eyes. "I've tried for ages to build up a clear picture of our systems, and this"—he taps the pad in front of me—"does it simply, and you just produced it in three hours of talking to us."

I frown a little, not quite so ready to accept my little diagram is remotely up to scratch or accurate. "Well … of course, it won't be *totally* correct …"

"I bet it's 80–90 percent right." He scans over the paper, body tilting forward, torso brushing my shoulder, and I can't move because, if I did, I'd rub up against him. He smells of soap and Downy and warm male. His hand is right there, and I'm mesmerized by his high-tech watch, the slight ridges on his nails, the jut of his thumb. The way his hand flexes on the paper. My breath pushes at my ribs like water. Is the touching deliberate?

He taps the map. "This one here. Hong Kong. I think that isn't quite right, but I'm not sure we've got the full picture to tell you exactly what the situation is there. The office is new, recently set up but growing fast." He turns his head and his face is inches from mine. "You might need to talk to people on the ground for that one. Travel out there."

I'm so breathless all I can do is nod and grin like an idiot. He must think I'm a nutcase. I can see where he missed a bit shaving this morning. Someone coughs, and he straightens, striding back to his place at the table and looking around the expectant faces. I sit there, feeling hollowed out, like someone cut the cords that were tethering me to the room. He nods at the table, avoiding my gaze.

"Okay, everyone! Have we done enough for now?" he says.

Janus has finished so the meeting is over, over, over. I blink as people start to move, snapping notebooks shut, clicking laptops closed. I shoot to my feet, gathering my stuff and packing my bag like I'm on autopilot. Janus gives me a nod as everyone drifts toward the door.

"Thanks, Jo. Can you scan and email the team that map?" he says.

"Yes, and I'll send you a plan to sort the immediate problems quickly and then start on some of the other weaknesses."

"Matt's in charge of that, so forward it to him. Can you start on this tomorrow?" He glances at his wrist and his lips do a half quirk. "Today even?"

I nod, almost plopping back down in my chair. "I'll need an upfront payment, so we can pull resources onto it fast." I hold my breath.

"No problem." Janus's gaze flicks to Matt. "Make it happen," he says and then strides from the room, pulling his phone out of his pocket. I can't help a quick glance at his backside. It's as delicious as the rest of him.

*

When I shake everyone's hand at the elevator, I'm still reeling from the speed of the decision making. But internally I'm cartwheeling all over his fancy office space. Janus Industries security! Holy moly! I'm bouncing on my toes with the idea that I have landed this job, and, fingers crossed, *enough money to cover payroll.*

As my eyes scan the desks, Janus appears in the walkway, head down, engrossed in something on his phone. The back of my neck prickles as a hot sweat starts on my chest. I focus down on my phone trying to appear busy and not at all bowled over, or worse, gawking at him as every woman must do. I'm scrolling through Slack, not even reading, when sneakers appear on the gray carpet by my feet, and my eyes travel up his body to find him looking at me with that lopsided grin on his face.

"We meet at the elevator twice in one day," he says, sliding his phone in his back pocket and pulling his shirt tight across his chest. He rubs his hands together. "What are you doing now? Fancy grabbing a coffee and a sandwich? I'm starved, and the opportunity to chat about software would be cool. I'm always surrounded by marketing people." He scans my clothes and makes a mock grumpy face.

I'm taken aback by his overt friendliness. He wants to talk tech with me? *Janus Phillips* is asking *me*? Surely he doesn't have the time. I've never met someone who's actually appeared on gossip sites, and on the heels of this thought comes another: his reputation is terrible. Even Bob was aware of it. Would people misread me leaving with him? I survey the wide-open space, but it appears deserted. Unfortunately, he's too sharp not to notice what I've done, and he leans in and raises an eyebrow.

"Scared, Jo? Tut, tut." He looks me up and down. "Where's the rebel I saw on the way up here? The woman with the smart mouth and smart clothes who tries to confuse the hell out of poor unsuspecting chief execs? Making them think she belongs in marketing maybe?" He tilts his head and is outright grinning at me now. My face goes hot, and as I open my mouth, the elevator pings and I suck in a breath: saved by the bell.

Shooting through the opening door, I roll my eyes at him. "I have a reputation to protect you know," I say, "unlike you. I can't just be seen heading out for a sandwich with the biggest wolf in the business." For effect, I lean out of the door doing an exaggerated check around, then turn around and quirk my lips at him.

He bursts out laughing, leaning forward to press the button for the lobby, and the doors grind closed behind me.

"If that's my reputation, then I'm keen to protect that," he says, as he fiddles with a silver ring on his finger. "Wolf, eh? Who knows what kind of interesting women a reputation like that might cause me to run into?" He raises an eyebrow. If he gets any cuter, I think I'll spontaneously combust. I'm not surprised models are falling all over his smart mouth and crazy hair.

"I wouldn't exactly class you as a poor unsuspecting chief exec." I screw up my nose as his eyes scan my hair, my face. He gives a little head shake.

"Well, you certainly managed to pull one over on me in the elevator. I don't forget things like that or take them lightly, so you'll need to watch out for me getting my own back."

"Is this invitation for a sandwich one of those times?" I fake a concerned frown. "Should I be worried? Are you going to put laxative in my coffee?"

"You mean the invite you've not yet accepted, that's causing me untold amounts of stress because I've asked a girl out for the first time in a long-ass time, and she's not said yes?"

"Asked me out?" My voice comes out about two octaves higher than normal, my heart leaping into my throat at his choice of words. Good God, is he … is he … No. He's a player—they all come out with lines like this. I straighten my face into what I hope is a nonchalant expression.

Janus waves his hand. "Yeah, well, I'm going in for the kill because I think you're stalling." He studies the floor, and through the tousled top of his head I can see the white teeth of his smile, then he peeks at me from under his lashes. He is such a flirt. If he wasn't so cute, it'd be painful.

My mind is whirling. "You know"—I stare up at the floor numbers slowly ticking down on the console and pretend to think hard about what I'm saying—"I've never met you before, and it's been a total honor by the way, but you need to stop doing all the standard guy pickup moves. They are way too obvious. Do most girls you meet fall for this kind of thing? Is this the approach you use to get everyone to say yes to you?"

Tipping his head back, he laughs out loud.

"I think I'm a bit rusty." He nods for emphasis. "Perhaps you could help me with my technique. What's your method for getting people to say yes?"

"Squiggles on paper," I deadpan. "What I write down is actually nonsense, but the tech guys who run companies like to look smart and it works every time. The more complex and incomprehensible the drawing and lines, the better."

Janus's face is a picture as he gusts out a bark of laughter.

"You were particularly gullible." My smile creeps slowly over my face. "You actually came and looked at it closely. Although I'm rather disappointed that you thought it was real; I use it as my standard intelligence test." I try to look crestfallen as I lean toward him, lowering my voice in what I hope passes for regret. "Not sure you passed that one."

He cups his face in his hands, fingers pressing into the corner of his eyes, and lets out a rumble from deep in his throat. The sound reverberates, making me think of warm naked skin and hot hands, and the heat creeps up my neck again.

"Tell me the map was real, *please*," he mumbles, as he raises his eyes to the ceiling like he's praying and runs his hands down his face.

I can't hold back the broad grin spreading across my face. "Yes, I'm messing with you. It was genuine, but"—I circle his face with a finger—"I'm loving this response so much that I could happily start a rumor about it being a trick of mine ..."

I can tell I'm grinning like a maniacal idiot, enjoying the joke far too much to make any kind of sensible comment.

"Has anyone told you you're nuts?" He responds to my wide smile with one of his own.

Like my mom? The thought is there before I can squash it. I swallow it down and wave my hand at him in a dismissing gesture. "Yeah, *yeah*. But is there any other way to be? You can't be sensible in this business."

Janus puts his head on one side. "You know, I kind of like you," he says, and I'm almost sure he didn't mean to say this out loud. He looks away and bites his lip, a faint pink tinge resting high on his cheekbones.

Yes, but how long would you like me for? I'm not exactly arm-candy.

We're rescued by the elevator grinding to a halt, and I leap out like a cat avoiding a sprinkler into an almost empty lobby. I say the first thing that comes into my head: not a strategy that works well for me usually.

"I'm sorry about earlier." It bursts forth before I can stop it.

He frowns at this as we head across the atrium toward the doors.

"What do you mean? In the elevator?"

"No—well, *yes*—in the elevator, of course. That was so stupid, pretending not to recognize you." Words are stumbling out too fast. "But I meant in the meeting. You made a comment about my map and I suppose I ... I guess I thought you were being sarcastic about producing a silly little drawing."

"Ah, that!" His face relaxes. "I wondered why you looked so sort of ... off."

"Yeah, I'm sorry. I have a bit of a chip on my shoulder with guys who ridicule what I do: a surprisingly common experience for a woman working in this industry. They don't expect me to understand anything and are often thrown when I do."

Janus shakes his head. "No need to apologize—I've come across enough prejudice in my time about my age, my appearance, my reputation, *my hair*. Being told things 'aren't possible,' that we should 'take time and think about it.'" He makes air quotes with his hands. "As you can probably tell, my nickname here is Mr. Impatient, although no one says that to my face; they all call me it behind my back. I'm raging mad half the time, and don't get me started on how often I yell at people."

I can picture him doing all this. "Glad I'm not the only one."

"What you shout at people too? Somehow I can't imagine that."

His wide smile reaches right down to my toes and my head is empty, not even a hint of any coherent retort. I mumble out a "no," desperately swinging back to concentrate on where we are going. I'm so out of kilter here—saying inappropriate things, turning into a blathering idiot. God help me.

We emerge out of the building, and I lift my hands over my head as a downpour hits my shoulders. The traffic swishes past, cars throwing cascades of water onto the sidewalk of rushing pedestrians.

CHAPTER 3

Janus

Talking to Jo Williams feels like holding on to a bare electric wire. I hung around spying on reception, waiting for my team to disappear, hoping to catch her before she vanished. When I first saw her in the lobby, I checked out the pink lips and the tight skirt and acted like a typical guy: who *was* this getting into my elevator? But then she poked fun at me and turned up in my meeting. *So far so interesting.* But then that *map*? This girl is glowing from the inside out, and all the hairs on the back of my neck feel like they're standing on end. I've not met a woman like her in a really, really long time.

Over the last few years, I've dated a lot of beautiful, self-obsessed women. Andi, who spent all night pulling up videos of key scenes in her films. Melissa, who spent the evening on her phone posting pictures, checking likes, and videoing *everything*: the meal, me, the waiter, the event, me again, kissing her on the cheek, holding her hand, *picking her up and swinging her around.* Crazy. None of these ladies *eat.* I mean, I get what being the head of my own company gives me, but what am I *doing*? They're interested in my position or my money or who they think I *should* be. They want to go to parties and be seen. They don't know me or care about the things I care about. Nothing that comes out of Jo Williams's mouth is boring or predictable.

I stare at her soft red hair and laughing green eyes as the rain turns her shoulders from light to dark blue and I can't tear my gaze away. Am I a wolf? I don't feel like one, but the media have painted my reputation in a particular light, and I know first of all that Jo Williams really isn't that kind of woman, and, second, I could totally scare her off.

"I should have brought an umbrella," I say, smiling through the downpour, trying my hardest to be charming. "Where would you like to go?"

Her lips part over perfect white teeth as she chews on her bottom lip. She's done this several times this morning, and every time she does it I—

"Somewhere close?"

Her voice hesitates and a pink blush washes over her cheeks, and I examine the freckles all over her face. She's been blushing on and off all morning. I could see it in the V of her shirt. How far down her body does it—

She raises an eyebrow, and the cold seeps into where my shirt is sticking to my torso. What were we talking about?

"We could stand here and think about it?" I say.

She puts a hand on her hip. "Yeah, I could stand here quite happily, in this glorious sunshine."

Something nameless bubbles up under my skin. My company is this ravenous beast that's eating my life one huge bite at a time until I no longer know who I am, and it's been getting worse lately: the expansion into so many countries, hundreds of people joining, endless conference calls. I don't recognize most people in my elevator these days. It feels like only yesterday there were ten of us in a tatty little building in Brooklyn. Talking to Jo is lifting the boulder off my chest, like I can leave the worry and stress of millions of dollars of contracts in a heap right here on the sidewalk.

"Well." I fold my arms over my ribcage slowly and deliberately, as the rain soaks into my shoulders. "Let me think. Luchadores on the corner does tacos and Mexican takeout and their quesadillas are to die for." I lean forward, feeling the wet stretch of my shirt. "Then there are a few places on the waterfront or healthy places like Sweetgreen or Westville, I've been there a few times before and ..." I tail off as she slaps my arm.

"Janus!" she exclaims. "Quit messing around, we're getting soaked."

I look around in confusion. "What? In this sunshine?"

This time she gives me a different laugh, one that's thick with devilment, and it makes me high that I've managed to get that out of her.

"Just take me somewhere before I drown," she growls.

So I grab her hand, pulling her through the bouncing raindrops to the nearest shelter.

CHAPTER 4

Jo

Janus's wet hand slides in mine as we run along the sidewalk, people hurrying past us and diving into doorways shaking their dripping umbrellas. The *flirting*! Oh my God, my heart is a wild flapping beast in my chest. Exactly *why* am I so ridiculously flattered here? His reputation is *terrible*. He's a playboy. It's industry lore that he's never been involved with a woman for more than a couple of months. And I can't say I blame him or them: he's young, free, single, and Mister-I-am-cute-smile and why wouldn't you take advantage of that?

Anything with him could blow my reputation and take my business down like it's been hit by a nuclear missile. The very idea of him "asking me out," of being photographed with him, of any kind of press speculation, makes bile rise up the back of my throat. Images of what my father went through on my behalf flood my mind, the confrontation with the school, the press interest, the whispers behind hands every time we went anywhere. And Janus is so much more high profile than the local papers in some small town in the middle of nowhere. My company is just starting to get traction: Janus Industries called me in because they'd *heard* of me. I swallow the sinking sensation down. I need to keep him in the friend zone.

I peer down at my hand in his. "Where are you taking me?"

We stop on a crossing, and he meets my gaze. "There's a great Thai place about a block away."

I carefully remove my hand from his, and he glances at me as he ushers me across the road, hand shifting to the base of my spine. Is that better or worse?

Water is streaming off the sidewalk, running down the grates and washing away the dusty feel of the city. A man about to cross gets soaked by a plume of wash from a car, a dog gives itself a full-body shake. I search my head for something, anything, that will put us on a *friends-who-lunch* footing and not a *this-is-a-date* footing.

"Tell me all about these amazing women you date." *Awkward, Jo.* I swallow down the lump in my throat. "You've been out to some incredible places and events, that sounds all kinds of interesting."

We slow to a walk under a construction tunnel on the sidewalk, and my stomach dips as I glance up at him and see his raised eyebrows.

"Um …" He pauses as his Adam's apple bobs. His long throat has a shadow of hair where he's shaved, and he flexes his hand. "You really want to hear about that?"

I give him what I hope is a professional smile. "Well, you have quite the reputation in this industry. You must have had some amazing experiences. As a newbie, I'm looking forward to the day that guys are falling over themselves to go out with me."

My skin prickles with how gauche and stupid this sounds.

When we emerge from the tunnel, he takes a sharp left into a double doorway and yanks the door open with more force than necessary. His hand is an irritated flap as he gestures for me to go first. Ugh, I'm messing all this up. But my churning stomach vanishes when a small round Thai lady bustles up, all waving hands; then she spots Janus behind me and her face breaks into the widest smile I think I've ever seen.

"Mr. Phillips, Mr. Phillips!"

She jostles me to one side, and all I catch is his tousled hair and delighted grin as he bends down to have his cheeks kissed and rubbed.

"May, call me Janus," he mumbles in such a way that I get the impression that this is a conversation they have every time he comes here.

I tear my eyes away to look at the stripped brick walls, mismatched furniture, and the room full of hipsters, and raise my eyebrows. I've never been to a Thai place that looks anything like this.

He grins at me … Jesus, he needs to stop with the stuff that makes my insides swoop and dive. Finding him cute is going to break me. May turns to take me in and, if anything, her smile gets wider.

"Who is this?"

"May, meet Jo—a friend of mine."

"Ah, you are a lovely lady!" she exclaims, pulling me in for an assault similar to the one she gave Janus. "Come with me!" she says as she pivots on her heel to head off across the floor.

Janus dips his head. "May used to run a traditional Thai restaurant, but it was old-fashioned and struggling, and she asked me what 'all the young boys with money liked in a place to eat.' So I told her"—Janus waves his hand around—"and she created it. She and her husband ripped the place to pieces and did this. She's packed now, and her coffees are the best in Manhattan … and her muffins!" He laughs. "If I came here too often, I'd have a gut like a bear." His stomach makes a hollow thud when he pats it like there's no spare flab there at all.

I glance down at where his hand is resting, and his wet shirt is transparent and sticking to his body; I can see the outline of muscle and a trail of dark hair. Jesus. I jerk my head up instantly, pursing my lips, looking around for anything to distract me from the body beneath those clothes.

"I love it. The only thing that gives you a sense it might not be totally hipster is the lucky fortune nodding cat." I inhale a deep breath and incline my head toward the counter.

Janus laughs. "Yeah, but I kind of like the quirkiness of that. I like the fact they still have that."

"I've always wanted one of those. I like the waving thing."

"The what?"

"Someone wrote this poem: 'Not Waving But Drowning.' About a man who's sinking underwater, and he's moving his arms to signal for help, but nobody realizes that's what he's doing. Sometimes I see that cat and I wonder whether it's desperately waggling its paw and actually inhaling water."

My chattering voice bounces around my head. So much nonsense has been coming out of my mouth today, honest to God, I could slap myself. But Janus is still smiling, and his eyes hold a question as they meet mine.

"Do you think about stuff like this all the time?"

He's thinking I'm a crazy cat. Definitely. He's going to regret giving me this security contract, never mind anything more personal. Which you absolutely don't want, Jo. *Jesus.* My head sinks into my body, shoulders drooping, but he shakes his head, nudging my shoulder with his.

"You should know I like it. It's all kinds of cute."

He thinks *I'm* cute? I'm saved from having to respond coherently to this by May waving us to a table in the back, and we squeeze past packed tables to where she's standing, still beaming. The distressed pine tables are as clean as a pin, the floor some wonderfully aged patterned tile, the chairs a battered metal. Heads turn as Janus moves past: Is it because people recognize him or because he looks good enough to eat?

Once we've sat down and tried to shake the water from our damp clothes, I lean toward him over the table. "I think I'd rather be hot, not kooky and cute. How else am I going to pick up all these guys when my company grows enough to give me some kudos?"

It's a ham-fisted attempt to circle us back to our earlier conversation and settle us into a more friendly vibe, but my brain can produce nothing more coherent.

Janus's brow creases as his Adam's apple bobs. "It's not all it's cracked up to be," he says.

CHAPTER 5

Janus

I fiddle with the leather strap on my wrist, cold sinking into my skin. Somehow, I don't think Jo's going to have to try too hard to find guys who are interested in her, but what woman asks a guy about other dates the first time they sit down together? Usually, this is the last conversation anyone wants to have. The only thing that swims up in my consciousness from previous dates is sour eyes and bitchiness. Maybe she's so involved in the tech world she hasn't experienced a lot of that, but it strikes me that she doesn't have much of a filter, and my heart goes out to her. I like her openness and the way she says every thought that pops into her head, but the world will treat her brutally for being so open and honest.

Tendrils of red hair are escaping from her bun, dark with the rain. Her face is completely bare, and a slight sheen from the wet and the warmth in the restaurant makes the pale freckles sing across her face. Eyelashes brush her cheeks as she peers down at the coffee that May has magically produced in front of us. When she brings her head up, all I can do is stare at her lips. They're tiny and candy pink. A faint flush starts to build on the side of her face, jerking me out of my reverie as I clear my throat and focus down on my espresso, running my hand around the edge of my T-shirt.

"I can't believe she did that," she says in a hushed tone, leaning forward.

"What?" I whisper back, even though speaking quietly is totally unnecessary given the racket around us. I grin, bending my head toward her so my nose is inches from hers, glad to have the distraction of some intrigue.

Jo sinks back into her seat. "Brought us coffee without ordering. This is Manhattan. People are the most demanding I've ever come across. If you did that too often, people would throw it at you."

I like the visual of a coffee fight. "But there's something appealing about cutting across all that. The ease of not having to make a choice? We're too obsessed with having all these options; I think it makes it much more difficult to decide. I want someone to decide for me."

Jo's lips tip up in a half smile, and she tilts her head sideways. "I love it actually. I wish someone turned up at our office every day with my lunch like a random potluck exercise."

Her finger picks away at some flaw in the wooden surface of the table. She has tiny hands—the freckles almost perfectly matching the ones on her face.

"Yeah, someone to decide about all the trivial things," I say.

"And to do them all, too: washing, cooking …" she says.

She must see something in my face because she snorts.

"You have someone to do all that, don't you?"

I nod and make a face at her, and she bursts out laughing. May appears again like a genie twinkling at us like we're two cute kids she's matched herself, and gives me a knowing smile. It occurs to me that I've never been in here with a woman before. She's worse than my mom. In her outstretched hands are two plates piled high with quiche and salad. We didn't even order.

"Sorry, I always eat the same thing here." I grimace. Oh, God, most women are so picky about their food … I've listened to endless conversations about the merits of different kinds of diets. But Jo just nods, beaming at the plate in front of her. Christ, could she be any more low maintenance? She is fucking perfect.

"Someone in the tech industry—possibly Steve Jobs?—used to have like six sets of identical clothing because he didn't want to spend time deciding what to wear," I say.

"Yeah, Zuckerberg did that too. And it was always jeans, sneakers and a black T-shirt or turtleneck or something."

"That sounds great actually. I could totally get on board with that plan."

She waves her fork at me, chewing. "You're always well kitted out."

I am? But as soon as I remember why, I wrinkle my nose at her. The backstory behind this doesn't paint me in the best light, and sharing stories like this comes later—months later. I'm trying to act cool here. But, of course, Jo is way too sharp to let this go.

She draws a circle around my face. "What is this expression?"

I sigh, staring over to where a team of Thai baristas are making coffee behind the counter, and inhale the familiar smell of grounds. Can I avoid answering this question? I don't want to be looking at Jo when I tell her this. She taps my hand and, keeping my gaze fixed at a point on the wall above her left shoulder, I start to talk.

"I was *that* tech guy: awful hair, band T-shirt and jeans—and not trendy ones either—often filthy. I think I didn't wash much actually." I shrug, heat creeping up my neck. I'm not sure she needed that particular detail. "I got marginally better at college, but when I graduated and set up Janus Industries, at some point we appointed a PR firm." I take a forkful of quiche and chew thoughtfully. "After a few interviews where I turned up unwashed after days of coding and it got some press comment, they decided to take me in hand. They arranged to have a company come every quarter and basically turn over my wardrobe and give me a new set of clothes."

My eyes drop back to hers to find her open-mouthed and staring at me.

"*Seriously?*" she says.

I nod, grimacing. That's not all of it, though. Something about Jo makes me want to spill my innermost secrets.

"Someone also comes and styles me for events."

"*No way!* Like they come and do your hair and makeup and stuff?"

"Yep."

Her eyes scan over me, snag on what I'm wearing. "I thought you looked a bit different from the photographs I normally see."

Ugh. I'm vain enough that this comment makes me wobble.

"Don't tell me that! Tell me I look as amazing as my press shots."

She ignores my plea entirely and waves at my hair. "Okay, tell me about this."

This has gone way farther than I wanted it to.

"I'm not sure I—" I start, but she gestures impatiently at me. Why am I being so open with her? No one knows about this shit.

"Once a month a team …" I tail off, wincing at the word. "… Come and do my hair, nails …" Jo's eyes shoot down to my fingers. I raise my eyes to the ceiling. "God, I sound like the vainest man on the planet. You've no idea what grief my best buds from college would give me if they knew about this."

"And is this appreciated by all these women that you go out with?"

I shake my head at her, grinning. I'm struck by how odd this conversation is: We've only known each other a matter of hours, and we're already diving into such personal stuff. I don't have conversations like this with anybody else. Surely we should be chatting about tech?

"I think it just sort of happens when there's a lot of scrutiny. People start commenting on all sorts of stuff you wished they didn't notice," I say.

She stares at me, nodding, before taking a bite and chewing on it contemplatively. "What do your friends do?"

"Fabian is a hacker, and Adam also has his own startup. Both techies. We got into this sort of pact at college—"

"Like the Unbreakable Vow?"

Why am I not surprised she's a Harry Potter fan?

"More like the three musketeers. We agreed to be friends for life, that kind of thing. That sounds incredibly cheesy when I say it out loud." I stare down at my plate, suddenly not hungry at all. What with this and the comments about clothes she must think I'm the biggest douchebag alive.

"That strikes me as pretty cool actually. Do they live here in the city?"

I nod, unwinding a little.

"Yes. Fabian lives in Brooklyn, and I go and hang with him from time to time." I stretch my neck to the side. Fabian is something of a mess, and I don't see him anywhere near as much as I should.

"What about Adam?"

And now something cold slithers through me. I'm not sure what's happened to my relationship with Adam over the last few years; I can't even remember when I last saw him. Shit. I should give him a call. But how often have I had that thought and not done anything about it? I've been running scared with the business, terrified that the success will slip through my fingers like sand.

Before I can answer, Jo says, "Fabian's a hacker? Why didn't you ask him to help with the company?"

Why didn't I? It's a good question, and I have no answer to it.

CHAPTER 6

Jo

The office is cool and relatively quiet when my phone starts vibrating on my desk, and I glance down at the screen. Dad. He's a lovely man but hard to chat to when I'm swamped and a bit wound up. I watch it thrum against the wood. Damn. He's on his own and I should talk to him.

"Hi, Peach," he says when I pick up.

"Hey, PJ."

A delighted snort fills my ear. I started calling my dad (aka Peter James Williams) this at thirteen when I felt too old and sophisticated to call him Dad. I haven't been able to call him anything else since.

"How's my beautiful girl? Not too busy to chat with your old man?"

"Not sure about the beautiful bit, Dad, but definitely a girl."

"Come on now, with that red hair, how could you be anything but beautiful? How are things in the Big Apple? Proud of you, you know."

Oh dear. He's in a sentimental mood.

And something soft and warm seeps through me. I was desperate to escape the small South Carolina town I grew up in when I went to college. I love and miss my dad, but I was buried there. Buried by girls that taunted me every day and followed me home. The red hair that just acted like a siren call to every narrow-minded asshole in the place.

I remember the last time Darcy and her crew set on me. The way they grabbed the woolen hat off my head, came at me from behind, *because that day I hadn't done enough checking*. Darcy called me "carrot top" and her whole posse snickered. She ruffled my hair as she stopped in front of me, tight, mean eyes scanning my head. I remember seeing school just around the corner as everyone hurried past, heads down, ignoring us, and I didn't blame them. No one ever wants to get on the bully's radar. Then Darcy narrowed her eyes and declared that they should cut off all my hair for the warmer weather. I tried to push past then, tried to escape. But she just snapped her fingers, and before I knew what was happening someone had produced scissors. I started really fighting then, catching Darcy on the chin, hitting anyone, anything. As I kicked and scratched, she told her posse to hold me down.

My dad clears his throat, and I blink at the damp patch on the wall of the office. What the hell were we talking about?

"I'm proud of you, too," I say, and goddamn it, I am. He's a quiet man, living a quiet life in a quiet town. Because the other thing I know is how he fought for me. Fought the bullying girls, the school, the press, everyone who thought we were pariahs. I carry his silent strength around with me every day. Cut me through the middle like a tree and my rings would be made up of pieces of him.

I draw in a deep breath and say the first thing that pops into my head. "How's things at home?"

"Oh, the usual. The roads are terrible, being retired is as dull as ditchwater, but on the plus side I got some freelance work from Northeastern Tech."

"Oh yeah? Dad, that's great."

I close my eyes. My dad might have waded in for me, but he never does it for himself. He's never pushed himself forward. He's a brilliant engineer who worked a lowly job in a manufacturing company for thirty years. They treated him like shit, eventually compulsorily retiring him at fifty-five. They gave him a handshake and a pen for thirty years of unwavering service. Before I went to college to study computer science, he spent hours and hours bent over a bench with me soldering and making electronic circuits. I've been waiting all my life for him to get the recognition I think he deserves.

"I said I'd give them a hand in their lab."

"They're paying you though, right?"

"No, I volunteered to do it, Jo. I can't *charge* them." His voice cracks and my stomach sinks. "They're a publicly funded body. They need all the help they can get."

I poke at a hole in my jeans. That right there is the trouble with my dad. He's always thinking about the other person's problem, and that would be great, lovely even, but he's not exactly flush with money. He's been on his own since my mom died, and I don't remember a time when we weren't owing money to someone. We always struggled. We maybe had a couple of vacations when I was young. He says he's helping people out; I see all the bastards that take advantage of him. Sleepless at 3 a.m., I see the same fate for myself, the threads of my mom and dad running through me.

"Dad—"

He tuts at me in that way only parents can do. "Don't start, Jo." A deep sigh.

I bite it all back down. Change the subject.

"How are your hands?"

My dad has had some stiffness in the cold mornings over the last few years, and the doctors have warned it might be the start of arthritis. The idea that his hands might stop him doing the electronics he's loved all his life makes my shoulders droop.

"Good, actually. You remember Joan?"

Joan lives over the road and I think she's been sweet on my dad for a long time. Not that he'd notice. She takes him homemade muffins and feeds our old dog, Mitzi, on the rare occasion he's away.

"She told me about this Pilates thing she goes to that's helped with her arthritis. So I'm going to that with her. Ach, I think the hands are a bit better."

The very idea of my dad doing an exercise class with Joan and her friends in their Lycra rolling around the floor makes me grin into my phone, and the tightness in my shoulders starts to loosen.

"You go for coffee with them afterward?"

"Sometimes," he says, and I laugh out loud at this. My dad likes to talk about engineering, about how to solder a board. The Internet is his passion because people are generous with technical stuff online, and he's learned to do and share more than he could ever have dreamed of. He's the last person on earth I can imagine relaxing into the gossip of a coffee morning.

"Do you discuss politics?"

He harrumphs at this. "I don't like your mocking tone, young lady."

"At least put the world to rights?"

"Ailments. That's what we talk about. How our bodies are giving out on us."

CHAPTER 7

Jo

S tanding in the line for my morning espresso, my eyes land on the waving
cat. This is good, right? Switching it up. Coffee from May's. I'm not hoping
to run into Janus. Nope, definitely not. Ugh. I can't shake him out of my head:
his long fingers wrapped around a coffee cup, thumb stroking the handle, the
curl of his lip in a grimace, the soft dark hairs on his forearms. Somehow, the
idea that he was a mess when he was younger just makes him all the more
attractive. I was a mess, too. I'm still a mess.

Code. Code and networks. That's what I should be thinking about: getting to
the bottom of how the hackers got around his systems. From what Matt's told me,
their network defenses seem solid. And it's complicated; so the hackers are good,
and they know what weaknesses to look for. I need to add some extra security
layers to fox even the ones who think they're super smart. I should head out and
visit some of his offices. Talk to people. As I raise my head, I catch a guy farther
up the line watching me, and he winks. He's tall, broad-shouldered and good-
looking with short spiky blond hair and the kind of smile that makes women drop
their panties. I grin back. Andy: former coworker, former partner in crime. I give

a little wave and then gape at him as he steps out of line and heads toward me.

"You lost your place!" I gasp, but he grins at me. "That's line heresy in my book," I mutter darkly at him.

This gets me a laugh. "I saw a hot woman, what can I say?" He shrugs, and not for the first time I find myself admiring his clean-cut jawline and sharp suit. I've always got on with his dry sense of humor. If he wasn't a complete womanizer, I might have been interested, but oh my God, the way he goes through women; he's probably worse than Janus. Sourness coats my tongue. Why are all attractive men dicks where women are concerned?

"How's Triton?" Triton Securities was my last proper job before my business became more than a side hustle.

He shrugs. "Oh, you know, same old, same old."

I can feel a sly grin creeping over my face. "And how is the manwhoring these days?"

It's my standard joke to rib him about this. I lived vicariously through him when I was at Triton: I helped him with the technical side of the job and he took me out to clubs and stopped me being such a nerd, giving me a detailed account of his manwhoring escapades. Some of the things that women do … honestly, he's had blowjobs in more outrageous places than I've had hot dinners. We used to have a scoring system for the quality of the oral sex and the riskiness of the place where it happened.

"Well, since you left Triton, I have no one to discuss blowjob points with the following day." He lifts a sexy shoulder with a half smile.

As the line shuffles forward the man in front of us half-turns, clearly catching something in the conversation, probably the word *blowjob*. My inner devil starts to rise, and I grin at Andy and raise my voice a little; might as well make the guy's morning even more interesting.

"Well, you could always text me to discuss it," I say, pretending to mull it over, "preferably with a photo—a picture of your dick and her mouth?"

Andy begins to laugh, and the guy in front of me makes a choking noise but doesn't turn around. I wink at Andy, and he's smiling so wide as he stretches out and pulls me into a massive hug.

"Fuck, I've missed you, Jo Williams. Life has been insufferably dull since you left."

Leaning back, he places both hands on my shoulders and my frame is so small they cover me from my neck to the tops of my arms. He's looking at me quizzically.

"You're a gorgeous lady, how come you never went out with me?"

I think my skepticism must show all over my face. "Andy, you don't go out with women. You have one-night shagfests."

He wags a finger at me. "Two nights if she gets ten on the scale."

I giggle. "Any tens recently?"

"Oh God, I got one better than that."

"An eleven?" That usually means a very risky location. "Wow, where?"

"She gave me a blowjob under the table at an awards event." Mischief is written all over his face.

"How the hell …? I need to hear more about this, I've missed living vicariously through you," I say, peering at my watch. "Can you spare fifteen minutes for a quick coffee before I head into work?"

He nods enthusiastically. "How's it going anyway?"

For once, I've got good news. "Great." I lean over to give the girl behind the counter my order. "I've got the contract for Janus Industries security. It could really put me on the map."

CHAPTER 8

Janus

I've almost forgotten about Jo Williams. Well, okay, that's a lie. But the meeting and lunch that followed feel like a distant dream. I'm drowning in Excel spreadsheets, staff who are leaving, employees who are sick or hate their jobs, contracts for new premises, legal documentation for ten different countries. The chasm between what I know and what gets put in front of me widens with every passing day, and I have to step back and trust everyone, ask the right questions. I have no way to pull back, to stop the runaway train.

Two weeks out of the US and what have I got to show for it? A balloon that is slowly deflating in my hands, that's all. Rubbing my eyes, I hunt for the details of my flight from Singapore to New York on the board: *delayed*. Am I even going to make this conference I'm heading home for? The business lounge is quiet, the wide white counters loaded with pasta, crackers, and cheese, more booze than any one person could reasonably drink. People are huddled in groups of soft chairs, engrossed in their technology, *one last problem sorted*. Tiredness seeps into my limbs as I study the 1,562 emails sitting in my inbox, and these are just the important ones: my assistant, Maddie, has culled, sorted, and responded to the rest. Well, with the two-hour delay, I could hack through some of these right now. I'll have to go straight to the conference when I land in New York, and sleep will be an elusive beast unless I can relax on the plane. Not something I manage to do that often, something about the hum of jet engines doesn't quite work for me.

An insistent vibration in my pocket makes me pull out my phone and peer at the screen: Matt. A frisson of nerves runs through me: Head of Security is one person you don't want to hear from too frequently. I hold the phone to my head.

"I think I'm in love," he says.

"What the fuck, Matt?"

His laugh is a mad bark in my ear. "Had any sleep yet?"

How well he knows this gig.

"Heck no, I've been up for …" I glance at my wrist. "Twenty-three hours and counting."

"I knew you'd be out of contact for a while, so I thought I'd call now."

"So, you're in love with …"

"Jo Williams." His voice drops. "Who else?"

Something white hot shifts in my chest and I stare unseeing at the gray geometric carpet ubiquitous to airport lounges all over the world. He'd better not be. Matt rattles on oblivious.

"Oh God, Janus, this girl is amazing. She's all over this, digging into the nitty-gritty, the speed with which things are happening is almost frightening. Her brain, man, it's sexy as hell."

I lean forward in my seat—finger pressed in my ear—trying to shut out the announcement of boarding for another flight; then I get up and pace away from my chair and the distraction of my laptop. Matt's one of my favorite employees, but right now I'm plotting his murder. I let myself have a brief fantasy that Jo's personal commitment to this is because of me, but she couldn't have made it clearer that wasn't how things stood when I took her for lunch. In any case, I can't afford to let myself be distracted by the fact I'm smitten when we've got such a critical problem.

"Matt," I growl, "she's a supplier; that's inappropriate in a major way."

"Okay, I know. I *know*. A man can dream though, right?"

My gut clenches with something hot and dangerous. How many men does she have chasing after her? How many men like Matt? The map she drew at the meeting, everything written in this perfect tiny script; different colors between every connection, each symbol drawn with a quirky flourish. I could almost taste her desire to nail everything down. What a warm contrast to the chaos that seems to be sweeping over everything else in the company. She and Matt are working so closely together, I'm pleased he likes her but—*goddammit*—I don't want him to be *that* keen on her. I want him focused on our security problems. We need to build additional layers of defense. I try to drag my tired brain away from all things Jo Williams. If this blows up with our clients, then we could have a serious issue.

"How's the damage limitation with customers going?"

"I've talked to all of them now. The big companies are scheduled for lunches, which is a sensible thing to do anyway, so in a twisted way this is an excellent excuse to see them. One or two of the important ones are in your diary. We're running an internal security session next week to go through the nitty-gritty. Jo's going to run that."

"And?"

"Well, they're concerned obviously, but they're also relying on us to sort it out. Nobody has threatened to move business because of it."

I blow out a breath. Jo Williams might just be saving our asses, and with a bit of luck I might even be able to chase after her ass if I ever make it back to the US. I search the flight notifications on the board again. I'm back on my home turf for a few weeks after this. Fucking Matt is not getting a look in.

*

Twenty hours later, I walk into the huge steel-and-glass conference center, my limbs moving like I'm swimming through molasses. Thank God I'm not doing a talk; all I have to do is chair a couple of discussion panels. Seven hundred emails and two hours of sleep out of the whole flight, despite the seat in business class. Little wonder my thoughts are woolly and my brain is taking ages to process anything anyone says to me.

I head down the ramp toward the smattering of people still milling around outside the main hall, a speech booming behind the pale wood doors. I want to encourage other entrepreneurs to set the world on fire; so many people helped me, but I won't be contributing much today. My fires are growing a little *too* warm. Perhaps I should talk about that.

I briefly glance at the woman behind the fancy reception desk. Her eyes are like saucers.

"Janus Phillips?" I say, perusing the name tags set out on the table.

"Oh yes!" she flusters. "Mr. Phillips! So glad you could make it. Let me find Catriona and—"

"Janus!"

The voice comes from somewhere behind me, and the next minute I'm enveloped in a warm hug and a sickly cloud of perfume. Not, I reflect wryly, the smell I'd like to be surrounded by. Why do women wear cloying scent anyway? I take a step back.

"Catriona, good to see you again." I eye her glossy lips and perfect ponytail warily. "How's it going?" I've met Catriona before, she seems to organize every tech conference in New York, and she makes the back of my neck prickle. She's just the wrong combination of oblivious and gossipy.

"We started about an hour ago," she says, taking my elbow, and I steel myself not to jerk away. "But I'm so glad you made it! I got the message from your office about the flight delays. What a *nightmare*. Are you okay? There are seats reserved at the front for people who are going to be on the stage."

I nod noncommittally. I don't want to be drawn into a discussion, or talk about how exhausted I am. No one wants to hear about the struggles that come after you've made your company a success; they only want to hear about how rewarding it all is, how the grind is worth it. As Catriona sashays quietly down the aisle in front of me, trying not to disturb the presentation, I scan the space looking for familiar faces. I catch a glimpse of red hair and my pulse picks up. Could I be lucky enough that …? Keeping my fingers crossed, I squeeze into the last chair at the end of the long row. Several people lean forward to nod silently at me and my stomach tightens as a pair of green eyes meet mine. Her lips curl up. *Hallelujah.* The day has gone from being vaguely interesting with the hope of a quick nap at the back of the hall, to being something completely different if I can hang out with Jo. I could spend the lunch break with her. My whole body starts to crank up, the lack of sleep and heavy limbs receding like a wave.

Two hours later and I'm sitting in an almost empty auditorium in the first interval grinding my teeth. The smell of coffee wafts in from the lobby, but I'm not leaving until the pack of guys surrounding Jo on stage have stopped fawning all over her. She gave an impressive talk about current security issues, but they're circling her like a pack of wolves. The light is dim, her final slide is still up on the screen, and she laughs up at a good-looking guy. Another man in chinos and a band T-shirt indicates a path off the stage, and Jo nods as yet another holds out his hand to help her down. His long fingers wrap around hers and a growling beast starts up in my chest.

It's been a long time since I've had a woman deal with me like Jo, and if I was in a more rational frame of mind, I would probably decide it was teaching me some kind of lesson. Instead, it takes me right back to college sitting on the edges like some nobody. A shudder runs through me: Have I really become *that* arrogant? I push up out of my seat in the darkness and head back toward the coffee, trying to squash everything down. Jo is *gorgeous* and in *security*, THE hot topic right now. She's going to be seriously successful if she can make her business take off, and having Janus Industries on her client list will give her a huge step up. I'm glad of it, I want to see her do well, but what is this possessiveness? Over lunch, she was clearly fending me off. I have no idea how to get out of the friend zone she's put me in.

As I walk into the break room, I nod at various people I recognize, scanning for her red curls as I make my way to the hot drinks. A woman materializes at my elbow.

"Janus Phillips?"

My heart sinks, and before I can take evasive action several more people appear and then I am surrounded—people asking me questions, a few women fluttering their eyelashes at me. I'm starting to despair when my phone vibrates in my pocket and I let out a breath I didn't know I was holding.

"Hey, Matt."

"Is Jo with you? They told me she's at the conference I think you're at." The slightly brusque tone to his voice makes my spine snap straight.

I smile at the people surrounding me and move away to try and find a quieter spot, looking out over the sea of heads. Where is she?

"She's here. I'll need to find her. What's up?"

"Someone has had another go at the system. They didn't get through, but Jo has put some stuff in place to alert us whenever anyone tries and track them, too. I just need to talk to her about it."

"Fuck, okay. Damn." My mind grapples around the edge of the problem as I push my way through the hordes of people, then I catch a flash of red hair. "I've found her, Matt. Hang on."

I fight my way through the crowd, my earlier sourness bubbling up again; dammit she's *surrounded* by guys. I tap Jo on the shoulder, and she turns around, and I feel ten feet tall when her face dissolves into gratitude. My insides do a strange wobble.

"Hey, Janus."

I gesture at my phone, handing it over to her, and she leans toward me, the sweet scent of lemon and soap drifting up.

"I've got Matt on the line for you," I say.

And God bless Jo Williams—she's the consummate professional. She turns to the men behind her and makes our excuses as she grabs my elbow.

"Matt. Let me find somewhere quieter," she says into the phone as a good-looking guy says loudly, "Has Janus Industries got security problems?"

It's a harsh reminder of how this could all blow up, but I'm too busy following Jo to do anything more than glower at him over my shoulder as I follow her across the plush brown carpet into the main auditorium. Her voice echoes in the dark emptiness as she sinks into the nearest seat and I ease into the row in front of her, idly watching as a couple of guys on stage fiddle with the microphones for the talks after the break. She's so calm, I can almost sense Matt subsiding on the other end. She eventually hands my phone back to me with a smile.

"Hey, Matt."

"Thanks, Janus, we're all good. I'll see you later." The edge has disappeared from his voice, and he almost sounds embarrassed. I want to tell him he shouldn't be, that she has the same effect on me. But he hangs up, so I grin at Jo, pocketing my phone.

"How come you're always so calm?" I say.

She looks away, chewing her lip. "My mom suffered from depression and died from an overdose when I was eight. I'm calm because I feel like I looked into the abyss and nothing will ever be quite that bad again."

What? I can't believe she's just come out with something like that so bluntly. I gape at her.

"Jesus, Jo, that's terrible. I'm so sorry."

She nods and swallows. "I don't think she actually meant to kill herself. She just felt so bad and didn't know what to do with it. It was a long time ago."

I'm beginning to realize Jo's a wide-open book. "I feel like an asshole for asking …"

She gives me a wobbly smile, interrupting. "No, it's me. I have a bit of a tendency to open my mouth and blarrgh"—she makes a hand action for words spilling out of her mouth—"out it all comes. As I think you've seen before." She grins then nudges me with her hand. "Sorry for just coming out with that."

I laugh. "Don't apologize. I like how open and upfront you are."

And I watch as a blush stains her cheeks, so I gesture at the phone in an attempt to change the subject and save us from the awkward silence we've descended into.

"Do I need to be worried?"

I can almost see her pulling herself together as she straightens. She shakes her head. "They've tried again, which isn't unusual. They're testing your system, and it looks like they stopped when they realized they were being tracked. If they're serious, they'll probably bypass my surveillance quite quickly. I'll ask someone at the office to sort out a different tracking mechanism."

She's already tapping into her screen as she talks. "The upside is there should be some data we can dive into. Matt's going to dig into it with James to see whether we can find out anything. If they've been careless, we might find clues as to who they are."

I nod. "Sounds good. I appreciate what you're doing." Ugh, that sounded so stiff. "I liked your talk."

"Oh, thanks, I was so nervous!" The rose blush I like so much blooms on her cheeks, and she tucks a red curl behind her ear: I want to reach out and twist it around my finger. I examine the pink lips, the dusting of freckles, her turned-up nose. The color on her face grows. What were we talking about?

"You didn't come across that way at all," I manage.

"Thanks, that makes me feel much better." Her eyes track across my face, and I wonder whether the fact I spent all night on a plane shows. Her next words confirm it.

"How are you doing? You look tired."

Everything in my body sinks into my sneakers. She's being kind, but I'm not sure this is the impression I want to leave. I shrug, twitchy in my awkwardness.

"I've been in Asia for the last two weeks. Everything's been crazy." I glance around again, anything to not meet her eyes.

But she claps her hands and I start, zeroing back in on her. "Asia! How exciting. Crazy good or crazy bad?"

I laugh at this, and in this strange instant of time, sitting there in the half darkness with her, it occurs to me that Jo Williams is a bit of a life force. She could easily be beaten down, but she isn't. She has an enthusiasm for life; no, that isn't right; she has an eagerness for life's obstacles. Yes, that's more like it. A sort of "bring it" attitude, but not in a macho, I-can-take-any-shit way, more in a determined, "I love fixing problems" kind of way. Whereas I tend to bulldoze my way through everything, she calmly sorts. I run my hands over my face and into my hair, no doubt making it even more disheveled.

"God, so many headaches. You wouldn't like to work for me, would you?"

She laughs. "I thought I *was* working for you?"

"Oh yeah. Damn." I pause, letting the sweetness of it all wash through me. "It was good, Jo. We're setting up offices all over Asia, and you're right, it is exciting, but I'm exhausted. I've hardly slept."

She nods, wide green eyes blinking at me. "Your company is doing so well, Janus. It's never easy; I'm really impressed."

My chest swells. As if I need more evidence of how nice she is, there it is. Talking to her is like that moment when your code unexpectedly starts working after weeks of effort. She understands the pressures, the self-worth that is bound up in this thing we do, the desire to win.

"I've never done anything special, Jo. I just set things up and get going. I like people, and they respond to that. I guess I know how to push."

People start streaming back into the auditorium for the next session.

"Can we chat over lunch?" I say.

The tightness in my body that has been dogging me all day eases when she nods. "Yes, I'd love that."

CHAPTER 9

Jo

I hardly engage with any of the talks after the break. Janus is sitting in the row in front of me, and somehow his tired, gloriously rumpled state just makes him better looking. His head nods forward as his shoulders slump and something soft burns through me. He must be under a crazy amount of pressure, and yet he's here, holding it all together. The guy on stage pulls up another chart of figures, and my eyelids droop as I blink down at my notes.

Should I have told him about my mom? I'm so unused to dealing with men like Janus that I just get flustered, and then what comes out of my mouth is a total crapshoot. But there's never a right time to tell people about some sad history. I used to watch her wandering around at night, in her white nightie muttering to herself and feel like it was all somehow my fault. Then afterward, trying to deal with that knowledge that a certain set of people have: that loved ones can be ripped away and there's nothing you can do about it. After she died, my dad picked up all the threads of me and him and somehow wove us both back together. And I wasn't exactly straight with Janus. I'm calm because it holds me together, like a safety pin in a skirt;

otherwise I'd be climbing the walls. I close my eyes.

An hour later, the talks drag to a close. I roll my shoulders as the two guys I was chatting to in the break pause at the end of my row. I fall into step with them as we stream out of the main auditorium, searching for Janus over the crowds of delegates starting to gather around the buffet tables. My stomach grumbles. One of the guys takes my elbow.

"What would you like to eat, Jo?" And something in his smooth tone and false solicitousness makes something shrivel inside me. "Do you want to find somewhere to sit?"

"Actually, I need to talk to Janus Phillips."

The guy frowns like I am inconveniencing him, and my impression of him morphs from pest to asshole.

"Have they got security problems?"

Alarm bells go off at the slightly salacious tone of his voice. It reminds me all over again why I need to be careful: both with Janus and because my business is starting to hold some of the biggest secrets of the tech industry in its hands.

"No—"

It isn't a lie, not really. I've sorted out their first-line defense problems.

"But as in any top software company they want to be at the leading edge of security developments. As I was saying in my talk, you can't afford to fall behind. The risks are too high—there are too many smart hackers looking for an opportunity." A reasonable spur-of-the-moment response, and I quirk my lips at him hoping to dampen the slight sting in my words.

A tap on my shoulder forces me to turn, and Janus is standing there, staring at the good-looking asshole with a frown on his face. His hostility bristles all over us and a little thrill goes through me at his expression.

As the guy turns away to assess the buffet, I lean toward Janus, whispering, "Let's get out of here. These guys are creeping me out."

His scowl dissolves, and the way his forehead clears and his eyes brighten makes me want to do that for him over and over again. I turn to the guy next to the asshole and smile, murmuring, "Hope to see you in the second half."

He nods and gives Janus an assessing look before they wander off to join the line for food. I take a deep breath and swing back to a smiling Janus.

He gestures toward the stairs, glancing sideways at me, eyes crinkling, as we head for the exit. "I thought you were looking forward to the day men were falling over themselves to chat to you up?"

I grin at him, shaking my head. "What was I thinking?"

He nods with a rueful smirk. "You get a lot of creeps, too."

"Creepy *women* exist?"

"Like you wouldn't believe." He shakes his head. "Chances are I'm going to sound like a complete dick when I say this, but the airheads who think highly of themselves are the worst. I've hidden from women like that. Fabian is *ruthless*. I mean he's crazy to be honest, but he can't stand women who are bitchy or silly. He even got to the point that he started asking them what their GPA was before he talked to them." He starts to laugh. "He's a fucker."

"I'd like to have met you guys in college. You sound fun."

"I'd loved to have met you, too."

He sounds so unexpectedly sincere that it makes my insides twist. We've reached the outside of the conference venue and I'm flustered, like I always am whenever Janus makes one of his comments that suggests something more. I scan the street. Noticing a retro-looking coffee place, I turn back to him, only to find he's staring at my mouth. Every time I'm with him, we're plummeting into some new intimacy. I angle my head up the road, and he takes a deep breath and nods before we stroll in silence up to the steaming warmth of the shop.

"So much better than conference food." I eye up the options on the counter. "Oh, *God,* look at that pastry."

Janus laughs, leaning forward to ask the woman for a piece of pie and a couple of coffees. "You should come and meet Fabian; he's got a bit of a cake fetish thing going on, too," he says over his shoulder.

Something about the word *fetish* coming out of his mouth curls around my ribs and my eyes drift to the way his shirt stretches at his waist, the twist of his body. I examine his one-sided grin from the side before I realize I've been completely distracted from where he's paying for our lunch. When he turns, I try to crumple some dollars into his hand, hand shaking, fingers brushing his, but he stares at me like I'm mad. My cheeks are flaming.

"Does he bake?" I'm desperate to stop my mind wandering, to take myself out of the sea of awkward I always seem to inhabit around Janus.

"I don't know. If he does, he's kept it pretty quiet. He codes for fun, though. He's got serious kit."

"Kit?" Now here's a comfortable space I can settle into. "I can't remember the last time I coded for the sheer joy of it."

His face falls. "I can't recall the last time I coded at all. How depressing is that?"

Woah, really? "You don't write software on planes?"

He shakes his head. "Not anymore, too many emails."

"That's no fun."

He screws his face up in a gesture that says *tell me about it,* and we gather our coffees from the end of the counter and head over to two red armchairs that are facing each other in front of a floor-to-ceiling window. The sun spills through the panes warming the wood of the low table between us.

As soon as we're settled, Janus turns to me. "I've got a favor to ask," he says as he swirls his spoon through his coffee and sucks off the foam. "I need someone to talk to." He grins as I raise my eyebrows, but holds up a hand like he is expecting me to give him shit. "About the *business.* I'm finding it hard to find anyone who understands. I can't talk to people who work for me: Bob is an excellent sounding board, but I'm paying him to worry and track the detail. This is more strategic. Someone who'll mull over those big decisions, be positive, help me step back and think about what I need to be working on. I'm spending way too much time firefighting."

"Sounds like a tremendous idea. Who are you thinking of?"

"You. That's the favor."

"Me?" I sink back into the depths of the chair, staring at him. Then my eyes land on my frayed jeans, the token jacket I put on this morning. *If we hadn't got this contract, we wouldn't have met payroll this month.*

"You're kidding, right? You're way more experienced than me—if anything it should be you mentoring me."

"Well, I'm happy to do that, too. Potentially we could help each other?"

"You'd actually mentor me? You do realize you're kind of like … like the person in this industry I admire and look up to." It just comes spilling out of me, and the familiar tightness starts in my neck that heralds a blush. I can't meet his eyes. Is he seriously suggesting this? I'd love to support him, and to have his help with my business would be beyond awesome, but I can't believe he thinks I would know anything about running a company the size of Janus Industries.

He's giving me that cute smile again. "Can we put that out there somewhere, that people look up to me as some kind of shining example?"

I swallow. "We almost went under this month." I want to be honest.

He laughs. "Yeah, it's always like that at the start. Touch and go."

He went through this? "You want to do this?"

"Fuck yeah."

I keep looking at him while he fiddles with his wrist strap, think about our flirting when we first met. That attraction doesn't feel like it's fading at all; in fact, if anything, it's getting stronger. No matter how much I might want to, how gorgeous he is, I know I can't go there; it's the only fly in the ointment. I narrow my eyes at him.

"Just business."

He stiffens like I've insulted him. "Of course. Cross my heart." He makes the movement across his chest. "You're a supplier anyway." He looks away, shrugging like this is a dealbreaker for him.

I can't quite sort out what that statement does to me. There's a curl of regret in my stomach that I don't want to examine too closely. I want the thrill of his interest. And that thought shouldn't even be there, skulking in my subconscious.

CHAPTER 10

Janus

I am never sure why Fabian insists on meeting in odd places. Maybe it is our thing, or possibly his thing: He never goes anywhere with me where I might conceivably be able to pay for him. But the Brooklyn Bridge on a windy day must be one of the worst: I am fucking freezing, the traffic is a thudding assault, and there's no readily available coffee. I hunch down in my jacket as the early-morning light dances across the white waves of the East River. The ironwork is rough against my back as I lean back watching the people power-walking their way to work. I think Fabian likes messing with my comfort levels. I once arranged to go to a nice restaurant with him without his knowledge, and he turned up, gave me the finger, and left. We have this odd relationship that's at once competitive and then suddenly supportive—the kind that only guys who have sat sweaty and unwashed coding in front of screens for four years at college can probably have.

Fabian's hacking activities take him to all sorts of dark depths, and to say he leads an unconventional lifestyle is to undersell his tendency toward oddness. As the tourists and cyclists stream over the wooden walkway, it strikes me again that, even though we've known each other since college, he wasn't the first port of call when we discovered we had a security problem. He's one of my closest friends, but I'm dubious about the world he inhabits. More than once I've thought he has no scruples, no morals, but then he has also been the most loyal friend. Large parts of his life are a mystery to me, but he's said enough things in passing, when we're staring at screens or mulling over the meaning of life, that have made me wonder why he's not in jail. And, despite all this, our friendship still sits deep. There is some part of me that burns with what he burns with and always will; that desire to know and to expose, to bring these people, who think they can get away with fleecing or lying to the rest of us, to light.

But now I've been sucked into playing a corporate game, and I'm envious of his alternative lifestyle, that fuck-you attitude, his willingness to walk an unconventional path. When I first started my cloud computing business, I thought I was forging my own rebellion—it all felt so different from my family's expectations—but I've drifted to a more conventional place.

Fabian's experimentation through college and after taught me more about the tech world we inhabit than any lectures we attended. The problem is his desire to try new things doesn't end with technology: He does drugs, conducts scientific experiments (usually on his own body), has bizarre relationships with other people, and collects weird people around him. I've had to rescue him more times than I'd care to count. That debt goes both ways, though. As I stand on the walkway looking down at the traffic and the metal framework, I'm half-expecting to see Fabian thrown out of a speeding car.

But as my eyes scan along the bridge again, I pick out his hunched figure in the distance and I smile to myself. He's sheltering behind a pillar, a thin jacket hugged around his equally thin body, trying to hold back the gale. As I stride toward him, his face breaks into a reluctant half grin.

"All right, you fucker," he shouts as I approach, garnering a look from one or two passersby—the usual Manhattan radar for crazies—but as I get closer, concern starts to wash through me. He has sores on his lips and his skin is a gray wash.

"You look like shit."

He stares out over the water and shrugs, and I deliberately wait. When I don't say anything, he turns back to me impatiently.

"What? I always look like this." He hunches over in on himself as if he's trying to hide.

My gaze wanders over his gaunt face and too-thin body.

"What are you taking?" I'm starting to sound like my parents, dammit.

He answers my question with one of his own. "Why are you always so suspicious?"

"I went to college with you, remember?" I say, leaning on the railing next to him in a bid to mask the extent of my concern. "I saw all that shit firsthand."

Fabian almost died from an overdose in college by not being clear about what he'd taken, and some enthusiastic doctor in ER gave him the wrong thing. It nearly killed him. I can still remember the panic of that night: the crash team swarming around his body, getting kicked out and spending nail-biting hours in the waiting room until a consultant walked down the corridor to let me know he was all right.

He laughs and shakes his head, looking to the side with pursed lips as if he's wondering what to say to me. I'd trust Fabian to always give it to me straight—we made a pact the night of the overdose—but I know sometimes it isn't easy for him to do this: He wants to protect me from the truth of his life. We've argued on and off about this for years. He's told me he doesn't want me to worry or to land me in trouble; I've told him that I'm one of his best friends and I can handle it.

"I have no idea what I've taken," he says, and I gape at him.

He waves a hand at me. "It came from a friend, okay? He wouldn't give me shit."

"You're kidding me, right?"

He doesn't *know*? But why am I surprised? The thought of losing him makes my breath seize in my chest. If I lost this friendship—this bond we've always had from the first time we found each other and coded together—it would rip me apart.

He jiggles his legs and arms like he's trying to reboot his circulation. "I'm fine, *I'm fine*. Whatever it is, it's nearly out my system now. It was just a bit of a bad trip, that's all." He gives an unconcerned shrug, pushing his hands in his pockets. The wind whips strands that have escaped from his man bun all over his face.

My throat contracts with everything I want to say, but I can't keep repeating the same old reproof. We came close to falling out at college when I ranted and raved at him. I wish with all my heart that whatever makes him do all this crazy bullshit would somehow get sorted.

I knock his man bun to one side with my hand. "What is it with this fucking *hair* anyway?"

And his lips turn up in a reluctant smile, half-thanking me for giving him crap and moving this conversation on. He reaches out and ruffles my hair in return, and I try to jerk backward out of his way. He studies his hand in disgust.

"Gel? And you have the nerve to mock *me* about my hair? I just can't be bothered to cut it. At least I don't style it, you asshole."

"Can we go somewhere fucking warm and get a coffee? I'm fed up with your crazy meeting places." I sound more grumpy than I intend.

"Got to keep switching it up, Janus." He grins at me like a maniac and punches my arm. And I'm irrationally pleased with this exchange; our groove has been worn smooth through a thousand similar conversations. "Don't want you to be a dreary old corporate drone, do we?"

"If fucking only, something boring and desk-bound would be bliss right now. I've been in more countries in the last couple of weeks …" I trail off and narrow my eyes at him as we move to head over the bridge. A guy whips past us on a bike not holding the handlebars, headphones on, nearly taking Fabian out.

"Fucker!" he says.

"You don't want to come and work for me, do you?" I ask this every time I see him. It'd be fantastic to have him involved in our software. "Lots of crazy shit happens when you start new offices in new countries; enough to keep even *you* interested."

He laughs, knowing I'm not really expecting an answer. "Never mind me working for you, when are you coming over to code with *me*?"

Fabian's Aladdin's cave of an apartment in Brooklyn is packed to the rafters with kit, like one of those obsessive-compulsive hoarding people you see on television, except all high-tech gadgetry. His bedroom is command and control central, a huge rack of servers and screens, endless amounts of things to fiddle with to your heart's content. I sigh, scrubbing my hand over my face. I haven't managed to get over there in so long.

"I would kill for some cake." His words interrupt my musing. "I'm ravenous. Interesting drug this one; I'm so fucking hungry."

I roll my eyes at him, try to picture my calendar. "Next weekend. I'll come by then." I need to keep more of an eye on him. Taking his arm, I drag him across the bridge in search of that elusive Manhattan rarity—homemade cake.

CHAPTER 11

Jo

I dump my bag on the floor by a cluttered table, and Kate looks up from her papers, squinting in the setting sun. The light casts a warm glow over the wooden tables and floors and Manhattanites catching up after their hectic workdays and even more frenetic gym sessions. Kate's residency in ER keeps her too busy saving lives for us to meet up as often as we'd like, but the McNally Jackson Café has become our go-to place to hang out. I glance around at the pastries and the magazines littering every surface and feel my body ease. When I turn back to Kate, her face is lit with a broad smile.

"Hey, geek girl."

"Dr. Dull."

Kate screws up her face in a hilarious approximation of outrage and sticks her tongue out. This is our routine, honed over time in a shared room at NYU and ultimately a rented apartment near campus where she still lives with Liss, the final leg in our three-legged stool. Studying medicine meant that Kate's course was longer than ours, so she's still got years to go.

At college, I started helping people set up their IT systems to pay my way, which morphed into my small just-about-surviving business that buoys me up every time I think about it. When the Caltech contract came in, we had to double in size in six months, and Des and James have recruited like crazy as I've watched our cash flow get more and more precarious.

I let out a long breath, and Kate raises an eyebrow at me, gesturing to the counter of food.

"Are you eating?" she says.

Warmth seeps through me. She isn't pushing for explanations concerning my no doubt panicked expression. She's letting me be ... or perhaps she's just hungry.

"Oh God, yes, are you? I'm half-starved, no time for lunch, and I worked out this morning, too. My body is shouting, 'Give me carbs right now!'"

She laughs. "Go order. Another coffee and a muffin wouldn't go amiss while you're there."

As the barista swirls a pattern into the top of our two flat whites, my eyes land on a newspaper in the rack next to the counter. Caltech's problems quickly came to the attention of the press, who wanted answers about who was going to sort it. Thank God they had a decent PR agency that protected me. Feeling that kind of heat, having that lack of control over what people were saying, the public scrutiny, was too close to how the press harassed my dad and me at home. They camped on our lawn for weeks. A shudder runs through me: It all got out of hand so fast.

And how much fallout could there be with Janus Industries? Janus is already in the public eye, and if it became known that his company had a security issue, the press would be all over it like a rash. Getting my own publicist would make a lot of sense. But given how close we were to the edge this month, how could I afford something like that? I almost laugh at my whirling mind, cutting and dicing possible options and solutions; mentally drawing flowcharts for absolutely everything.

When I return to the table, Kate reaches out to grab one of the coffees from my hand. "I've been so looking forward to catching up," she says, leaning into the table expectantly as I slump into my seat.

I grin at her, shoving down my worries. "You know I'm working with Janus Industries?"

Kate shimmies her hands as she tips forward, knowing eyes locking with mine, voice dropping to a reverent hush. "I think I'd just spend the whole time gazing at him in meetings. I'm presuming you've actually *met* him?" She drops her voice like she wants me to share the greatest secret. "So, *spill*. What's he like?"

"Oh, of course, he's gorgeous." I stare out the window at the street lit up by the evening sun and the stream of worker bees heading home. How can I even begin to describe Janus? "He's impatient but considerate … fun, too. I can see why women swoon all over him."

"What about this woman with me?" Kate asks, making circles with her pen over the table at me. "Is she swooning all over him?"

I let out a groan. "Honestly? Yes, I am. *My God*. He's totally irresistible." I put my head in my hands. "When he smiles at me … I could spontaneously combust." I fill her in on my idiocy in the elevator, the lunch that followed, and the conference where he asked me to mentor him. "But let's be honest here, I can't afford to be involved with him. First, I've been employed by his company, and second—*hello?*—I'm just beginning to build my reputation as a serious player in this industry, I can't be sucked into anything that would destroy that."

"Why would it destroy that?"

"Can you imagine? 'She only got the contract because she's sleeping with him,' yada, yada, yada. They'd have a field day. I wouldn't look like a genuine business proposition at all. I'd be like some sleeping-her-way-to-the-top floozy. There'd forever be this question mark over me. Of course, guys can do this, no problem; they'd just be nailing a 'hot piece of ass.'" I do air quotes with my fingers, and Kate laughs. I lower my voice and lean over the table. "And if we had a fling and split up? All bets are off. With his media profile, I could be *crucified*. At the conference, people were already asking questions about why I was talking to him and whether Janus Industries had a 'security problem.' Everyone in the industry is interested in him and his success. Thank God they didn't probe any further. Can you imagine?" A shudder rolls through me. "I don't know how he handles it."

"This kind of double standard drives me nuts."

I laugh. "Why do women even have to think about this stuff?"

"Sounds like he might be interested in you, though."

My heart knocks on my ribs when she says this, and I don't like the spike it causes in my chest.

"Why do you say that?"

"Come on, Jo, accosting you at the elevator and practically begging you to go to lunch?" She leans toward me, eyes wide, finger tapping the wood surface between us. "He even flat-out said he asked you out, and that he hadn't done that in a long time."

She's enjoying this. She's told me before that she thinks the guys I choose are as dull as toothpicks. I think they're calm, steady, committed. *Safe.* No one in their right mind would describe Janus Phillips as safe.

I groan. "Don't remind me. It won't help me resist the Phillips charm. Anyway, he's a player; they all say things like that."

She does a little dance in her seat, and I can hardly bear the gleeful expression. "Janus Phillips is keen on a friend of mine," she sings.

"Shhhhh," I say, flapping my hand and looking around.

"Maybe you're worrying unnecessarily?" she says.

"Maybe I am, but I really can't afford to take the risk."

Her face falls. "Oh yeah. Don't get me started on the risks working in medicine. There was this cute guy yesterday …" She stops, blushing slightly.

Now I am all sorts of interested. Kate almost never notices guys; she's way too involved in her studies. Although calling her "Dr. Dull" is our joke, she *is* completely subsumed by her career, and she'd be the first to admit it.

"He was unconscious."

"Comatose. The best kind of man. I like them when they can't speak."

She starts to giggle. "Oh don't. We can't talk like that; I could be banned from practicing medicine before I'm even qualified."

"Anyway,"—I pat my hand on the table—"spill."

"I don't know, there was something about him. He'd taken some drug—"

She purses her lips as if she's running his medical symptoms through her head. We've talked a lot about this kind of thing in the past. "It had knocked him for six. And then he came to halfway through the night and wanted to leave: He was still spaced out."

I stare at her open-mouthed. "And?"

She shrugs. "He signed the piece of paper and left."

"That's it? You let him go?" I say, my voice rising.

She wrinkles her nose at me. "We can't make them stay if they're determined to go. He was dizzy, disoriented. I watched him weave down the corridor as he was leaving." She frowns again. "I hope he was okay. I'm still wondering whether I missed something."

"Didn't you want to follow him home?" I can hear the appalled squeak in my voice.

"Well, I did, but purely for professional reasons." She winks and shakes her head at me.

I put my chin in my hands and inspect the blonde hair brushing her face. When did she last talk about a guy? Even found one worthy of comment? A warmth flutters up inside me seeing *this* Kate return, a Kate that's not ground down by the slog and responsibility of being a doctor, the pressure of her overperforming family, the sting of past relationships; a Kate who escapes the worry of every diagnosis she's ever made. I settle in, happily throwing my own worries out the proverbial window.

"Tell me what he looked like," I say.

CHAPTER 12

Janus

The door squeaks as I push it open, and I take in the warm lofty space and inhale the sweet smell of baking and coffee beans. Hopefully no one will recognize me here. The wood floors are scuffed with the tread of hundreds of sneakers as I step up to the counter, my eyes scanning the beard and piercings of the guy behind it, his hand movements lazy, precise, a cat appearing slowly on the surface of the foam.

"That's impressive, man."

He raises his eyes to meet mine and laughs.

"What can I get you?"

Once I've collected my order, I saunter through the nooks and crannies until I find a quiet sofa in a sunny dusty corner, and sink down gratefully into the cushions. Tucked away at the back of the coffee shop, I'm caught up in my phone when the chair opposite me is pulled out. As I look up, my chest squeezes. It's a version of Jo I've never seen before: her coppery hair is piled haphazardly on her head, red tendrils spiraling softly down her neck, and round shiny pink glasses sit on the bridge of her nose. Skipping down her body, she's a mess of trailing scarves, ripped jeans, socks that look suspiciously like they have rocket ships on them, and a pair of blood-colored Doc Martens. She looks like an exotic bird, some tech guy's fantasy. If I had been smart enough when I was younger to draw a tech girl hero, she would have looked just like this. Even the glasses are hot. I swallow. All my blood drains to my groin. I want to remove the glasses slowly and watch those green eyes widen as they meet mine. I am so deep in my fantasy I don't even notice the odd expression on her face.

"Janus?"

I motion my hand up and down. I can't ignore the fact that I've just done a whole-body scan.

"Is this what you wear to work?"

Oh! Wow, Janus, way to go with the idiot comments.

"Yes, uh, why?" She glances down at herself as her voice catches, and I am a dick for making her feel that she looks anything other than fucking amazing.

"No, God, no." I flap my hand, too quick with my response, and I groan inwardly. "You look great. Like a girl tech hero." I swallow hard. I've never sounded so stupid. I've promised I won't hit on her. Be professional, Janus.

Fortunately, she laughs, sinking into the seat opposite and unwinding a scarf. "I guess you've only seen me in my executive outfit before now." She looks around the café and inclines her head toward my laptop, open on the low table between us.

"How's it going?"

I wave my arm around the warm wood interior and the gray wool sofa I'm sitting on. "Being out of the office and somewhere different is great. I've been making some notes on things, made some decisions. We need to find someone to head up the Asia Pacific region: having a person in place would make the process of setting up there so much easier." I stop myself in mid-flow. "That's so *obvious* when I say it out loud."

Is there a woman in the world who wants to hear about the plans for my management team? As a young nerdy guy in school, I got used to being dismissed by girls. With my slightly overweight frame, unkempt clothes, and temperamental skin, girls handed me their phones to fix and never *once* looked at me. It wasn't until I went to college and Fabian took me in hand— screamed *move* at me on weight machines and treadmills and stopped me living off pizza—that I started having any sort of success with girls. That guy still lingers inside, rearing his ugly head when I talk too much about tech or meet a woman I like, but as I look at Jo her eyes are clear and bright, never straying from mine.

Okay then.

"Less travel for you?" she says.

I nod. My tongue feels welded to the roof of my mouth, but her earnest expression makes something unwind. I wonder if she was the same kind of nerdy teenager that I was. I straighten my legs, easing back into my seat.

"The traveling over the last six months has been insane. I've been to so many countries and seen so many hotel rooms I can barely remember them. Hopping from country to country"—I shake my head—"as a backpacker it would be a blast, but all I do is see lawyers and offices. I love writing software, but the reality is I might never get back to having fun with code again."

She's nodding.

"Friday is my coding day actually. I protect it in my calendar." She laughs and leans forward to stir her coffee. The light catches a piece of her hair, setting it on fire.

Some scent I can't define grabs me in the back of my throat, a sort of citrus perfume, and I want to lean over and sniff her. I almost laugh out loud at how inappropriate *that* would be.

"I count the days to it. Sad geek." She mumbles the last words with a grimace as she lifts her cup to her mouth. I take in the wrinkled nose, the sweep of her lashes. I want to kiss her cheek and lick her freckles, see if they taste like chocolate, sweet and exploding on my tongue.

"Janus?"

Ugh. What the *hell* were we talking about? Coding days. Yes.

"Excellent idea. I should try and do something like that. The real problem is the time you need to get your head around it. The chances of me getting a whole day now without interruption are just …" I shake my head.

She reaches over and puts her palm on my forearm.

One.

Two.

Then her hand is gone.

I am branded. The buzz of her touch moves all the way down my body, and I only just stop myself leaning right over the knee-high table and kissing the perfect pink shine off her mouth.

"You need to keep doing the things you enjoy, don't you? It keeps you sane. Do you do hack days in the office?"

"No. Actually, well, to be honest, I'm not sure … I don't manage that area anymore." I shrug, heart sinking, as I study the guy on his laptop at the table behind Jo. "I just get the reports."

"Maybe you could set something up, or even join in. I bet there would be a real buzz if the CEO came along and hacked code. Make the techies feel like they're the lifeblood of the business."

"They are the lifeblood of the business," I growl.

Her eyes skirt away from mine and then back.

"Don't bark at me. You're talking to a geek, I know they are."

"Okay, okay, apologies." I hold up my hands, palms forward. "Shit. I hate how developers are used and abused. They create all the value."

She slumps a bit as she smiles. "I think I've hit a sore point."

"Yeah, sorry." I'm being an ass.

"Perhaps we could code together sometime?" she says.

I gawp at her. This sounds like all my best fantasies rolled into one.

Nervousness chases across her face like a cloud scudding across a perfect sky.

"I mean I'm sure I wouldn't be anything like as good …"

I wave my hand at her, shaking my head. "That would be awesome," I choke out, trying not to crumple at her feet in adoration. "You'd do that?"

"Well, of course! It would be a blast. You could come to a coding Friday at my company if you like. The tech guys would be so excited."

"I'd love to do that, too. The thought of getting stuck into somebody else's problems for a change would be fun."

Warmth hums through me as I bring my coffee to my lips, but I'm somewhat ashamed that I've set this all up because I am a jealous prick who didn't like other guys hitting on a girl he was interested in. I have so many ideas buzzing through my head now. I should have thought of her skill and insight first, not all the other inappropriate thoughts. There is no way I am good enough for this girl.

CHAPTER 13

Janus

I have my first Sunday off in what feels like forever and I'm almost light-headed as I head out of Clark Street subway and into Brooklyn's leafy streets. The brownstones wrap around me like a protective blanket, and the sidewalk is almost empty, so unlike the downtown frenzy. Sun glints through the trees, bouncing off the buildings and the frosty sidewalk, warming my face and my arms. Tension slowly seeps out of me into the cold January air as I walk toward Fabian's. A sudden shout snaps my head upward.

"Janus Phillips, sex god!" Fabian is leaning right out of his top-floor window.

My lips curl up and I wave. Turns out he hasn't forgotten one of our ongoing jokes, this one from a newspaper headline that ran above three pictures of me all taken in the same week, each of them showing me kissing a different woman. If anyone knew how little sex I got now, they wouldn't find my life quite so amusing. I certainly don't. Then I'm laughing at him as he's hanging out the window, shirtless, waving what appears to be a spliff at me.

"Come do dem drugs," he yells, and I wince as a couple of people stop chatting on the stoop over the road and observe him in confused silence.

He cackles loudly as he slams the frame down, and I wonder how much he's smoked and how stoned he might be. Fuck. I didn't do dope at college, not from some moral high ground; I just didn't like the lack of control and had no time to be high anyway. But God, today with all that is going on in the business and the constant jitters from my crush I am trying to hide, it has never sounded more appealing.

The buzzer unlocks the door, I take in the out of order sign on the elevator and the battered hallway, then trot up three flights of stairs. Fabian meets me at the doorway to his apartment, all naked tattooed chest and the dirtiest, roughest denim I've ever seen on anybody. I narrow my eyes on his face, but I can't see any outward signs that he's high at all. I nod at the joint in his hands and at his jeans. He peers down at himself and winces.

"Let me take a shower."

He hands me the spliff with a grin before disappearing into the bowels of the apartment. "I have no idea when I last washed," he shouts at me over his shoulder, and the familiarity of this conversation makes a soft laugh bubble up my throat.

I look at my hand and take an experimental drag, bending double as the smoke hits my lungs. Am I trying to suck in air or exhale as fast as possible? Jesus, my ribs are like iron bands around my chest, eyes starting to stream. Fabian's head appears in the bathroom doorway.

"Don't fucking finish it," he growls before disappearing again, and then the drum of running water starts along with his tuneless whistling.

I squint at the glowing ember in my hand. One inhale had that effect on me? I head down the hallway, walls plastered with all kinds of crazy art various "friends" of Fabian have given him, often in return for IT help. A patterned kilim sits on the dark wood floor. It's all remarkably clean, but Fabian was never particularly messy or dirty; he just accumulated things. Lots of things. I wander into the fifties kitchen, the bright orange cupboards and food everywhere in such contrast to my own. Setting the spliff down gingerly on a saucer, I busy myself making coffee. He starts singing loudly in the shower some tune I vaguely recognize. Every time I come here, I'm a student again and

Fabian's living the same life we lived in college like he's stuck in a time warp. But he's such a lovable nut, and I'm not sure whether it's being here or the effect of what I've just smoked, but—as I add milk to the cup—the worry of the business, Fabian himself, and Jo, all start to fade away.

Coffee in hand, I wander idly into his bedroom and scrutinize what's on his screens as I sip. Rows of servers blink and hum. A whole wall is covered in boxes of kit. I'm in the middle of working out what program he's running when he appears bare-chested behind me, rubbing his wet hair with a towel.

"What do you think?"

"Damned if I know. What is it?"

"Password AI. I'm trying to hack into the National Archives. I got chatting to some chick online, and she said they had the most amazing data in there. I thought it'd be easy to go in via the back door but everything's pretty up to date, so this is my next line of attack." He frowns at the code as if he could understand the problems with it through sheer force of will.

Fabian can't be bothered to ask anyone for permission to do anything. He's got access to a huge variety of national institutions, databases, classified documents, and he works to keep those things open, to have all this information at his fingertips. I could ask him anything and he'd know or be able to find the answer. Crash investigation? He can locate all the confidential reports. And I suspect that I don't know the half of it. He's told me in the past that he's good at covering his tracks, careful not to get on anyone's radar. I have no real idea how he makes money. Some people seem to pay him to fact-check, but I'm sure he does all sorts of other illegal stuff, too. I scan the screen: black boxes filled with lines of code. At least this one doesn't sound *too* shady.

"What's tricky about it?" I say.

He sinks into the chair next to me, towel around his waist, long hair dripping water onto the keyboard. I lean forward tracking a loop as his fingers grab the mouse from mine, following the script down the screen.

"I've got a problem right there," he says with a harsh scowl, jabbing his finger at the offending code.

I nudge him. "Get dressed. Give me time to run through it."

Fabian swivels around, still in the chair, dragging a random T-shirt from the floor and stretching it over his head. He zips backward to the computer adjacent to the one I'm sitting at, signs in, then stands and grabs underwear from a drawer by the bed, pulling them on before tugging on clean jeans from a crumpled pile on a seat. The warmth settles inside me, the keys under my hands, the huge screen in front of me, even Fabian's long hair shedding water like a wet dog. He plonks himself down beside me on a sharp exhale, and for a blissful minute I'm that guy again, coding next to his friend.

I cuff the back of his head with my hand.

"Wrap something around that ridiculous hair of yours and stop soaking me."

He laughs, leans over, and shakes his head over me and the keyboard.

"Fucking hell."

He sits back and clicks over the screen, booting things up, but I quickly realize that he's working with a bunch of software tools I've never seen before.

I nudge his elbow. "Show me what you're using."

He grins over at me, starts to explain, and before long we are buried in problems.

Time tracks shadows across the ceiling and eventually Fabian leans back in his chair and rubs his eyes, saying, "Fucking starved." And the hunger I've been studiously ignoring for the past couple of hours ignites in my stomach. I glance out the window at the darkening sky visible above the buildings over the road, before looking at the time on my monitor. Seven p.m. *Holy shit*, we've been coding for about eight hours straight. I widen my eyes at him, and he laughs, scrubbing his hands down his face.

"Pizza?"

I am struggling with some particularly tricky code my mind won't let go of, so I nod vaguely at him, turning back to the screen. Only half of me hears him ordering the food on his phone. He chuckles, patting me on the shoulder.

"There's the Janus I used to know."

I laugh at the warm thickness in his voice.

"Fuck, this is great." I gesture at the monitor. "How long will it take you to crack this, do you think?" We've made solid progress today, but I have no idea how much work he'll need to do before he's got something workable.

He shrugs. "How long is a piece of string? Sometimes I get lucky and find a weakness. Other times it takes weeks."

"That sucks."

Fabian stretches, laughing. "I'm going to go and play Xbox for a bit—give my head a rest. You want to join me?"

"Nah, I'm going to carry on with this problem." Something is just out of my reach snagging at the back of my mind. I want the satisfaction of some kind of breakthrough: code that doesn't throw up any errors.

His chair complains loudly as he pushes back too sharply and pulls himself up. He disappears into the living room next door. The screen in front of me has started to turn into squiggles I can't separate. I blink up to the wall, my eyes wandering to his computer, the crazy Post-it notes he's got all over the wall reminding him of passwords and things he needs to do. I try to pull my head back into what I was doing, staring down vacantly at the papers lying across the desk, and as I focus on the haphazard pile between the two screens, I almost do a double-take when I see the word *Janus* written in his curly writing on a piece of paper jutting out from some others.

My brows knit together, and I tip forward, lifting the sheets up gently and scanning the page. A diagram of some sort is scribbled there in Fabian's distinctive scrawl. As I lean closer, blood starts thundering in my ears. *What is this?*

Standing, I move the stack off the one I'm interested in and place them face down, so I can put them back exactly as I found them. I hold my breath, listening for a second like a thief. The sound of distant gunfire comes from the living room.

My eyes crawl over the diagram, mind churning. What am I looking at? It's not dissimilar to the one Jo was drawing in our meeting. Is this our *system*? Nausea bubbles in my gut. Picking it up and studying it closer, I notice access keys all over it.

I put it on the desk and whip out my phone, snapping several photos and closeups, before carefully placing it back with the other papers on top. I cock my head at the pile. Does it look like it did before? A shout suddenly erupts and I whirl around, shoving my phone in my pocket so fast I almost drop it. But the room is empty, and I hear Fabian curse loudly in the distance. Heart hammering, I sink back down into my seat and blink at the floor, unmoving. I pull up my phone and examine the photographs. Why would he have stuff about my system written down? I stare at the mess of papers, hoping they'll give up their secrets. It makes no sense.

Could *Fabian* be our hacker? The idea keeps trying to push itself into my thoughts. But why? Why would he do it? *You could just ask him*, a little voice says. My stomach lurches. I don't want to have that conversation immediately; I'll sound panicked and accusing. I have to get out of here and examine it properly before I do anything.

The door buzzer startles me out of my thoughts. I listen for a beat, two, realizing belatedly that Fabian won't have heard it with the noise of the game. So I head down the hall, pressing the button to let the delivery guy in, and in minutes we have warm pizza on the kitchen bench, and I am searching for clean plates and beer. I resolutely put whatever that piece of paper was to the back of my mind. I'll think about it when I'm home.

CHAPTER 14

Jo

Sun streams in over the mismatched desks I bought cheaply at an auction house when I had to find an office fast; I paid so much in rental that I shook with the thought of spending money on anything else. You could pretend the space is boho chic if you were high and lacking mental faculties, but, in all honesty, it's okay, despite the age of the property and the decrepit furniture. The single room runs all the way along one wall of an old downtown office building. Tall windows let the light stream in, and the battered desks, rescued from an old garment factory by the saleroom, are lined up perpendicular to the wall, like soldiers on parade. The only exception is my workspace, where a desk is placed perpendicular to two desks that face each other. A glass meeting room sits behind me, and a breakout area occupies the other end of the room, with tall shelves, a blue slouchy sofa, and bean bags. Next to it is a small kitchen.

I gaze absently over the top of my screen at the dark blue paint that covers the long wall of the office. Des, James, and I decorated it one Saturday night when we were working late and drunk. I can still see the uneven patches. Des's tight curly blond hair that he wears in a short crop looks white in the sunlight, and he quirks an eyebrow at me over his glasses, snapping me back into the real world. I've been gazing at him for ages. I shake my head in apology, giving him a grin. He's cute, gay, and everything I could hope for in a right-hand man.

"I know I'm gorgeous eye candy, but stop staring at me," he says, pretending to concentrate on whatever is on his screen, a small smile hovering on his lips.

I grin. "How is that love life? Caught any guys ogling at you recently?"

He wrinkles his nose. "God no, just my boss, and she's a woman." He makes a sort of strange screwed-up-being-sick face and I burst out laughing.

"If you must know"—he pauses for effect, pushing his Robert Marc black frames back up his nose—"I'm fed up with it: the hooking up, the thankless boring dates. Why are people so obsessed with their social media? No one has any fun anymore. If anything exciting happens, everyone stops, so they can take pictures and post it." He sighs theatrically.

James peers over at him from his desk that runs across the end of our two. "Have you had anyone do that while you've been ..." He tails off making some obscene gesture with his hand.

I snort. This type of thing always makes me want to start a blog about our crazy office conversations, but who wants that kind of exposure and shit; isn't that Des's point?

"Don't be rude, Jimmy-boy." Des eyes him over his glasses, trying and failing to look offended. "Anyway, what world do you live in? Of *course* guys want to do that, but I have a no pics rule. I mean can you imagine the *trauma* if Uncle Tommy came across a picture on some site?"

"I agree with you actually," I interrupt, "about the thankless boring dates. I haven't managed to find anyone I'd even want a one-night stand with."

Des's head snaps back to me, the picture of enthusiasm. "You want me to set you up?"

"With a *gay* guy?"

"Of course not, you dolt." He makes an impatient face while I grin at him. "But I could find you a gorgeous hetero guy."

"You don't know any hot straight guys," I scoff.

"Janus Phillips?" James slyly lobs a grenade into the whole conversation.

Both of them are staring at me expectantly. I roll my eyes at him, glancing down the row of desks behind Des, but only a couple of people are sitting at their screens.

I rub my nose. "What?"

Des throws his hands up in the air. "Come on, girl."

I lean into my screen. "Shh!"

Des glances around, before leaning forward and lowering his voice. "No one's here. And all your dates are as dull as ditchwater."

I'm ignoring that comment.

James folds his arms on his chest. "He is like the hottest guy in New York right now."

"And you know him!" Des nods, his head bobbing excitedly. "God was not smiling on the world when he decided Janus Phillips would not be gay," he mutters, ducking into his screen to stare at something.

I spread my hands out in a shrug. "Don't be ridiculous—he's a client!"

"And?" James is looking at me closely.

I roll my eyes. "Can you imagine the epic fallout if I started up something with Janus?" I start to laugh, but they're looking at me like I'm some raving cat woman. Oh, God, they're right, I need to get laid. Janus and I have met twice now for our "mentoring" sessions, and each time we meet all I want to do is kiss that smirking grin right off his mouth. The real worry is that I am going to be tempted into doing just that. How embarrassing would that be? I need another guy to distract me. I'm not even concentrating that well on my work at the moment.

"You mean the kind of epic fallout when one woman says to another: 'How sensible is she, banging the pants off that incredibly hot guy?'" Des shakes his head at me.

"Or says, 'I'd tap that if it was within fifty feet of me,'" James adds, and he and Des high-five each other from their swivel chairs.

"Come on, guys, not Janus Phillips, okay? He's a womanizer. There are loads of pictures of him kissing women in the press—usually models—sometimes different ones in the same week. He's known as Mister-Couple-of-Months."

James waves a hand in dismissal. "I'm sure that was ages ago."

"I'm sure it wasn't," I mutter into my keyboard.

Des pretends to think about this. "I can't convince myself he's a womanizer. I don't think he's a liar or a cheater. He just has the opportunity to take out a lot of stunning women, and why wouldn't you? Well, if you weren't gay, *obvs.*"

"And he's into you." James points a pen over the screens at me.

I gawp at him. I kind of know this, but I'm trying to ignore it and other people definitely shouldn't be thinking it. Janus takes beautiful models to social events. There was a picture of him in the paper at some red-carpet thing last night, so he's clearly not that into me, or he would have asked me.

Okay.

No.

Just … No, Jo.

Where did that thought come from? I want to slap my head. He's a client. He's sleeping with numerous women. A stone sinks to the bottom of my stomach.

"He's not into me," I say.

"That's not the gossip on the hotline." Des smirks at me.

My head snaps up. *What the hell?* Has there been something on social media I haven't seen? Des is one of those people who has eyes and ears *everywhere*. He always knows someone who knows someone. A hot spear shoots through me.

"What *gossip?*"

"Don't have a conniption. A friend of mine at the TechConn conference said Janus was fighting off hordes of men and dragging you away."

Honestly, the tittle-tattle in this industry. All my fears and hopes rush up my throat. Rumors about Janus and me are the last thing I need.

"That was when we got the call about the second hack attempt, okay? He had Matt on the line and needed to talk to me."

"Oh." Des is clearly deflated, but a thousand horses' hooves have started up in my chest. If my staff are gossiping, how many more people are?

James shrugs and goes back to his screen. "Still, it'd be hard to find anyone hotter than him."

Ugh. I wish he hadn't said that.

"Guys," I say, "we need another candidate."

At that, their heads both snap up and Des gives me an evil grin. I groan as I realize what I've said: I've agreed to their nefarious plan to set me up with some guy.

CHAPTER 15

Jo

The following morning I'm back in Mays inhaling steam and espresso grounds, trying not to overthink the conversation with Des and James about my lack of a relationship, my lack of dates, my lack of *everything*. Trying not to think about the gibberish I spout around guys I like. After I got home last night, I googled Janus Phillips and *my God* the number of women he's been photographed with. My guilty secret? As I was scrolling, I found a picture of him in board shorts on vacation somewhere, which I've screen-captured. It will do nothing to help me behave normally around him or help me sleep when I wake up in hot sweat. I'm contemplating the chalkboard of new coffee blends when a kiss lands on the back of my neck, and my whole body locks.

"What the—" I spin round to find Andy grinning at me. I can hardly handle my plummeting stomach. That will teach me to stop daydreaming about Janus Phillips when I should be thinking about work. Am I so deep in my daydreams that I could convince myself that he would be kissing my neck? The words "You're a supplier" float through my head.

"Don't pile your hair on your head if you don't want guys having hot fantasies about being behind you and smooching the back of your neck," Andy says.

He's smiling.

He's an absolute menace.

"That's assault actually," I say, completely failing to appear stern. "My hair gets in the way when I'm working and I pile it on my head, you dick. Just 'cause guys like you think that—" But he's shaking his head at me.

"Jo. No one could see your neck and not want to kiss it."

"Andy …" I circle my face with the finger of one hand. "Very annoyed face."

He holds up his hands in mock apology, grinning widely at me. "Okay, I'm sorry I attacked you—goddamn feminist!"

I grin at him, not at all offended.

"You see, this is why I could never go out with you. You assault me and then—"

"Oh, shut up!" he mumbles good-naturedly. I don't mind being assaulted by Andy. He's harmless, and underneath all his whoring ways is a heart of gold; he just needs to find the right woman to be faithful for.

I smile sweetly at him. "Met any more elevens recently?"

"Unfortunately, no, but I'm glad I ran into you; I've got a favor to ask."

He glances off to the side and my ears prick up.

"You can say no, okay?" The words are almost dragged out of him, and he chews the side of his cheek, glancing around without meeting my eyes.

His normal effusive confidence is being replaced by an Andy I've never glimpsed before. I've never seen him so … so … unsure. I gesture with my hand for him to spill the beans.

"I've got a problem with a girl at the office and I need to take someone to a dinner that isn't from work. I don't want to show up alone."

His words come out in a rush, a flinching tremor in his voice. "I don't want any more drama. I'm genuinely worried if she kicks off they might fire me. I thought of you because we're friends, and I thought you might like to go and catch up with everyone from Triton? It's a work do."

His eyes are cast down as if the floor will answer his prayers, and he runs his hand around the back of his neck. I stare down the line to where the barista is making coffee. Seeing the guys from my old office again would be amazing, and I had a good time at Triton, but Andy's modus operandi with women is not usually like this. I turn back, considering his bowed head intently.

"How bad is it with the girl?"

"We hooked up at a bar one weekend and since then she's been on my case," he mumbles, blowing out a long breath and staring at the wall behind my head. "She's told me she's pregnant." The last bit comes out on a whisper.

"She *what*?" Too late I realize my voice is way too loud—pulling a few stares from the surrounding customers—and he shushes me with a hand, grabbing hold of my arm and dragging me in close, finally meeting my gaze. He hunches his shoulders and gives me puppy-dog eyes.

"Don't tell anyone, okay?"

I almost laugh at this request. I'm in our office twenty-four seven; who would I tell?

"She fucking tricked me into not wearing a condom, and now she's telling me she's expecting a baby. I just don't believe her. What are the chances the one time I don't wear a condom she is—she gets—"

He can't even repeat the word and screws up his face in defiance.

There is so much wrong with that sentence I think my head is going to explode. "Andy—"

He shakes his head at me, like he's heard it all before, like he knows how dreadful his hookups are, and my mind drifts to Janus and the picture of the girl he was with the other night. Was she his hookup, too? Does he spend time dealing with this kind of thing? I can't believe it. And would I be that girl who expected more? Every sharp comeback sinks back down inside.

"So, fairly bad with the girl then?" I half-joke.

"Her best friend told me that she's not pregnant." He scuffs his foot against the floor, and the barista leans over the counter and asks for our order, all the while drawing an elaborate pattern in the coffee he's making. I swing around, requesting two flat whites. When I turn back, Andy is staring over my shoulder. The normal grinning bonhomie has completely disappeared, and his eyes are turned down, deep grooves on either side of his mouth, so I reach out rubbing my hand up and down his forearm. What if he *has* got this girl pregnant?

He sighs, running his other hand through his messy blond hair, and I gesture to some stools. I need to stay and talk to him, despite all the work waiting for me at the office.

"I don't know what to think," he says, leaning into me on a half whisper.

"Surely taking someone else will make it worse?"

"I'm hoping to flush out the truth. She's being all doe-eyed and tearful on me. Her friend told me she'd done it to another guy before." He picks at a nail and sighs. "What a mess. I thought maybe if she saw me with someone else it would force her hand—I'm sorry, Jo, but some girls are just—"

I know what he's trying to say. There's a certain type of woman that likes to manipulate guys, and, despite being a sexist dog, Andy is upfront about the fact that he's only interested in hooking up. We weave over to the stools at the bench by the window and hitch ourselves up. People are streaming along the street, headsets firmly in place, coffees clutched in their hands. I still have to pinch myself sometimes. *Manhattan. I have a company here. So what if it's touch and go? I escaped.*

"You're the only girl I know who'd have my back in something like this," Andy says, pulling me back into the conversation, and something softens inside me.

"Everyone thinks I'm a player, but dammit, Jo, I'm straight with the girls I do all this stuff with. I'm *always* clear about it."

I can't find it in my heart to berate him. My gaze roams over the broad shoulders and smart suit, a patch of blond stubble on his chin. Not for the first time I wonder what his deal is and why such a good-looking guy goes through women like water. But he's been a good friend to me in the past. He helped me out with a persistent client we had once who seemed to want more than his software worked on. I lean over and ruffle his hair, and he smiles a sad and crooked grin at me.

"Okay."

"You'll do it?" he breathes, and as I nod he leaps up, dragging me off my chair into a hug.

"I'll need a full briefing," I mumble into the shoulder of his suit where he's suffocating me, and he pulls back, nodding enthusiastically.

"I owe you huge, Jo." He takes his face in my hands. "I can't thank you enough."

He plants a soft kiss on my cheek, and I grunt, embarrassed, placing a hand on his mile-wide chest. "Okay, okay. Enough."

What have I just agreed to?

CHAPTER 16

Janus

Jo Williams is being pulled into a bear hug by some good-looking blond guy the size of a linebacker. As he kisses her, she puts her hand on his chest in a way that is so familiar that red-hot pokers push through my stomach. Why didn't she tell me she was seeing someone? But, frankly, I'm an idiot for never considering that question. I hunch my shoulders. No wonder she's been so careful with me: I'm a client and I've been coming on to her. I sink back behind a pillar and out of the line. Coffee will have to wait.

Sweat trickles down my spine. Seeing him come up behind her and kissing her neck—where the freckles form a swirling pattern that disappears into her hairline—it's branded on my eyeballs. Jo Williams had started to feel like she belonged to me. But this explains all the friend-zoning, all her reluctance. I watch them with their heads close together a bit longer, and she smiles at him as he gives her a knowing grin.

"Two mocha lattes!" the barista suddenly shouts over the hiss and bang of the machine, and I start, looking around wildly. I can't stay here. I skirt backward, nearly sending someone flying, and apologize profusely as I shoot out of the door like I've been stewing in the steam of a thousand coffees. I roll my lips together as my head pounds. The traffic swooshes past, horns blaring, a couple argue on the sidewalk right next to me: thousands of people carving out their lives in frustrated hopes.

By the time I reach the office, my head is hot enough to explode. Well, fuck it all to hell—if I'm in a shit mood, then I'm going to make use of it. Some things that have been bugging me at work are going to be sorted today. I need something to make me feel fucking better. I snap my fingers at Maddie, my PA, and she startles, eyebrows shooting up into her hairline—I never do that kind of shit—but she gamely grabs her pad and follows me into my office like her feet are on fire.

When lunchtime rolls around, I've bawled out so many people about the network and our clients that people are hiding from me. Maddie has sat through the whole thing, frantically making notes as I've hauled every team over the coals about the issues that aren't getting sorted anywhere near fast enough for my liking.

"Shall I order in some lunch?" she says quietly.

I sigh, stare at the glass wall of my office and the sea of desks outside—a few hardy souls are still there braving the onslaught of the tornado. Some of the fight seeps out of me. "Sorry, Maddie."

She grins at me. "No worries, I like seeing you on a tear. I don't know what's got into you today, but sometimes things need shaking up."

She's a great assistant, the best. I want to explain, but I can't do that; it wouldn't be professional. I turn to look out of the window at the view. The sun is bouncing off the office buildings, and the water under the Brooklyn Bridge shimmers like a mirage. *Brooklyn. Fabian.* Bingo.

I wave her away. "If you could make some notes on everything that was agreed this morning, I'm going to head out and get myself something to eat."

The phone picks up after twenty rings—and I know this because I'm counting them, willing him to not be passed out in some drug den in Harlem.

"'Lo." Fabian's rough grumble echoes over my phone.

"You are having lunch with me," I growl at him.

After a long silence, he chuckles on the other end of the line.

"Okay," he says, "but you're coming to Brooklyn."

CHAPTER 17

Jo

My stomach is sinking through the floor.
Down.

Down.

I swallow a yawn. Never again will I let Des and James organize my dating life. I glance around the dimly lit restaurant, the dark bamboo dividers and intimate seating. There's a couple at every single table, and this makes my heart reside somewhere near my boots. I'd rather have gone bowling. Making small talk is a nightmare when you find out you've got nothing in common. Note to self: Make sure any first dates are at places where entertainment can be had— movie theaters, bowling alleys, ice rinks.

"—And, of course, then I had to rewrite the code for the compiler—"

I tune out again. Lewis is doing an outstanding job of convincing me that I shouldn't be dating someone from the software industry at all. I thought we'd have shared interests, could bond over a mutual love of all things tech, but I clearly didn't tick the sense of humor box. I knew he was a bust when I made a joke about his shoes, and he just blinked at me. He probably thinks I'm incredibly rude.

My phone vibrates on the table, and the illuminated screen shows a photo of Des making a face at me over his computer. His text is four question marks one after another. Lewis and I both glance at it at the same time, and I curse the fact I put it out on display. I snatch it up, smiling a watery smile at him.

"Sorry."

"No problem, where was I …?"

"Compilers?"

"Ah yes!" His eyes light up as he sits forward. "I'm so happy you're into this stuff, Jo. Normally women are not interested at all."

I nod numbly. I wish I could text Des back.

I glance down as my phone—now on my lap—vibrates again. Fortunately, Lewis is in full flow and doesn't pick up on my lack of attention.

"Do you need rescuing?" Is all it says and I'm light-headed with how much the idea appeals.

Suddenly, the screen switches to an incoming call, and the name Janus Phillips appears. My date stops talking mid-sentence as I hold it up to my ear.

"Sorry," I mumble, "I've got to take this."

I'm sure he'll think that's rude, too.

"Hello?"

"Hey, Jo, apologies for ringing this late on a Friday night."

I give Lewis what I pray is a placating smile over the table.

"That's okay; I'm just out for a meal."

"Oh, yeah, anywhere nice?"

"Zenkichi."

"Oh, awesome place! Is it a special occasion?" he says.

God, I hope not. I fiddle with a strand of my hair as heat rises up my neck.

"Um, not really, um … just a date," I mumble, and the handset goes quiet.

"With your boyfriend?" he eventually says, and my brows furrow in confusion. Boyfriend? What the hell is he talking about?

"Ummm," I say, voice rising, and a strange silence balloons as panic fills my chest. But I can't grill him on this now. Lewis is watching me, listening in to every word.

"Anyway, none of my business," he rushes on, filling the dead air. "I wanted to find out if you could come into the office tomorrow. I'm sorry to ask on a Saturday, but I've got something important I need to chat to you and Matt about."

"No problem, what time?"

"About 11 a.m.? That work for you?" He's all business.

"Sure, sounds fine, I'll see you—"

But the phone goes dead before I have a chance to say goodbye.

CHAPTER 18

Janus

Matt and Jo sit across from where I'm standing at our big board table. Looking out through the colored-glass walls, I can see a few lights have been activated by our walkthrough, but otherwise the office is dark and weirdly quiet. No pieces of paper or files in here. My gaze returns to Jo. They're both slightly rumpled: Is it because we're meeting on a Saturday or the fact that they had a wild Friday night? A sharp stab pierces my ribs. Jo's hair is tied up today, the wisps skimming down her neck, cheeks bare of makeup. I wish she'd mentioned her boyfriend to me, but perhaps I can't blame her for that: I'm a high-profile client and it's none of my business. She was thinking it was one thing, and my thoughts were somewhere else entirely. I should have worked out some guy would have snapped her up ages ago. The first time I met her, I practically forced her to have lunch with me then asked her to mentor me. My chest caves in. I'm sure now that she's been trying to tread a line of putting me off while also being professional. I'm going to be one hundred percent business from now on: no more flirty conversations.

"Nothing we are about to talk about goes any farther than this room," I growl, pacing down to the end of the room and back to where they're sitting.

"Why all the cloak and dagger?" Matt says, leaning back in his chair with his hands behind his head, a frown creasing his forehead.

I'm even thinking we need a secret code word. I stop and run my hands through my undoubtedly already crazy hair.

"I've got something to show you guys."

I tug my phone out of my pocket and pull up the pictures, placing it on the polished wood table in front of them as I sink down into the opposite seat. They both frown as they lean over the table to look at it.

"What am I looking at?" Matt says.

"Some kind of system diagram," Jo murmurs, tapping the screen as she angles forward.

"That's one of our name servers, a map of the connections into it," Matt adds, magnifying the image with his thumb and forefinger.

I've studied these photographs all week and I lean over the table, too, a warm hum buzzing through me that he's noticed this straightaway.

"Those are the access keys for the servers in Delaware and Cincinnati," Jo says, and my body straightens as the tightness that has sat in my chest ever since I found the paper starts to ease.

"Right. Denver and San Francisco, too," Matt mumbles as he examines the list. Their heads are bent over my phone, Matt's mouth getting increasingly pinched.

"Is this just on your phone?" he says.

I close my eyes for a beat. "Yeah. It's not synced anywhere else." We encrypted my phone a while ago.

"Why are you showing us this? Where did this drawing come from?" Matt narrows his eyes on me.

"I'll explain in a minute but let me ask you a question first. How big a deal would it be if someone outside the company had this information, these keys?"

"Well, potentially they could get right into the system—"

"Did you find them outside the company?" Jo is looking at me curiously.

I nod and their eyes widen. "I have a good friend from college who's a hacker." I pause. I've mentioned Fabian to both of them before and I wonder how much more to say about his alternative lifestyle. "He's very, very good at it. He's got into places that you'd need to leave the country for hacking into. As far as I'm aware, he's never been discovered or arrested. I noticed these written on a piece of paper on his desk when I was at his place coding last Sunday."

"*What*? Have you ever given him the keys for any reason?" Matt asks.

"No."

"Has he ever worked on our system?"

"No."

"Maybe you left some access open when you went there in the past—"

"No. Definitely not."

His eyes narrow on me. "Logically, that's what makes the most sense," Matt says. I know it does—nine times out of ten these things come from human error. Fabian has told me this himself.

"I haven't been to code with him for a long time. Our first hack happened four weeks ago. I've been all over this. So it's unlikely—"

"You think he's been hacking into the system?" Jo says. Her brow is wrinkled as she chews on her lip.

"You said he was a college friend. How close are you now?" Matt asks.

And questions pile up like cars on a highway, thick and fast. They're the same things I've asked myself over and over.

"Very close." I run my hands through my hair again. "I don't know, Jo, I don't know what to think. I'm completely thrown. Fabian and I are more like brothers than friends. We've rescued each other from scrapes too many times to count."

"And this is his handwriting?" Jo taps the phone screen again, eyes staring vacantly at the windows opposite.

I nod again.

"Could he have inadvertently got a password from you in the past? Something you left at his place? Even if it was a long time ago? Help he gave you with something?" I don't mind the fact Matt is pushing this; I want them to think of all the possible options.

I mull that over for a second, trying to think back, but Jo taps a colored pencil on the table interrupting my train of thought.

"We changed the passwords; it'd have to be recent," she says.

"I didn't take anything with me. I worked on his machines," I say.

"*Why* would he be in the system, though?" Jo says. "Do you trust him?"

"Up until now I'd have said I trusted him with my life, and I undoubtedly have on one or two occasions."

Matt blows out a breath.

"What kind of hacking does he do?" Jo asks, and I tip my chair back to stare at the ceiling. It's a hole in my knowledge about Fabian. A big fucking hole.

"I don't know to be honest. He's more of an information gatherer, I'd say. I wouldn't peg him as selling a lot of government secrets; he's more about exposing corruption. He likes to know stuff, particularly about legal cases, big ones with the government or businesses, that kind of thing."

"Perhaps he's being blackmailed?" Jo says.

"Doesn't that only happen in movies?" Matt mumbles. He's pushed his chair right back from the table and is now sitting with his elbows on his knees, hands wrapped around the back of his neck as he stares at the floor.

The thought had crossed my mind. He wouldn't want to tell me, thinking I'd offer to help, give him money. "He's certainly got an alternative lifestyle."

Matt looks up. "How alternative?"

I shrug. "Drugs and stuff mainly. He experiments with some crazy shit, using his body like a chemistry lab."

"Jesus. He could be involved in some big narcotics thing." Matt sits back, pushing his unruly mop back from his face. "This might explain everything that's been happening recently, the security breach—"

"I don't really see how a drugs thing—" I start.

"I guess the things people like that would be into—blackmail, extortion, fraud—the data you hold is probably a holy grail for them," Jo says.

I run my hands up my face. "I don't really think that's the kind of drugs he does. He takes things no one else would take. They're not generally things that people would sell, even illegally."

Matt harrumphs at this. "We need to get a P.I. on him, find out who he's seeing, track his movements."

"God, I *so* don't want to do that," I groan. "He's my best friend! He's paranoid—if he catches on someone is watching him, it might scare him unnecessarily."

"Have you thought about just asking him?" Jo chips in, and I try not to stare at the freckles and perfect skin.

"He doesn't tell me much. He's said in the past he doesn't want me dragged into anything illegal through him. If there's some trouble driving why he's doing this, then there's a reasonable chance he wouldn't tell me."

"Yeah, there might be other reasons he's not telling you stuff, people on drugs—" Matt starts.

Jo interrupts. "If I was able to access his apartment, it might be possible to set something up to track the activity on his computer."

And oh! I hadn't thought of that. Ugh. The thought of doing something like this to Fabian—

"You'd have evidence of what he's actually up to," Jo says.

"But not *why*. God, I don't want to do something like this."

"Janus, we need to get as much info on this as we can," Matt says. "If he's innocent, he'll forgive you. Come on, man, this is the company you've built from scratch; you can't let it be damaged like this."

Matt's so laid back normally, but here he's staring at me intently, eyes narrowed, and I'm impressed all over again with how professional he is. He understands how much trouble our recent security breaches are causing, and what could happen if it gets worse. Jo's doing an amazing job, and we've kept it out of the press, but it could only be a matter of time. Caltech were hung out to dry. He's right. He's right. I hold up my hand.

"Okay, okay. Let me get my head around it. Let me get to the point where I can accept I'm going to do this to my best buddy. I'll get there, okay? This is so fucking mercenary, all because my company is worth a billion fucking dollars." My hand lands on the wood of the table with a slap.

I thrust my seat back, pace to the window, and look out at the cold gray twist of the East River below. I swore I wouldn't do this kind of shit because the money was too important. Now I'm planning to investigate my closest friend.

I lift my head, and their faces are tight, worried. A wash of gratitude spills through me.

"Thanks, I appreciate you coming in and—"

Jo shakes her head. "Can we think of any better ideas?" she says.

I walk back over to them and sit down. She's right to pull us back; we need to explore all avenues. We all look at each other glumly.

Matt nods grimly, rises from his chair and heads toward the flip chart. "Let's brainstorm."

CHAPTER 19

Jo

My Brooklyn rental is the garden apartment in one of the brooding brownstones that hang over the streets in this part of town. The guy who owns the building lives on the top floor and works on some kind of financial trading desk. When I told him I worked in tech his eyes lit up, and as I probably didn't look like the sort to give him trouble, he gave me a good deal when I had to move out of our college apartment. I miss Liss and Kate, but it's warm and peaceful despite the tiny rooms. The living-cum-kitchen space opens out onto a plant-filled yard, and my favorite thing to do on the weekend is to sit outside buried in a book with a cup of coffee.

I've staved off Des and James setting me up on any dates by telling them about this thing tonight with Andy, although I was careful to avoid the backstory. The full-length mirror shows my taupe lace dress in all its glory; with my pale skin, I look like I'm wearing nothing. If only I had the courage to wear Doc Marten boots with it, but I'm Andy's date, so I've dusted off some elegant suede shoes and a handbag. Yet another disguise. I turn to look at the dresses piled on the double bed; there's a million miles of lace here. I skim my hand over the pile, peering over my shoulder at myself in the full-length mirror. I look like a petite fairy princess: no ass at all. My phone beeps with a text.

"Are you ready? A."

"On my way."

Calico, my gray cat, winds around my ankles. "No time for any of that, buster, I'm going out."

I grab my wrap and slip my feet into my shoes. When I appear on the sidewalk, Andy's standing there next to a car, a tux molded to his frame, blond hair slicked back. His eyes scan over my dress and his mouth is a perfect O.

"Jesus Christ, you look amazing," he says, waving his arm up and down the lacy dress. "Remind me why we never hooked up again?"

I stick my tongue out at him, and he drops to one knee. "Please say yes, Jo," he says, raising his eyes to the sky with a grin.

I put my hand on my hips and glare at him as he pops to his feet, dusting down his trousers. He peeks at me through long blond lashes. "Worth a try though, right?"

The jittery feeling about tonight intensifies. I point my finger at him. "Not at a dinner, okay? No messing around. I'm not giving you blowjobs under the table. I'm not saying yes to any proposals. We're not doing anything except scaring this girl off. Promise me you'll behave: no picking up anyone else."

The last bit is an afterthought, but, God, Andy is a loose cannon. My stomach growls at me; either with food or nerves, I'm not sure.

He crosses his hands across his chest. "I'm on my best behavior, Jo, I swear." But I roll my eyes at him as we move toward the waiting cab.

Once we're settled, I examine his sharply shaved jaw.

"So this is just a meal, right?"

"Industry dinner."

"Industry as in …?"

"Security."

"Security?" Even I can hear the squeak in my voice.

Andy frowns. "Yeah. I told you Triton was taking a table."

Of course he did, but my stomach dips realizing I didn't put two and two together.

"The girl … is she on the same table as us?"

"Yep. She works at Triton."

I've clearly paid far too little attention to this. Some of my clients might be there. How is it going to look if I'm on the Triton table with Andy? I rub my forehead.

Andy grabs my hand as we leave the cab and doesn't let go. A faint tremor runs through his fingers and I'm like a rabbit trapped in the headlights. What a pair we are. Ugh. This was not a sensible decision. As we step inside, I look around the hall and immediately recognize several people from top New York tech companies. Blowing out a long breath, I straighten myself up. I'm here now, right? I can work this room like a pro; I'm not very comfortable doing the *chat-up-all-the-right-people* thing normally, but needs must where the devil drives. After thirty minutes, Andy is nowhere to be seen but I've found some useful people to speak to and some of the tension in my shoulders is starting to ease.

Someone comes to talk to the hardware guy I'm with, and I use the distraction to study the atrium, the roar of conversation, the glittering chandeliers overhead. A head of peppered hair near the doors to the dining hall catches my eye, and I shift position. Bob Sugar? Janus Industries is not in the security space specifically; why would he be here? A man shifts in front of me and I catch a glimpse of tousled dark hair. My heart takes off at a gallop. *Janus?* Craning my neck, I try to peer over the crowd. The two men I'm with are in a deep discussion and I take a step away, waving my empty wine glass like I'm going to find a drink. The man I was talking to touches my arm.

"Call me, Jo, yeah? I want to examine our security more closely."

I beam at him, nodding. Perhaps tonight won't be so wasted after all.

I shift through the crowd. Someone puts a flute of champagne in my hand. Several people step back and, even from the back, I recognize Janus. Grinding to a halt, I feel fluttery panic setting in: I *really* don't want Janus to see me here with Andy. As my eyes scan over the group, I realize Janus and Bob are deep in conversation with an older guy I don't recognize. I start to turn away but, as if he's aware he's being watched, Bob shifts his gaze over Janus's shoulder and spots me, his face lighting up as he waves me over. Damn. Then Janus turns and his eyes wander up and down my body, almost before he can stop himself. *Lace dresses, always the best choice.* I smile widely at him, and something working behind his eyes makes my whole body sit up and pay attention.

"Hey, Jo," another voice says suddenly at my side, and I turn to find Matt grinning down at me. Janus's expression tightens as he pulls me into a hug.

"Cool to see you here," Matt says.

I've become good friends with Matt over the last month; we're on the phone almost every day. Maybe I can stop the schmoozing for half an hour and have a normal chat with someone, but as soon as I think this, Bob draws me forward.

"This is the lady you want to talk to Jack," he says, turning to me. "Jack's one of our clients and runs a payments company. We were just chatting about security."

I smile widely at the guy and start probing into his business, and then he's asking me about mine and what we do. Slowly I notice two women on the periphery of the little group. One of them is Bob's wife, Mandy, and—I work out with a sinking heart—the other one is with Janus. She shifts closer to him, her hand curling around his arm and pulling his attention down to her by talking to him in a low voice. He studies her face and then he grins, and I suck in a sharp breath as a wild beast stretches its claws and digs in. I turn away to stop myself staring at them, but I want to take in every detail of how they are together. Is she one of his women who last a couple of months or something more? My heart is thumping out of my chest. Laughter forces me back into the conversation with Jack and Bob, but my mind skitters like it's on ice, her body shifting against his in my peripheral vision. *You've no claim on him, Jo.* Suddenly, an announcement echoes over the PA system that dinner is served, and I'm not sure whether to be pleased to escape or annoyed I can't watch their body language anymore.

"Give me your card, Jo," Jack says, and as I'm fishing in my bag, a hand lands on my lower back. Andy.

I take a peek at Janus as I swing around, but Andy is completely oblivious, smiling that big grin at me. And I don't know what comes over me; all I know is that I want Janus to experience some of the destruction that's burning through me, so I go up on tiptoes and kiss Andy on the lips. To his credit, he doesn't turn it into a full smooch.

"Hi," I say, pulling back as my face goes hot with the weirdness of this moment.

His eyes narrow on me; he's too smart not to realize I've done that for a reason, so he leans forward and whispers in my ear, "Who was that for? Janus Phillips? Because he's watching me like a hawk."

My stomach sinks. That was so childish. My face feels even redder when I turn and smile at the group to say our goodbyes. Bob and Jack are beaming at me, but Janus is staring at Andy, and my heart tries to fight its way back from the floor where someone has stomped all over it.

"Great to see you all. Hopefully catch you later?" I say, and Janus rubs his hand round the back of his neck, body tight.

I grab Andy's hand, dragging him away as fast as I can into the banqueting hall.

"What was that all about?"

I shake my head at him.

He stops, pulling me to a halt.

"Jo. What is going on? He looked furious."

I stop and turn and stare at him, my gut roiling like a hurricane. "He was with a gorgeous woman. I'm his supplier. Why would he be mad?"

Andy puts his hands on his hips. "You tell me. You're working with him, right?"

"It's nothing," I say, shrugging and moving down the aisle toward our table.

"Are you two playing some kind of game?" he says.

I shake my head. I don't know what we're doing. We're racing forward then retreating like two armies trying to take a battlefield. I look down at the tremor in my hand. *He goes out with women all the time.* I need to calm the hell down and stop doing things that are going to land me in no end of trouble.

CHAPTER 20

Janus

One a.m. The spreadsheets on my screen are more of a green-and-white blur than a coherent set of numbers. I toss back the rest of my whiskey and it burns all the way down, sourness and heat making my throat close. I want to drown out every thought, focus on what's in front of me, but the alcohol is clouding everything. I tip the bottle on the table—how full was it when I started? Snapping the lid shut on my laptop, I pick up my glass and the bottle and kill the only light in the room. Swivels, my cat, stretches in the bean bag next to my desk, getting up and following me as I pad through to the quiet hum of the kitchen. It's times like these I love Manhattan the best, with the dim glow of the kitchen cupboards and the glittering panorama of downtown spread out before me. Up this high, the clatter and honk of New York is a distant soundtrack.

What was I thinking, taking Aubrey this evening? I'd wanted to prove to myself that I could do what I used to do before: go out with a woman casually and have a nice relaxing night. I had no thought that Jo could be there, but of course it was obvious. She was inspecting us out of the corner of her eye, looking like a nymph in her naked lace dress; I think every man in the place was watching her. I swirl the ice in the glass, almost melted and gone, rattling against the edge.

She kissed him. My hands tighten around the tumbler. Of course she did. I place the glass in the sink and snag a beer from the fridge, moving over to the long windows along one side of the apartment. Unlocking the door, I step out onto the balcony, blocking Swivels exit with my foot. The cold makes my breath catch.

I spent most of my night trying to spot them at their table, much to Aubrey's disgust: She wanted my attention on her and her alone. Eventually I found out he was from her old company—some guy named Andy—and they looked close. Of course they did. A soft sofa beckons and I sink down, resting my head on the back of the chair, staring up at the stars. We've not yet hit the warmer nights that start to creep through in spring and the bitter chill is seeping through my white cotton T-shirt, so I pad back inside to grab a coat and a blanket before heading back outside.

Slumped back down into the soft gray fabric, I turn my phone over in my hand and force myself to concentrate on something other than Jo Williams.

"I enjoyed our hack," I type, hoping Fabian will be up.

The response comes through immediately. "Yep, like old times. Come over anytime."

I've got to take Jo over there so we can try to put something on his system, but after seeing her last night with her boyfriend, spending a whole afternoon with her will be torture. I wish she was meeting Fabian in more honest circumstances. I just hope what we're doing doesn't ruin my friendship with him for all time.

"Can I bring someone next time?"

In seconds my phone is vibrating in my hand, and it pulls a reluctant grin out of me: I knew he wouldn't let that go by. His laughing voice fills the line.

"How did I know that suggesting bringing someone to your lair would trigger a call?" I say before he can get a word in.

"Where are you?"

My voice slumps as I answer. "At home, working on spreadsheets."

"God, man, I thought you had different flavors-of-the-week women to drag you away from all that shit."

"Well …" I turn the beer in my hand, examining the label like it holds some previously unknown truth. "This person I want to bring round is a woman actually."

"Seriously? What's she do? No, let me guess … An actress? Model?"

"Nope, try something a bit closer to home."

"Media … Marketing?"

"She'd like you to think that, but she's a techy, too."

"Be still, my heart."

I laugh at the thrill in his voice, and how closely it echoes my thoughts from when I first met Jo. Women are as rare as hen's teeth in the tech industry.

"She's gorgeous, Fab."

I press the cold bottle to my chest and let the icy fingers slip into my blood. Fabian will know from this one comment that I'm smitten; I'm incapable of being cool with him about girls that interest me. He has a way of getting to the truth, and I'm like an over-enthusiastic dog; I was always a crap poker player. But all this is from college days. I've never talked to him about any of the women I've dated more recently, and I've certainly never taken any of them to meet him.

"It must be serious," he says.

"Oh God," I groan. I'm behaving like a lovesick schoolboy. "If only. She won't give me the time of day. She's got a boyfriend."

"Are you kidding? Do we need to persuade her you're a much better option? You're a good-looking guy and a rich one, too. What's not to like? Oh yeah,"—his voice drops—"I forgot about the small penis."

"Fuck off."

"Seriously though—"

Pulling myself out of my seat, I lean over the railing that sits behind the greenery edging the deck, taking a slug of beer. I peer at the antlike life below, the myriad of people here, lives that lurch from one crisis to another, deals and loves won and lost.

"God, I'd love to persuade her that I'm a better option. She's determined to friend-zone me—believe me, I'm trying." I'm not talking to Fabian about how I took another woman to an event for some stupid-ass reason.

"Whisk her away, man. Hire a private jet and take her to a tropical island. For fuck's sake you've got the money." Dishes clink and a tap turns on in the background.

"What are you doing?"

"Been coding all day, need something to eat," he mutters, and my stomach tightens with envy for the life he leads: every day like the day I spent with him, hunched over a computer examining code. "Can't you do some big gesture?"

I sigh. "No, not really. I need approval from the board for everything. The value is tied up in the company, not hard cash."

"Well, just tell the directors you want to get laid, and they need to sign off fifty grand for you to hire a plane ..." His laughing fades away and the click and crunch of the microwave door echoes down the line before his voice comes back stronger. "I can't believe she's resisted the Janus Phillips seduction techniques. Usually they're all over you."

"They're all over me because of my money."

"They're really not. Come on, man, even at college you got all the girls."

"That is so not true." Fabian pulled all the interesting, edgy women: the ones like Jo in fact. Perhaps I shouldn't introduce the two of them.

"Nadine—"

"God, remember Nadine—"

We both simultaneously come out with the same thing and I laugh.

"She was a head case," Fabian mumbles like he wishes he could forget.

I move on. Neither of us want to talk about the car crash of a relationship that ate him up at college.

"I'm depressed about the whole thing. I saw Jo with her guy in the coffee shop last week, and she hadn't told me. Not that she needed to tell me, but—"

"How did you meet her? What's she do?"

"She's been consulting for Janus Industries. She does network security."

"Seriously?" I can hear the thrill in his voice. "I love her already. How decent a hacker is she?"

"She's on the other side, Fab."

"Yeah, but you can't be good at one without being good at the other."

"Is that right?" I say.

"Are you good at both?"

"Are we still talking about hacking here?"

Fabian snorts. "Why's she helping you anyway? You been hacked?"

Curiosity worms through me with this question. How much does he know? Why *did* he have a map of my system on his desk? He'd know about my hacking if he was involved, but of course he'd need to pretend he didn't. Yuck. I hate this kind of double thinking. Then he pulls me back into the conversation.

"I thought Matt was pretty hot on this."

"Yeah, he is. But we needed an independent eye on it."

"Why didn't you come to me?"

How do I answer this? Surely he can't be doing anything if he's asking me questions like this?

"It wasn't really my decision, to be honest. Bob knew Jo through her professor at college. She's got a good reputation."

"Jo Williams?"

"Yeah. You know her?"

"I've come across her name a few times. She was part of that Caltech thing, wasn't she?"

"Yep, we've had one incident that she's sorted out, but she's sorting out some other security on our network anyway."

"Pleased to hear it." His tone is neutral, and I can't judge it. "If you need my help, let me know. Bring her over. I want to see with my own eyes that she's not into the godlike Janus Phillips."

"Shut up," is all I manage to get in before he mumbles something about his mac and cheese and hangs up on me.

CHAPTER 21

Janus

"She's lovely."

Fabian's voice is right in my ear as he sneaks up behind me in the kitchen like a genie, leaning out and grabbing a wedge of feta and popping it in his mouth. I've been tasked with lunch, and the bench littered with crumbs, plates piled high with food. Although I think Jo's amazing, something warms inside me at my best friend giving her the seal of approval. My face breaks into a huge smile as I stare down at the knife in my hand.

"Lucky bastard," he mutters as he leans back against the counter and crosses his tattooed arms across his chest, watching me slice avocado onto a piece of toast.

I shake my head. "Oh, she's not mine, believe me."

"Only a matter of time, yeah? Trust me."

I laugh and lean into him, nudging his shoulder. "She might have a friend," I say, and he snorts at this.

"No woman who's friends with Jo would go near a guy like me."

My eyes narrow. I've watched Fabian hold on to normal life by a thread since we were at college, but even I can see he's slowly unraveling and disappearing down some rabbit hole. He's getting thinner and more erratic, and I don't like the way he's starting to look—the gaunt tinge his face is taking on. Not for the first time I'm unhappy with myself for being too involved in my company over the last three years. I've got to come by more often, code with him regularly. I put the knife down carefully, turning to take him by the shoulders.

"Fab …"

But he doesn't meet my eyes and he shakes his head, so I stare at him for a few beats before moving back, picking up a piece of cheese and swallowing down the lecture that was bubbling up my throat.

In the uneasy silence that follows, I press a fork through the avocado with far too much vigor. "You're amazing. Any woman would be lucky to have you," I mutter into the bench. Sometimes the best you can do for your friends is to try and defend them against themselves.

But the whole conversation is making my body droop. I'm about to put some tracking code on his system. He's a decent guy. Why am I not just talking to him? For several seconds, I'm tempted to let it all spill out, but Jo's on her own in the tech room and I need to keep him in here chatting. I'm too far down the path to pull back now.

"What've you been working on? You still looking at that library system?"

"Yeah, still busy with that. Got a bit farther, but not there yet. Can't tell you about the other stuff I'm doing, though." He winks.

"Story of our lives. Did that person respond about the Python script?" I don't care what he talks about now as long as he keeps talking.

This is our usual conversation, and he's off, telling me about the tools he's discovered recently and the chat room stuff he's been reading and a whole tale about some guy who claims he's taught his dog how to code. I putter about making coffee and trying to think of anything but why I'm here. He pulls up the video, and we watch as the guy puts his Rottweiler in his seat with its paws on the keyboard. Fabian is bent over laughing, and, as he doubles up, I see Jo leaning against the door frame, eyes wide and smiling. How long has she been standing there watching us?

"This is like the best tech tutorial," she says, and Fabian straightens and grins at her, reaching out and ruffling her hair.

"Yeah, watch and learn, little girl."

Jo screws her face up and sticks out her tiny tongue at him, and then asks him a question about password AIs that blows my mind, and Fabian raises his eyebrows as he struggles to find any kind of sensible answer.

I start to laugh at the expression on his face, then she stretches up and ruffles his hair.

"Watch and learn, little boy," she says, and then we're all laughing. And oh, the joy of this! The unbelievable idea that I might have found this cool woman who is so awesome she can give Fab a run for his money. My throat thickens and I have to turn away. I'm pretty sure he understands me well enough to get what a dreadful softie I am. His hand comes out and touches mine briefly, ostensibly to help with the food, but I know what he's doing.

She's got a *boyfriend*.

Boyfriend.

Janus.

Boyfriend.

I suck in a sharp breath and stare at the three heaped plates on the bench, turning back around to hand her the now-cold toast piled high with feta and chili.

She gapes at me. "How much do you guys eat?"

It makes me laugh, and I clear my throat.

"Come on," Fab growls, grabbing his plate, "I want your thoughts on this library system I'm trying to hack into."

The whole afternoon goes by in a blur of watching them chat about hacking and exploring tools on the Web. I'm slightly envious at how they share stories, the way she jokes with him. But I also don't think Fab has many strong, calm, organized people in his life, and it's nice to witness. Eventually, Jo and I are out on the street turning our collars up against the cold air that's spreading its icy fingers over the trees and cars around us. My brain is lit up, refreshed. The weak February sunshine has long since disappeared; I've never felt less like ending an evening.

"He's great." Her voice is concealed behind one of her scarves, and she shifts it down, smiling up at me. My gut tightens.

"He's a lovable nut for sure."

"But God, so knowledgeable, Janus! Knowing I've got someone like that on the other end of my attempts to keep systems safe is terrifying."

I wave my hand in the vague direction of the Clark Street subway, shrinking down into my jacket as I study our feet on the sidewalk. My beaten-up old sneakers, her short steps.

"Yeah, I know." I pause. "Did it go okay?"

She nods and her breath comes out in a whoosh. "Yes, I put it on there. I've buried it well but"—she chews her lip—"he's seriously switched on, Janus, and so paranoid; I can't guarantee he won't find it."

Her cheeks are pink with the wind and her lips look bee-stung, as if she's been thoroughly kissed. I groan inwardly. I can't keep my brain in gear when we're together; my whole body wants to lean into her. Stomping my feet against the cold, I try to shut down the swarm of thoughts.

When I pull myself back into the conversation, she's chewing on a finger. "I'm worried about this, about him. What if this is something bigger than him? What if he *is* being blackmailed? Some of the things we talked about today ..." She hesitates. "He's involved in a lot of highly illegal stuff."

I nod. "I know." Pursing my lips, I blow out a long breath.

"Um—"

I turn to look at her tilted head.

"What?" I say.

"He's not that stable, is he?"

The fact that Jo can see this when she's only just met him makes an iron fist tighten around my throat. In a heartbeat, my mind leaps over all his problems to Jo's code on his machine, and my thoughts barrel forward and out of my mouth before they're straight in my head.

"I'm concerned that you'll be sucked into some sort of problem, too."

But she immediately shakes her head. "Don't worry about me. I'm in security, we're always doing this"—she waves her hand around and shrugs, but my sixth-sense alarm is pinging like crazy—"delving into the hacking world one way or the other. There are other people like Fabian. He's extremely good, but it was weird meeting him today and knowing that he's breaking into systems, because it doesn't seem like we're on opposite sides of this game at all. He's a nice guy."

Despite her tiny frame and losing her mom in such an awful way, she's not in the least bit fragile. I inspect her earnest face and wonder for a beat if she might ever think I'm a nice guy, too—or are my impatience, the women, and what they print about me in the paper all too much for her? I glance down the street at the disappearing red lights of a car. I don't know how to resolve the situation with Fabian, and I'm still conflicted about the code on his machine.

"What are you doing now? Do you want to get some dinner?" I didn't even know I was going to say that until it was out of my mouth and I hold my breath; then she smiles and all the air rushes out of me in relief.

"Yes, and I know a great place not too far away," she says, beaming up at me, and my desperation takes on a totally different edge.

CHAPTER 22

Fabian

The traffic is squealing and honking as I cross the street, damp seeping everywhere. The lack of sleep and remnants of drugs in my bloodstream are causing me to zigzag, and the few people hurrying along are studiously ignoring me in the way they do in big cities where there's too many crazies to count. Jo's good, I have to give her that; I only found her code on my network by accident. Engrossed in some other problem, I decided to look at the work we did on Sunday and found some timestamps that looked odd. I've left her stuff in there happily tracking an irrelevant part of the system; it'll buy me time to have this little chat.

She's fucking betrayed Janus. I stamp my feet, trying to warm up, and tamp down the swarm buzzing in my chest. She's friendly and lovely with that flowing long red hair and tiny body and, Jesus, who would blame any man for being smitten with that? I growl to myself. Someone must see Janus as a way of getting to me, and the escalation, using someone like Jo to put code on my system, is terrifying. The Russians have been a worry ever since I hacked into some military servers and found all sorts of eye-popping documents tracking Western defense activities. I'm not sure what I am going to do with that information, and I've covered my tracks, but the hacking world can be brutal.

I stare up at her building. Most networks across the city are easy enough to access if I need to find out something simple like where someone lives. It might have been safer to call, but I want to see her expression when I confront her. The red brick glows in the pale light of the rising sun as it peeps over the haze of the buildings. I glance at my watch, noticing a tremor in my hand. *Goddammit.* Six a.m. and I've got the full-on shakes. Coffee. I need coffee. A guy on the other sidewalk carrying a cup snags my attention, and I shoot across the road, loping up to him. He startles out of his early-morning daze, and I gesture at his hand, but he takes one look at me and doesn't stop walking, waving behind him up toward the intersection and muttering something about an all-night convenience store. In a burst I am up the street and in the blissful warmth, helping myself to a two-dollar coffee from the dispenser. I scan the energy bars, hungry, but my stomach is fragile these days and I don't want to puke.

I'm out of the shop in minutes. Fortunately, there aren't many people around, and the warmth of the cup is blissful as the February chill seeps through my clothes. After another half an hour of freezing my ass off, a small slight figure, bundled up in more wool than you'd find on a sheep, appears at the door. I jog over the road and call her name. Her gray woolen hat jerks backward, and her eyes go wide as they latch onto mine.

"Fabian? What are you doing here? Is everything okay with Janus?" And the concern and worry on her face make everything inside me want to curl up and die. Fuck, she likes him. I turn my head to look up the street: That makes no sense at all.

I bring my eyes back to hers, trying to read her before we say anything more, and she frowns in consternation.

"You're freaking me out right now."

"I found the code," I say, studying her, and I blink as resignation crosses her face, then a half smile. I jerk back. What the fuck? Where are the blustering denials?

"You're pretty impressive," she says, and the respect in her voice takes me by surprise. "Three days. That was fast."

"What the hell, Jo?" She's so calm, but pressure is building in me like a spring that's wound too tight. I scan around half-expecting some henchmen to appear out of thin air.

She pulls up a sleeve, searching for her watch, nodding like we are discussing some small trivial error. "Let's find a coffee place and go chat."

I try to calm down by talking to myself positively in my head; I can rarely make techniques like this work for me, despite everything past therapists have told me.

We end up in a rough-looking place with steamed-up windows around the corner. I glance at the occupants, staring at a large threatening-looking guy at the back, but he doesn't even lift his head. After we're settled in, she puts a calming hand on my arm, and her eyes are fixed and clear, gaze never shifting from mine. No wonder Janus is so head over heels for her.

"I don't know how much to tell you, but I'm not a natural at hiding things, so I'll just tell you the story." She blows out a long breath. "You know someone has been trying to hack Janus's Industries systems?" I nod. "Well, Janus found a map of his system on a piece of paper on your desk."

"*What?*" The alarm cracks out of me. Bloody hell, of all the things that were a possibility, this one never crossed my mind. The spring that has been winding tighter and tighter begins to unravel with frightening speed. *Janus* instigated this?

I'm fucked.

I'm seriously fucked.

He thinks I hacked his system. An age-old dread mushrooms like a virus in my stomach. All the people who cared for me have disappeared in one way or another, but he and Adam are still around: the only people I trust.

"*Janus* asked you to try and track what I was doing?"

I'm practically shouting, and, leaning forward, I catch the eye of the man at the next table. The big guy in the corner raises his head. The hum of conversation disappears as a hush settles like a shock wave.

"Fabian, *please* …"

Jo's hand comes out but I'm on my feet in seconds and her eyes widen, mouth dropping open as I jerk to my feet, adrenaline flooding my system. Several people are gawking at me openly now.

"Fabian, for the love of God, just listen to me. He was tortured about whether he should do this …"

This confirmation is enough to send me right off the edge. I'm not even listening as fear grows like a weed. The number of things Janus has done for me. I need to talk to him.

Right.

Fucking.

Now.

The clatter of my chair hitting the floor follows me as I shoot out the door, and my arm is out for a taxi before I even reach the edge of the sidewalk. A panicked shout behind me sounds miles away.

Go, go, go.

As a yellow cab pulls in, I catch her voice, closer now, but I'm in the back and shouting directions before she even reaches me. *Thank God.* The detail of what Janus asked her to do I'll only be able to listen to when I'm calmer, when I've made this right. A hand slaps on the window as we pull out from the roadside into the thick traffic.

I fidget with my ring and my phone as the driver watches me in the rearview mirror, frowning as I'm muttering to myself and bouncing around on his back seat, leaning out of the cab to shout at some old guy stuck on the crosswalk. There's nothing good in this, nothing at all. Finally, the steel-and-glass tower that houses Janus Industries looms down the street, and in a flash I'm out of the door, flinging a twenty-dollar bill at the cab driver before racing past surprised pedestrians and barreling into the reception.

"Janus Phillips, right *fucking* now."

The receptionist's eyebrows twitch, and she examines me warily before consulting her screen. Jesus. I don't have time for this. My name comes at me from behind, and I spin to see Jo coming through the doors, wool coat flapping.

Dammit, she *followed* me? I turn back to the receptionist.

"Janus isn't here today, sir." Her face doesn't shift, even though I must be snarling and red-faced. The rational part of me distantly registers how professional she is.

"Like fuck he isn't. I need to see him, *now*," I growl, leaning over the counter toward her, and out of the corner of my eye I see the security guard start to move forward.

"Fabian." Jo's breathless voice is close beside me. When I turn, her white face is right there. "He's away in Israel right now; he'll be back tomorrow." She pulls on my elbow. "Come and talk to me."

I groan and pull my arm away from her calming hand, slamming my hands down on the polished marble desk.

"Fuck!"

"He didn't mean to—"

My head snaps back. "I've screwed up the only real friendship I've ever had." The words are wrenched from somewhere deep inside me.

"What? No!" Her shocked voice washes over my distress.

I lean forward, putting my head on the cool marble of reception, rocking from side to side. "He'll never forgive me."

"What?" Her voice is hesitant, surprised. "Why would you think … What have you done?"

CHAPTER 23

Jo

The chase has started a fast flutter in my heart, breath sawing in and out. It feels like ... *Tamp it down, Jo.* Dealing with Fabian is like trying to quiet an enraged and slightly unstable tiger. Trickles of sweat make their way down my neck, and I'm hot with the thought that I might have damaged his friendship with Janus. Worries chase themselves through my head one after another. *Is* he the one hacking into Janus's systems? *What is he doing?*

He starts pacing agitatedly up and down in front of the desk, and I scan his pale face and red eyes, the tremors running through his body. Grabbing his arm, I smile my apology at the receptionist and the security guard who's hovering with his hand on his belt like he wants to taser us. I drag Fabian out through the revolving doors. Coffee: we need strong, black, *good* coffee. What's open this early? *Financier Patisserie.* I pull him around the corner to the small bakery tucked in a backstreet, breathing a sigh of relief as I push him into a wicker chair reminiscent of a Parisian café. He groans and I stop, looking at his chalky white face, ghostlike. But then I shake my head and move to the counter, staring at the waxed moustache of the guy in his black apron as I order, gaze switching between Fabian, the blackboard, and the card in my hand, pulling in breath after breath. Fabian's sitting with his head in his hands when I shuffle back to our table with two espressos.

"You have to help me sort this, Jo."

Okay. That's not what I was expecting him to say. On the surface, he looks much calmer, but how well do I know him? I take a deep inhale of air. I thought he'd be evasive or mad, but instead he seems worried that Janus will be annoyed with him. I don't get it, unless he's been trying to destroy Janus's business for some reason. *Would he go that far?*

"I don't understand."

He rubs his hair back and forward in his hands. "I don't want to lose him"— his voice cracks—"You get that, yeah? He's my best friend, and I don't have anyone else. You've got to promise to help me."

I shake my head at him. "I'm not going to agree to anything until I understand what's going on. Why are you afraid that Janus is going to be upset? Why aren't you angry with him for putting something on your system?"

Fabian lifts his head with his hand over his mouth and focuses on the benches outside, on the street starting to hum with people talking into their headsets as they walk to work. The counter is getting busier. He stirs his coffee, sips it, and stares out the window some more.

"You know I hack into some fairly dodgy places?" he starts.

What the hell is coming next?

"Define dodgy." I don't like where my stomach goes when he makes a face. I cross my eyes at him, and he laughs.

He waves his hand. "All this stuff I do"—he pauses—"I'm pretty careful. They don't usually find out. But I've been wondering recently whether someone has noticed that I've been poking around."

Perhaps he *is* being blackmailed.

"Define *someone*."

He shrugs. "I've dug around in a lot of systems over the years, and I don't do anything with the information generally. Well, what I mean is, I don't sell it.

But you understand better than anyone that I need to keep out of the limelight to do what I do."

He's right. He wasn't someone who was familiar to me when Janus mentioned him.

"I've explored a lot of systems: the Russians, Chinese, North Koreans—"

"Holy *crap*, Fabian, *why*?" I say, my voice rising. Breathe. Breathe.

"Um—I'm interested, okay? I went into a tricky Russian system more recently—" He holds up his hands when I roll my eyes at him. "I was *careful*, but I think they worked out someone was in there. So I set up a test. There's some brief written information on the Web about me, and I can monitor who's looking at it and I picked up some activity from Russia—pretty fucking amateur of them—although they possibly wanted me to know they were looking me over. It could even be the Chinese wanting to make it appear like the Russians. Anyway, who knows about any of this shit? I'm sorry, Jo, I'm as paranoid as hell." He stops and inhales. "Then I got a warning."

"You were *threatened*?" My heart sinks. Once you've gone beyond hacking online and they've located you ... I mean, wow. That's serious.

"Yeah, some random guy came up to me and said I needed to 'watch those that were close to me.'" He makes air quotes around the words. "He was right in my face, and then he was gone. I chased after him but then lost him in a backstreet. Since I don't have much family to speak of, I wasn't too worried, and I thought it was some kind of joke." He shrugs. "The usual crazies you come across in Manhattan. But then I picked up some chat online about Janus Industries' security after the TechConn conference, and it made me wonder ..."

They know what Fabian *looks* like and followed him? *Oh shit.*

"... whether they might be trying to get at me through him, that perhaps it really *was* some sort of warning. So I went into Janus's system and put some code in there to track what was happening and see if I could work out where it was coming from, who it could be, what might be going on. It's been a bit trickier to access the network lately." He smiles wanly at me.

This is so like what I've done that I could laugh, but Fabian is staring down into the dark swirl of his coffee, eyes shuttered.

"I've tried hard to make sure none of my activities ever touch him," he mumbles. "Finding a connection between us online is quite difficult."

He's been trying to help. I slump a little in my seat, placing my hand over his on the table. He grips my fingers in return like I'm the only thing anchoring him here.

"Do people employ you to do this stuff?"

The curiosity about how this all works for him brings a million questions into my mind. No wonder he's paranoid.

"Yeah, sometimes. Occasionally I sell information that's not too controversial. But more often I'm testing systems to find the holes, and they pay me well for that." He flexes his shoulders back. "I could probably charge a lot more, but I'm pretty wary."

I stir my coffee, thinking. "The Russians, Chinese, or whoever … they haven't tried to hack into your system?"

"They can't."

"What do you mean *they can't*?" I raise my eyebrows at him.

He starts ticking things off on his fingers. "The ports are locked down. I wrote my own kernel and verify the code mathematically. There are two operating systems checking each other—I've developed a lot of my own tools. It's pretty impregnable, even for the best hackers."

I gawp at him. "That's insane amounts of work."

His smile is a small flash of pride, and he pulls himself up, sitting a bit straighter. "Yep, I've been working on it for years." But then he wraps his arms around his thin body, closing his eyes.

"I can't believe that I've done this to Janus," he whispers.

I reach out and tap his shoulder. "Why are you worried? He was beside himself when he thought you were hacking into his system; he'll actually be delighted you've been trying to work out who it is."

He sits up again and blinks at me, hand pressed to his chest. Then he shifts his gaze over my head as if to look at some faraway unseen object.

"But … But … I'm responsible for other people being in there," he says.

"You don't know they're there because of you, and you've tried to sort it out.

He was torn on whether to just talk to you about it. He thought he'd lose your friendship if he went behind your back. Trust me, he won't be mad. Why aren't you mad at him?"

Fabian shifts, and his leg bounces as he plays with the leather straps on his wrist. I wonder if he's ever taken them off: They're worn and soft like an old, battered shoe.

He laughs. "I could be mad, but I didn't talk to him either." He shrugs. "Perhaps we're equally culpable. I'd feel a lot better if I could tell him something about the hack."

"Wouldn't we all?" I mutter.

For a while we sit in silence. I sip my coffee. The shop is filling up with early-morning commuters, and the machine hisses and pops as the barista fills another order. Fabian has curled in on himself and I scan his body: God, he's so thin. He could pass out at any moment; I've never seen anyone so gray.

"Let me get you something to eat."

He shakes his head at me. "I'll puke. Drugs." He gestures down himself like it explains everything. "I keep getting admitted to the ER. Often unconscious," he mutters the last bit under his breath.

Unconscious. The word echoes around my head. I look at the hair piled on his head, the translucent tattoos over a too-thin frame, the kind of guy I know Kate goes for. My God, is *Fabian* the guy who she treated weeks ago? If he was …

Fabian squints at me.

"Look, Jo, why don't you come and work with me on it? Chances are we could find out where this is all coming from … I've gathered quite a bit of data on who's been accessing the system that we could sift through. I could help you with protecting bits of it?"

Ugh. It would be heaven to have his assistance, but … do I trust him? It always takes me a while to trust people, and I don't want to do anything that might be deemed to be confidential or outside our contract.

"How can I be sure—"

"You can check everything I've done."

I purse my lips and frown at him.

Fabian rolls his eyes at me. "You're a worrier."

"I signed a confidentiality agreement." My voice has a touch of outrage, and he laughs, standing suddenly and grabbing my hand.

"You should appreciate better than anyone that these contracts are a crapshoot. Come on, you can't reveal anything I don't know already; I've been in his system before, remember?"

CHAPTER 24

Fabian

"Look at these," Jo says, and I swivel around from where I'm pouring through network data on my computer as she crosses the room to me, a wad of paper clasped in her hand.

Jo retired to the sofa several hours ago with printouts. When I asked why she wanted to look at printed data, she said she sometimes missed things looking at a screen all the time, and that she liked to switch it up, *use colored pens*, and I laughed.

I screw my face up at what she's showing me.

She's highlighted various parts of a log file printout with fluorescent markers, and the repetition on the different pages is immediately obvious, but why is this interesting?

I scan over the colors. "Lots of recurrences. Yeah. What are you thinking?"

"As you'd expect across days and months." She purses her lips and winds a long tendril of red hair that has escaped from the messy bun on her head around a colored marker.

I nod at this, studying the patterns more closely. I swivel around to my desk and try to compare the bits she's highlighted with what I've got on my screen.

"This one here repeats over and over again."

"Yes, and some other ones appear only once."

She leans over, eyes fixed on the paper. "Let's spread it out." She taps her pen against her lips.

An hour later we've got paper all over the floor. We've identified about a hundred regular patterns and I'm back at my screen writing a program to identify them all but particularly looking for unusual log patterns going back in time.

She stretches and glances at her wrist, and I peer at the screen on my computer. Eleven-fifty. We've been at this for hours, ever since I melted down on her in fact. She's been remarkably unruffled and her calm, quiet clear-headedness makes me feel like I'm filling my lungs with fresh air.

"I need to go into the office," she says.

"Come back later," I mumble. "I'll try to make progress this afternoon, and we can work on it this evening."

I look up at her to find a broad grin on her face.

"What?"

"Good to have you on the team," she says.

"In the normal run of things, I'm not a team player," I mutter into my keyboard, cracking my neck and shifting in my seat.

She just laughs, gathers up her stuff, and blows me a kiss before she leaves.

CHAPTER 25

Janus

The floor is strewn with the debris of a long-haul flight—napkins crushed, headphones discarded. We're an hour out of JFK and the sky is dark with a pale strip of pink along the horizon, the lights of the Eastern Seaboard sparkling like jewels below. I roll my head on my neck, stretch out in my seat, and my spine pops. Jet lag has been my constant companion for years now, and I idly wonder what Jo is doing now, perhaps she's curled up around her blond hunk of a boyfriend. Ugh. If I go home, I'm just going to pace around the apartment like a caged tiger: I can't sleep after sitting stationary for thirteen hours. Going into the office doesn't appeal either.

I've only been away a couple of days, but the more I think about the code we put on Fabian's computer and what I found on his desk, the more unhappy I am with what we've done. I feel his loyalty down to my bones. He must have a valid reason for what was on that paper. I drum my fingers on the arm of my chair; maybe I could turn up early and drag him out for breakfast before heading into work? The charming flight attendant who's been looking after me all flight bustles up asking me if I want more coffee.

Before long, I'm comfortably wrapped up in the warmth of a cab. It's cold after the spring temperatures of Tel Aviv, and, as the familiar streets whip by, all too soon I'm in among the brownstones and the old factory buildings. New York waking up after the chill of winter is a delight of spring sunshine and people out walking. I stream through some extra emails and Slack messages that have accumulated while I was in the air, and by the time I hit Fabian's street in Brooklyn, I'm feeling like I've got a head start on the day.

The old metal door to the building opens as someone heads out, and I sneak in, crunching the doors of the rusty elevator open. Three floors tick by with a creak and a groan of old machinery coming to life. By the time I reach his floor, I'm grinning to myself at how early it is on the luminous dial on my watch. Fabian frequently pulled all-nighters at college and I'll bet not much has changed: He might not have even gone to bed. I drag open the elevator doors and in two seconds I'm banging on his door shouting, "Get out of bed, you lazy hippie!" I press his buzzer twice, already grinning at the battered door in front of me. But the silence stretches out and I cock my head, before hammering on the door again. A dog barks in an apartment somewhere below, and I stand still in the eerie calm for a minute, ears on stalks. Behind the door, there's a distant noise followed by shuffling footsteps getting closer, and some words I can't make out.

The door is flung open with a muttered curse and Fabian is standing there looking exhausted: hair all over the place, tattoos snaking all over his body—I swear he's got more of them since I last saw him half-naked. He's dressed only in his boxers.

"What the hell?" he says, grimacing and running a hand through his hair. "I thought you were in Israel?"

"Morning," I say with a smirk and push past him into the hallway. How does he know where I was? Has he hacked into my calendar? "Tel Aviv actually, and having just landed, I thought I'd come and take your lazy ass out to breakfast."

A rustle of movement drags my attention down the hall, and I pause for a second putting two and two together, then turn and give him a knowing smile.

"You got company?"

I don't think Fabian has women on any kind of permanent basis, and I've certainly never met a woman at his apartment. I raise my eyebrows at him. He hasn't mentioned anyone to me. I thought the car crash at college had put him off relationships for life: Someone staying over is all sorts of interesting.

Fabian is standing stock still with an odd cast to his face, a sudden tightness around the eyes, and he runs a distracted hand down his chest.

"Um …" he starts, and I don't understand his expression or the strange tone in his voice.

The whole thing happens in slow motion. I turn around as someone appears in the door of his bedroom. Bare legs and red tousled hair and a T-shirt that can only be his. My heart drops like a stone in my chest—down through the floor and all the stories of the building below. Sound washes out like I'm swimming underwater. My hand connects with something solid and I turn to look at it in surprise, frowning at the silhouette of my fingers slapped against a white wall. The world slides sideways. I can feel it when my pulse takes off, and suddenly I'm fighting like a beast to control a tidal wave of nausea that's rising and rising. My hand twitches with the desire to punch it into the plaster, into Fabian. I can't stand here; I can't stay and bear witness to … to … what? He *slept* with her? Sourness coats my tongue. I have no idea what the fuck to say, except perhaps to release the scream that is building in the back of my throat. I swing round, hands clenching into fists at my side. Fabian flinches as soon as he sees my face and puts his head in his hands. "Fucking hell!" is all that comes out of his mouth.

"Janus!" Jo says. "What are you doing here?"

I can't look at her again in so few clothes having just had sex with my best friend, so I stay facing Fabian who is slowly shaking his head, eyes fixed on mine.

"Janus—" he starts.

"Fuck this, fuck all of this."

It's all I can manage, and before I explode with everything raging through me, my feet take me out of the apartment and down the stairs of his building toward the street and fresh air.

*

The creased T-shirt, the red curls in disarray, his black boxers. Jesus. I tip my head back as everything swims. Am I madder at him or her? He knew, he fucking knew I was into her, and he went and did that? I clench my fists, bouncing as I walk up the road; I could fight, I could. The empty street echoes around me, a blur of red brick. A rough snarl tightens my neck. I wrench my phone out of my pocket and stare at the screen, but I have no idea what I'm looking at. *What? What was I fucking thinking?* Uber. As I press on the app, a shout from behind me ricochets off the buildings and I turn to see Fabian running toward me, barefoot and clothes askew. I don't need any more evidence that he just left a warm bed curled up with Jo. Something about his bare feet eats at me. He met me at his door in his *boxers* for fuck's sake. Were they naked? Vomit crawls up the back of my throat again.

"It's not what you think, Janus," he shouts as he runs down the sidewalk, hands chopping, either in agitation or in an attempt to calm me down—I can't tell.

And then he is there right in front of me and hot lava boils up inside and a deep sense of betrayal and before I know what I'm doing my arm has swung out and connected with his cheekbone, which gives a sickening crack. He goes down like a sack of potatoes.

"You fucking bastard!" I shout, leaning over him to make sure I'm right in his face, and my cab is forgotten in my rage and the satisfaction of being able to lash out. He moans and rolls onto his back on the damp sidewalk.

"Goddammit!" He shakes his head. "What are you doing?"

"You bastard," I growl, taking three agitated paces away from him before stepping back. My leg twitches with the need to kick him.

"I didn't fucking sleep with her, okay?" he groans, looking up at me. "My fucking face!" He sits up holding his cheek. "What the hell did you do that for?"

Spitting, face hot, I reel away from him. "You knew, you bastard. You knew I was into her and—"

"I didn't have sex with her. Fuck, Janus, come on, I wouldn't do that, you know I wouldn't." He's shouting as loudly as me now, face twisted and flushed.

I'm glad the street is quiet, the blank windows the only things witnessing this meltdown.

The words seep into my skin. I pull myself up, focus on him properly, but I don't see any guilt; only knitted brows and a sharp rosy bruise appearing on his cheek. Honesty always, that was our motto, no matter how bad.

"Calm down," he says, and it almost makes me laugh that he's the one saying this to me. I turn away, running my hands through my hair and groaning. "Fuucck!" My voice bounces off the red brick of the buildings.

He pushes himself forward and gingerly probes his face. "I think you've broken something. That fucking hurt."

He sits with his head bent between his knees as I pace up and down the sidewalk.

"Janus. I didn't do anything with your girl. Honest to God, man, when have I ever even looked at a girl you were interested in? Seriously? You know me better than that. She came over to code last night, and we got on a roll and before we knew it, it was 3 a.m. and I gave her my bed and I slept on the sofa. All my bedding is still there; you can come and check."

Blood thunders in my ears. Is he telling me the truth? Coding? I'm supposed to believe that?

"Why the hell were you coding with Jo?"

"I found your tracking program on my system." He prods his face again, wincing.

And just like that my stomach falls through the floor. Oh! This is the worst possible thing. Apologies and explanations rush up my throat, but then it occurs to me that sleeping with Jo was possibly some kind of retaliation for him, and bile bubbles up again. The fucker.

"So you slept with her to get your revenge." I fold my arms on my chest.

"No, *hell* no, you cunt." His voice rises as he waves an arm dismissively, talking loudly like I'm a small child. "I know you found a map of your system on my desk; I know why you put the code on my computer—I'm not mad about that at all. After I discovered the tracking software, I went to see Jo, and she told me you'd chanced on your system diagram in my flat. I panicked that I'd messed this up"—he motions between us—"*That's* why she offered to come to my place to help, to have a more detailed look at your network with me."

What is he talking about? "Why would you think you'd fucked this up?" I make the same gesture between us that he made.

"Because I hacked into your system, man! I thought you'd never trust me again."

So, he *is* our hacker? Oh, *holy shit*. I turn away and stare at the red brick of the buildings disappearing down the street.

"What the hell were you doing, hacking into my systems?"

But he doesn't answer the question; he just eyes my pacing and says, "Are you going to lay into me again?"

"What? No!" Somewhere in the course of this conversation my blood has cooled. I hunch my shoulders in on myself. There was no excuse to lash out like that. My dad always encouraged me to apologize quickly. The words "Rip the Band-Aid off fast" echo in my head.

"I'm sorry about your face," I mumble, unable to meet his eyes, and a different kind of heat climbs up my neck.

"S'okay," he mutters into the sidewalk, dropping his hands between his knees and staring at the ground. "But I probably need to ice it." He stares off to the side and silence envelops us. "Let's go back to the apartment, and I'll tell you the whole story about why I was in your system, why I had that map."

I stretch out my hand, and he surveys at me warily before grasping my fingers as I pull him to his feet. I eye his cheek. Purple is coming up under the reddening skin, and I grimace at him in what I hope resembles some sort of apology. He gives me a half smile, then winces, and we drag our feet back toward his building, keeping a decent distance from each other as if neither of us can believe the fight is over and any second one of us won't lash out. We're both silent on the stairs, and, as we walk through his front door, Jo is sitting on the sofa, fully clothed and turning her phone over in her hands. She jumps to her feet, gaze flicking from mine to Fabian's, letting out a loud gasp when she sees his face.

"What's going on? You hit him?" She's looking at me like I killed a panda.

I nod, desperately willing Fabian to keep his mouth shut, but he waves his hand.

"I deserved it," he says.

"Is this about the tracking program? Because—"

Heat rises up in my body and I focus on the ceiling, anywhere but meeting her eyes. Fabian, God bless him, shakes his head.

"I've told Janus that I understand about the code you put on my computer. I've talked to him about you and me working together, and he's cool with that. We should bring him up to speed on where we've got to."

Work is a perfect excuse for my odd behavior, and I latch on to it like a drowning man, but her eyes are narrowed on the pair of us. What is she thinking? Does she think I'm a lunatic for reacting like I did? Being pissed that it wasn't my T-shirt she was in, my bed she slept in? Jo's hand flutters up to her hair, trying unsuccessfully to smooth the wayward curls.

"We were up late last night examining your system. I gave Fabian full access. That's probably breaking the contract I signed, but we've been flat out since I explained everything to him yesterday."

She gestures to the bedding still on the sofa, like she's trying to demonstrate how busy they've been. She doesn't need to explain herself to me; I don't care about some damn contract. I try and pull up a proper response, ridiculous though that clearly is.

"Of course, Jo, I'm glad you've been working on it closely. Thanks for sorting it all out with Fab while I've been away." I'm coming across as a bit stiff, but my gut is curling in on itself with this whole conversation; we need to move on from all this awkward.

So I don't have to look at them, I sink down onto the blankets on the sofa and start talking.

"I didn't want to go behind your back like that, Fab. We—"

But he's already shaking his head. "I get it."

"Tell me why you hacked into the system in the first place," I say, and he drops down beside me and puts his head in his hands, sucking in a deep breath before straightening and staring at the exposed brick of the wall around the large windows.

"When you told me your company had been attacked I got concerned," he starts.

And then he's off, telling me about the dodgy places he's been hacking, how he thinks he might have been traced by some Russians or possibly the Chinese; about being stopped in the street; his worries about my business, about me being targeted for some reason. And, finally, he tells me that he wanted to check that my system was safe without me knowing. Jo seats herself in the battered leather armchair next to where Fabian is perched on the sofa, absorbing every word.

"I'm so sorry if this is anything to do with me," he eventually says, eyes fixed on mine. "Jo and I worked some pretty sophisticated tracking code into your system last night, so, if they have another go, we should be able to work out who it is. I want to make sure you're not affected."

I nod at this. "Why didn't you just come to me first, explain?"

Fabian shrugs and picks at his nails.

"You've suffered through enough of my crap, Janus. All these years—" He rubs a shaky hand around the back of his neck. "Shit, man, you shouldn't have to do that for me. Bail me out, sort me out. I'm no friend to you at all."

I put my hand on his arm, staring down at where my fingers have wrapped around muscle and bone.

"Don't fucking talk like that, okay? We're here for each other when we need it, remember?" I examine his red-rimmed eyes, the flat line of his mouth. My eyes drift to Jo, distracted by her freckles stark against her white face and pale bloodless lips. They're both putting everything into this. The last remnants of my fury seep out of me, and every hour I spent on the plane throbs in my back and my head.

"Breakfast?" I say, and this gets me a reluctant half smile from Jo as Fabian's mouth quirks.

"Are we finished hashing this out?" he says.

"Yeah. Do you have any incriminating information on whoever you think might have done this?"

His face creases into a grin and it breaks through the gloom that has settled like dust. "I've got incriminating stuff on everyone, man, that's the whole problem. Let's go find something to eat, and we can talk about it."

CHAPTER 26

Jo

The sky is a heavy gray outside the window as I mosey around my little kitchen. All I want is to grab a bowl of cereal and hole up under the covers with my laptop and sugared snacks. As I stare absently at the machine chugging through its brewing cycle, a few raindrops start to appear on the windowpane behind. Well, at least I have no excuse for avoiding the pile of work now.

Over a week later, and I still feel bad about the fight between Fabian and Janus. After we worked late, Fabian insisted, at 3 a.m., that I took his bed and handed me a T-shirt. Then, in an embarrassed flurry, he showed me his shower and changed his sheets, mumbling something about being ashamed of the state of everything, and my heart went out to him. He's such a nice guy under that crazy exterior. He swore he was fine on the sofa and, in fact, "often slept there." The following morning, Janus was there looking like a thundercloud and then he left, and Fabian ran around the apartment like a mad thing, saying that Janus thought we'd slept together. I mean Fabian is so unstable, I'd no more think of sleeping with him than fly a kite. But he chased Janus down the stairs, and when they came back it was clear they'd been fighting, and I got no sense from either of them.

I've been working with Fabian almost constantly since, despite the fact that joining forces with a known hacker to work on a billion-dollar company makes all the hairs stand up on the back of my neck. But, to be fair, he *is* a friend of Janus's and has been a godsend this week; his knowledge of how hackers operate has been nothing short of incredible. He's lounged around our office several times, ostensibly to work with me and the guys, but mainly to tell us about the drugs he likes to experiment with. I also have a sneaking suspicion he enjoys the company. Des has a complete man-crush on him and his spectacular tattoos, and just smirked at me when I told him I'm sure he bats for the other team. The memory of Des plonking himself down next to him on our sofa yesterday makes a wide smile break out across my face.

Back in my bedroom, I'm just getting hunkered down when my phone buzzes, and I lean right out of bed to pick it up from the floor.

"What are you doing now?"

Janus. A little thrill runs through me.

"Looking at your system," I type, adding a smiley face, because honestly what else can I say? Caught working in bed.

"Seriously? I need to be paying you overtime."

I start to reply that we're doing extremely well from his contract—thank you very much—when I see the writing icon appear again.

"You do your coding day on Friday?"

And I immediately want to write this in my diary: Janus Phillips remembered something I told him weeks ago.

"No." The truth is that my time in the office is getting harder and harder to protect. "Too many company problems to solve." Another smiley face.

"Tell me about it. How do you fancy giving up on my system and coming over and writing software with me?"

I laugh at the kind of invites that make your pulse race when you're a girl in tech. He thinks I'm worth coding with: another entry for my journal. In fact, never mind that: Janus Phillips just invited me over to his place.

Although we have another mentoring session scheduled in a couple of weeks, I've not seen him in ten days, and I can't contain the buzz in my bloodstream. My finger hovers over the text box. What do I do here? Spending one on one time with him at his apartment strikes me as madness, but so help me God, I've got a ton of work in front of me, the day is miserable, and the idea of doing something that I love with him right now sounds like the best thing in the world.

The typing icon starts again.

"Warning: my mom and dad are here and I'm actually looking for an excuse to not have them nag me twenty-four seven about my laundry or the state of my apartment."

There are so many things about this statement that make me smile so wide: Janus Phillip's parents give him a hard time? He's scared of them, so he needs a cover story? Priceless.

"How can I resist an invitation like that?" If his mom and dad are there, then how much of a risk will it be?

The writing starts and stops on his phone several times, and when the words come through my heart skips in my chest.

"I'm working on being impossible to resist."

Ugh, he's clearly an expert at the flirty text thing. He's good because he does it a lot, I remind myself. How many dates has he been on in the last ten days? Is he still seeing that woman from the tech dinner? I squint down at my phone. I hadn't intended my response to be suggestive, but our interactions always have some edge, a line that we never quite step over. Clearly I'm silent too long because a follow-up message appears.

"Didn't mean to imply anything inappropriate by that."

Yes you did, I snort to myself as I peer at my screen: 9 a.m. I've been up for hours but it's still early for a Sunday. The giddy sensation comes back: This is Janus Phillips texting me, inviting me over. What is my life? I tap out the words, hands shaking.

"What time?"

"How soon can you get here?" Then immediately followed by another text.

"I've got fresh croissants."

Be still my heart.

"The way to a girl's heart is through her stomach," I reply. "See you in an hour." And I leap out of bed and race into the shower.

CHAPTER 27

Janus

I place my phone carefully beside me on the kitchen bench and blow out a drawn-out breath. The offer of food was a stroke of genius. I press my hand to my chest. Swivels winds around my ankles, mewing, so I reach out and grab a sachet from the cupboard.

My parents are lovely, but they've been here for five days now, visiting me and my brother—a teacher in a deprived area upstate—and we are getting on each other's last nerve. I understand that they have my best interests at heart, but they've nagged me from the minute they got here about how hard I work, how that's the reason I don't have a girlfriend, and I probably don't have a girlfriend because what sensible woman would want to spend time with a man who leaves his apartment in such a state? My mom is a DIY supremo, and, despite bending over backward to force her to relax, she has fixed all the dodgy drawers and dripping taps as well as installing a new control on the shower. My dad has cooked me some of the best meals I've had since living here. He's been waxing lyrical about how it's the most relaxing thing he's ever learned to do, and how this year he set himself an objective to learn how to make Indian food.

My freezer is piled high with tubs of brown and yellow sauces.

When are they going to accept that I'm thirty-one, and they don't need to look after me anymore? The relief that they're off out for a day of exploring New York without me buzzes through my system. For once in a long-ass time I'm at home and I have a free day. And now I'm going to hang out with Jo. But hell, I don't want them to get any hint of a woman coming over—I straighten up— they must be out of here before Jo arrives.

"So, what's your plan for today?" my dad says, peering over his glasses at me as he sits at the granite kitchen counter eating his croissant. This question or a version of it got asked every weekend morning during my childhood over the breakfast table. Old habits die hard. I'm not sure if my parents grasp that I'm running a huge tech company; they seem to think they still have to chivy me into having a productive day. But something about this well-worn routine is like a pair of comfortable old shoes that I've slipped on after finding them at the back of the closet.

"A friend's dropping by and we're going to code together," I say.

This is good. It won't trip their radar. Ever since I got into computers when I was younger, someone has always been coming over to code.

"Sounds like fun, honey," my mom says absently as she peers into the dishwasher. "Hmm, funny smell in here." She wrinkles her nose as she straightens, and I can already see her cogs whirring about how to take it apart. "How do you know this guy?"

My heart sinks with this question. Now I'm stuck. Do I correct her?

"It's someone I work with," I say, neatly avoiding the gender problem without giving too much information. I blow out a breath I didn't know I was holding.

But my dad is clearly way too smart for that and snaps his paper before placing it down on the bench. Damn.

"And does this someone have a name?"

"Jo." I want to do a little victory moonwalk that Jo's name could actually be male or female.

"Well, that'll be lovely," my mom says, like she ever had any idea what coding involved. She never checked on us. Honestly, we could have been watching porn when we were younger, and she would have been none the wiser.

I start clearing away the dishes and sorting the kitchen, and my dad shuts the paper and moves over to one of the large gray sofas in the open-plan space. My heart sinks. This is a surefire sign he's settling in to read. Swivels reads it like a pro, too, jumping onto his lap and getting comfortable. My skin itches, and I wipe the countertop down to distract myself.

"Aren't you meant to be heading out?" I say, looking at my wrist and—damn—over twenty minutes have passed. I have no idea how long it will take Jo to get here. Perhaps I should meet her at a coffee shop and keep her out of my apartment?

My dad inspects me again over his glasses. "You keen to get rid of us or something?"

I don't like how assessing his stare is. He always had some sixth sense about my nervous ticks. I try and force myself to relax.

"No, just wanted you to make the most of the day." I keep my tone light, glancing out of the wall of windows that face 21st Street, blithely wiping down the bench again so I don't have to meet his piercing stare. He's one of the few people who can still make me feel like I'm sixteen again, waiting for my girlfriend to come over. Although, to be fair, that never actually happened to me because I was an uber-geek and girls went for the sporty, jock types.

"We should stay and meet this friend of yours," my mom says firmly as she settles on the sofa next to my dad, and I kick myself. I should have known—they are always mad keen to check out anyone I know.

"Excellent idea," my dad says, disappearing behind the paper. "Make me another coffee there, would you, Janus?"

"I'm not sure—" I start, but my mom flaps her hand at me.

"Don't be silly, Janus. It would be rude if we headed out before meeting this friend of yours."

"Well, not so much a friend as a colleague."

"From your company?" My dad's voice drifts out from where he's still buried behind his newspaper.

I've taken my parents into the business numerous times in the past, and we went in yesterday because I wanted them to see the offices we've moved into since they were last here. They enjoyed meeting everyone, and my mom told me it was, "all very nice," but my dad didn't say much, spending the entire time nodding and agreeing with my mother. This is nothing new: My whole life they've treated my achievements like this. I'm not sure why, but I *have* realized that they have no clue about what it takes to run a business like this. My dad's an anthropology professor at the University of Wisconsin–Madison and lives in the past; my mom works in a nonprofit. Their idea of something big is a trip to New York to see their sons. When I mentioned in passing that the traveling was getting me down a bit, my mom lectured me on "staying home more" and told me she "didn't understand why people wanted to go to all these foreign places." When I explained we were setting up offices in the Far East, she asked me if we "needed to do that." My dad coughs, and I'm pulled out of my reverie: His paper is down, and his eyebrows are raised. I realize there's no way I'm dodging this.

"Someone who's doing work for us. A subcontractor," I say, getting my head around his earlier question, although something feels off about calling Jo a subcontractor. I am probably never going to hear the end of "that nice girl" if they meet her.

I'm pulled out of my thoughts by the noise of the buzzer. Oh, fuck. She's here.

*

I shoot out of the apartment like the devil is on my heels: I've got to give Jo some warning about my parents; they could say anything to her. Catching my reflection in the mirrored aluminum walls of the elevator, I realize that I've not touched my hair since I got out of bed this morning and tufts are sticking up on the crown of my head. I try to flatten it into some resemblance of style. The black T-shirt I'm wearing was on my bedroom floor this morning. I tentatively sniff my armpit. Not too bad. The doors slide open, and I nod at the concierge as I catch Jo's eye across the lobby. As she starts toward me, too late I register how she's dressed. A thin white T-shirt sits under a huge dark green sweater that swamps her tiny frame, her ubiquitous ripped jeans winding around her legs. Her hair is down and curling madly over her shoulders, fluffy and soft and my fingers clench and unclench like I have no control over them. It reminds me of the first time I saw it like this, and her smile shifts to uncertainty as I wrench myself out of my head.

I grimace at her and her eyes go wide. "Is everything okay?" she says.

"I need to warn you about my parents," I start with a wince. "I tried to get them out of the apartment but ..."

"Why? What's wrong?"

"Um, they wanted to meet you?" My tone rises at the puzzled crease between her eyebrows. "I told them I had a friend coming over to write software, but I didn't tell them that you're a ... you're a ..." I wave my hand as my words trip over themselves.

She frowns at me in confusion as I spit out "girl" at her.

"Is that a problem?"

Oh, God.

I groan and run my hands over my face, stomach sinking; any minute the heat building in my neck will be all too obvious. Why did I ask her over? Oh, yeah, because she's wonderful and I want to spend time with her.

I clear my throat. "My parents, like a lot of parents I guess, are keen to see me settle down and I've never introduced a woman to them. The fact that you've come over to code with me?" I shake my head, color creeping up my cheeks. "All bets are off. I have no idea what they'll even say to you, but it'll be mortifying for me, have no doubt about that."

Jo's expression completely changes as I say this. Her eyes dance with amusement, and she shifts a little in front of me, almost bouncing.

"Oh, I'm so looking forward to this. I don't think I've ever seen you do 'embarrassed Janus' before. How excruciating will it be? Will they quiz me on marriage and baby plans or give me some kind of test?"

I shake my head, laughing. She's a nut.

"You're enjoying this a little too much."

"I love them already."

I gesture toward the elevator distracted by wild thoughts of Jo standing next to me in a church, a small girl with tumbling red hair. My throat locks up. Where are these thoughts coming from? But as I'm standing next to Jo somehow none of it sounds off-putting at all. I turn toward her, reaching out to press the button.

"I've no idea what they'll say, okay? They can be a bit crazy. They're going out to explore New York today. I was hoping they'd have gone out by the time you got here."

"Do they know about all your women?"

I frown at her, trying to work out what she means. "What women?"

She studies me patiently. "All these ladies you go on dates with?" she says, something rushing across her expression before it disappears. "The gossip mags? I'm just scoping out what they might say to me, or even assume about me." She mutters this last bit under her breath as if it has just occurred to her. "Oh God, they'll be expecting a supermodel." She glances down at her clothes and makes a face.

Woah, woah, where did all that come from? But I'm distracted by the heat rising up her cheeks in my favorite blush. Talking to her is like chasing a bolting horse. We're on a different conversation from the one I thought we were having. I shake my head as we head into the elevator. "They won't think anything like that. My mom might have seen one or two pictures of me taken by the paparazzi, but they live in the suburbs in Madison, Wisconsin, and I don't think either of them reads any kind of celebrity news"—I wave my hand—"Not that I'm saying I'm a celebrity or anything." Could I sound any more up my own ass? "My mom did ask me once about a picture of me she'd seen in the paper, and I told her there were work things that I had to go to sometimes."

I'm making it sound like people take pictures of me all the time, which is bullshit. Tension ripples across my shoulders. I can't pull myself out of the thought that Jo has this perception of me that isn't who I really am.

"Oh, okay."

She stares at the elevator panel, and my stomach sinks lower with each floor that passes. I run my hand down my cheek. This was a bad idea and I have no clue how to put it right, and we've not even spent the day together yet. I stare glumly at my reflection in the doors and pray that the next thirty minutes will be over as quickly and painlessly as possible.

CHAPTER 28

Jo

Janus is silent beside me as I fidget with the cuff of my sweater. Why did I ask him about his women as if it mattered? This is not that. I hitch my backpack farther up my shoulder. He said his parents might assume I'm going out with him. Will they think I'm some kind of gold digger? They've got to realize how wealthy he is, right? The thought is there before I can even sit on it. Ugh.

We head out of the elevator in silence, and his uncertain, apologetic smile as we reach his apartment door makes me melt inside. I think about my own dad and how he might react to meeting Janus: how he'd tell him about all the neighbors and his bowling. I grin and wink at him.

This makes him laugh. "Behave, you," he says as he scans his card at the door.

I eye the sensor, another interest blooming immediately: There might be all sorts of state-of-the-art tech in this building. The idea is enough to pull me right out of my hot sweat, and as we step into the entrance, I draw in a sharp breath at what's unfolding in front of me. The white marble floor expands into polished wood and the largest open-plan space I've seen in a New York apartment, wide windows stretching all down one wall, a skyline of skyscrapers beyond. As I turn to look at Janus, he gives me a cocky smile, his eyes roaming over my face.

"It's beautiful," I say.

"Yes, it is," he says, looking at me.

And I take in the tousled hair, crumpled blue T-shirt and the stubble on his jaw where he's not shaved this morning, and the urge to go on tiptoes and place my mouth against his is almost unstoppable. I wrench my eyes away and blurt out the first thing I can think of to stop the blush building like a clarion call.

"Are we still planning to code?"

I need to distract myself from the view, the awesomeness of the space, Janus's unrelenting cuteness and, my God, his parents! I might explode with trying to appear normal.

Janus moves forward, mumbling under his breath something that sounds a lot like "We are definitely coding unless you've got any other ideas?"

At this comment, I can't stop the heat that creeps up into my cheeks as we come fully into the apartment past a glorious light-wood kitchen. Sunlight cuts across the floor, casting a glow over an older couple who are sitting forward expectantly on a large gray sofa, one of three that are arranged around a modern, swirling rug, the windows and view providing a glorious backdrop. The man is gray-haired and handsome, a pair of thick tortoiseshell glasses resting on his nose; the woman in jeans and a soft smokey sweater, short dark brown hair tousled on her head. They are both looking at me open-mouthed, and as I smile, Janus's mom's face dissolves into the widest, happiest smile I've seen in a long time.

"Mom, Dad. This is Jo, she works for a firm that is working on our security." His voice is tight, clipped. "Well"—he corrects himself—"it's Jo's business actually."

Both his parents rise up, smiling, his mom hurrying over to grasp my hand. "A *girl!*" she exclaims with what appears to be giddy excitement, and her warm acceptance, and how thoroughly normal and *mom-like* she is, makes me ache to my bones.

"Mom," Janus says low and deep.

His dad chuckles before his eyes come to rest on me, and for a split second his lopsided grin is so like Janus's that something stutters in my chest.

"Your own business, eh? That keep you as busy as it seems to keep my son?" His sharp eyes twinkle at me.

"Well," I say, smiling back at him, "I certainly don't have a lot of free time."

"Would you like a tea or a coffee?" his mom asks, fizzing with suppressed energy.

Janus stiffens at my side. "I thought you guys were going sightseeing?"

"All in good time," she says, patting his arm. "Jo has just arrived, and we need to say hello."

Janus frowns, folding his arms over his chest before looking at the floor. He doesn't shift.

"Are you going to make the coffee?" she asks.

"I'll do it," his dad mumbles, mouth twitching.

"Espresso would be lovely for me," I say, trying to cut through the weirdness that has appeared from nowhere.

"Honestly, Janus," his mom huffs as his dad heads toward the kitchen. "I don't know why you can't relax. We're not ogres."

"That remains to be seen," he says dryly and gestures at me to sit.

Soon I am chatting away to his mom asking her questions about Wisconsin, and before long she is pulling out pictures of their dog and their house. Her head bends over my phone where I'm showing her some photos of my own, and she laughs at the ones of code and says she'd be sure to find this kind of thing on her son's phone if he ever gave her access to it. I lift my head to smirk at Janus only to discover he's watching me from the other sofa with an odd expression on his face. I frown and mouth "What?" at him, but he smiles, looking toward the windows and shaking his head. His dad appears with the tray, eyes flicking between Janus and me. I can feel the heat return to my cheeks, but his dad just nods and turns to Janus.

"How long have you and Jo known each other?" he says.

Janus bristles, and I can hardly blame him: What a loaded question. It's something you'd ask a couple.

"I think the contract you've been doing with us started at the beginning of January, didn't it, Jo?"

His dad's eyes are like an owl's through his glasses, unblinking, all-seeing. What would it have been like to have a father like this who demanded everything? He tilts his head as though he has so many questions bubbling under, and I smile at the deep frown on Janus's face. This prickly, defensive version of Janus is a surprise, but it's cute how eager his parents are to see him settle down. Perhaps they are more worried about all his dates than he realizes.

"Yes, I've been getting my head around the security on Janus Industries' systems." I try valiantly to keep this about business.

"There was a breach—although that's highly confidential," Janus adds as an afterthought.

His dad frowns again. "Is it serious?" he says.

"Worrying enough to get Jo's company on board, but hopefully with her help we've managed to contain it; well, more like totally sorting us out actually," he mumbles. Then he laughs and runs a hand through his hair. "You've made some significant improvements to what we were doing." And the warmth in his voice as his gaze catches mine makes my eyes skitter away. His dad clears his throat, and my eyes swing back to find him watching Janus thoughtfully: He's not missed either his son's warm tone or my response.

But all his dad does is look down, mumbling, "That's good," into his coffee before taking a sip. Janus's mom inhales sharply and smiles at me, patting his dad's hand before standing and picking up the tray. "Well, we need to be going, Robert. Leave these two young people in peace."

"To code," his dad says dryly, and I can't tell if he's making a joke like we were planning to do something else. I blush to the roots of my hair, although I'm not sure why: We really *are* going to code.

"Yes," Janus says, heavy creases appearing between his eyebrows as he squints at his father. "I don't get much opportunity to do that now. I'm counting on Jo putting up with my rusty programming skills."

My blush just won't go away, and his dad chuckles as he pulls himself up from the couch. He heads over and bends down to kiss my cheek.

"Lovely to meet you, Jo," he says, straightening. "I hope we see you again in the not too distant future. You keep this young idiot in check."

I laugh up at him. "Of course," I say, winking at Janus. "That goes without saying."

CHAPTER 29

Janus

Sun is streaming into the study despite the cold spring day and the blinds protecting us from the glare outside, so I drag my sweater up and over my head, the static pull of my T-shirt making my hair crackle. When I emerge, I catch Jo's head turn, but when I look at her she's engrossed in something on her screen. I stare at her bent head, wisps of wayward red hair escaping from a hair tie she produced from somewhere. She's sitting on my large bean bag, one foot tucked up underneath her bottom with Swivels wedged in beside her, fast asleep. He always curls up in here when I work, but he doesn't seem perturbed by having an extra guest in his bed: He's stretched out on his back, paws folded on his chest as if he hasn't a care in the world. Jo is swamped by the bag, her glasses perched on the end of her nose, and as I turn my attention back to the screen her eyes flick to mine, color rising in her cheeks.

"Okay?" she says.

I nod at her, pretending that I've not been watching her each time she shifts and her T-shirt twists and molds itself to her frame. I can't remember when I noticed that she wasn't wearing a bra, but I wish I hadn't. Now I can't seem to drag my gaze anywhere else. Every time she asks me a question about Python, I have to pay attention and listen to the drumbeat in my head that keeps repeating *eyes up, eyes up*. I want to concentrate on my software. I do.

The sunlight is casting a zebra pattern over the desk, and when I look at my monitor, the code there looks like hieroglyphics. God. Leaning back in the chair, I straighten my arms over my head and make my spine pop. Is it too early for alcohol? The time on my screen says 5 p.m., thank Christ. Jo's eyes are narrowed on her laptop, and I risk a glance at her chest like a creeper. The soft curve of her breast and the outline of her nipple sends a shiver through me. I almost groan out loud. How have I got myself into this tortuous situation? I move my eyes away, but her gaze has shifted to me.

Friends. Friends. Friends who code.

"He's cute," she says, stroking Swivel's tummy, and he stretches all his paws out and opens a lazy eye.

Lucky cat. I'd give my right arm to have her stroke my stomach like that.

"He's a menace," I say, rolling my shoulders like an idiot. "Time for a beer?" I shift out of my chair and head to the door, throwing a casual "You want anything?" over my shoulder.

"Oooh, wine would be lovely," she says as I head out of the study, and I can hear her straightening herself in the way her words come out. I resist the temptation to look back and ogle her body. My socks scud over the warm floor to the kitchen, and I pull a cold bottle out of the wine fridge, setting it down on the countertop before resting my hands either side of it and breathing slowly in and out through my nose.

Her voice floats through the walls. "When are your mom and dad back home, Janus? I don't want them to think we've been drinking all day or anything."

Instead of what they were thinking: I'm still half-mad at them for that.

"They didn't say, but don't worry about the alcohol: They're partial to a drink or two themselves. Would you rather be gone before they come back? I appreciate that they're a total pain in the ass and I can—"

"God no, they're lovely, although somewhat invested in their son finding a girlfriend." The laughter in her voice sounds much, much closer, and I turn my head to find her standing in the gap between the island and the wall, dust motes swirling in the warm air around her. I ease back from where I'm gripping the bench like my life depends on it.

"Are you okay?"

"Yeah, sure." I bite my lip and start rummaging in the drawer for a bottle opener, popping my beer open with jittery hands and grabbing a wineglass from the cupboard, all without looking at her once. *Get it together.* "Stuck on a tricky problem, you know?" The lie trips so easily off my tongue. I unscrew the wine, and the golden liquid coats the side as I pour. I turn to press it into her outstretched hand. The light catching her hair makes it look like smoldering embers. I swallow.

"You fancy doing something else?" she says.

I gaze at her, dumbfounded. The silence that follows goes on far too long.

Her eyes widen, and she reaches out to tap my arm, a pink flush starting up on her neck.

"That's not what I meant! Get your head out of the gutter. I thought we could watch TV or something?"

I tip my beer back, grinning. "Definitely 'or something,'" I mutter around the bottle, and I'm gratified when her mouth twitches, eyes darting away like she doesn't want to acknowledge what I've said. Her gaze drops to my neck as I swallow, drifting up to where my lips are firm on the glass. It gives me a hot thrill.

"You've got games?"

She clears her throat and nods to the controllers sitting on one of the sofas opposite my huge screen and my stomach sinks at the neat subject switch, but I obediently play the distraction game.

"I'm a guy?"

I raise my eyebrows at her. I rarely bring women here to the apartment: I have never had a girl ask me about computer games.

She purses her lips and scans my body, and then that half smile appears again as she starts to walk around me. I like this playful version of Jo: I prefer her to the calm business Jo that I see more often. Is she more naturally the first than the second? Why is she walking around me? But she pushes me away from the bench so she can go all the way around, looking me up and down. The touch of that push travels right down to my toes, and, as she circles, the penny drops.

"Well, you say you're a guy, but you don't look like a typical macho male …" she says, trailing off.

She's questioning my masculinity?

I hardly let her get the words out of her mouth before my hand snakes out and delves into her stomach to tickle her. She lets out a loud shriek that makes my ear ache before racing into the open-plan area of the living room. But I stand there completely dumbstruck, my fingers are still tingling from where they connected to what appeared to be rock-solid abs. She works out? That was so hot I have to close my eyes for a couple of seconds, take in a few tenuous breaths. Fortunately, she's not looking at me as my words crank out like a rusty engine that's stuck on old tracks.

"Were you trying to suggest that I'm somehow not as manly as …?" I say, clearing my throat as I turn toward her, but she's grinning at me, shaking her head and waggling a controller.

I frown at her. "Prepare to have your ass kicked, lady."

She gives me a wide-open smile. "Oh, I'm no lady. You're about to find that out."

CHAPTER 30

Janus

The wind is whistling in the background alongside labored breathing. I take the handset from my head and stare at the number on it before placing it back against my ear.

"Hello?" The word comes whipping through the turmoil at me.

"Jo?"

"Yes? Janus!" The words come out on a gasp accompanied by a long noise that sounds like someone opening a packet of chips. "God. Hi. Sorry ..."

The noise abates for a second, then starts again, and I hold the phone away. When I put it back to my head, all I catch is a heaving breath.

"... Let me move ..."

"No worries," I say.

She doesn't reply when I say this, just another sound like ants crawling over a microphone before her breathless voice returns to the line.

"Where are you?" She might be out of town. Crap.

"Running along the Hudson. Why?"

She's a runner? If I'd known that, we could have run together. I could have found endlessly creative ways to spend time with Jo Williams. The thought of that tiny body in tight Lycra ... I snap my thoughts off right there, gripping my phone so hard my hand starts to ache.

"We've got another problem."

"*What?*" Her voice is a sharp crack over the wind. Then the buffeting noise abruptly disappears, like she's gone into a building.

"Somebody has hacked into the Hong Kong server."

This gets me a raspy inhale. "Oh, God, Janus. Damn." She's quiet for a beat. "Ugh. They've been looking for weak points, and they've found one. That means we're being specifically targeted. Damn, damn, and double damn. I half-expected this given that they'd already had another try ..." She trails off.

"Yeah," I say, grinning at her damning. In the silence that follows I can almost hear her brain ticking, see her hand making flow diagrams on paper.

"Can we find some more resource ...?" I start.

"We're going to need to go out there, aren't we?" she says over me.

The tension in my neck eases. She said "we."

"Yeah."

"Could it be somebody internally? You know this whole thing with Fabian could just be a red herring," she says. 'It might be nothing to do with him.'

And damn me if she isn't going through the same thought processes that I've had. I've done a run-through of the team in Hong Kong, but it got me nowhere. I'm too distant from the people and the day-to-day operations; we need to have boots on the ground.

"It could be. I'm not sure of the detail of the team and I don't want the general manager to think I'm investigating his employees just yet."

I probably ought to brief a private investigator to dig into it, though. We can't afford to delay. Our Sunday of fun and games is a world away from the harsh reality of this.

"Yeah, I get that," Jo says.

"Who'd you want to send out to Hong Kong?"

"I'll go. I understand your systems better than anyone now."

We're in the middle of a shitstorm but the fact that she'd step in on something like this, that she's not leaving it to her team, makes me warm inside. I'd been wondering whether it would be enough to send Matt out there, but the thought of spending a long flight and few days out there with Jo sends more warmth buzzing through me. My sad guy brain goes straight to us having seats together and her falling asleep on me. I daren't let my mind stray any farther than that.

"Who's going from your side?" she says.

"Me."

Jo's silent on the other end of the phone.

"Could you go off tonight?" I push. "Straight from the office?"

"No problem. Let me sort my stuff out and pack, and I'll come in as fast as I can." All professional business.

"Thanks, Jo. I really appreciate it. I'll see you in … what?"

"I'll be with you in about an hour, maybe ninety minutes? Don't worry, Janus. I'm delighted to do it. Taking down hackers is my thing. It's why I do this."

She's a godsend. I put the phone down and shout for Maddie, who hustles into my office.

"We've got a hacking problem in Hong Kong. Can you find Matt? I need to talk to him now. We also need two flights out there today for myself and Jo Williams. Whatever we can get, but I'm not doing anything less than business class and I want flatbed seats. Someone needs to go to my apartment for a few clothes and anything else I'll need for the trip. Jo will be here in about an hour and a half, and we've got meetings to do here first before we can leave. Get the PR agency on the phone. I need to brief them about possible media fallout if this gets out."

She's frantically scribbling away. "Your personal PR or the company one?"

"Both."

"Passport details for Ms. Williams?"

"Call her."

No doubt if the shit hits the fan on the security breach, then it will heat up around me as well. Julie, my personal PR, is there to handle the press interest if I attend some event, but I'm only too well aware that going to Hong Kong with a woman could lead to speculation if the media pick up on it. I'm heading into the eye of a storm.

CHAPTER 31

Janus

Jo pulls out drawers and peeks into pockets as she settles herself into her business-class seat.

"Okay?" I say.

Her eyes are wide, and Fab's comment about taking her away on a private jet pops into my head. I should have listened to him; he always had a talent for impressing women.

"How amazing is this?" she whispers to me, leaning back into her chair as the flight attendant hands her a glass of champagne. She blinks at it like she's never seen anything quite so delicious and takes a small sip, smacking her soft pink lips together. She waves an arm around the cabin, oblivious to my ogling.

"Private jets are even better," I lean in to say quietly, and, as she stares at me, I want to press her backward and taste the bubbles on her tongue.

"You've done that?"

"Yeah, once or twice when I've had no alternative."

I busy myself extracting my laptop, finding my headphones, and getting settled. The flight attendant greets me by name, like they always do with people who fly a lot, and puts my glass down on the little table that folds out of the dividing wall before moving up the aisle.

"I'm sorry about how last minute this is, Jo. Is your boyfriend okay with you going away?" I ask as conversationally as I can manage, eyes down on my bag. If we're going to be working together for four days, it would be easier if we were more relaxed and open with each other. I like Jo, I want to get to know her better, and—boyfriend or no boyfriend—we don't need awkwardness on this trip. My eyes shift to her freckled face and her brows are a hard slash on her forehead.

"My boyfriend?"

"Yeah."

"Um …" She tilts her head at me. "Who's that?"

I smile at her. She's cute. "You've got more than one?"

"I wasn't aware I even had *one*," she mumbles into her glass, knocking far too much back and spilling some over her chin. The flush I like so much starts on her neck, and now it's me who's frowning.

"The guy you were with at the dinner, the blond one? I saw you with him before that as a matter of fact, at the coffee shop."

She wipes the liquid off her face with a careful hand, grimacing. "At the coffee shop …? What coffee …?"

Her face clears, and she starts to laugh—actually fucking laughs. My stomach is about to dissolve from this conversation. I take a deep breath.

"Andy?" She covers her mouth, shaking her head. "Good-looking, blond, smooth?"

I nod tightly; the tension in my chest won't let me speak. Our voices are hushed and I'm confident no one can overhear us, but I consciously try to relax my face.

Amusement is still dancing around her mouth. "Andy's not my boyfriend. He's an ex-colleague." She leans forward, oblivious to my internal meltdown. "There is no way in hell … Honest to God, Janus, if you knew …" She shakes her head. "He is such a dog. He used to come into the office and brag about all his conquests. Mainly all the places he'd persuaded women to give him blowjobs—he's with a different woman every night. I went to that event with him because he thought he'd got a girl pregnant"—she waves her hand—"but that's a whole other drama."

And I can't even be interested in the pregnancy story, because I'm still stuck on the words *he's not my boyfriend*. My entire body collapses in on itself, like a deflating balloon—all tension gone, whizzing through the air in a random arc. I close my eyes. I can't look at her face. *Not her boyfriend?* How did I get this so wrong?

"Janus?"

My eyes pop open, and I try to temper a smile that would be dopily wide if I let it escape, hoping the adrenaline coursing through my body is not showing in my face. *How long has this been eating away at me?*

"Okay. Good."

I'm not making much sense, but better words are trapped behind my tight throat. Her eyes go minutely wider, and she blinks, fiddling with her hair.

"What about your ...?" She hesitates, and I instantly understand where she's going with this. She's talked about my dates before in a teasing way, but not in this way, not right after a conversation about a non-boyfriend. Suddenly, I want to give her every reassurance I can.

I shake my head. "For several years now, the company has been all-consuming, and I haven't had a relationship in a long time. I've seen women because it's sort of expected at the events I go to and need to be seen at."

"So just hookups, huh?" she says, looking down at her hands.

I shake my head, but she's not watching me. I don't normally pay much attention to journalists and what they write about me, but, in this moment, I feel sick with it. I hate how it sounds. I hate the hesitancy in her voice.

"The media love to take photos of me with some eligible woman or other on my arm, but it was rarely more than a pleasant evening out. I've hooked up a few times, sure, but way less than people think."

She glances up the aisle to where a flight attendant is helping a businesswoman settle into her seat. "So, this thing about you only seeing a woman for a couple of months …"

I take a deep breath and start counting: one, two, three … I've chosen to run this company; to have a profile in the press. But I loathe the idea that the media have created a false impression of me. The desire to set the record straight makes my words come out in a rush.

"The assumption is whoever I'm photographed with is my 'partner'"—I make air quotes around the word—"so by the time I take a different woman to the next event, papers like to write that I've 'split up' with the first one, even though we hadn't been actually dating." I roll my shoulders in an attempt to release the tightness. "It gets them readership, I guess." I squint at the darkness of the window behind her, trying to remember how often I've seen a woman after a function or even slept with one. One or two were nice, but they blur into one in my mind. It's difficult to recall any other women with Jo sitting right in front of me.

"I've gone out with someone like that a few times—dated a woman again after an event, I mean."

I'm well aware all this probably makes me seem sketchy, whereas I've never really had the time to think about it or met anyone who grabbed my attention. I can tell she doesn't really buy this explanation, but I don't know what else to say here.

"I reckon you missed out on a golden opportunity. Some of the women you went to those events with were gorgeous." Her smile is teasing but her voice has an edge I can't quite put my finger on. But … hang on … she's looked me up? I immediately deflate: Of course she looked up a potential client, and all those pictures are probably front and center.

I take another deep breath. The rest of it is going to sound even worse.

"It's all arranged," I blurt out.

"Arranged?" Her eyes are like saucers.

"Yeah. My PA, Maddie—the one you met when you came to the office today—has a friend who's an agent, and she coordinates invites to red-carpet events for me."

She gawps at me. "Are you serious?"

Her head turns sideways, a muscle ticking in her jaw, and my heart sinks. Fuck. Not good.

"I'm going to the men's room; I feel like the biggest jerk right now."

But she shakes her head and laughs, stopping me when I'm half out of my seat with a hand on my arm. She bites her lip, leaning forward with a half smile.

"Do you get lots of invites?"

I'm flattered she thinks this, but I'm not going to lie to her. I want her to understand.

Sinking back into the leather seat, I say, "At first, I was flattered, you know. You can't help it and it sounds amazing, right? Thrilling, even. But in all honesty … while occasionally I do have a nice evening, mostly it is"—I hesitate, run my hand through my hair—"just awful. Some of these women are"—I wonder how to put this nicely and come up blank—"quite self-obsessed."

Some of them expect you to be so thrilled in their presence that all you want to hear about is them. One woman talked about herself for three solid hours.

"Only twice did any of these women ask me about the business," I say. I can't recall who, but I remember this clear as day.

"You're kidding, right?"

I shake my head. To my surprise, Jo's hesitancy has all but disappeared, and she makes a sympathetic face.

"That sounds like a whole lot of disappointing, like going out with Ryan Gosling and finding out he's an insufferable bore."

"You like him?" My blood fires up.

She laughs. "God no, not my type."

"What is your type?"

We're skating on thin ice now. All I want her to say is *me, me, me,* while also knowing she won't say anything of the sort.

She taps her lip with her empty glass, and the champagne I've consumed makes recklessness climb up my throat.

"Dark-haired, gorgeous, works in tech?" I say. I have thrown myself right off the cliff now. I described myself as "gorgeous." No. Just no.

But she just laughs again and picks up the gauntlet I threw on the floor.

"Sounds amazing actually. Where do you think I could find someone like that?"

"Oh, I don't know, work is always a good place to start," I say. The ever-present pink is unusually absent from her face. I look at her lips.

Her eyes meet mine and she raises a quizzical eyebrow. "Are you flirting with me, Janus?"

I smile down at my hands, shaking my head. "Yes, definitely."

CHAPTER 32

Jo

The effect of several glasses of champagne and Janus Phillips with his floppy turmoil of hair and smirky smile catches up with me in my suite. Oh, my God, the conversation on the plane and the flirting. Sitting so close to him, every time his gaze rested on my lips—I don't think he realizes he does it—it made my body hum. Those chocolate-brown eyes, the thick lashes. I hardly registered a thing he said.

We talked about tech, too. Damn. The memory of his hands as he explained something to me: forever-long fingers, neat nails, the dark hairs on his forearms. I'm tired of pretending. I've had enough of looking at his no doubt gorgeous body in tight shirts and fitted T-shirts and not knowing what's underneath. I'm sick of acting as if I don't want to rub myself all over him whenever I see him like a cat in heat. We have four days here and something wild and careless in me wants what he's so clearly offering. I'm not sure if I believe all the things he told me about his past hookups, the red-carpet events, but, dammit, I like him.

The bathroom is all glass and gleaming mirrors, and I examine myself as I rub gel over my freckles; I've long since given up trying to cover them up, settling for an all-over sheen. The red lace dress I packed so carefully before I left is draped over the side of the tub. With my matching hair, I'm going to turn heads. Am I reckless enough to wear it here? What am I doing exactly? If I slept with Janus, would we be hooking up or something more? I can't even bring myself to think about that; there's no evidence he's ever done anything long-term.

And am I crazy to think no one would know? We're away from New York— does anyone care here? Would anyone think of taking pictures? Surely the local tech network doesn't stretch this far. Ugh, my crazy rolling thoughts. I need to stop trying to persuade myself that this is somehow okay. I strip off my yucky plane clothes and step under the pulsing heat of the shower; I want it to dissolve all my worries like sugar on my tongue.

CHAPTER 33

Janus

The pounding water echoes the thump of a pulse in my blood: I'm off the goddamn plane. I tip my head back letting the water run over my face and hair, washing away the grime and tension, grasping for the bottle the hotel has provided and lathering soap over myself as I sink into the warmth.

The hack feels like it's taken over everything recently, but I just want to park all the worries for tonight and focus on Jo. Chances are I'm the kind of guy Jo avoids like the plague, and my half-assed explanations of my history with women will only make her aversion worse. I'm well aware how it looks—like I'm someone who can't hold down a proper relationship—whereas I feel like I'm just a bit of an introvert who's easily flattered and likes things to be uncomplicated.

Rinsing off, I step out of the shower, pulling the towel off the rack and rubbing myself down, scrubbing through my hair. I pull on a fitted white shirt, ripped jeans, and a leather bracelet, slipping on the ubiquitous silver ring. Fabian and Adam have them, too: We got them one drunken night in Amsterdam bonding over too many Belgian beers and the wonderful chaos of a European city. Fabian said they were our brotherhood bond, and the reminder is good.

My crazy hair is sticking up all over the place, so I stick some gel in it, messing it up even more. I'm doing too much fiddling around with my clothes tonight, especially after I met Jo dressed in a T-shirt from my bedroom floor on Sunday, but I've never felt particularly confident with women. When I thought Jo was attached to someone else I couldn't mess it up, but now I'm on shifting sands, standing at the top of a cliff tipping off the edge, about to either crash or spread my wings and fly. I take one last glance in the mirror, frown at the reflection, bare my teeth to check nothing horrible is stuck in there, and force myself out and into the corridor.

Moments later I'm squaring my shoulders in front of Jo's door. The sound of my rap echoes down the hallway, and I peer left along the dimly lit carpeted space, twisting my ring around my finger. Feet shuffle behind the sleek mahogany, the lock clicks, the door swings open and …

Holy.

Shit.

Her face and lips are glowing, almost transparent, dark lashes curling over pink cheeks, auburn strands cascading all over her shoulders. A red lace dress clings to every tiny curve, and when I reach the see-through bits my mind screeches to a halt, my whole body going tight, mouth falling open before I snap it shut. I want to push her back into her room and take her apart on the bed.

"You look unbelievable."

My voice is a dry croak, but she blinks away, and the telltale pink starts on her neck as she fidgets with the scooped neckline. In a blur of confusion, I immediately reevaluate what I'm doing tonight. Did my overt flirting on the plane make her uncomfortable? Is she wearing this dress for me? I can do low-key, friendly. I don't need to seduce her right now. We have four days here. I give her what I hope is my best amiable grin.

"What? I'm not allowed to admire how you look?"

She shakes her head. "Getting dressed up and going out for dinner with you is all sorts of weird."

I laugh. "We're friends, aren't we?"

Her blush deepens, and she peers into her handbag as if she's checking for something, but it seems like acquiescence.

I duck my head, trying to meet her eyes. "How do I look, friend?"

She stops searching and studies me as a small smile starts to play around her lips. "Sharp." She's looking me up and down now, and the sparks start everywhere her eyes land. "Smooth." I do a slow spin, and she laughs, tapping my arm when I stop.

"Come on, we need to eat before I pass out from lack of food."

My eyes roll to the ceiling. "Thank you, Lord, for giving me a restaurant companion who actually eats meals."

Jo giggles, and I gaze down at her smiling face. Her shimmering lips are right there, and, as her mouth opens and her tongue appears, my eyes track all over her face. I want to adjust myself, but I can't, and the next few minutes are torture as we head along to the elevator.

The cool of the restaurant by reception is a welcome relief: plush booths, velvet banquettes, dim lighting. Each table its own private oasis. The waiter flutters around us, settling us in and handing out drinks menus, saying he will bring us water, before gliding off to the kitchen. I'm trying to tamp things down, but something is building in my body, and I know from bitter past experience that it's never good if I hold this feeling in. If she turns me down, so be it.

"Can I ask you a question?" It's out of my mouth before I've thought to speak.

"Oh dear, I hate conversations that start like that." Jo wrinkles her nose at me. "Is it a difficult one to answer?"

I shake my head, pursing my lips and blowing out a breath. I stare at the partition behind her head, take a step closer to the precipice, tentatively stretching my wings.

"Are you interested in me as more than a friend?"

She gawps at me.

"What …?"

"I thought I'd worked it out: You had a boyfriend. But you told me on the plane that that's not true. When we first met, you seemed keen to keep it all businesslike. I mean, I understand completely if you think I'm an arrogant asshole. I get you can't say things like that to a client like me, but we're here for four days together and I want to be upfront."

She blinks at me a few times, pulling back. I've gone straight in with this. Way to go, Janus. Then she looks down at her hands in her lap and shakes her head at me.

"Do you think I'm a player?" I say.

She raises her head and grins at me and then puts her hand out, moving it side to side in a rocking gesture that says the jury's out on that one.

Fuck, I like this girl. Even in the middle of a serious conversation like this where I've shocked her, her instinct is to push me just a little. She's dodged my first question, but perhaps she needs me to say what she can't.

"I like you, Jo. I've got no problem being with one woman; I've just never met one I particularly wanted to be with." I am done messing around and second-guessing all of this. I want to be crystal fucking clear.

Her throat moves as she swallows, and something in her expression tells me that she's nervous, that she isn't quite sure about what I've said, or ready for how blunt I'm being. She's staring at the tablecloth as if her life depends on it.

"Why me?"

I laugh. "Is that an actual question?" I lift my hand to push an errant red curl off her shoulder and out of her face, and she pulls back. My stomach sinks to my feet. "You have men running around all over the place after you."

"So have you—women, that is," she says, picking up her glass of water and swirling the ice about. Why do I suddenly think she's stalling? I glance around for the waiter. I'm not a big drinker but I've never needed something alcoholic more.

"You've been to events …" She trails off.

I frown. "What events?"

"You went to that security dinner—"

"With Aubrey?"

She shrugs. I've explained the women in the papers: Does this bother her more for some reason?

My words come out in a rush. "Aubrey is an old friend from college. She's married to a trader; he lives on adrenaline, a complete asshole. She sometimes wants …" I sigh. "She needs a hand reining him back in. I said if she ever needed me, I'd help her out … I mean, they have a complicated relationship. He has affairs; she uses being seen with me to pull him back."

She wrinkles her nose but nods at this; I can't read it. Aubrey and I do have an odd friendship, but then, she's a strange lady.

I groan into my hands, run them up over my face and into my hair, stare over at the waiter helping a couple at the next table with the wine list.

"Let me down gently." I'm pretty sure now that this conversation won't have a positive outcome, but with it all pressing so hard on the inside, I can't hold it back anymore.

She blinks away and to the side. Then her eyes drift back to mine and her face is warm and conflicted all at once.

"I *can't*, Janus." She closes her eyes, muttering, "You know this is a bad idea."

Wait. My heart takes off at a gallop. Not quite the response I was expecting. She's not saying she doesn't like me.

"A bad idea?"

Her eyes pop open. "What if people find out we're together? It will be a disaster for my business, *for me*. People will jump to all the wrong conclusions: They'll say I got the contract with your company because we're sleeping together."

I like the idea of that so much I'm momentarily sidetracked. But seriously? This is what's worrying her?

I grin at her, inflating inside as if someone has released a band that was constricting all my organs. This is what's holding her back?

"So, you don't think I'm bad looking or a player then?"

She rolls her eyes. "Come on, Janus, you know what you look like."

I lean forward, grinning. "I'm very happy to hear you say that. I thought you were immune to my charms."

"I'm so far away from resisting your charms, it's not funny," she says with a quiet growl into the tablecloth that I have to bend in further to hear.

This sends an electric thrill through me. We're close right now, heads practically touching. Her hands are playing with her cutlery, and I lean in a little more. She smells like sweet rose and citrus. My whole body tenses right back up.

The waiter chooses this moment to arrive at our table in a flurry, and if I could reach out an arm and grab his collar and tell him to go away I would, but he's out of range. Jo shifts, taking his proffered wine list and scanning down it, asking him a few questions before dispatching him with an efficiency that makes me wonder whether she wants him gone as much as I do.

I lean back, trying to calm my blood, pulling the thoughts from earlier forward. We have four days. Four days to persuade her I'm worth it. I know what the problem is now. I just have to knock the bricks down, one by one.

"Maybe it could be perfect for your business; perhaps the publicity could be helpful? Why has being with me got to be negative?"

"You've got no idea how women are viewed in this profession."

"Yeah, I do. I just don't think you should pay attention to it. Somebody has to lead the way. You can't not have relationships just because of what the industry might say."

My gaze roams over her red hair and freckles as a half smile flits across her face. I reach out and cup her chin with my hand and her eyes widen, before skipping down to my mouth. I tilt forward, giving her plenty of time to move away, and her eyes are on me right up to the point I'm too close. I brush my lips across hers. They are so small and soft and hesitant, and I'm shaking with how much more I want to do, but I lean back trying to take it easy. But, to my shock, her hand sneaks onto my thigh as she leans into me, and I don't know how the second kiss happens, but somehow her mouth is soft on mine all over again. My cock tightens painfully in my trousers, ideas of slow disappearing like water down a plughole.

She draws back, bending her head down to the table and drawing a pattern on the white tablecloth. I examine the red lace on her shoulder, her bare arms. I run a thumb down the one nearest me. My hand is ridiculously large against her tiny arm, a myriad of freckles under my fingers, like jewels flung on cream silk.

"I like you too, Janus." Her voice vibrates, and I only catch what she says because I'm leaning forward right into her space.

Sitting back into the red velvet seat, I take in her bowed head, my jaw loose. In four days, I hoped I might get her interested in me, but I threw away any thoughts she might be sold already: She's been skittish with me so many times.

I open my mouth to say God knows what, but the waiter appears out of nowhere at my shoulder, making us both start. I'd love a weapon right now.

"Sir, madam." He gives an obsequious little tilt of his head. "Can I run through the menu?"

"Steak," I say, looking down but not seeing the list in front of me on the table. "Fries and green beans on the side."

"Filet de boeuf. Pommes frites," he mumbles into his pad, and I slide my gaze sideways to Jo, who's doing the same to me with a smile on her lips.

"I'll have the same," she says.

He nods. "Would sir and madam like some wine to accompany your meal? I can recommend—"

"A bottle of champagne," I interrupt.

This is not the right thing to have with steak and the waiter pauses infinitesimally. I can tell he's wondering whether he should suggest a red and risk offending me.

He makes to open the wine list, but I shake my head.

"Your choice of maker will be fine."

He doesn't flicker, and we both sit in silence as he gathers up menus, inclines his head and drifts away.

Picking up her hand, I turn it over and trace the lines on her palm, then, tightening my hand on hers, I stand, pulling her up with me.

Her eyes widen. "What are you ...?" she starts to say.

When I'm halfway out of the booth, the waiter comes hurrying over.

"Mr. Phillips, can I help?"

God love all fancy hotels because they will give you anything you want: That's their job. At this moment I've never been more grateful for it.

"We're going to eat in my suite," I say. "Can you arrange to have food brought up there?"

"Certainly, sir." He stands to one side and I pull on Jo's hand, but she just pulls back.

"What are you doing?" she hisses.

I lean into the soft hair near her ear, lips brushing her skin.

"I might want to kiss you again, and I'm not making out in full view of the restaurant."

She blinks down at my hand in hers, and I close my eyes and take a deep breath, tightening my fingers.

The waiter bows and shifts away, giving us privacy.

"Your suite?" she says. "I'm not sure …" She shifts on her feet.

I lean back, raising an eyebrow at her. "It might be easier to continue this conversation somewhere more private."

Her warm eyes roam over my face and then she nods, so I let go of her hand as we walk quietly past the other booths, diners' heads bent over elaborately arranged plates. No one looks at us. I take her hand again when we reach the elevator, and she smiles at me while we wait. She tilts toward me, and I curl my hand into the hair at the back of her head, kissing her forehead. Stepping forward, she leaves a paper-thin gap between her body and mine.

"I thought I would die when I saw that guy Andy kiss your neck," I say quietly into her hair.

"What? When?" She tips her head back.

"At the coffee shop." I draw back slightly to look at her. "You don't remember? Your hair was all piled up, and he …"

The elevator pings, and we move into it, pressing the button for our floor. I turn around to see she's nodding, lips pursed.

"I remember." She lets out a little laugh. "Andy's a liability. I can quite safely say I have never been interested in him."

Given where my head was a few days ago, she can't say enough of this kind of thing. I reach out to snag her hand, rubbing my thumb over her knuckles.

"What do you want, Jo?" I'm liking the direct approach tonight.

"Oh God, Janus," she groans. "Don't ask me things like that."

"Tell me. I've suffered through all this time with you, thinking you were attached to someone else, trying to keep things businesslike. I need to know ..."

Everything tightens inside me, so I cup her face in my hands brushing my lips across hers. Her mouth opens, her tongue tentatively nudging mine, before pulling back, licking the bow of her lip like she's tasting me. I can't remember a time when a woman I'm with has been so obviously reluctant. My blood is thundering through my veins as my cock hardens painfully. I want this with a desperation I don't think I've ever felt before.

CHAPTER 34

Janus

Something washes through Jo's face as she stills my hand creeping up her torso.

"What?" I raise myself farther up on my elbows on the bed so I can see her face better. "What is it?"

She purses her mouth, worrying her bottom lip with her teeth.

"I'm small, Janus."

"What do you mean *you're small*?"

"My breasts are small," she whispers, and her cheeks flush, eyes dropping away to the side.

I can't help the smile that bubbles up, and I bury my face in her neck as she stiffens under me.

I lift up again on my arms, shaking my head. "Did you actually just say that? You need to understand how long I've thought about …"

She's tense and motionless under me. "What …?"

I shake my head again. "Okay." I close my eyes and let my lips quirk up. "So, let's think. Small, beautifully pale, with a smattering of copper-colored

174

freckles spilling across creamy white skin, perfect brown nipples sitting high and tight." I'm getting increasingly hard describing what has been so vivid in my imagination for so long and, as I push my erection into her, her ribs shift as she takes a sharp inhalation of breath.

"Okay, I'm going to go for bust here and tell you that I even searched 'redhead's small breasts' on the Internet." Heat inches up my throat with this admission, so I collapse back down, burying my head back against her ear.

Her whole body slumps under me, and I feel her cheek curving against my temple, so I pull back as her unchecked grin dissolves into a delighted snort.

"What's so funny?"

"Let me get this right," she gasps out. "Janus Phillips—*the* Janus Phillips— the one who's built a billion-dollar tech company—searched for 'redhead's small breasts' online? How come you haven't been arrested?" Her whole body starts shaking with laughter, and warmth slips through me. Maybe I'm managing to diffuse this.

I grin at her. "If you have to ask me this, then you don't understand how many times I have imagined these breasts." I inch my hands upward to rest on her dress covering the small mounds, not confident enough to do anything more with her, even thumb her nipples. They harden minutely under my palms, and I lean forward to nip her lower lip.

As her laughter fades away, her eyes roam back and forth between mine. "I just don't want you to be disappointed," she whispers. "You've dated some of the most gorgeous women—"

I close my eyes, groaning. I've never regretted my dating history as much as I do right now.

"It wasn't like that. They weren't proper dates and anyway, it's *you*," I say, wanting her to be over this anxiety, to understand. "I don't want you because you're beautiful, although you absolutely are, I want you because you're *you*." I close my eyes swallowing. "I don't want anyone else."

"Including my small breasts?" My eyes pop open to catch her scrunched-up face, clearly trying to lighten the intensity that's descended like a cloud. *Too much, too soon, Janus.*

But it feels wrong to hold back now, wrong to make jokes, even if I understand why she's doing it. I growl and grind my erection into her, closing my eyes.

"I can't joke about this, I'm …" I push up on my arms. "You have no idea how thrilled and anxious I am about this, do you? I didn't think for the longest time you'd want this, want me. You seemed so determined to keep me at arm's length, so turned off with my reputation …"

I need some distance, so I sit back on my heels and run both hands over my face. I want to be honest. She opens her mouth, but I barrel on. "I know you saw the pictures online and decided to stay away, chose to be colleagues and possibly friends, and I've regretted every evening I've spent with other women, knowing it could drive away the woman I really want."

Her lips part. She sits up, sliding her hands up my jean-clad legs, hands coming to rest on the creases of my hips, tantalizingly close to where I really want them.

"I always wanted this too, Janus. I just didn't think I was glamorous or beautiful or famous enough for you, and I didn't want to be second best, being compared and not reaching some gold standard."

"Fuck, no." I growl. "How could you even think that?" Damn, that's crazy. "With what you do, what you've achieved? How gorgeous you are? Couldn't you tell how into you I was every time we saw each other?"

She licks her lips and stares at me, mute. There's a long thrumming moment when I'm looking into her dilated pupils. The air conditioning hums, water drips somewhere deep in the suite, muffled footsteps pad down the corridor. Eventually, she pulls back and stretches behind her, unzipping her dress and peeling it down her torso, and I lean backward, tugging it down and off as she lifts her hips. She's all freckles and white lace. She unclasps her bra and lets it fall down her arms, lying back on her elbows.

My breath stutters in my chest. Seeing her for the first time … I've imagined this too often to be healthy. I want to touch, and I don't. I want to put off knowing the feeling of her skin because, after that first stroke, I'll want it again and again. Rushing through all these firsts … just … *no way*. A low rumble builds under my ribs as her eyes meet mine. The reality is *infinitely* better than my imagination, patterns in the freckles, pink tips to her brown nipples, small and beautiful. I know without touching them they will fit my hands perfectly. I want trace and learn every mark.

"Good?" she says, her hand sneaking up my thigh again, and the scratch of her tiny fingers brings out goose bumps all over my body.

"You have no idea. Is it acceptable when you're with a woman for the first time to spend hours staring?"

Her lips tip up. "You tell me. Although,"—she nods at my shirt—"I might well want to do the same."

I laugh and she sits up, copper curls falling over one shoulder, reaching up to feather her lips over mine, her nipples brushing my chest and, with one tug on the back of my neck, my shirt is up and over my head, tossed roughly behind me.

Her mouth is a perfect O, and it is so fucking hot watching her shift back to look at me, eyes snagging on my nipples before concentrating on my happy trail disappearing down into my jeans.

"Good?" I echo her words.

She swallows. "I've imagined this, too … Well"—a pause—"maybe I've also looked at pictures of you online."

I love Jo's lack of filter sometimes. *Here* is the evidence she's been interested; that I'm not just persuading her into this.

"So, you searched for 'Janus Phillips half naked'?" My eyebrows disappear into my hairline.

She grins, her hands coming up to trail down my chest, and my cock presses harder against my jeans as she feathers her fingers down the center of my stomach, playing with the soft hair there, skin jumping under her touch.

"Oh yes, but I only found one or two decent pictures. They're my guilty pleasure."

I can hardly stop myself from throwing her back on the bed and growling at her. I stare at her naked breasts, much closer now.

"Why aren't you touching me?" she whispers, eyes meeting mine then dancing away again. A faint pink is blooming on her cheeks.

I roll my eyes. "Let me enjoy, okay? Once I feel how soft you are, I'll never forget it. It will be better, but I don't want to rush through the firsts; the first time I saw you naked and stared and stared." I nod at her breasts and groan again. "I want to come all over you." As soon as the words leave my mouth, I want to swallow my tongue: Have I no filter either? But her eyes dance at me.

"Please?" she says, voice wobbling.

I shake my head; she deserves better than me behaving like an overeager kid.

"Oh yes, Janus, that's so hot."

She wants this? "Can I …?" I hesitate. "Is it weird?" Fuck it sounds weird to me—weird and creepy.

She shakes her head, and I push myself up on my knees and start on the buttons on my fly. She closes her eyes and emits a noise I've never heard before, halfway between a growl and moan. Something about that sound coming out of her tiny body makes me laugh.

"What?" I say.

"You're not the only one with fantasies you know." She licks her bottom lip before worrying it with her teeth, eyes fixed on my hands.

I pop the last button, and she leans forward, peeling the denim back, pushing my jeans down my hips as I lift onto my knees. Standing, I shuck them off and return to the bed. She's staring at the outline of my cock straining against my black stretch boxers, and she runs her finger around it softly, sending crazy tingling all through my crotch. My legs tense. Christ. I still her hand, shaking my head, and her pout is a work of magic. My lungs no longer seem to be working as I desperately try to suck in air, giving a hoarse laugh.

"As you can probably tell, I'm beyond turned on here." I hold on to her hand. "This could be fast, but I don't want it to be. I don't think I'm going to have much control first time around." I try and swallow, but my throat is like sandpaper. I want this to be good for her.

She nods, settling back on her elbows again and I stare at her breasts, the freckles winding around her torso and disappearing into her panties:

two together right next to one nipple. I lean forward, and her hand hits my stomach, fumbling under the elastic waistband of my boxers. Her lips part as her fingers graze my tip.

"Can I …?" she says and slips her hand around me, her thumb exploring gently as her gaze fixes on mine, pupils dark and wide against the sea green of her eyes.

"You feel …"

I nod and nod and nod, eyes fluttering closed. No way. No way. A fire has started on the forest floor, out of control. My head snaps back at the feeling tickling down my length as she runs her thumb back and forward over the head.

"Janus, I …" she whispers, and I tip my head forward to find her expression full of awe, hips shifting on the bed.

Sweat prickles on the back of my neck. I look down at her breasts and fight to hold off orgasming in about thirty seconds flat.

"Shit. Fuck. Slow down." Gasping, I pull back, but her gaze is riveted on how I'm jumping in her hand, and she follows me up, not stopping, not holding back for a second. Her other hand scrabbles at my hip to push my boxers down.

"Don't hold back." Her teeth press into my chest like a prayer. "I want it to be fast, I want to see what I do to you."

"Bad girl."

My jaw pops as I grind my teeth, and through half-closed lids I catch the wicked smile stretching her mouth. It reminds me of the Jo from the elevator; the impish one that doesn't often come out to play. There are all these different, mysterious Jos and I want to own every one. She pulls me forward as she lies down and I straddle her hips, staring down at how her nipples have hardened to a pinky rose. Her hand and circling thumb rub and rub, and the visual of coming all over the miles of creamy skin in front of me almost finishes me off. I bend forward, wheezing.

"Oh, *Christ.*" Her hand is slick with pre-come. "I'm desperate to touch you." I groan, curling down and burying my face in her neck, but she just grips me harder and plays with the underside of my cock. My orgasm hovers just out of reach, coursing down my legs and climbing up my length, swelling and tightening. She's shifting under me and a telltale warmth spreads through my pelvis as I straighten, thrusting into her hand, messy and frantic. She tightens her grip in the best way, and before I can stop it, I am holding myself on one arm shaking and shuddering, spilling all over her chest. Her smile is so unrestrained it lights up every dusty corner.

"What?" I rasp. Fuck, I can't breathe. The room swims for a moment. Heart pounding, I collapse down over her. The quiet ticks around us and sweat pools on my forehead and runs down the side of my face.

"You're right, that was fast," she says, and I nuzzle into her throat before pulling back to catch her dancing green eyes, the freckle right under her left eyelash. How come I didn't notice that one before?

"Fuck, I'm sorry." I shake my head with regret. "What a dick I am."

I shift to kiss her cheek, my own heating as my apology spills forward. "What guy comes first, and so fast, his first time with a woman?"

But she's still smiling and shaking her head. "You're kidding, right? I love how quick that was. I'm ridiculously proud of the fact that I made Janus Phillips come in about sixty seconds flat."

Her eyes are clear and bright and—fuck me—they're happy. I feel like a king. Trailing a finger down the center of her chest, I pick up the liquid and circle each nipple. She blinks down at my hand before closing her eyes.

"I need to play now," I say as a slight pink color builds on her neck. Fuck yeah. I'm not sure about the reality of my mess all over her, though; whether she likes it.

"Let me find a cloth to clean you up." I wander into the bathroom, dick in hand, and when I come back she's watching me, still smiling.

"What?" I say.

"I don't know. It makes me happy seeing you walk around naked, doing intimate man things."

I've never felt a woman liked me for precisely who I am. At college I was inexperienced and awkward, and since then I've done what's convenient: I can't explain the distance that's developed. I feel bare here. Real. Relaxed for the first time in a decade. I want to wrap Jo in cotton wool and keep her in my bed forever. I walk on the bed on my knees wiping her down carefully, stretching over and putting the facecloth on the nightstand. Her hands scratch down my chest, and I lean down to brush my mouth against hers, tasting fruit and coffee.

Finally, I let my hand stroke her breast and settle down at her side to watch myself do it, running my fingers around each flawless freckle. She arches into my hand, and I circle gently around the edges, avoiding her hard nipples still damp from the cloth. So fucking soft.

I groan. "Your breasts are amazing."

I glance up at her face, and her cheeks are flushed but her eyes are doubtful. Tilting my head at her, I say, "What? You don't think they are?"

She purses her lips. "No man has ever thought my breasts were amazing. One guy told me they were 'really small.'" She makes air quotes. My jaw tightens with a crack. Some dick gave her a complex? Fuck that.

"Well, he's clearly an idiot, as he gave up these." I stroke over the tips, and her breath changes, emitting gusty little exhales. "What sane guy would do that?"

Bending forward, I take a nipple into my mouth and flick it gently. Her skin tastes sweet, like warm apples.

"Please." She pushes up. "Janus."

Thumb on one stiff peak, I use the flat of my tongue to wet the other tip which stiffens as I play with it. Blowing on the damp freckles, I draw back, and she squirms, reaching out to tug me closer. I shake my head.

"Guys like to watch. I want to make you come apart with my hands and my mouth. I want to taste you." The idea makes my whole body tighten, and I trail my hand slowly down her body.

"Janus," she whimpers, as my hand drags down her stomach to her panties. I've come all over her chest, and she's not even naked. My cock lifts again at the mere thought of seeing how hot and wet she is. I slip my hand in, and she wiggles, clearly desperate to give me room to explore.

"Oh, your hands." She exhales on a long gasp as I reach the start of her mound.

I stop, laughing, hand pressing down. "What?"

She groans. "You remember those hot fantasies you had about my breasts?"

Where is this going?

"Well, I had those about those long fingers." She nods down at where my hand is resting, lips parting as I slide my hand lower, gliding over the smooth skin to her clit and down and down into the wetness below. She pushes into my touch.

"Shit, Jo."

No stopping now; she's soaked and slippery and I haven't even touched her. My whole body vibrates, like a dog shaking off water. I groan, rolling into her and burying my face in her neck, nuzzling and licking her skin, tasting sweat and more soft sweetness.

"Fuck. So wet."

Her hips shift into my hands as I move my finger, words jerking out of her. "At that first meeting you put your hand next to me on the table … your hands and arms … God, I could barely … oh God … tear my gaze away." She gasps, turning her head into my naked chest and her mouth is open and wet, gusting hot against me, licking at my sweat.

"You …" I start, hardly able to believe what I'm hearing, "you liked me when we first met?"

She felt like this from the *beginning*? I pull back as my hand stills, and she groans, nuzzling into me farther. I need to see her face.

"*Seriously?*"

She lifts her head and clear green locks on me, brows pulled down.

"Come on, Janus, you know how you look, how you are with people. You could have any woman you want."

I close my eyes. Her words are so different from my usual mental dialogue that I want to pick her up on them, but questions crowd everything else out.

"But … so long ago? You never gave me any hint you were interested, just the opposite in fact. Was it some kind of game?" A prickle works its way down my spine: I've tortured myself about this for months.

She groans again and moves her hips against my hand.

"I'm not doing anything more until you explain this." I'm spoiling the mood, but seriously?

She sighs and rolls onto her back. I follow her, finger slipping out of her, my hand still in her panties.

"We've talked about this. Your reputation … I knew if we did anything and it got out it could kill my company. I'm just getting started. People are vicious with women in this business." Her forehead creases, eyes fixed on the ceiling like she's studying a cloud I can't see, and it dawns on me she's still thinking we shouldn't be doing this. She's not all in by any stretch.

"Jo, that's not going to happen. You're only going to get good things out of being with me."

It sounds weak even to me; like someone saying "believe me" when they're the last person you should trust.

She laughs. "Like an orgasm sometime soon you mean?"

I straighten by her side. She's keeping this light. My instinct is to push, but maybe that's the wrong response here; I can see her doubts bubbling away under the surface. If we're going to do this, I have to make sure nothing blows back on her. I slide my hand back down and inside her, and she gasps as I lean in to capture her breath.

"More fingers," she wheezes, hips lifting.

I need better access, so I help her push the lace down as she flicks her feet. I inspect her tiny body, but before I've had my fill, her head comes up to mine, capturing my bottom lip in her teeth, whispering, "More," against my lips, and my chest aches with the need to give, give, give. I run my tongue along her lower lip, watching her eyelids droop as I move my hand. She might be worried, but she's desperate for every pleasure I can give her. Fuck anything else; I never want this to end. I am fully hard again, and I don't know how.

Gradually pulling my finger out, I add another, and she widens her legs, head tipping back as I use my thumb to brush lightly over her clit. Her neck is damp with sweat as I trail kisses up to her ear, biting her lobe gently. "How many orgasms are you going to let me give you tonight? How many times can I watch you fall apart; watch myself doing this to you over and over and over again?"

The slim length of her is stretched right out, my erect cock by her hip. I rub it experimentally against her. She snakes her hand down to touch me and I maneuver away.

"Uh-huh." I shake my head as my eyes meet the confusion in hers. "This is about you. I want to watch."

She pouts through a half smile, and I curl over to capture her mouth.

"As long as I get to play later," she mumbles against my lips.

I can feel the accumulated frustration of the last couple of months disappearing like air whistling out of a pressure valve.

I laugh. "Oh, you can count on that."

"As many times as I like?"

Fuck but I love how her inclination is to give as good as she gets.

"I'm not sure how many rounds you'll get out of him, but you can do anything you like to me."

CHAPTER 35

Jo

My eyes blink open onto a dark ceiling in a dimly lit room, and I frown into the heavy silence. No vague honk of New York traffic, no distant conversations through walls. I blink a few more times and stretch, and my outstretched hand makes contact with cool skin. *Janus.*

Twisting my head to look at him, I can't help the grin that breaks free. He's stretched out on his side next to me, mouth open, dark hair sticking up in some huge tuft on his head, a crease down his right cheek. Just above the sheet around his waist I can see his abs disappearing under the bedclothes. I shift fully onto my side to stare at his slack-with-sleep face in the half-light: Imagine waking up to this every morning.

I've never had someone in my bed like Janus, and my chest tightens with the idea that I passed out so quickly I didn't savor the first night we spent together. The *first* night? Who knows how long I might get this for? Swallowing it all down, I glance at the clock on the bedside table: 10 a.m. I'm sure Janus didn't arrange anything at the office until this afternoon.

His hand is resting on the mattress inches from my head, so I kiss his outstretched fingers. *He's naked.* A little thrill goes through me. I can't resist touching his smooth chest just lightly enough that I don't wake him, but he twitches on a sigh. I should let him sleep: He doesn't get much chance to rest. But then he rolls onto his back and the movement tightens the sheet and, looking down, I can see the outline of where he's hard beneath the covers. My God. I want to touch. Leaning forward, I skate my tongue over his soft nipple, and it instantly goes hard in my mouth. I can feel the moment he jerks awake. *Bad girl, Jo.*

"Jo," he croaks, voice full of sleep, and I want to lock his dopey gaze somewhere deep inside me. I can see the moment he remembers last night, because his eyes widen as his tongue wets his lips, and he scrutinizes every part of my face. Then his mouth turns up at one corner, gaze dropping to my lips, and my whole body warms.

"Don't look at me like that," I say.

But he just grins and shifts his naked body until he's right against me, eyes never leaving mine, and my blood runs thick. He's too much this close up.

His grin gets impossibly wider as he presses his erection into me. "Impressive," I mumble, half-laughing.

He closes his eyes and runs a hand over his face, smiling. "I'd say I'm sorry, but I'm also kind of not. It's a morning hazard—"

I stretch up and kiss his lips, and he rolls me onto my back and into the soft sheets, growling. His hips fall through mine, and I widen my legs and wrap them around his, holding on to him and urging him on all at once. If he thrusts forward, he could be inside me in seconds. But he props himself up on his elbows as he inspects my hair and my face. Ugh. Is my hair as wild as his?

"You okay?" he says.

I am. My God I am. I take his head in my hands, stretching up to place another soft kiss on his lips.

"More than okay; very, very good in fact," I say.

"You liked what we did last night?" He's chewing his bottom lip, and it makes something soft and warm light up inside. I want to him understand how good this feels.

I smile at him, nodding. "You?"

"Yes, fuck I want more," he says.

What does *that* mean? Sex or something else? A shiver runs through me, *something else* feels like far too much right now. I search his gaze, but his face is still sleepy and warm, and so I tilt my hips and his length slides forward again through my wetness. He pulls back and I pout at him.

"Let me get a condom on," he whispers, stretching down to run his tongue along my lips. "Let me touch you first."

As he nibbles on my skin, his hand slides between us to find the smooth skin of my mound and goose bumps break out on my arms and chest. I flatten my hands on his sides, sliding down, digging my fingers into his butt and squeezing—hard.

"Oh God, this ass." My voice breaks on an exhale, and it forces a laugh out of his throat. "I can't believe …"

He pulls back slightly out of my grip, propping himself on both hands. "You can't believe what?"

"That day at the elevator …"

"When we first met?" he asks, and I nod, teeth sawing over my bottom lip. "What about it?"

"You were gorgeous, ridiculously cute, if I'm being honest. I just never thought …" I trail off, whispering, "I never thought we'd end up here, that we'd actually *do* this."

He's frowning at me, and my throat constricts. I don't know what we're doing here. I've been holding a hand up and now I feel like I've dropped it, and the thought makes me cold. But Janus just gives me cocky grin and moves closer, rubbing his nose with mine. How can he be so *cute*? *I want to trust this.*

"I was chatting you up," he says, tilting his head. "You weren't having any of it. I was desperate to find out who this beautiful woman was getting into my elevator."

Beautiful? Is he kidding? "Yeah, I reckon you're not great at picking up women." Deflecting is my only defense; otherwise I'd just dissolve into a puddle.

He screws up his face like he's trying to look offended, and that expression with his hair makes me snort. How bad were we in the elevator that day? I was a goof and he came out with some awful lines. But my snort vibrates all the way down to where he's resting against me so I shift my hips and he groans, leaning forward and sticking his nose into my chest, dragging it over my collarbone and biting the edge of my shoulder.

"Jo."

The sensation of the tip of his cock resting against my folds makes me shiver. I want to talk but I also want to be here like this with him. I reach down to wind my hand around his length, rubbing my thumb gently over him, and it makes my heart turn over to see his eyes pinch as he struggles for breath.

I push on his chest and he looks down at my hand, but I don't release the pressure, so he sits right back on his heels as I hold out my hand.

"What?" he says.

"Condom," I say.

He laughs, tipping sideways over the edge of the bed to rummage through the crumpled heap of clothes on the floor. I swallow and stare at the map of muscle, tense as he's bending, running my hands up and down his thighs, grinning as his cock lifts and his hands fumble. Eventually, he finds something in the back pocket of his jeans and twists back up, pressing it into my hand. I turn it over, peering at the crumpled packaging.

"What?" he says, looking at it with a frown.

It looks like a herd of wild beasts have trampled all over it. *He had a condom in his back pocket.* His odd relationship history niggles away at the back of my brain.

"Is this your 'getting lucky tonight' condom you keep in your jeans?" I say.

I catch an almost imperceptible flinch as he rubs his hand over his chest. I shouldn't have said that.

"If it is, the state of it doesn't say much for my success rate."

Okay, Jo, it's worn because it's not been used.

"But no actually,"—he gives me a mock frown—"this is the 'be prepared' condom that went in my pocket *before dinner*," he says, stressing the words.

"For when we both got completely carried away and couldn't make it back to the room."

I raise my eyebrows at him, but warmth seeps through me. "That sounds like fun actually."

I shove the unsettled thoughts to the back of my mind, and he leans down and gently bites my neck. I track a path down his spine with one hand, and he plucks the condom from me, opening it with his teeth. The crown of his brown hair flops forward as he looks down, and I watch the ease with which he handles himself, rolling the rubber down slowly as he sucks in a deep breath. I've imagined this situation, but the idea of him being inside me … This morning, I want to feel everything, *enjoy* everything. He trails a hand down my stomach, long fingers delving right into my folds, and his eyes jerk up to mine when he finds out how hot and slippery I am.

"*Jo.*" He groans, pressing and circling my clit with a steady rhythm.

My eyelids start to drift down.

"So hot seeing you put that thing on," I mumble.

He leans forward, rubbing himself against my folds, pressing and releasing, slipping and sliding, our heads tilted together to watch. My hand digs into his ass again as my gaze flicks up. *Ooof.*

"Feels amazing," I gasp.

My fingers land on his stomach, playing with his abs and the curl of hair in the center. I scratch him with my fingernails, watching with fascination as his whole body tightens. God, I could watch this forever.

"*Janus,*" I can't get my voice above a harsh whisper, "I'm so turned on just looking. Look. Look at this."

He grins up at me as I slide an exploring hand down to the base of his cock and my fingers wrap around his balls, gently stroking.

"Yeah?" he says, and just like that he's slipping lower and finding my entrance; I shift to meet him, both watching as he pushes slowly forward.

I never expected him to be so careful, so keen to give me pleasure. Never thought about the mechanics of why some guys are good at sex, always feeling somehow that my orgasm was my responsibility, my job to get my head in the right place. But Janus isn't like that at all. He's so focused on me, so unconcerned about his own satisfaction. And I'm small with small parts, so I'm not the kind of girl that gets so wet the sliding in part is easy, but oh my God … Here? Right now? It absolutely is. The stretch of him has pulled everything tight.

He's pushing somewhere deep, and my skin is hot with the pressure. Sweat is beading on his temple, color resting high on his cheeks, that crease mark still visible down one side of his face. My muscles tighten involuntarily, and he lets out a long groan, looking down at where we're joined, not moving.

"I don't dare move because I'll shoot off like a teenager," he says.

I laugh at this, tilting my hips, and he inhales sharply.

"Give me a little movement," I say, and he closes his eyes and grimaces like it's an impossibility.

Most guys would take this request and let go; they're often careless, bent on their own pleasure, and the thrusting in and out of me is just … well … not my thing? But the still pressure of him on the inside is ratcheting it all up, layer by layer. Then he does this shifting slightly back and forward thing with his hips, and the movement's tiny but it makes goose bumps break out all over my body.

"Oh God," he says, resting his forehead on my chest, still watching where he's moving. "Fuck, Jo."

He pushes in and rubs his pubic bone against me, and I arch right up and grab his ass all in one movement, eyes rolling into the back of my head.

"You like that?" he growls, and he starts this rhythm: a short thrust inside and a rub, and I can hardly hold on to myself; I'm fraying around the edges. My open mouth presses into the hot damp of his skin, my tongue tasting the salt of him and there's nothing I can do—just the impossibility of breathing and the need to take, take, take what he gives me. The wet suction of him as he pulses, he's whispering into my collarbone, fragments of breath and speech gusting over me.

"Fuck."

"Holy …"

"Jo."

"So."

"*God.*"

I start to move my hips tentatively, and he swears, hands coming around to grab my ass in a punishing grip as he pushes right into me, long and slow, rubbing all over me before pulling out and doing it all over again.

"Jesus Christ," he grits out. "Jo …" He lets out a husky groan as he grinds against me. Heat burns down my spine and sets up a dull throb behind my belly button and down into my sex. I'm slippery with sweat watching how turned on he is. I feel emboldened. My thoughts flap loose as I dig my heels into his thighs and push up into his thrusts.

"Yes, Jo, yeah. Fuck."

His hand slips between us, and I was close anyway, but as soon as his thumb finds my nub, it's game over. His teeth sink into my neck and I gasp as the tightness builds, like racing up the staircase of a slide. I'm teetering on the top as sensation moves up from toes to hands to shoulders, and the wave in my body is rising and rising and rising.

"Oh *God*," I whisper.

"Please."

"*Janus.*"

Seconds tick by with my mouth open, his gaze moving from one eye to the other, narrowing as he gives one more twist of his fingers, and my whole body jerks as I come, forehead thudding forward into his shoulder. My eyes flutter closed but not before I see how his are fixed on me wide and wild. And then he's swearing up a storm as his movements stutter and his ass tightens under my hands. My head slumps back and I see his face contort as he jerks, his cock pulsing inside me, shudders moving through his body, and something about the sweet pressure of it all—along with the dying pulses of my own release—makes tears leak out of the corners of my eyes. I can hardly breathe. Janus sinks into me, forehead buried in my neck, slippery as his shoulders curl over. Shakily, he presses his lips into my collarbone.

"Fuck, I'm ruined," he mumbles into my skin, and a giggle rises up as he trails his nose up my throat. My fingertips skate over his back, relishing the sweat and the muscle definition, as all the oxygen is sucked out the room and quiet settles over us like a blanket of snow. The room comes back slowly: the muted hum of the air conditioning, the cotton sheets at my back, and I'm drifting when he groans, grabs the base of the condom, and moves, lips ghosting across mine as he mumbles, "I'll be back."

Next thing I know he's curling in behind me, arm snaking around my waist and warm breath floating through my hair. There are dim noises in the distance, a door closing down the hall, the distant rumble of voices. His heart a solid thunk-thunk against my back.

"That was amazing," I mumble, squeezing his hand on my stomach.

"It was," he says quietly, kissing my hair. "I wish we could lie here forever."

And this brings me back to earth with a bump. "What time do we have to be in the office?"

Janus lifts his head, looking at the digital clock on the nightstand. "In about two hours, I reckon we can laze here for a while yet."

I sigh, snuggling back into him, and he hardens slightly behind me; it makes me smile into the pillow. I half-turn my head as he grunts, burying his face in my nape, his hand gripping my hip to keep me still.

"Stop turning me on, woman," he grumbles.

Grinning outright at the bedside table, I flip over to face him. He groans, putting both hands over his eyes.

"Don't show me your breasts."

I've never been with a guy who likes my body as much as he seems to.

"How am I going to keep my hands off you all day, now I know what these are like?" His hands come down and he cups one breast, eyes tracking his thumb as he rubs it over my nipple. "All these amazing freckles—the pattern is so perfect."

I've never liked my freckly skin, but I'm seeing it with new eyes. He draws me into him and I rest my head on his pecs, feeling the hard muscle under my cheek as his chest rises on a deep inhale.

"I've never had sex like that before, Jo," he says, and I snort. He pulls back and tips my head to meet his gaze, brows drawn tight. "What?" and the firm command of his voice sends a hot thrill through me, but as his eyes wander over my face, hesitation creeps into his expression.

"It was good for you?" His voice slips a little, and my heart is like a bird in my chest. This vulnerable side of him is killing me. I want to trust him with my soft side, too, trust him with *everything*.

"Good?" I grin. "I think it was a bit better than that. I've never done anything like that either. I don't know what happened, it all just exploded."

Some of the confident, smirking Janus reappears in his face. "Move into my suite with me? I want to sleep curled around you for four days straight."

My stomach dips—whether from thrill or anxiety, I can't tell.

"Just sleeping? Really?" I say.

He grins as I make small circles on his chest. When I look up at him, his warm brown eyes are still fixed on me, and I take a deep breath, gaze returning to the smooth skin in front of me.

"I feel like I owe you an explanation. I feel like I've been so reluctant—"

"You don't owe me anything, Jo. I understand that I'm—"

But I just shake my head at him. It's me, not him.

"I want to explain…" I raise my head to look at him. "I was badly bullied at school. It started out small as these things do, you know: people tripping you up in the corridor, pulling your hair as you walk past, taking your textbooks. Small things. Things I could ignore." I take another breath, looking at my freckly hand on his smooth chest. "Then a gang latched on to how much fun it was to try and catch me before and after school, and they started following me home. A neighbor told my dad how nice it was to see me walking home with my friends. What irony. But I couldn't *confide* in my dad; he's this quiet, peaceful man, and he struggled on his own after my mom died." I swallow it all down. "I didn't want to drag him into something so ugly."

When I look back at Janus his smile has completely disappeared, and his voice is a harsh rasp when he asks, "What did they do?"

"Oh, all sorts of things: setting fire to my hair, cutting holes in my clothes, putting food down my neck—" My voice thins out.

Janus is completely still. "Sonofabitch."

"Yeah." I trace a line down the center of his chest buying myself time. "Then one day it got really out of hand." I prop myself up on my elbow. "They cut off all my hair."

When I look at him his eyes are closed, a muscle ticking in his jaw, and my stomach roils.

"There was five of them, and they set on me on my way to school. When they got the scissors out, I didn't know what they were going to do, so I started fighting back, my hands got quite badly cut." I look down my hand again, and Janus's eyes pop open and flick down as he picks it up, thumb smoothing over the small scars.

He shifts against the headboard, hand tightening into a fist around mine.

"I struggled away and ran into school. A teacher saw my hair and the blood on my hands and took me to the nurse's office. In the meantime, the bullies had followed me in and gone straight to the Principal. They said I'd attacked *them* with a pair of scissors. I was called in to give my side of the story, but I could tell that she wasn't going to do anything, despite the fact half my hair was missing. It was my word against theirs."

"Fucking hell, Jo." Color is sitting high on his cheeks, brown eyes almost black.

"When I got home, my dad took one look at my hair and went berserk; questioned me until the whole story came out. He called the Principal at home, went around to her house. There was a big fight between him and the father of the girl." I swallow, her name stuck in my throat. "Darcy, the ringleader. When the school refused to take sides, my dad went to the local newspaper. I'd never seen him so mad. I was on the front cover; pictures of me with my hair chopped off and the injuries on my hands. You can imagine how the paper loved a juicy story like that."

Janus pulls my hand up to his mouth and kisses my palm, stormy eyes locked on mine.

"Darcy's father went berserk and wanted revenge. He was a local councilor, so, of course, the paper also printed his side of the story, saying his daughter wasn't a bully. I mean the slightly unfortunate thing was that they had no injuries: I'd defended myself against scissors and I'd lost all my hair. But the local paper didn't care about any of that; it started to take their side—I guess he was too important locally not to. We became pariahs. People started whispering behind their hands, saying I did it for the media attention. That I'd cut my own hair."

"Jesus Christ! I—" I squeeze his hand with mine."I can't *believe* you …" he starts again, and I shake my head at him. I need to get the whole sorry story out.

"I don't know what happened to my dad. He flipped. He took them to court."

Janus's eyes widen. "To *court*? Fucking hell. What happened?" He cups his face in his hands and presses a long finger into the corner of his eye. "Please tell me that those assholes got nailed," he mumbles.

If only. I shake my head again.

"Nothing so satisfying. It dragged on and on; they kept trying to put things in the way, raise questions. No one wanted to testify. A lawyer friend of my dad's took it on, but she was under a lot of pressure, and we had no money. Eventually, we had to give it up. I'd gone back to school by this time, and it was like I was invisible. No one talked to me. The small number of friends I'd had before drifted away. The bullies ignored me, too; I think they had been warned by their parents to stay away. But I sort of lost trust in people, in friends, in adults, in how the whole system works. I started doing things for attention. I made trouble. In the end, I had to homeschool. My grades weren't great, so I didn't get into college on merit. But I had an interview, and because of what my dad had taught me, they let me in."

I raise my eyes to his, feeling full of fire and regret. "I never feel like I'm good enough."

"*What?*" His voice comes out in a sharp crack as he sits forward on a jerk. "That's insane—you're amazing at what you do."

I shake my head, putting my hand on his shoulder to push him back down, and he blows out a long breath, running his hands through his hair before turning to look at me. "Can we go after those assholes now? I'd love to …"

Warmth seeps through my chest. "It's a long time ago now."

He lies back, and I watch his face as he winds his fingers through mine, closes his eyes and lifts my hand to his mouth, pressing shaky lips against my skin.

"I'd like to meet your dad. He sounds amazing." I look at his dark lashes, swallowing.

"He is. Amazing that is. But he's quiet, too."

"Some of the best people are. Quiet, that is."

He looks down at our hands now entwined together on his chest and rubs his thumb over a small mark.

"So that's where the troublemaking comes from, then?"

This makes me laugh, and I sag into him. I'm glad he's asking questions, making it light. We need to share our histories, no matter how awful.

"I suppose so. I wanted to tell you because I find trusting certain people—I guess I'm always skeptical, always looking over my shoulder." I feel soft and hollow inside, like I'm never going to be good enough to make it, to step out from under my own shadow.

"And that's why you worry about the press?" he mutters.

I nod.

He squeezes my hand and then pulls me into a tight hug. "I'm so sorry that happened to you, Jo," he mumbles into my hair. "Thanks for trusting me."

CHAPTER 36

Janus

Slumped at a row of desks, I study Jo across the bank of screens. Hing Ko is leaning forward and frowning at the workstation in front of them.

"I could write a script to examine this," Jo murmurs.

Hing Ko points at the monitor and narrows his eyes, saying something in a low voice I don't quite catch. Jo's cheeks are pink, her lips are still slightly swollen, and I pull my gaze back to my screen reluctantly, code swimming before my eyes. Everything I'm doing today is probably a total crapshoot. I scroll through more system data, trying to pretend I'm working on something concrete.

Despite the tiredness and the underlying crevasse of the hack that could derail us at any moment, a bubbly feeling is fizzing and popping inside me, a warmth that's seeping deep into my bones. I can't stop watching her. My God, the way she asks for what she wants, tells me what she likes ... she's *demanding*. And what happened to her at school? How is she still okay? How is she still on her feet and fighting? She's like a rod of iron. But ... I get it. I understand her reluctance now, and I'm on fire with how much I want to show her what this can be, to keep her safe.

The cool air of the fiftieth floor of the Waiwei building washes over me, and the bank of windows is dark behind Jo, the city spread out like an array of shiny coins sparkling across the harbor. There was a point a couple of years ago when the value of Janus Industries became more visible, and everyone I met seemed to want something from me. My response was to draw back, to deal in superficialities. Although my experience is nowhere near as bad as hers, Jo's not the only one who's withdrawn into themselves. My dating life is like some perfect echo of how disconnected I've become. I've used women for publicity, accompanying someone to an event, never having to properly engage. The thought is sour in my mouth; how easily have I fallen into this? To be fair, they benefit from the arrangement, too, but still. How exposed Jo and I were in bed with each other last night and this morning—I haven't talked to someone like that in a long time. The company has been eating away at me, and I know that—I'm tired and busy—but I don't think I'd fully grasped the long slow slide into myself until now. And my history isn't like this; my parents didn't bring me up to skim superficially through life. They've been on my back about keeping in contact with people and particularly my brother. Bryn and I were close when we were younger, but even when my mom and dad were here, I didn't meet up with him. Right enough, we're both insanely busy and caught up in our own lives—he's dedicated to his school and the deprived kids he works with—but I could reach out. I pick up my phone and squint at the time; 6.35 p.m. local time. Pretty early for the East Coast, but, knowing Bryn like I do, he might be up. I fire off a text, and I snort when one comes back almost immediately.

"Who are you and what have you done with my brother?"

I grin. We're so not used to complimenting each other. "You running?" I type back.

"*Yes*." And I can almost hear his impatient sigh. A reluctant laugh huffs out of me.

"I'm in Hong Kong trying to fix problems."

"Hahaha, it's goddamn freezing here."

"Catch up when I'm back?"

"Definitely. You need your arrogant ass kicking."

Bryn loves ribbing me about the business and what he calls my "New York lifestyle."

When I raise my head again, Jo is looking at me, and I wink at her. She rolls her eyes and goes back to the computer in front of her.

"Are you doing anything useful over there, Mr. Phillips, or just laughing at cat videos on your phone?"

I tap the screen. "My brother," I say, putting it down and frowning at the monitor in front of me. I need her calm head to help me focus.

"Come here and help me sort out what the fuck I'm looking at," I grumble. "I need some actual brains on this job; mine are mush."

This gets me a grin, and she wheels her chair toward me, pushing on the ground with her heels. She's all sorts of cute with her hot glasses and the disarray of red curls I washed in the shower this morning after round two, or was it three? She complained bitterly it would go wild and curly, and, fuck me, it has.

"I love your hair like this. I love knowing I made it look like this," I murmur under my breath as my gaze roams over her head, inhaling clean woman and citrus perfume: I'm giddy.

"You're a total caveman," she grouches quietly.

I have to restrain myself from burying my face in her neck and sinking my teeth into her; I can't remember ever feeling this possessive about anyone. She peers at my monitor, and her steady thinking face returns as she tries to work out what I'm looking at.

"What have you done so far?" she asks, her gaze swinging to mine, calm and expectant.

A laugh huffs out of me. "Not one single thing—for some reason I'm massively distracted."

Her lips curve up into a warm ripple of a smile. "Men. A couple of rounds of hot sex, and they're mush. No wonder the best spies and assassins were women." Her gaze flicks to Hing Ko, before drifting back to the screen in front of us.

She's a tiger underneath that soft curly exterior. Apart from the first day in the elevator, her wicked streak isn't often in evidence. She's so calm in work, so rational and professional, but I like the Jo with the runaway mouth that I think she must keep on a tight leash. I lean in, smiling.

"Are you all set for another round?" I murmur. "Ready to have my mouth all over you?"

She observes me steadily through her glasses, and her gaze is so close and so earnest on mine. I can see the freckles on her nose and the dark flecks in her eyes, speckled like her skin, and she gives me a half smile as her eyes track to my lips and back again.

"You're a flake, Janus Phillips, be honest with me now; you didn't build this company, did you? It can't possibly be you because you clearly spend all your time trying to distract people in the office."

I smirk back at her, dropping my voice. "My mouth. All. Over. You." And damn me if she doesn't shift a bit in her seat. I'm getting to her.

Then she leans closer to me and my eyes flick down to her chest—I just can't help it—I'm already hard and this conversation isn't helping.

"How about my mouth all over you?" she says, so quietly I wonder if I've heard right. "Hot, wet suction. Licking,"—she hums a little, making me wait—"rubbing that bundle of nerves with my tongue."

I groan and bury my face in my hands, moving to ease the tightness in my jeans. I've had so many fantasies of Jo doing that to me; on her knees in front of me, my fists in her hair: I want to tell her them all. When I lift my head, I find she's holding her hands in the air and wiggling them in a little victory dance. Hing Ko's eyebrows are knitted together: I hope to hell he didn't hear any of that.

"Think I won that round, don't you?" she murmurs, and I roll my eyes at her.

"You're a menace," I say. "I'll exact my revenge later."

"You'd better." She laughs. "Now get your head in the game and explain to me what we're looking at here." And she tips her face toward the screen.

*

I stretch myself out in my seat and examine the white trims on my sneakers under the table. The three earnest faces sitting opposite me are steady, unwavering. I like the team here; they seem straight, professional. *And I've got a P.I. digging into their backgrounds.* Ugh. This hack is causing me to distrust everyone.

"So, what have we found out so far?" I say.

"Well, we're pretty sure they got in via a password breach." Matt's voice echoes down the line from New York.

"Seriously?" I lean forward, resting my chin in my hands. "Do we think that's what happened in the US?"

Jo shifts in the seat next to me. "They were in and out and left no clues. We've been through mountains of data and not managed to pinpoint it," she says, making a face that shows just how unhappy she is with that statement.

"Goddammit, we could just be leaving ourselves wide open here. How did you find it here?" I say.

Matt's face looms large on the screen at the end of the meeting room. "The team's much smaller, so it's been easier to look for anomalies in the data. Hing Ko's done an amazing job on forensics." Hing Ko beams at me across the glass table. "It could easily be passwords here in the US, Janus," Matt continues. "I talked to James yesterday, asked him to use Hing's work to look for anomalies in the US data around the time of the hack."

"We did change all the US passwords at the time, even though we weren't sure," Jo adds.

"Change them again." I growl. "Matt, I want passwords changed in every office, company-wide."

"I thought you might say that," he says dryly. "Bob's on it. Communication is going out this morning. We've got a couple of people lined up here to coordinate it all."

I nod at this, and Hing Ko is nodding at me quickly. "I can help. We have been very secure with the passwords, Mr. Phillips." He gives me a faltering smile.

I keep telling him to call me Janus, but he doesn't seem to settle happily into that. And I get this comment: he's worried I'll be pissed.

"All of the passwords have been changed here now, properly generated," Sonia, Hing's number two, pipes up from where she's sitting next to him, and I look at her short black hair and trendy red glasses. I like her, she's a real straight shooter.

Hing Ko stiffens and turns toward her, frowning. "They were properly set up when we opened the office."

Sonia shifts in her chair and looks down at her hands, like she knows what people do with passwords, and this isn't quite the truth.

Jo looks down at her notepad, and I glance over at her, doing a double take at the detail of what I assume to be a drawing of the Hong Kong system. "There were a number of passwords that were outside the password management system."

Hing Ko's eyes go wide as he straightens in his chair. He's not used to this kind of directness. This kind of scrutiny. "If there is a mistake, I will resign," he says.

I inwardly roll my eyes, reaching out to pat his arm. "Hing. Chill. We're not losing you on top of everything else."

My patience is wearing thin. It's been a long day. I need the staff to be over their worries of making some kind of mistake I don't fucking care. It's done. We need to sort the problem in front of us. I stare at Matt's blond dreadlocks on the screen again.

"I'm thinking there's a reason that Hong Kong was targeted specifically," I say and they all look at me, surprised. I try and doodle a cartoon dog on the pad in front of me, failing completely. "What's here that isn't anywhere else? Why here?"

"You said this office was new," Jo says. "It could just be simply that."

"I know, but they'd have to know it was new."

"It has not been a secret," Hing Ko adds. "We got a lot of publicity around Janus Industries opening in Asia. Well-respected US company." He smiles at me.

Jo shakes her head. "Maybe it's just a distraction, a lucky accident. Maybe they found a way in here and are just playing cat and mouse with us."

Matt grumbles over the line. "Yeah. Maybe this was their plan all along. They knew they could get in here, and this is just the next stage in whatever it is they're planning."

I *really* don't like that idea. It's like someone has got a noose around my neck.

Sonia purses her lips. "There are some well-known hackers in Hong Kong, you know, links to China, the gangs. Maybe there is something …" She tails off.

I stare out the window. Fabian's comments about it being the Chinese pretending to be the Russians echoes in my head. That could also be why they picked Hong Kong: close to home, relatable.

"Good thought."

"It could be because of something Fabian's done in the past in China, Hong Kong even," Jo adds.

Matt cracks his neck. "You know, maybe they were just trying to avoid our tracking code."

Jo laughs. "Yeah, it's always the simplest explanation."

We've got lots of ideas, but it feels like we're casting around with no concrete answers, and I bury my hands in my hair.

"We need to narrow it down."

"I'll chat to Fabian and see what he knows about the Chinese, if he's been in any Chinese systems," Jo says.

"I can look into hackers here in Hong Kong and China in more detail." Eric, the third member of the team, nods from next to Sonia.

"I'll start spreading that tracking code around every part of the system," Matt adds.

At least we're taking some action. All the staff here seem so good. I can't believe any of them are involved in anything nefarious.

CHAPTER 37

Janus

As we head up to my room, we both slump against the side of the elevator like we're in a permanent curled-over-a-screen position. The mirrored wall behind Jo is reflecting a cascade of red curls, and I examine my sneakers as I flick my bracelet around my wrist. We've done a lot today, shut down some clear loopholes, I've talked to Hing Ko in detail about all the staff ... but it still feels like we're eons away from the root of the problem. Part of me had fantasies of sorting it all out day one and keeping Jo in bed for the other three, ridiculous though that clearly is.

"Food?" Jo says.

"Room service," I say, a scowl twisting my face.

She raises an eyebrow at me as I stare at her pink lips. I watched her rub some kind of gel on her face this morning and paint the jet lag circles out from under her eyes, before making her eyelashes thick with mascara. Only the black lashes are still in evidence. I want to bury my face in her neck and inhale. The elevator judders to a halt, and we head down the thick gray carpet to my suite in silence. I hold the card on the panel on the door, and as soon as the door swings open, my hand lands on Jo's hip and my lips find her jaw as I turn her into the wall and kick the door shut with my foot. She gives a shuddering exhale as my hands cup her face and my mouth finds hers; then my fingers are between us fumbling with the buttons of her jeans, her hands dropping to work over mine. When the last button gives in, my knees hit the floor and I tug the waistband over her hips, pausing to kiss her stomach, nibble at the edge of her briefs. Her sex is bare beneath the white lace, and I slow for a second to watch my thumb slide under the fabric, moving it back and forth over her silky smooth skin before pulling the material aside, opening her up as I nuzzle into her warmth.

My first taste makes me frantic, and a faltering "Oh, fuck" falls from her lips as her hands flutter and land in my hair. I wondered if she'd be as relaxed about this as she seems to be with everything else, but she's pushing at her jeans in an attempt to widen her thighs and give me better access. And I'm all over her, messy, sliding my fingers down and into her, mouth anywhere I can get it, peeling her underwear and jeans down and off. Using the tip of my tongue, I flick her several times and her whole body twitches, nails digging into my scalp. I'm so hard I shift, trying to ease the pressure.

I press my tongue, sliding and rubbing as her sounds take on a more ragged edge. I ease up a bit; but I'm drunk on this, on her, on the sheer impossibility of her skin, on this secret time in Hong Kong, on finding her in my bed every morning. I could stay here with her and never go home, never go back to anything.

"*Janus.*"

The word is forced out of her on a sharp exhale. Even though we were joking when we talked about it earlier, this doesn't feel like a game at all. When I was working minimum-wage jobs to earn enough money to struggle through college, even with my fantasies about the company, about what I would do when I "made it," I lacked the imagination to come up with anything as good as this.

Jo pulls on my hair, desperate for more pressure where she wants it, and I stand and lift her in one movement, carrying her through to the bedroom as she wraps her legs around my waist and presses into my erection. I try to rub against her, catching her open lips with mine before collapsing forward onto the bed.

"You taste of me," she whispers, and I groan.

A chocolate that's been placed by the staff after turning down the bed rolls down from the pillow and I stretch over and pick it up in my teeth, holding it for her as we both bite down. As it melts, I move my head smearing the mess over her lips and chin, sweetness exploding on my tongue as I lick it off. My shirt comes off over my head while I'm propped on one arm; she undoes my jeans, and they come off with my shoes as she sits to peel her soft T-shirt off over her head. Having watched her dress this morning, I knew there wasn't a bra under there—another reason I've been hard on and off all day. I lean forward on one hand and squeeze her bare breast with the other, nipple hardening against my palm. As she reaches between us, the feeling of her soft hand squeezing down my length makes my eyes roll into the back of my head.

"Jesus *Christ*," I say.

I drag my nose down her body, finding her wetness and parting her with my thumb and forefinger, pulling in a deep breath to try to slow myself down. Cool air seeps into my lungs.

"Janus," she whispers, an embarrassed tilt to her voice.

"Shh," I say. "This is too gorgeous for words." And, as I bend down to kiss her folds, she gives me a strangled "Oh God," before a soft thunk tells me she's collapsed flat on her back. Giving oral sex to a woman is wonderful, that feeling of swelling under my tongue, but Jo takes it to a whole new level, lifting her hips up into my mouth on a plea. I give her what she wants, moving in rough fast circles on her clit, pushing her legs wider to dance my fingers down to her entrance, teasing, relishing every shift, every shudder. Goose bumps form beneath my other hand, heavy and tight on her stomach, holding her in place for my circling tongue; and she's tiny under my hand. Her surrender makes me want to roar. Up until now, I've had mechanical sex—decent sex, sure— but it followed a set of actions, a script. What I've done has got me off fine, but I've never been lost in it like I'm lost in this; lost in the feeling that I could do this forever and never end the anticipation of what we're doing together.

I slide a long index finger inside her wetness, and she's so slippery I delve lower to taste. She raises her head in protest and I'm instantly back there, pushing at her swollen nub again: She's close. I hook into her, rubbing her inner walls as she clamps down on my finger and I push up, thumb pressing where my tongue has been, looking at my hand moving, the rigid cast of her body as everything tightens. She gasps, and her eyes snag mine for a brief second before they fall closed, lips open on a gasp, face tightening into a grimace.

"Oh God."

"Janus."

"Please."

"Oh my, my ..."

And fire burns through me watching her face as she falls.

*

The airport cab is one of those old Mercedes cars you find in poorer corners of the world, with worry beads dangling from the mirror and huge holes in the foam seats. The driver is part maniac, part magician, as he weaves us in and out of the traffic, muttering under his breath, occasionally singing along to whatever is looping through the radio. I stare out the window at the passing buildings, the guardrail whipping past. This is ending—we are going back to separate apartments and different lives—and I hate it. I stretch my hand into the seat between us, catching her fingers.

"Okay?" I say.

She takes me in, eyes roaming my face, lips curling up.

"I've had the best time," she says.

I smirk at her. "I know," I say, and this gets me my favorite Jo laugh.

Something settles down in me with this exchange. We're doing okay. Hong Kong is locked down tight; passwords right across the network have been sorted. Matt's making good progress with the tracking code. Fabian is as agitated as fuck, but he's started delving through his hacker networks. It's good to have him on board; he understands the hacking underworld better than we do.

Jo and I have still got to have a conversation about how we're going to behave in work when we're back home, but there's plenty of time to sort out how our relationship is going to work. *Relationship.* I'm still not sure I've got her on board with the idea that I want more, but I need to sit on my desire to hustle and give her some space.

"I'm really pleased with what we've done here. We can use this as a blueprint for elsewhere. That office is like Fort Knox now," I say.

She grins at me, and I wonder for a minute what she's going to say. I'm never quite sure which version of Jo is bubbling to the surface.

"I've got other ideas I'd like to implement, too," she says.

What is behind that knowing grin? I gesture at her face. "What is this? You had some thought there, didn't you?"

This makes her laugh. "You betcha."

"Going to tell me what it was?"

"I was wondering what exactly was the blueprint? The picking-up-a-woman blueprint? The fucking-all-night blueprint?" She leans forward, a devilish glint in her eye. "The oral-sex blueprint?"

Her eyes sparkle. I'm speechless. Will I ever recover from what we did to each other in that suite? It was the hottest oral sex of my life, giving definitely, but receiving? My God. My ability to stay calm with her was rather sketchy from the get-go, but Jo wasn't having any of that; she made it go on and on. She made me promise I wouldn't take over, that I'd her allow her to do what she wanted, and I'd said yes, not knowing what I was letting myself in for. She tortured me for a whole hour, bringing me close time and time again. Her tongue on the underside of my cock, right on the bundle of nerves, playing with me and only occasionally sinking all the way down. The thought makes my breath hitch; the frustration, the ache in my balls I can still feel an echo of even now. I clenched my hands so fiercely, so many times, I could hardly type the next day. How hard I came at the end of all that? Fuck. I lost the sensation in my fingers and toes.

I'm silent for a bit before I lean into her and say, "it's the Jo Williams blueprint. Amazing things happen when this particular lady is around." I trail my finger down her arm as she groans.

"Good God, man, that was the worst line I've ever heard."

A reluctant laugh huffs out—will she ever stop poking fun at me? Will I ever hear *I love you* out of her mouth? Woah, woah, woah. Where did that thought spring from? We're way too early for that. But some old certainty is churning in my gut—so deep I hardly dare lift the lid of the box—I'm all in here, buried by these mountainous feelings coursing through my body every time my eyes pop open to red curls spread over a white pillow.

CHAPTER 38

Jo

Kate's smooth blonde hair is bent over a textbook at our usual table when I bounce into McNally Jackson's the next day. After the turmoil of the last few days and the long flight home, I can hardly contain myself. I'm exhausted but strangely elated. With frantic days and even busier nights, I went out in a dead faint on the plane home and slept all the way, too tired when we arrived to do anything other than curl up around Janus.

I weave through the busy tables. "Kate!" I say, and her head snaps up as she grins widely.

"Hey, tech princess." She rises from her seat and I pull her into a warm hug. The give of her body is so familiar, so solid and warm, that it brings a lump to my throat. I'm desperate to offload the swarm of bees lodged in my chest. I need her sensible perspective to quash the giddy thoughts. For the first time in my life, work is buried under something else.

She narrows her eyes. "No comeback to that one?"

I shake my head. "Sorry, Doctor, too distracted today; I'm no use to anyone. I've been longing to talk to you."

She raises an eyebrow at me in typical restrained-Kate fashion and motions at me to sit like she's doing a consultation. "Fire away," she says.

I take a deep breath and gesture to the coffee counter, heading over to place my order before coming back and plonking myself down opposite her. I hardly know where to start.

"So how was Hong Kong?" she says before I can get a word out, and I put my head in my hands and groan.

This gets me a typical Kate laugh.

"That bad, huh? Was resisting the life force that is Janus Phillips a problem?"

"I didn't resist him." I talk down to the wood grain of the table.

"*What?*" she wheezes, leaning forward and whisper-shouting, "Oh my God, why didn't you call me immediately? Holy shit, Jo, you kept *this* quiet? This is epic. I bet you guys are so cute together, discussing HTML or whatever you techy people get so excited talking about."

I give her what I hope is a patient look, but I can see from her face that she's thrilled, and in this warm moment I understand suddenly that *this* is the reaction I was looking for; some reassurance that I'm not a lunatic for doing this. Shushing her with my hand, I lean forward, and the woman at the next table glances over at us as I lower my voice.

"I didn't call you because I wanted to tell you face to face," I say, and she grimaces at me in a way that tells me what she thinks of this.

"I needed time to process where my head's at, but oh God ..." I roll my head on my neck, trying to pull my thoughts into order. "Thinking about it on my own is making it all worse."

She's grinning at me in genuine delight now; the way only a proper friend will do.

She holds her hand up, palm forward in my face. "I want to know *everything*," she says. "You can talk about how you feel in a moment, but start with what he's like in bed." Her smile is pure evil. "Are the rumors true?"

I think about the first night—Janus coming so fast—and laugh. It was like being a student again, the awkwardness, both of you having next to no experience, fumbling your way through a maze of how to give pleasure to each other.

"What rumors?" I say, still smiling, but I can't quite squash down how much I dislike the idea of rumors. I don't want there to be rumors about his sex life; he already feels like he belongs to me.

She tips toward me, talking quietly now. "That he's a sex god?"

Someone walks behind me and jostles my chair, and I pull it forward, glancing back and letting my gaze skim over the people at the next table, the windows softly steaming up with the coffee and the breath of a hundred customers, the people hurrying past outside. The loud bang of the barista emptying coffee grounds jerks me back into the conversation.

"I don't know about that." I think about his quiet intensity, his soul-baring, his focus on my pleasure and his delight in giving it. "He knows how to look after a woman in bed."

"Oh! Oh no, missy. You are not getting away with a statement as bland as that. I need details."

"Only if you are prepared to give me the lowdown in return." I quirk an eyebrow at her.

This will fox her: Kate is notoriously uptight. Sure enough, she sinks back in her seat, making a face at me.

"I like the way you think I'd have anything juicy to share," she grumbles, stirring her coffee. "My sex life is as quiet as a graveyard and about as exciting." She stares down at the cup and her lips gradually lift up. "So … you're thoroughly satisfied right now?" Her smile grows improbably wider.

"Oh God, Kate. On the one hand, I absolutely cannot do this, I cannot do this with Janus Phillips. He's well known. If it gets out, there'd be so much scrutiny, and it could scupper everything. I've worked so hard. Am I really going to risk it all for a guy? But …" I let it all roll over me, all the things we did and said, and I meet Kate's eyes. "I like him. I mean, I *really* like him. We have fun together, and the sex …" I take a sugar lump from the bowl on the table and pop it in my mouth, "I've never been with someone where I wanted it to go on and on." I drop my voice, shivering. "Usually, it's one orgasm if you're lucky and that's it … you know? But this? I think he could give me one orgasm after another—"

Kate raises her eyebrows and I grin at her.

"—And he did," I say, and she stretches out her hand and high-fives me, both of us grinning like a couple of teenagers.

"And you know … it would still not be enough."

I want so much from Janus, but I'm shying away from examining it because every time I do a vice squeezes my ribs. Something about Kate's easy acceptance is unwinding all the tightness coiled inside.

"Not enough?" There's a light in Kate's eyes I can't interpret. "Why … What …?" She trails off.

"It's something about the focus, Kate, the way he's focused on me; the desire to see me tip over the edge, over and over again … And I can tell it gives him more satisfaction than getting there himself. He wants to give that to me."

"God, he sounds like a wonder. I'm green with envy right now. One orgasm not of my own making would be an amazing addition to my life right now."

I laugh at her. "You're too busy for orgasms. You've told me that in the past."

"Yeah, shoot me now. ER is insane," she says, and she unexpectedly sounds so down that I blink at her. I've turned up here obsessed with some guy, and all is not well in Kate land.

"How's it going?" I say, and she's quiet when I ask this, looking down and picking at a bit of loose skin on her dry hands. She's talked about how difficult ER is with me before, and I'm no psychologist, but even I can see the effect of her demanding, no-fail, perfectionist family on her.

"You're a superstar, you know that, right?" I say, reaching for her hand over the table. I don't want her to give herself such a hard time, I want to soothe and help in my own clumsy way: give her some of the acceptance she's given me.

She waves me away with her hand.

"I understand what the criticism from my family and the constant comparison and demands for more, more, more, did to me, and usually I can control my negative head noise, but in ER … I can't explain it, it's like"—she wrinkles her nose—"a growling, anguished beast comes out and I can't shut it down. He's not in my head. It's me: I'm this wounded animal and it scares the living daylights out of me."

A wounded animal? Jesus.

She straightens. "Anywaaaay …" The word is drawn out. "Janus?"

I laugh. "Way to change the subject."

"Yeah, I don't want to talk about me—denial is my friend—and anyway, I've made this a depressing conversation. I'll do something about it, Jo, I swear. Tell me more about Janus, what's going on under that calm exterior? I've never seen you so rattled. I know you like your safe, steady guys."

"Yeah." I pick my nail. "He's definitely not that."

She taps my hand. "And?"

"I don't know why I like guys that are safe and steady."

Kate purses her lips at me. "I mean, *so* much happened to you when you were young. Your mom committed suicide … and you get such a lot of erratic behavior with a mental illness."

I stare out at the blank windows of the shops on the other side of the street. Yeah, I remember my mom's erratic behavior all too well.

Over the last few years, I feel like the business has given me some control. When I was younger, I was carried along on a tide with no way of stepping out of the flow: the bullies, the press, losing my mom. My whole life I've battled for some solid ground, and now I've finally I got to the side of a mountain, out of the tsunami. But maybe it's all some impossible dream—fleeting, transient.

"I'm scared, Kate."

"Of what?"

"Getting too attached and then … I don't know, I guess … losing my footing. It's not the safe course of action, is it?"

I turn back to her sympathetic face.

"Sometimes you need to take a risk," she says.

CHAPTER 39

Jo

My coffee cup is glued to my hand as I push through the old glass doors into the office building the next day. After the conversation with Kate yesterday, my shoulders feel lighter, like I'm no longer going to be torpedoed from below. Janus was dragged into meetings until ridiculously late last night, but he's texted me already insisting he's not spending another night on his own, and I'm bouncing on my feet. Goddamn him. He's so into this … this … whatever it is we're doing. I shake my head.

And I must have some kind of happy aura around me this morning, because the eyes of the two secretary types waiting by the elevator widen on me as I approach. They're both wearing tight sweaters and figure-hugging skirts, looking at me with their heads tipped on one side, like a couple of curious birds, so I smile at them. My work clothes sometimes prompt this odd reaction—the ripped jeans and oversized top—but with the long red hair, I'm used to people scrutinizing me. High school wasn't the only place that happened. There's the usual clunk as the doors open, and, as I follow them in, one of them turns.

"Jo Williams, right?"

"Yeah." She's in my building, so I've probably met her before. Damn. "Um … I'm sorry." I tilt my head. "Did we meet …?" I wave my arm around and my coffee tilts dangerously. I'm not usually so bad with placing people.

"Not really." The woman giggles. "I saw you in the paper." She leans forward conspiratorially. "I think everyone is envious," she says, beaming at me. "Well done by the way."

What *is* she talking about?

"Um, thanks?" I lift my cup to my lips, take a hot sip.

"Janus Phillips!" The second woman says with a huge smile, leaning forward around her colleague.

Something crawls up my spine. An article must have appeared about the fact we're working for him. Damn. I hope to God Janus Industries hasn't been exposed.

"Yes, they want to make their security world-class," I say, floundering for a response.

"And a gorgeous guy," she adds with a wink. A hot sweat breaks out on the back of my neck. This is exactly why Janus is a problem: Too many people know who he is and are invested. I push my glasses up my nose.

"He's built an impressive company." I say the first thing that pops into my head, hoping it might deflect this conversation on to safer ground.

"Is he as amazing as they say he is?" They're both smiling so wide now.

What do I say to this? "He's an exceptional businessman," I manage. God, I need to find out what they've seen and where.

One of the women frowns at me. "Well, it looks like you were having a good time with him in Hong Kong." The other one winks at me again.

"Looks like … where …" I can hardly get the words out.

"*The Gazette* is such a great paper," one of them says on a sigh.

"I get all my news from there." The other one nods in confirmation.

All the blood drains from my face. The worst gossip rag in the US.

Oh, holy shit.

I stare at the pair of them. There's a picture of Janus and me in Hong Kong in *The Gazette*? Sweat breaks out all over my body.

No, no, no.

The elevator shudders to a stop and they smile at me. "You're so lucky!" one of them simpers as they head out onto their floor, and I catch a glimpse of my white reflection in the mirror on the wall opposite the elevator before the doors slide closed.

Oh, God.

Des and James are both out when I step through our door, thank God. Coherent conversation is beyond me. I greet the few staff who are in before scurrying into our glass meeting room, pulling out my laptop and clicking through to *The Gazette's* website, hands shaking. Relief washes through me when I don't see anything on the first page that loads. But when I click through to the gossip pages, there it is, the first article. Shit. *Shit.* A photo of the pair of us laughing outside an ice cream parlor sits under the headline. And oh my God! We look … I don't want to think about how we look. We'd finished a long but fruitful session at the office and walked down the road looking for some coffee and found this amazing place instead. Fifty-three flavors of ice cream, including some weird Chinese ones. This got us talking about obscene-tasting ice cream: He'd invented pussy flavor, and I'd said I wasn't sure about fur in a cone. We're laughing, happy, we're acting like we're … My chest constricts painfully at the intimacy written all over our faces, I can hardly bear to read the text.

Has Mr. Right found his Tech Sweetheart?

Janus Phillips, the gorgeous tech entrepreneur known for his rotation of different flavors of women, may be a leopard about to change his spots. He was spotted on a four-day "business trip" to Hong Kong enjoying time with none other than Jo Williams, another startup founder, and our sources tell us the couple have been hanging out together lately. Jo's company, Williams Security, has recently been awarded a lucrative contract with Janus Industries. It looks like Jo is not only taking care of security, but also the main man himself.

Ugh, *business trip* in quotation marks. I skim through the rest of the article. It's all about previous women he's dated. Pictures, too. Yuck. My palms are damp with sweat, and the sickening feeling in my gut has only intensified. *They caught us together.* I thought we were safe from prying eyes out there: I am the most naïve person alive.

I look up from the screen at the glass walls, the bent heads of the team outside: all oblivious to the fact I am dissolving inside.

Kate.

I almost don't care if she's saving lives in ER. I know she won't answer if she's in the middle of something crucial, but, God, I need my calm, balanced friend right now. I pull out my phone, my thumb slipping as I press her number.

"Dr. Thurman." Her voice is cool ice and I've never been so glad to hear it. I suck in a deep breath.

"*Kate,*" I say in an urgent strangle. Ugh.

"Are you okay? You sound—"

"Stressed?" I finish. "I've got a problem." My heart claws up the back of my throat.

"What's up?"

"There's a photograph of Janus and me online."

Of all people, Kate will understand. She shares some of my paranoia about career dreams evaporating.

"Let me find an office," she says, and her shoes click heavily on the floor, ringing phones providing a background clamor. A swing door whooshes and thuds.

"Are you busy? I don't want …"

A pause.

"No. I'm okay at the moment."

"You save lives on a minute-by-minute basis, and this problem is not the same level of crisis as that."

She snorts at me down the phone. "Quiet, you. Stop with the feeling guilty about calling me at work. We're not busy at the moment: I can take five."

Another door opens and clicks shut, and the hospital noises disappear. I can hear fingers tapping on a computer keyboard.

"Okay, I'm online," she says, blowing out a breath. "Site?"

"*Gazette*, gossip section." I chew my nail, pick at a hole in my jeans.

She hums a little into the phone. "Right. Let me see … Got it. Cute picture of the pair of you. Let me read." The line is quiet for a minute. "Okay," she eventually says, "I presume you're freaking out on about fifty different levels right now."

"Oh, God, *yes*, Kate. Jesus."

"I hate the way newspapers write about women," she grumbles. "'Looking after him' indeed. Goddammit. He runs a billion-dollar company. Hopefully by now—because, you know, he's an adult—he can take care of himself."

A strangled laugh huffs out of me, and the fluttering in my chest that started in the elevator eases a bit. I would hug her if I wasn't on the other side of Manhattan. She's given up her precious emergency time for this. She gets how women are judged; she gets the sting in the article for me.

"What are you planning to do?" she says.

"God, I don't know. All I'm doing right now is kicking myself for getting involved with him in the first place."

She hums a little more. "I think that horse has bolted now, Jo. I know you: Don't give yourself a hard time about something you can't do anything about. You can't go back."

I nod into the phone despite the fact she can't see me. This is a typical Kate response: practical, clear, shutting down avenues that would cause me to spin my wheels.

"Whatever happens, you want to try to control this." I can almost hear the cogs whirring. "Even if this dies away, being with Janus is inevitably going to involve scrutiny, exposure of one form or another. You have to decide if he's worth it, but you also must take charge of it, too. You can think about whether he's worth it, and the effect on you and your career, later. Put that aside for now. First things first: Find someone to control this for you."

Caltech. It's the first word that pops into my head. And although that wasn't personal, their PR person, Carly, handled everything, and deflected the heat in an almost magical way.

"You're right. God, you're right. I should have prepared, done something before this photo got out there. I knew this was a potential problem."

"Stop giving yourself a hard time. No one thinks about this kind of thing until it happens; otherwise, you'd tie yourself in knots trying to cover a thousand different contingencies. Like me," she mutters the last two words under her breath.

"I'll get on it." The lump in my throat rises up again and I can hardly speak.

"Let me know how it goes. I'll let you press on and sort. You want to catch a drink later? Come over to the apartment and talk it through a bit more? I could come to you?"

"Oh, God, would you? Would you come to my place? I don't want to …"

"Perfect. Girls' night in. I'll bring wine and we can order pizza. Should I see if Liss is up for it?"

Both of them. I let out a breath I didn't know I was holding; this is just what I need to get through this day.

"Sounds wonderful. God bless you, Kate."

Her hearty laugh echoes down the line before she rings off.

I shift from the table to stare out of the window. Carly was so utterly professional with me and the company, as well as being a tech industry wizard, but I'm not sure she'll be the kind of person who is happy handling such a personal story. Although I'm still sick to my stomach, I scroll through the phone until I find her name and press call.

"Carly Miller speaking." Her crisp voice echoes down the line.

"Carly, Jo Williams."

"Jo! How lovely to hear from you. How are things going? I hear you're working with Janus Industries now as well as Caltech. Sounds like things are going well."

And only a few months ago we couldn't meet payroll. I cross my fingers. "Yes, they are, thanks. It's the contract with Janus Industries I'm calling you about."

"Oh Gawd," she says in a voice reverberating with years of press shenanigans. "Are the media trying to do a number on them as well? Security is so hot at the moment. Fantastic news for you, I guess. They have an unhealthy interest in Janus's personal life, that's for sure."

My heart deflates a bit with the idea that Janus's private life is worthy of comment.

"Yes, *exactly*, and I'm not sure whether you'll be able to help. Something appeared in the press today … Can I send you a link?" I move over to my laptop to find the page I need.

"No problem," she says, and we pause while we wait for it to come through.

"Okay, I've got it … Let me read." And she breathes quietly on the other end as I chew the pad of my thumb, staring out of the glass walls to where James and Des have now arrived and are bent over a screen together, sun casting a glow over the wooden desks and the white-blond tones of Des's hair. He glances up and waves, and I give him the best smile I can muster.

"Hmm," she says, "they do love their gossip *The Gazette. Are* you dating him?"

Damn. I'd forgotten how direct she is. How do I answer *this* question?

"Well, no." I clear my throat. "We're both techies, obviously"—I'm waffling here—"and we ended up mentoring each other. We went to Hong Kong together to sort out a problem with his office. We're good friends," I say more firmly; I need her on my side. "I've been terrified of the media misreading things, the harm it could do to my business, so I've"—my throat tightens and the next words come out sticky—"I've stayed away from any kind of relationship with him."

"Why would it damage your company?" Carly asks, a curl of curiosity in her tone.

"Oh, all the comments about me getting contracts because I'm sleeping with him, I wouldn't look like a legitimate business proposition at all; there'd forever be a question mark about my expertise, whether I can do my job. The gossip in this industry is terrible."

"I know," she says, crisp voice softening like bread in water, "and I understand your panic. The press treat woman roughly sometimes, but maybe we can come up with a positive spin on this."

The warmth in her voice pours honey over the sharp spike sitting under my ribs.

"I'll find a hard copy of the paper and see where they've put the story, and check if it's been picked up by anyone else." Her pen scratches on a pad, keys tap, tap, in the background. "Let's meet first thing tomorrow morning and figure out how best to handle this. My colleague Selena often works with me when business strays into personal. She's terrific at handling what I would call the more scurrilous parts of the press. Does 9 a.m. suit you?"

"Sounds great," I say. Having a professional looking at this makes the heaviness that's been weighing on me all morning start to lift.

"Janus Industries employs a public relations agency, and I'm just not sure if the same one handles the publicity for Janus himself. Given he's in the papers quite a bit, I'm certain he'll have a personal PR." She is clearly mulling over her questions out loud. "It could be useful if they were there? To make sure we're presenting a consistent story. We could meet at his offices; it might be more convenient. Would you like me to see if—"

"No worries. I'll talk to Janus and ask him to set it up," I say.

After I finish talking to Carly, I flip my phone over in my hand a few times. Everything is vibrating through my body, and I pull in a deep breath: I don't want to say something to Janus I'll regret. Without warning, my phone lights up in my hand, and the picture I took of him looking out of the windows in the office in Hong Kong flashes across my screen: He's staring at something in the distance, a frown on his face, jaw covered in stubble, dark lashes thick around his eyes. He's so unspeakably handsome, something stutters in my chest.

"Hey," I say, attaching the phone to my ear.

"I was thinking we could get some dinner tonight, chill out at my place?"

He mustn't have seen the article this morning because it'd be the first thing he'd mention, surely? Or maybe he doesn't worry about things like this anymore because his media people handle it. I clear my throat.

"I'm actually seeing Kate and Liss." My voice is tense. "But I was wondering if we could meet tomorrow morning, with your PR lady if she's free?"

"Meet?" His voice sounds confused. "Yeah, sure, what about?"

He definitely can't have seen it. He knows how I feel about being exposed like this.

"*The Gazette* published an article." I'm trying to keep my voice steady, but it wobbles perilously. "Nobody mentioned it to you?"

He makes a noise, and I pull my phone away from my ear and look at it, wide-eyed. He's laughing? I gingerly put it back against my head. He must have been clearing his throat. But no, he's still chuckling down the line. I'm sick to my stomach, and he thinks this is funny? I press my lips together, a sharp heat bubbling up.

"Yeah no, I've seen it," he says, amusement lacing through his voice. "It's fine, Jo, nobody is interested. Bloody hacks are always getting photos of me. It's no bad thing now we're back to have it out in the open. They won't be so curious in future if we're out and about together in New York. I'm quite surprised no one photographed us before now."

What? I stare at the dark blue wall of the office, the two programmers who are deep in conversation in the little kitchen. *This* is his reaction? I've opened the door to the arctic and icy air has swept in. The article implies all sorts of things about me, my reputation will be crucified. I don't understand. At the very least, shouldn't he be concerned for me? To be so cavalier …

"Jo?" he says.

"I was planning on having my PR lady issue a full denial as soon as possible tomorrow," I say, trying to keep a rein on the hot and cold alternating through my veins.

The silence on the other end of the phone goes on forever.

"Sorry. *What?*"

I repeat what I've said to him, pacing the words out and sounding like a robot.

"Issue a denial?"

"Yes, well, we need to get the facts straight. I can't have speculation like this washing around about me. My business. My professionalism."

"The facts? Speculation?" He sounds stunned. Good. At least he's starting to realize how important this is to me. "Well, it's not exactly inaccurate," he says, and I'm not sure what that tone in his voice is, but it lights a fire in me and I can't hold back my anger any longer.

"What do you mean by that?" I snap. "Perhaps you also think I got the contract with your company because you wanted to sleep with me?" And for the first time I wonder if maybe I did. The anxiety in my stomach turns into a ball of flames, like a match in gasoline. What the hell is he thinking?

"Where does it say that?" His voice is low and even.

"It implies it, Janus. All that nonsense about a 'lucrative contract' and 'taking care of the man and the company.' It makes me look utterly ridiculous. Unprofessional. People are going to have a field day with this."

"It's just a little salacious," he says. "I don't think it says that at all. I can't believe …" He hesitates and—oh my God—I want to breathe fire down the phone.

"It suggests I got the contract with Janus Industries by having sex with you; not because I'm good at my job, or, you know, fucking amazing at security."

My fury is making me swear and something about this feels so liberating: to channel this rage, this anger at my own stupidity for getting into something like this when I knew exactly what would happen, into an argument with him.

"It makes us sound like we're in a relationship." My heart dips a bit when I say this.

A long silence fills the other end of the line.

"We need to talk about this face to face," he says. "I'm coming to your office." And the phone goes dead on me.

"Fucking wonderful," I mutter and head out from the glass box to make a hot tea and brace myself for whatever the hell he's going to say when he arrives.

*

I'm back in the meeting room pacing the floor when he's buzzed up by the doorman. I flick my fingers trying to ease the cramp in my hands, sucking in a deep breath. Why, oh, why did I do this? When I stop and close my eyes, I can still see the jostling cameras on our bungalow's front lawn, people shouting my dad's name, *my name*, see that guy with the long gray hair and yellow fingernails. The door of the office swings open with a crash and I jump, eyes flying open.

I wish I could control how my body reacts to the sight of Janus; his lean torso wrapped in a faded T-shirt and jeans that always hang too low. I don't want to notice his boxers. I am not going to watch the way he walks. I stare at the screen on my laptop for a second, two, but then his voice responds to someone, and when I look up, my whole team is sitting up straighter, eyes glued on him. I grind my teeth. Des is out of his chair, and from the way he's fidgeting he clearly doesn't know what to do with his hands, except I'd hazard a guess he'd quite like to put them on Janus. And I realize—too late—that this is the first time Janus has been here; the first time he's met everyone, and of course they're all thrilled. As I head out of the room, James and Des both swing toward me, wide-eyed, along with the rest of the office.

"Guys," I say, through gritted teeth, waving my arm. "Let me introduce Janus Phillips."

"Great to meet you," James says, holding out his hand. Des's hand is pressed against his chest, practically swooning.

Then Janus gives them that grin, the one that makes me dumb to my toes, and says, "You guys are the best security team I've come across; I couldn't be more grateful."

Ugh. It's just the right thing to say, and as Des presses his hand farther into his white top like he's about to have a heart attack, I notice his T-shirt has "FUCK THEM ALL" written across the front.

"Oh, my God, I've wanted to meet you for the longest time. Can we take a selfie? My Instagram account would go wild for a Janus photo." His words are rising, giddy.

I'm not going to be lucky enough for the ground to swallow me up, and I'm about to open my mouth at the mention of social media, when Janus turns to me, smile getting impossibly wider.

"What do you think, boss?"

Fuck all cute men. Does he think he can melt my anger by sucking up to my employees? By flashing that grin? Shoot me now.

I nod my head in an effort not to appear surly, and try desperately to hold on to some of the fire I felt earlier now I'm faced with the Janus Phillips charm turned on full force. All my team are up in an instant, crowding around him and taking selfies and group shots, and I mentally calculate that this might actually help the situation if more pictures emerge of him with my team.

"I've got to chat to your boss now, guys," he says eventually. "But I would love to catch up with you all. Des, how about organizing a meet-the-team night out?"

Des is gazing at him with stars in his eyes. "No problem," he says. "How gay can I make it?"

Janus laughs, rubbing his finger across his chin. "I think that would be fantastic for my reputation, don't you?"

Des and James are laughing and agreeing like a couple of nodding dogs, and I turn on my heel, moving toward the meeting room. Him and his damn reputation. I want this conversation over, so I can go and dissect everything with Liss and Kate. I don't want him to charm me into backing down.

Janus closes the door carefully behind him and studies me for a beat, not saying anything.

"I like your team, Jo. You chose well." He gives me the adorable crooked half smile, and I don't need the reminder of how into him I could be if I let myself feel too much.

I nod. I'm not going to be the one to start this discussion. He carries on, looking at me.

"Tell me what you're thinking right now."

"Honestly? I want this conversation over, so I can go home and decompress for a while. I've had an entire day of *this*." I wave my arm around. "Discussing *this*. Not my company, or my clients' problems, or even your hack. I've wasted a whole day on one measly picture. This is not how I want my life to be; I don't want to be second-guessing what I do and say all the time, or having to deal with the fallout when I don't get it quite right and someone takes a photo and writes a shitty article."

Too many emotions are bubbling up inside and making me petulant, and I'm aware I'm not behaving brilliantly right now, but he's not exactly being sympathetic himself.

Janus runs his hands through his hair and stares at the floor, not meeting my gaze.

"I'm sorry, Jo, I really am."

What's he apologizing for specifically? I fold my arms. "You didn't seem to think it was that important on the phone?"

He shakes his head. "It's not that. Maybe I've had a lot of shitty things written about me and I've become immune to it? I try to ignore these kinds of things most of the time because I can't let myself be distracted. I'm sorry if it came across badly."

Is he apologizing? He sounds just a tad judgmental, like I should be dealing with this how he does.

"But you don't think it implied anything negative about me?"

Why am I pushing this? I don't like what he's doing right now: it feels like he doesn't agree and is trying to placate me. That this is somehow my problem, not his.

Long fingers scrape through his hair. "I think you have to be the judge of that, Jo. You have to make a decision about whether to react or not. Sometimes, if you respond, it makes it into more of a thing. They think you've got something to hide and do more digging."

So it *is* my problem? Ugh. Although I don't like what he's saying, I get that it can be a good idea to let things like this bury themselves. Carly said as much to me herself when we started working on Caltech. And maybe my dad stood and fought too much. But aren't some things too important to just let go? And why is it my responsibility to deal with this? Aren't we in this together?

"Okay."

What else can I say? He clearly doesn't agree with me, but I want to go home. I'm running away, but I need to think when he's not in front of me being cute.

"Are you still all right for talking it through with the PR people tomorrow?" I say.

He nods. "Of course. I've already called Julie, and she's coming to our offices at 9 a.m."

He walks toward me, but I don't know how I feel about him right now, and the entire office is pretending not to peer at us through the glass walls. My eyebrows knit together, and I tilt my head at the desks. He grins at me.

"They'll have to know sometime," he says.

And just like that, I'm doused in icy water. I shake my head at him, but *of course* they'll know. How stupid am I being right now? Killing this one story is not going to make the problem of having any kind of relationship with Janus go away. I won't be able to keep it secret indefinitely. If I want this, if I want him, then this is going to be part of the territory. I'm going to have to live with these kinds of comments being made about me all the time. The thought makes my stomach roil.

His gaze roams my face for a bit, then he shrugs. "Walk out with me?" he says.

CHAPTER 40

Janus

From my balcony, the lights of Manhattan resemble fireflies dancing across a dark field, the rumble and shrill of traffic a distant chaos. Cubes of ice are slowly melting in my whiskey, and the oily liquid slides as I roll the glass side to side in my hand. There's an ache just below my breastbone every time I think about Hong Kong, and now Jo and I have fallen down some damn rabbit hole. How much damage can a silly little article do? The way Jo denied we were in any kind of relationship today has left a bruise under my skin. I don't think she would have done that if the trip to Asia had meant to her what it meant to me. Am I imagining how intense it was in bed night after night? I could see the panic on her face today, hear the tremor in her voice, so I backed off. I didn't want either of us to say things we couldn't take back.

The last red-carpet event I went to, there was a huge bank of cameras and never-ending shouts of "Over here!" Did I even look at the papers the next day? If Jo's company grows like she wants it to, then they're going to be interested in her, and she'll be on the end of those camera lenses whether she likes it or not. This article is a tiny wrinkle in the pages and pages written about me, and perhaps it wasn't that complimentary about her, but newspapers always publish nonsense, so this all feels like a massive overreaction.

On my way to see Jo, I called my publicist, Julie, to fix the meeting for tomorrow morning, and she agreed with me that, if we wade in on it, the press will become more suspicious that something is up. We haven't responded to things which were much worse than this in the past—and why would we? The women involved have often wanted the publicity; that was the reason they wanted me there.

I fling the ice from my glass into the nearest planter, missing it and it bounces off the ceramic and skids across the tiles. When she said she wanted to issue a denial, I wasn't sure what she was saying. If this carries on, we'll have to be seen in public together *sometime*, so does this mean we can't ever have a relationship? My stomach drops with the thought. The wail of a siren reaches up from the street and sets my teeth on edge. She's doesn't seem to want to push past problems with me at all.

I pour myself some more whiskey from the bottle on the side table, and the alcohol burns my lips and all the way down my throat. How much will it take to tip me into oblivion?

My phone starts an insistence buzz on the low table in front of me and my chest expands. *Jo*. But when I turn it over, a picture of me and my brother appears on the screen and I slump back into the chair. The pair of us are standing on top of a snowy mountain next to a ski lift with the broadest smiles on our faces.

"Bryn. What are you doing up this late?"

"Well, hello to you too, little brother. I know you don't get home until godforsaken o'clock and I've just finished my marking. So I thought I'd catch you after a random and unusual early-morning call from Hong Kong. How the hell are you?"

"I'm good. Good. Yeah." I hesitate. "Good."

How many times can I repeat good here? "Well … someone's messing with our system, and we're not sure who yet, but we're trying to sort it."

"You must be keeping it quiet; I haven't seen anything in the papers."

Thank God Bryn doesn't read the gossip pages. And here's another thing: the press focusing on a relationship between Jo and I might be distracting them from the other problems the company's having. Ugh. I'm silent too long for my uber-observant brother.

"Stressful, huh?"

"Yeah, nothing unusual—you?" Luckily for me, he isn't one to push.

"Crazy kids, crazy lives, adults who are AWOL, the whole gamut. Rescued some kid from a playground in the dark the other night—he's only six—parents nowhere to be found, probably out doing drugs. Had to take him to emergency care. The poor guy was acting out like shit."

God, what am I doing in my ivory tower apartment when people's lives are falling apart like this? Not for the first time, what my brother has chosen to do with his life gives me a warm thrill.

"You get him sorted?"

"Yeah." He lets out a long, controlled breath. "As much as you can in this situation."

He fills me in on the kid's background, and listening to his problems makes the tension in my shoulders start to ease off.

Eventually he says, "You're quiet tonight, not talking my ear off like you usually do. Where's my impatient brother gone?"

"Oh, you know. Just mulling over stuff."

"Personal or business?"

Do I want to talk to him about this?

"Personal."

"Woah, really? I thought you had a drama-free situation there. Lots of compliant women falling all over you. Beautiful girls, premieres …"

I chuckle. He has such a distorted view of my life. "Yeah, I met a less amenable one."

Bryn will understand this—his wife is a firecracker. He gives me a hollow sound somewhere between a laugh and a cough.

"They're the dangerous ones. Don't get tied up in that."

"Uh-huh, not much chance of that. I've probably fucked it up already."

His throaty chuckle on the other end pours oil on my skittering thoughts. "What did you do?"

"Oh, some stuff in the paper she took the wrong way."

"Man, the way the press is interested in your life, how do you stand it?"

"Comes with the territory I think."

"Does it though? Why?"

"Well, they got interested as the company grew. There wasn't much I could do to stop them taking photos and commenting."

"You could try not accepting invites to the fancy events you like to go to."

This is very much an outsider's perspective. New York doesn't work that way, but his questioning makes me pause. You can easily be sucked into the crazy here.

"In some ways you're right. I don't *need* to go out and be photographed, but on the other hand, the events I've been to have been amazing and I've met some incredible people: smart, motivated, doing completely different things from me. I don't want to say no, despite the press interest."

He's quiet for a few seconds. "Yeah, I get that."

"And also, I don't want to live my life looking over my shoulder. Buried away in a hole. You can easily get paranoid and jumpy, and you have to get on with your life."

If there's one thing being in the public eye has taught me, it's this: You can't second-guess other people's reactions. I swirl the whiskey in my glass, stare at the open sky above the rooftops of Manhattan just beyond the plants on my roof terrace. Then the penny drops: The reason I'm resisting what Jo wants to do is that, to me, it's clearly the wrong path. Hiding, denying, it's a mistake. We need to confirm this relationship not disown it. And just like that, I know exactly what to do to sort this whole problem out.

CHAPTER 41

Jo

The pit that's opened up in my stomach since the story appeared yesterday morning is widening. Janus texted me late last night wanting to see me before the meeting, but I ignored it. I can't add more of his charm to the chaos of my thoughts. The conference room at Janus Industries is exactly as I remember it and, as Maddie bustles around sorting out drinks, a reel of images flickers through my mind: the way he leaned over me in that first meeting, the heat at my back, the muscles tightening in his forearms, how I have seen those arms over me and beside my head, have turned my head and licked them. We didn't resolve anything yesterday, and despite the tossing and turning in bed last night, I haven't pinned down what I feel about how he's responding to this: Is he making me the bad guy here? If I could transport myself back to the simplicity of Hong Kong right now, I would.

The door swings open in typical Janus-entering-a-room fashion and I can't stop my smirk. But as he enters, I'm shocked to see him in a suit. He looks sharp, lean, completely amazing. He catches my eye and gives me a small lip twitch as I try to focus on the woman following him in. And she's got PR stamped all over her: blonde hair piled on her head, a gray two-piece which is a bit too tight for her curvy frame, and a big, welcoming beam. Something in me eases at her friendly vibe. What must it be like spending your time fielding stories and photographs of Janus with beautiful women? And just like that my smile dies as something curdles in my stomach.

"Hey, you must be, Jo," she says, coming forward with an outstretched hand as I rise out of my seat at the table. "Great to meet you. I've heard a lot about you from this guy"—she jerks her thumb toward Janus—"bane of my life that he is." Her smile twitches wider.

Janus shakes his head at her. "You love explaining my dates to the media," he says, and she gives a rough laugh full of late-night gossiping and too many cigarettes.

Her laugh is suggestive and dismissive all at once, like every single woman is something to be handled, explained away. Adrenaline dumps into my veins. Will I be similarly swept under the carpet? After I've lost every shred of credibility I ever had? Does anyone ever think about how this affects the women involved? A rod goes up my spine: My dad didn't fight all those battles for me to throw it all away the first time some gossipy story appears. I'm not going to be lumped in with all these models Janus dates for two months and discards. I know he's explained to me that that's just how the press portray it, but all rumors have a grain of truth in them and, given what's happened with the photo of us, and his response to it, I'm not sure what I believe anymore. Maybe all his relationships have ended when some woman gets slaughtered in the press. Maybe he didn't defend them either. My blood starts to simmer.

Janus and Julie sink into the seats opposite us, and Carly smiles as she rises up, hand extended, and introduces herself. She sinks back down, pulling a sheaf of papers from her bag, tapping them together on the polished wood.

"I'd like to chat to Jo first for five minutes in private," Janus says, and all eyes swing to him. His are fixed on me.

I stare back at him. Am I going to let myself be persuaded by him playing it all down like he did yesterday? My chest aches for our time in Hong Kong: his half smile as he leaned over the bed and kissed me. I want to give him *everything,* but the monkey on my shoulder chatters on about how quickly people can turn on you and disappear, that I'd be trampling over everything I've worked so hard for if I ignore this. I slam the door on my heart and shake my head, and his eyes narrow. We're still staring at each other when Carly coughs, and I drop my eyes to the table, gesturing at her to continue.

"After Jo called me yesterday, I took the liberty of drafting a press release. Perhaps we could use this as a starting point for what we want to say and how we want to handle it?" She smiles placatingly at Janus, but his eyes are shuttered, a muscle jumping in his jaw as he stares somewhere over her head. She slides a single sheet in front of all four of us and I start to read.

Janus Industries and Williams Security note the recent speculation in the press. Both parties would like to confirm that Williams Security has been awarded a contract to enhance Janus Industries' security arrangements, supporting the company's aim of providing a world-beating service to its clients. A team of ten [?] people are being employed from each company to achieve this goal, and Jo Williams and Janus Phillips recently traveled to Hong Kong for four days to work with the office there on security. Any speculation these arrangements are anything more than an outstanding business team working together is unfounded.

Julie's eyes flicker toward Janus as his gaze scans the paper, getting stonier and stonier. I can almost see the storm brewing. Then Carly speaks from my right.

"We can say more than this, of course. When Jo and I spoke yesterday she said you guys were good friends, and I wanted to make sure we kept the right tone—"

Janus interrupts, eyes tight and fixed on me.

"You want to say we're *good friends,* Jo?"

Emotion is seething under his skin, in his eyes, and my heart takes off. After the weirdness at my office last night, something is going on here that I can't quite grasp. Why isn't he suggesting alternatives? Goddammit, why isn't he talking more? I think, too late, that we shouldn't be having a personal conversation like this in front of two undoubtedly curious PR ladies.

I shake my head at him, examining my hands in my lap.

"Perhaps *good friends* is the wrong term to use," I say.

"What would you call it, Jo?" His words have a sharp edge.

I lick my lips, stretch out my hand to wrap it around the glass of water on the table. I can't look at him again. He's like this ominous presence in the room, a dark cloud growing bigger with every second that passes.

"Maybe it would be helpful to mention our mentoring relationship," I say, aware of Carly furiously scribbling notes at my side.

"Are you *serious?*" Janus's voice comes out like the crack of a whip.

"Perhaps it would be easier if we don't call it anything," Carly says brightly, smoothing over the awkward. "We don't name it so to speak, we could just describe the regularity of meeting and contact ..."

Julie is nodding in agreement. "Yes, that works, I like it actually, specifics, meetings ..."

Standing up, Janus shoves back his chair with a muttered "Fuck!" He rakes an agitated hand through his hair and walks to the window. The sky is dark, splatters of rain starting to land on the pane. Julie's eyes narrow on him speculatively before looking down at the paper in front of her.

"If we put in the names of the team from each side working on ..."

Janus swings around. "*Fuck this*, Jo. You know these responses are bullshit. This is not what this was, and I, for one, am not going to lie."

The words drop into the room like oil in vinegar. Julie and Carly both turn toward him, eyes wide, their expressions no doubt mirroring mine. I open my mouth then snap it shut. He's never lost it with me. I've seen him agitated, but I haven't seen fury brewing like this: eyebrows knitted together in a sharp frown, lips curled, teeth almost bared; and everything is curling up and withering inside me. I don't want to have this discussion here. I've told Carly we're just friends. Heat crawls up my face. Oh, *God*. Why didn't I take the five minutes with him? Why wasn't I more honest with her? She said to me once she could hide anything if she knew the real story. When did I become a person who lied to cover things up?

"I can't—" I start.

Janus swings his arm out from his side as he strides back to the table. "I know you can't, Jo, and that's the whole reason this can't go on right there."

My heart hits a brick wall. Is he ... Is he ...? What is he saying? I close my eyes, trying to hold on to something, *anything*. My eyes snap open when he starts talking again, his stormy gaze flicking over all of us like we're being showered with hailstones.

"Right, Carly." His voice is tight, almost dangerous. "You can put out whatever Ms. Williams here deems is a fitting response. I'm having no part of it. Julie, if you are contacted by the press, then our line is 'no comment.'" He turns to me, and his gaze rakes over my face. "I hope that makes you happy, Jo," he says in clipped tones then walks toward the door, wrenches it open, and he's gone. It takes me right back to the first meeting I ever had with him.

I blink at the doorway before coming back to the two women who are staring at the empty space in astonishment. Julie does a little double take, but then her face relaxes, and she nods at me. Something slithers down my spine. How many other stormy meetings with rejected women has she sat through? Are the models the ones who are normally storming out?

"Can I stay and hear what you're planning to say? I'd appreciate you keeping me in the loop. We will say 'no comment,' but if they write more stories, that might need to change," Julie says.

I glance down at my hands, clamp them together to stop the tremor. "Of course," I say. I don't want them to see that my hands are shaking. What did he mean this can't go on? Is he saying he's finished with me? I try and swallow down the tightness at the back of my throat; all because I wanted to protect my reputation with him. A small slice of anger bubbles up again. That's shit.

Carly glances at me. "Are you okay?"

"Yes." I can't believe how calm my voice sounds. But I'm not even close to being okay. I hate myself. I hate this situation.

"I think we should put out a press release that doesn't even acknowledge this," she says, thoughtfully tapping the draft in front of her with a long glossy fingernail. "Let's not give oxygen to this sort of speculation. I don't think we should say you're good friends. I think we keep it professional: say you've been awarded the contract and keep the focus on big tech companies' security problems, on how Janus Industries needs to safeguard itself."

"Distract them from one story with another. I like that." Julie says, sitting up straighter, nodding and smiling. "Carly and I can work on it together, put out a press release from each company. I'm sure I can persuade Janus to run with that."

"Won't it raise questions about whether Janus Industries has security problems ..."

"I think you handled it brilliantly with Caltech, Jo, by saying big companies need to be at the forefront of the field in a fast-moving area of tech," Carly says. "We can play that angle. Are you happy to offer an interview if they want to talk to you about issues in security for large firms? It would be valuable publicity, arguably an excellent opportunity while the interest is high." Her tone takes on the enthusiasm of a PR person scenting a story they can twist.

"Won't I be grilled about our relationship?"

"Undoubtedly. We can say in advance you're not prepared to comment, but they'll still ask. I can coach you on deflecting the questions."

Something worms through me. Who willingly puts themselves in the firing line like that?

"You can always say 'no comment,'" Julie chips in.

"I could do the interviews with you, if you like? A buffer is often helpful when things are hot like this," Carly adds, nodding and smiling.

"Oh, that sounds ideal," I say, rubbing sweaty palms down my thighs and blowing out a long breath. Either something good will come of this or it'll be suicide. They must think I'm an idiot.

Julie peers down at her pad. "Janus did say he'd pay whatever costs were necessary ..."

Carly starts putting away her papers in her bag, and suddenly everything's agreed. I should be feeling a lot calmer, but somehow I'm not.

CHAPTER 42

Jo

K ate stirs her coffee, lifts it up to her lips, and takes a sip, blue eyes locked on me over the rim.

"So, when did you last hear from him?" she says.

Slumped in my chair, I stare at her glossy blonde hair and her turned-down eyebrows. I want to swing by Janus's office and kick him in the ass, but my chest has a huge hole in it that even coding can't fill. The press release has been out for six days and no more pictures or speculative articles have appeared; everything has died down. Janus was probably right. I probably panicked. Ugh.

Two requests have come in for interviews, both of which legitimately appear to be about the business. One is from a tech magazine which I should be excited about because they don't interview just anybody, but part of me is slightly resentful all this came about because of gossip, not because of my own expertise. But this is not the time to be sitting on some highfalutin principles; this is a business opportunity and I need to take it. I stare out at the rain pouring down outside; a woman dodges a puddle, umbrella held out stiff and taut. Where is the spring sunshine?

"Almost a week now," I say.

She grins at me. "If you could see your face right now, you look like you've lost your puppy."

I scowl at her and she breaks into a laugh.

"I am fed up with watching old TV series and eating takeout. All this stupid nonsense. I liked my life before." The whine in my voice makes me wince.

"Admit it: You miss him."

"*Of course* I miss him," I say, burying my mouth in my coffee cup. Why is that so hard to acknowledge?

"Are you still doing security for him?"

Oh, God. Sometimes Kate's ability to go straight at your deepest fears is a pain in the ass, but it probably makes her an outstanding doctor.

"Ugh. Kate. I've got no idea how long that'll continue. I'm fully expecting him to fire me."

She shakes her head at me. "That must be unlikely, surely?"

I shrug.

She raises an eyebrow at me. "What are you going to do?"

"I don't know, the radio silence is difficult to explain." I squint at her, biting my lip and staring out the window again, hoping for the distraction of a wet chihuahua or someone getting covered in spray. "I guess he was serious when he said this can't go on."

Kate tucks a blonde strand behind her ear, eyes following mine to the sidewalk. "Why don't you call him?"

My eyes dart back to her face. "And say *what*, exactly? You think I should apologize?"

"Would that be so bad?" she says, voice soft like I'm a recalcitrant patient who doesn't like injections.

"I don't know what to think," I growl. "He didn't think my point of view was valid and basically blew his top."

"Maybe he was as panicked as you were?"

My breath exits so fast it comes out as a snort. "I highly doubt it. He deals with this sort of stuff all the time. Manages his dates in the most convenient way possible for him. Does he even *care*? I mean he's got a full-time professional PR person to deal with the women he goes out with for fuck's sake. Who does that?"

Kate reaches over the table to pat my hand, and I want to snatch it away. My time with him feels like a piece of beautiful porcelain I've fumbled and dropped.

"He only lost it when you wanted to deny you were in a relationship. And what you told me about your trip? None of that smacks of someone who doesn't care to me."

I try to give her my best skeptical face, but I can't bear the spark I get hearing this from someone else. I look down at my lap and smooth my hands down my jeans. Hong Kong was … he was …

"Aren't you justifying your reaction to yourself a bit here?" she says softly.

"He turned on me, Kate."

She bites her lip and puts her hand on my arm. "Yeah, I understand why you see it like that; I just …"

Damn her calm reassurances. "Okay, super psychologist, why haven't I heard from him if he's so keen?"

"Perhaps you hurt his feelings? It sounds like he wanted more to me. He probably thought this meant you didn't?"

"Don't be daft, what woman wouldn't want more with Janus Phillips?" I lean forward. "He basically took me apart in bed and put me back together. No woman in her right mind would turn that down."

She leans over the table and whisper-hisses, "Yes but you wanted to deny it all, Jo. *No one* would take that well without a lot of behind-the-scenes reassurance, and he's a high-profile, somewhat egotistical guy. *Come on.*"

I groan into my hands. I gave him no reassurance at all. I lost my temper and backed off. Pretty much exactly the same thing—I realize with a sudden horrified clarity—that he did.

"Did you say anything about how it might work—you know, after you'd dealt with the press article?"

The window is misting up now, obscuring the chaos of a Manhattan commute in the rain. I am the queen of self-sabotage.

"Goddammit."

"Call him, Jo. I think you need to apologize."

CHAPTER 43

Janus

People are in the building, but you wouldn't know it. They are nowhere near my office. They have scattered like beads dropped on a floor. The very idea of not being disturbed should fill me with joy, but I want something—someone—to rail against, somewhere to park the agitation outside my body. Something to stop me thinking about the glittering jewel I had in the palm of my hand that I threw in the sewer, among the rats and the rotting toilet paper. I linger on the calendar on my monitor; it's a sea of meetings. *Seven days.* Raised voices seep in from Maddie's office; I'm sure I hear the word *asshole*. The blinking cursor on my screen is at the end of the line of text in an email written all in caps. The short sentence contains three swear words.

I spin my chair to stare out at the ocean of buildings outside the window, the background of blue, a shimmer of spring creeping in. Why did she want to deny we had any kind of relationship? I get her desire to protect her reputation, I do, and perhaps I didn't handle that particularly well, but am I not good enough for her to find *some* sort of compromise? Okay, being involved with me comes with a certain level of scrutiny—I know it's a big ask—but isn't she prepared to push *anything* aside for me?

Fabian has been a rock in a storm. I've been over at his place every other day sitting at his spare screen in grim silence. He's dealt with me with his usual stoicism: getting me involved in all his coding, asking no questions, and ignoring my surliness. I assume he's still working on my security with Jo, and I reckon he's been talking to her, but he hasn't done it in front of me. He's given me space to talk when I want to, which is not at all. After snapping at him one too many times last night, he casually mentioned it might be a sensible idea to chat about things: to "get the turmoil out of my head." What irony. He's the king of turmoil.

"I just don't see a solution," I said.

"To what?"

"*Jo.*"

This got me a long sigh. "Can't you protect her better, Janus? Can't you do something positive about this situation? It's bullshit, man. It's not like you. You're the one who doesn't let anything stand in his way; you've never been put off by little words like 'impossible.'"

I frowned at my screen and turned to look at him, taking in his scowl. Was I prepared to admit to the nausea rolling through my body? To him? He was way off the mark. With everything else, I took the risk because what's the worst that can happen? I lose my company and have to start again. I have a hundred ideas I could turn into something decent. But losing Jo? This woman who's so dazzling I don't see anyone else? This woman who deep down I think was made for me? It's a fucking mess.

"I'm fucking terrified," I said then, feeling sick to my stomach.

He laughed. "Yeah I know, man, but that's your superpower: You do stuff even though you're terrified."

What? "No. Hell no. You don't understand. I've never been in a situation where, if I mess up, I can't recover it. If I lose Jo, I won't find another woman like her. I mean … I don't want to find somebody else. What if I've already lost her? What if she never wants to talk to me again? Fuck. I'm just …"

He gawped at me.

"What?" I screwed up my whole face.

"First time I've ever seen you like this." He contemplated me for a bit, then gave me a smile halfway between patronizing and amused. "You can't mess this up, you know."

Fucking hell. "I already *have*," I growled at him, "I lost my temper. I didn't understand her point of view."

But he was shaking his head even as I forced the words out. "That's not what love is. If she feels for you what you feel for her, she'll forgive you."

I couldn't stomach his confidence and the way he made it all sound so fucking *easy*.

"*Love*?" I said incredulously.

"Yeah." He grinned at me then, and something hot and sharp kicked through me at his calm assurances. "What else would have you behaving like a bear with a sore head and around at my apartment every other night?" he said.

"If it's a problem, I can stop coming around," I growled at him, swinging my eyes back to the screen in front of me, sweat trickling down my spine.

His eyes fixed on the side of my face, his annoying grin like a taunt. "Yeah, I hate seeing you," he muttered, twisting back to his computer and putting his hands on the keyboard again.

"What if we're both too proud?" The words jerked out of me, surfacing hard and fast, and suddenly I wanted them all out of my head.

He leaned back in his chair, and I swung round to find him staring at the peeling ceiling, long fingers woven together behind his head. "The thing is I think you both *know*, you get that this is it. Don't you understand? You can't mess this up because you're on the same page: You've met the person who is *completely* right for you."

"I don't think she feels that way about me, Fab," I said.

"Yes she *does*, you dolt. *Of course* she does! The way she looks at you, fucking hell, I wish some woman would look at me like that. She might be upset, and you've got to sort that out, but she's as into you as you're into her."

I wanted to believe him. Christ, I did.

"Then why did she …"

"She's as scared as you are! She doesn't want to mess it up either. She doesn't want to ruin her company. Come on, man, she's worked a long time for this, just like you."

"Oh, *Jesus*." I put my head in my hands and rubbed my eyes with the heels of my palms.

"Look, you've got to show her that her worries are not a thing. God alone knows how, but …"

I looked up and stared at the bank of screens in front of us, not seeing them at all.

Then Fabian said, "You've got to take a chance. You've got to risk it all. You've got to make her to realize you'd do anything for her."

CHAPTER 44

Jo

When I arrive at my desk, I'm aware of Des's scrutiny. He's looking at me steadily and the lack of a smile makes me wonder if I've got something on my face, or my hair has gone particularly rogue on the commute into work. I screw my face up at him.

"You okay?" I say, meeting his unblinking gaze.

"You don't know, do you?"

"What?" Oh, God. Perhaps overnight someone has taken down a system we're working on? "Shit, Des." I put my hand on my chest as I drop into my chair. "What is it?"

"Janus has given an interview with the *Wall Street Journal*." Des's eyes are still fixed on me.

"Okay." I sink farther into my seat while my pulse takes off at a gallop.

"You need to read it."

"Oh, God, what is it? Is it something bad about the hack? The work we're doing?" Surely someone would have called me. "Has he fired us?" A public firing. That would be …

But Des is shaking his head, pursing his lips as he glances at James's empty chair, turning around to check out two programmers sitting at their desks, before swinging back to me and tilting his head.

"Read it," he says, looking at his monitor. "I'm going to send you the link right now."

A notification pops up at the bottom right of my screen, and when I click over to the web page, a heart-stopping picture of Janus appears. His hair is in disarray, biceps curving above his arms folded over some band T-shirt ... but it's the headline of the article that makes my heart seize.

Young and in love.

Jesus Christ. Nausea swells in the back of my throat, heat crawling up my neck. What am I looking at? The scrutiny has all died down—what the hell is this now? For God's sake ...

"What is he *doing*?" I grip the mouse tighter to stop the tremor in my fingers.

Des is frowning over the screens at me, and I glower back at him. I must look half-crazed because he shakes his head.

"Read it," he growls.

The page on my screen goes down and down and down as I scroll. Crap. I flick back to the beginning. The whole of the first part is about him and how he got started in tech, his company. He's charming the pants off the interviewer. My eyes stray to the name of the journalist: a guy. Well, at least it's not some woman who's fawning all over him.

"Press speculation has been building about security at Janus Industries, and two weeks ago a picture of you with Jo Williams surfaced in Hong Kong."

"That's right," Janus replies, "we were looking at the systems in our office out there."

The tight band that's taken over my chest eases a bit.

"And you confirmed recently Jo's working on protecting your company?"

"Yes. Every large organization is targeted by hackers these days, and we need to be at the forefront of what's happening in the field and safeguarding ourselves. Williams Security was recommended to us after they helped Caltech sort out a tricky hacking issue, and I think the public scrutiny around that made every fast-growing tech company take a long hard look at their systems. Jo Williams is brilliant; I've never met anyone who has the ability to visualize a network and highlight all the weak points like she does, plus the tech expertise to sort it out. The team at Williams Security is outstanding, but she's the jewel in the crown. She's made our system what it is today, without Jo and her professionalism we wouldn't be able to deliver the service we do to our clients."

I go back to the start of the section and read it again. He described the guys as outstanding, I trip over the words "jewel in the crown." My chin slumps into my cupped hands, eyes fluttering closed as I rest my elbows on the desk. He said *that* about me? My chest aches.

"And there's been some speculation in the press about a personal relationship between yourself and Miss Williams?"

Oh, *God.*

"That's right, but she's way too good for me," Janus jokes.

"You sound like that's something you regret."

I wince at the interviewer's questions; I want the floor to swallow me up. Is everyone in here reading this? My eyes flick over the bent heads. The thought of how quiet I've had to be; Kate has been my only sounding board. Heat climbs in my face as I focus back on the screen.

"Every guy would fall in love with Jo Williams, but she's been the consummate professional with me."

My stomach drops through the floor, and I try to take a deep breath, but my ribs are constricting the air in my chest. Is he saying what I think he's saying? I stare around the office dazed. Outside the window, the sun is streaming down, the hiss and thud of a truck rumbling past. What am I doing? I'm sacrificing everything I might have with Janus for some idea I'm being professional. Am I being the biggest idiot right now? Is he right? Am I good enough? Can I take this risk with him? I scan down the article, it carries on talking about his plans for the business. Before I've thought to move, I'm on my feet. He hasn't done what I wanted him to do. He hasn't kept it quiet or said, "No comment," he's deliberately gone out and made a statement. He's put his head right on the chopping block. It's the craziest strategy: He's not Fabian's best friend for nothing.

James appears at his desk and gestures at me over the screen.

"What?" I whisper when he waves the office phone at me.

"I've got Carly on line one and the Chief Executive of Samsung on the other," he says.

"*Samsung?*"

His eyes are bugging out, and he's giddy as he nods.

"Put him through, and tell Carly I'll ring her straight back."

An hour later, I hang up after the longest and most detailed call about security of my life. The guy had read the interview, and he wants us to review the system on their phones. I press a stretched palm into my chest; it would be a huge deal just to do the trial he's considering. They want me to fly out to Korea in the next few days. I'm reeling.

Des and James are studiously studying their screens, but their tension seeps across the desks: They've listened to every answer I gave.

"Damn Janus," I say, "he might have warned us he was going to throw a high-level bit of promotion our way. You guys better be ready to help me step this company into the big time."

"Samsung?" James says, his delighted grin giving it all away.

"This is huge." I bury my head in my hands.

"That sounded extremely thorough," Des says.

"Yeah," I mumble into my palms, dragging my hands down my face and looking at them over the screens.

With his hands over his head, Des starts making celebratory circles, and I can't stop the smile that breaks free.

"How big?" James says.

"With what they're talking about, I think we're going to need loads of people. Probably. Shit, I don't even know." The laughter bubbles up my throat. Tipping back in my chair, I focus on the ceiling as I mull it over, but my mind is already shaping the contract, what we're going to do. I straighten and meet Des's wide eyes before pointing at them both.

"You two are going to be helping me run all this." I'm asking a lot: They're young; it will be a mountain of stress.

"Oh, I'm so up for this!" Des says. "Can I have a pay raise? Can I be interviewed alongside Janus Phillips? Perhaps with my shoulder touching his?" Des makes a dramatic sweeping motion down his right arm.

James is laughing as I grin at Des. "You can be photographed hugging him for all I care after I've kicked his ass." But I don't have anything to kick him about. This is … I don't even know what this is. Unbelievably generous? And I hardly dare whisper it to myself … *unbelievably romantic*?

"I'll be Head of Operations, and James can be Head of Technology."

I'm laughing right now, but they're both nodding at me as if they've already agreed on this. I stare at the pair of them. If I could jump over the desk and hug them, I would.

"You guys okay with that?"

Des gets up from his chair and does a little dance around our desks. I want to dance, too. One of the coders glances up. The desks have filled up now, and everybody has been pretending not to listen in. I have to explain the article and the call. I stand up and clap my hands.

"I've got some exciting news," I say, and everyone turns to look at me.

CHAPTER 45

Janus

The plunk-plunk of rain dripping off the guttering and gurgling down into the street below is the only noise that cuts through the quiet of Fabian's apartment. I shiver in my hoodie. Saturdays like this used to be a complete rarity for me, but after my first few days of rampaging around the company like a wounded lion, I've been in the office once this week, drunk off my ass. I think Maddie got me out of the office and home, but it's a blur.

Fab arrived at my apartment today with a deep scowl and bundled me into a cab, grumbling that I might have thought to call him and that he'd been worrying about me all week. He dragged my complaining backside back to Brooklyn and into a shower and then a chair and gave me some hideous recursive coding problem to solve. I've been grimly trying solution after solution for hours. I want to curl up on Fabian's bed and sleep for a century.

Not a peep from Jo, despite it being six days since the article came out. I close my eyes, fighting the rising tide of nausea. When was the last time I took a risk and it didn't pan out? I growl at myself. That's what risk-taking is, asshole; it doesn't work sometimes. But I can't shake the feeling that I've blown it; she wanted no comment, for fuck's sake. What was I thinking? How much was hope driving me forward? I'm a fool. I need to do something, anything, but my head is as empty as the tequila bottles in my kitchen. She's not going to respond to a text, is she? I snort. *A text?* So fucking lame.

"Have you heard from Jo?" Fabian says.

What is he, a mind reader? I shake my head like a dog with a bee in its ear.

"You're making all sorts of weird grinding teeth noises over there."

"Shut the fuck up."

"She's in Korea," he says, and my whole body locks as I swing my chair round to gape at him.

"*What?*" I growl. "How do you even *know* that?"

He grins at me. "I'm following her."

"What the *hell*, Fab! You can't shadow her around like some creepy stalker …"

He flaps a hand at me. "I developed a tracking system some time ago. There were some questionable people I came into contact with and I wanted to"—he waves his hand again—"monitor them. It aggregates data from phones and social media …"

I gawp at him, but he just shrugs.

"You could make a fortune out of that," I mutter, swinging back around to my screen, but the news that she's out of the country pushes some of the bitterness and self-recrimination down for a few soft, warm seconds.

Fabian's hands are flying over the keyboard.

"Looks like—*goddammit*—she's at *Samsung?*" he mutters, leaning into the monitor.

"*What?*" I leap out of my chair. Samsung Digital City? My hands land on his shoulders as I peer over him. And there she is, a little dot on the map, halfway around the world. It eases something in my chest, but what comes out of my mouth is something else.

"What the hell? Why would she be there? If it was their security, it'd be huge for her. Maybe *that's* why I haven't heard from her."

Fuck. I said that last bit out loud.

His swings around grinning at me. The smug bastard.

"I like tracking your girl," he says. "This is the most animated I've seen you all day."

I roll my eyes at him. "Fuck off. And she's not my girl."

He nudges me where I'm leaning over him looking at the screen. "You should have seen how worried she was when I turned up at her apartment about the code you put on my system. She thought something had happened to you."

I scan his man bun and his unshaven chin. "She hasn't been in touch since the article."

He shrugs.

"Has she even read it? Anyway, give her time, yeah? Rome wasn't built in a day. You didn't think your company would *just happen*, did you? You can't expect her to roll over with one gesture. I can't believe I'm telling you this; usually you're the one giving *me* the lecture about patience."

A strange bark of laughter rumbles out of me. I'm not sure how I feel about *him* counseling *me*. He rubs his hands together like he's warming up to the role.

"You might have to do loads of stuff to convince her; you've only done one measly interview," he mutters, and his harsh words snap my spine straight. "Anyway, if she doesn't come after my buddy, she'll have me to answer to, so she should be quaking in her boots. You're the best guy in the world—after me, of course," he adds, swinging around again to tap away at the keyboard.

"I've done enough today," I say, sinking back into my seat and turning back to my computer.

"Now there's a set of words I've never heard coming out of your mouth. You want an IPA? Something stronger?"

I turn around to catch his devilish grin.

"Beer is good."

He gets up from his chair and stretches, puts his hand on my shoulder.

"She'll be in touch when she's back," he says, patting me before disappearing into the kitchen.

His tatty jeans are falling down his ass as he disappears through the doorway.

I stare back at my screen as nausea bubbles up again: I wish with all my heart I could believe it.

*

I lean back in the chair with a long sigh, staring up at the stains on Fabian's high ceilings. This could be an amazing flat if he wanted it to be, but I also like the dated fittings and the chaos, too. My phone vibrates on the desk and I feel irritation crawl up my neck. More messages on the work Slack channel. My team hid when I was on a rampage, and now I'm turning into an irresponsible drunk they're trying to include me in everything. *Goddammit.* I lean forward and grab it, opening the screen as a message drops down from the top. I just catch the first few words, "Hope you enjoyed your problems ..." before it disappears.

What?

I swipe the screen, scanning my notifications. *A text?* I click the app open. Unknown number?

"Hope you enjoyed your problems in Hong Kong. You should be more careful who your friends are, Mr. Phillips."

Cold floods through me.

"Fabian!" I yell.

He appears in the doorway with two beers in his hands.

"I've got a message. A warning, or shit, I don't know," I say, swallowing.

His eyes widen on me. "What? Where? How did it come in?" He plonks the beers on the desk and comes to read over my shoulder.

"Holy shit," he says, reaching over and taking the phone out of my hands as his thumbs fly over the screen. I rise out of my chair and peer at the phone.

"Text," he mumbles. "I guess that's good."

"Good?"

He inclines his head. "Well ... I mean ... it's unlikely that they've hacked your phone. They've just got your number. Although we probably shouldn't assume that," he mutters as if he's half-talking to himself. "Let me take a look at the message."

"I think we can assume they haven't hacked it. My phone's encrypted," I say. "We did it a while ago."

"Great." He walks over to his desk and sits down. He stares at the phone for a few seconds and then tilts forward, pressing his head into the desk. "Fucking hell."

"What?"

"It's all to do with me."

"We don't know that."

He snorts. "Come on, Janus—'friends'? It's got to be."

I sink down into my chair. He's right. If I'm being honest with myself, it's been obvious for a while. And who knows what someone that Fabian's crossed might try and do?

"Fuck." He slumps down in a chair, loosening his bun and burying his hands in the wild mess of his hair. "Why would they send us a text like this?" he mutters. "I mean, why not just go all in? It's like they're stringing us along."

Jo's comments about cat and mouse dances into my thoughts.

"What do you mean 'all in'?"

"Well, once they're in the system, they could do anything, destroy data, anything. What I don't get is why they haven't done it already."

Destroy data? My stomach drops out.

"Jesus, Fab, who are these people? Will that message tell us anything?"

"We can check, but they'll be using a burner for sure."

"Do you think it is this Russian lot?"

He purses his lips as if he's wondering how much to say.

"Come on, man, you don't need to guard your responses. I think we're way past that now."

He shakes his head. "It's not because of that. It's pretty complicated. Over the years there's been hundreds of people I've annoyed. I mean, I thought they didn't know what I was doing, but maybe I'm just being naïve here."

"Can you make a list? Like right now?"

He nods. "I'm already on it."

"They knew we were in Hong Kong, too." I walk over to stand behind him and stare at my phone in his hand. "I wonder if they've got some kind of tracker on my phone."

"You'd have to have downloaded something. I can look at it," Fabian says. Then he gives a half laugh. "Why am I even suggesting this? It's always the simplest answer: They probably just saw the photo of you and Jo online."

Ugh.

Fabian raises his head. "I'll check your phone, but we need to talk to Jo and Matt. I can do that if you like," he says carefully.

"Why would I need you to …?"

Oh right. I'm not talking to her because like an idiot I told her we couldn't go on with whatever it was we were doing. But fuck that. This is way beyond that.

CHAPTER 46

Jo

The engines are providing a resonating hum behind the dim lights of the cabin and the spotlight over my head casts shadows on my keyboard. Everyone is bedded down, under covers, sky inky outside the window. *New York*. I'll be glad to get home. Des is dozing across the aisle from me and the warm zing of business class hasn't dissipated at all. An empty champagne glass sits on a fold-down table one seat up from him, and the last conversation I had on a plane like this with Janus about my non-boyfriend slips into my head. That trip still feels like the best four days of my life. A life I threw away. My eyes flutter closed as my head slips back against my seat. I talked to him about trust, but I didn't trust his judgment, I didn't trust *him*. I fell at the first hurdle.

"Ugh, I wasn't drooling, was I?"

My lips curve up as I straighten and open my eyes. "You're fine." I nod down the aisle. "The flight attendant over there has been watching you sleep, though."

Des grins, stretching out in his flatbed and putting his hands behind his head. "He's cute." His eyes skim over me. "You not sleeping, missy?" His eyes narrow. "I think the Samsung contract is going to be okay."

This makes me laugh. "Yeah, you totally charmed the pants off them." I consider his sleepy face. "You were great, Des. Are you happy to lead on this one?"

"Sounds good." He lets out a huge yawn and turns on his side, so he can view me across the aisle.

"My feet haven't touched the floor since Janus gave that interview," I say.

Des gestures around the plane. "They literally haven't. I talked to James about getting people on board for Samsung by the way. You're not worried about that are you?"

I can't meet his eyes, so I stare at the window over his shoulder. "Not really."

Des doesn't respond, and I risk a glance at him as he props himself up on one arm arranging the blanket over his legs, gaze coming back to skim over my hair and face. "Are you thinking about him?"

I feel my cheeks go pink. "The flight attendant?"

He laughs. "I didn't mean him, you chump."

"Is it standard to call your boss a chump?"

"It is in tech and stop changing the subject. Want to talk about it?"

I sigh. I can't really share the whole Janus debacle with Des.

"I just want to see him," I say, and when I turn back, his face is warm and concerned.

"Did something happen between you guys in Hong Kong?"

He's fishing, and I smile as I look down at my hands. "Yeah."

Des grins that wicked grin of his, and I roll my eyes. "You are not getting gossip from me."

He leans forward, right across the aisle, whispering, "Was he *amazing* in bed?"

My face is on fire as Des wags a finger at me. "I'll take that as a yes. I'll get you drunk and drag the details out of you. That was an extraordinary article to do. He's got to be pretty smitten, you lucky lady."

I don't know what to say to this. I don't want to get into the whole media thing with Des. Maybe I'll fill him in sometime, but it feels too raw right now, like I was an ass. I owe Janus a massive apology, but I don't want to send him a half thought through text, or something lightweight, like "Thanks," "I enjoyed the article," or "What the fuck are you doing, breaking your no comment promise?" I've put my foot in it enough already.

Perhaps he was trying to show me that we can handle the media interest. That he will always do, perhaps not what I want him to do, but what's right for me. Ah, God. I press my hand over the ache in my chest like I can hold it all back somehow.

Des lies down again and pulls the covers over his head, and I pull an interiors magazine from my seat pocket; I need some distraction before I explode. As I flick through the pages, my gaze is caught by a picture of a woman I recognize; it's the one Janus brought to the industry dinner. She looks immaculate: the long peach nails I can still see curled over Janus's arm, the perfectly tousled hair. It all tastes sour in my mouth, and I look down at my sweatpants with the hole in the knee that I wore to be comfy on the plane.

Even her apartment looks amazing. I peer at the kitchen behind her, the glass table she's sitting at. The table looks familiar, like I've seen it before; in fact, the whole layout looks … My stomach jolts, heat burning up though me— this is *Janus's* apartment?

No.

Hundreds of apartments in New York are like this.

I turn the page and, *oh God*, the sofa is the one his mom and dad were sitting on. My gaze tracks down the page; it's all about her interior design business. Did she design Janus's apartment? And then the words "recently separated from her husband" leap out at me, and a crawling sensation makes my head swim. I stare off at two flight attendants talking around the curtain farther up the plane.

I skim back up and start to read the article properly. The first paragraph references her "extremely close personal relationship with Janus Phillips, the tech entrepreneur."

Extremely close? He didn't think to mention any of this when we were in Hong Kong?

Did I misinterpret that whole *Wall Street Journal* interview?

Maybe it wasn't about me at all. Maybe he was heading off publicity about their security, supporting "a supplier." He said, "Every guy would love Jo Williams, she's the consummate professional." And that also reads in a "well, of course, everyone loves Jo" kind of way.

That I'm terrific and I'm great to work with, but it's not a romantic thing. Did the journalist twist it like they make up every damn thing they write?

I groan. Janus is gorgeous and he dates models, and now he's got a beautiful woman sitting in his living room who's he's apparently "extremely close" to. The way she leaned into him at that dinner, the intimate smile on his face; they *were* close.

Maybe he's sleeping with her? He said he helped her rein her husband back in. What sort of "help"? What did he say? "I've hooked up a few times, sure."

We never talked about other people when we were in Hong Kong. I assumed he wasn't sleeping with anyone, but how do I know that? *Oh my God, Jo.* I flap my top, sweating.

*

My eyes jerk open to a roar of plane engines and a bump, bump, bump along the tarmac. After we've grumbled at each other all the way through security, I bundle a sleepy Des into a taxi, standing and watching the taillights disappear. How can I go and see Janus now? What if she was *there*?

Another yellow cab pulls up in front of me. My limbs move like lead and nausea churns through my stomach, so when the taxi driver jumps out for my suitcase and asks for an address, I give him mine. I stare out of the window as New York flashes past, thinking of her fingerprints all over his apartment and on his arm at the dinner. How many other women have had their hands all over him? The door to my apartment sticks and a whole pile of mail scrunches up behind the door before I kick it closed and stumble down the hall, dumping my bag and collapsing onto the bed. Five minutes. I close my eyes. I'll sort it all out after that.

I wake to a darkening sky outside and wipe my hand across my mouth, blinking as a dream slips away from me. The persistent buzz of my phone is making the table next to me vibrate, and I pick it up, jerking in surprise when a picture of James, taken at the office when he was looking over his glasses at me, appears on the screen. I swipe and hold it to my ear.

"James?" My voice sounds like dusty gravel.

"Jo, thank God I've got you," he says, words pushed out on a long exhale.

"What's up?"

"It's Janus Industries. Janus got a text last night, a warning, and then they got into the system half an hour ago, and they've been taking parts of it down: They want Fabian." His voice doesn't sound like him at all.

"What do you mean they *want Fabian*?"

"That's their ransom request."

"*Ransom request*? Who the hell are *they*?"

"Where are you?" he says.

"At home. Where are you?"

"I'm at Janus's offices with Janus and a couple of people from his team. Fabian's on his way, more of Janus's people are on their way. That pattern detection algorithm you and Fabian wrote is good, Jo, really good, and we've finally pinned down who they are: a bunch of hackers that Fabian has come across in the past. I think he's done some stuff that's got them pissed, but he's being tight-lipped about it."

"I'll come straight there."

"You don't have to, but I wanted to bring you up to speed. We're working on everything we can. I've got a couple of guys from the team in here with me."

Forget that. I want to help. "I'll come. I fell asleep after we landed."

Why didn't I contact Janus before I went to Samsung and while I was there? After what we shared in Hong Kong. After he gave me a contract with his *company*. I *work* for him for Christ's sake. Where's the professionalism he said I had? He could lose everything he's worked for if we don't get this right.

"Does anyone know?" I say.

"What do you mean? We all know of course …"

"Press? Have we done anything to keep it within his company, put out anything to employees?"

"Okay. Okay. I hadn't thought about it actually. I'll chat to Janus straightaway."

"Get some PR people briefed, and I'll see you in about …"—I look at my watch; how fast could I get there?—"… less than an hour."

CHAPTER 47

Janus

"How did they get in?"

"Don't know yet," Fabian growls, his forearms resting on the stark white of the desk, skin tight under the tattoos, fidgeting with his ring. I lay a hand on his arm.

"It's not your fault," I say, but he shakes his head at me, lips thinning, face like a late-summer storm before the thunder breaks, dark clouds pressing in. I glance around at the heads leaning into screens, hands skating over keyboards. Two guys are discussing something in muted voices at a desk at the end of the row. No one is smiling.

"Working through all the possible entry points is taking too much time. After you guys shut down Hong Kong, they must have gone looking for other holes in the system like rats running through sewers. But where?" he says. "Fuck!" His hand slaps down hard on the surface right beside where I am standing over him.

My phone buzzes in my hand and it's a picture of Jo, fast asleep on a sofa in Hong Kong, hair all over the place, mouth slightly open in sleep and—I thought at the time—all mine. My stomach contracts painfully.

"Jo?" I hold the phone to my ear. Some of her calm logic right now would be amazing. I draw in a deep breath for what feels like the first time today and squint at the wall. "Are you still in Korea?"

A pause settles over me like she's wondering how I knew.

"I'm back. I'm on my way in. James rang me. I'm so sorry—"

"Don't worry about it," I cut her off. I'm not sure what she's apologizing for; I'm the one who lost their temper. My voice drops low. "I'm sorry, too. I … I'm glad you called me."

She's in Jo professional mode; I can hear it in her voice. Fuck. I bury my free hand into my pocket, hunching over.

"Will I be able to get into the building?" she says.

"How far away are you?"

"About five minutes."

"I'll let the doorman know."

"See you soon," she says.

"Jo?" I pause, remembering Fabian's words—that it wouldn't take one thing to win her; one apology, one sacrifice. "I'm looking forward to seeing you."

Her long sigh whispers over my ear like a secret. "Me too, Janus," she says, and the line goes dead.

I pull back and stare at my phone, head down, a slow smile spreading over my lips. That's good, right? If she'd met my comment with silence, all bets would have been off. I turn back to Fab, take in his still-hunched position and glance over his shoulder at the screen.

"Jo's on her way in," I say quietly.

But he doesn't hear me. He's muttering under his breath, something about making the fuckers pay. My hands hover over his shoulders briefly. I've seen him on edge like this before. Damn.

He loops some code through a test, and the blinking cursor after it's run is an insult: nothing. Fab curses and puts his head in his hands. I lean back looking over the top of the guys working at the bank of screens. "I'm heading down to meet Jo," I say loudly to no one in particular.

Matt raises his hand over his screen. James looks up and nods, and I nod back at him. He's been so methodical, so organized in sorting this problem. At least half of Jo's team is in here now checking for breaches and locking down whatever they can, while he and Fabian work on trying to find the hacker's entry point. I head toward the door as he heads over to Fabian, sliding into the chair next to him and talking calmly to him as he touches his arm: Fabian straightens a bit in his seat. Good.

Heading down to reception, I examine myself in the stainless-steel wall of the elevator: not too bad. When I exit, an impending storm has made the space dark and the marble floor is washed with gray. I nod at the security guard behind the desk holding the fort on a Sunday, and he straightens: We must be ruining his quiet day.

'All right, Mr. Phillips?' he says.

'Yeah, Jock, thanks. We're working on some stuff today so there'll be a few people in and out.'

He grins a gap-toothed smile at me, nodding. He used to be a boxer, and I've offered to pay for a new set of teeth, but he's happy with the ones he's lost, says it makes him more threatening—apparently a good thing in his line of work.

A yellow cab pulls up outside, and my heart starts beating double-time as I try to pull something approaching a normal smile onto my face. It feels like months, not weeks, since I've seen her. In seconds, Jo is barreling through the doors and her clothes are twisted on her body like she threw them on damp skin, and she's so beautiful that a drumbeat starts in my body that I can't tamp down.

I almost want to laugh at how out of control her hair is—curling and frothing over her shoulders like a wave—and it sends me right back to the morning after our first night together. My gaze drops to her face and her smile is bare and warm, and as I step forward, she flings her arms around me in a tight hug. Fuck it all, before I can overthink it, I put my mouth on hers and my pulse soars; her small lips opening, all swollen and soft, tongue sneaking out to tangle with mine. *Oh, God.* I lift her up and spin her around, but my cock is way too keen on what we're doing, so I set her back down and pull back, breathless. Where do we stand? I have no idea, and I've probably taken it too far already.

"It's so good to see you," she says, eyes dropping away, and the pink I like so much creeps into her cheeks. "I'm sorry I was away."

My mouth is dry, and I wave my hand, words crowding behind the lump in my throat, not wanting to ruin any progress we might be making. "No problem, Jo. I'm glad you're here now."

I grab her hand, pushing us forward into this, whatever it is. "Come on, let's go see the guys."

*

I examine Jo surreptitiously in the elevator. Beneath the bounce I sense exhaustion. And I remember this so well: the elation and then the panic that set in when my business started to take off. Without warning I went from messing around with code to dealing with huge companies with huge issues.

As if aware of my scrutiny, she suddenly says again, "I'm so sorry this happened while I was away."

But she doesn't need to apologize; her team has been excellent. I shake my head at her and smile. "Korea, huh?"

"Oh my God, Janus, *Samsung* called. They saw your article."

My stomach flips at this detail. I'd convinced myself she hadn't read it. I tap my hand on my jeans; this is far too important a conversation for a short elevator ride.

"Thank you for being so complimentary about me, about my company," she says.

Is that all she thinks it was? I don't believe it.

"Janus, was that article meant to …?"

She won't meet my eyes as she tails off, but the door unexpectedly pings as we reach the main floor. Was it meant to what? I stare at her as the doors slide open, inwardly groaning. We have no time to sort this.

"Let's talk about it later," she says.

But I don't want to talk about it later. I rub the back of my neck as heat climbs up my body. I laid myself out in public, and she didn't respond. Now it sounds like she's taking it as nothing personal. That's any guy's worst nightmare. But as I step out of the elevator all I can hear are raised voices echoing across the space, and Jo's wide eyes find mine as we both swing toward the noise and start hurrying down between the desks to where James is bent forward over Fabian's screen.

"I think Fab's losing the plot," I mutter.

"What? Why?" I can hear the shock in her voice.

"No, no, *no no no*." Fabian's voice rises above the general murmur as James straightens, running his hands through his hair.

"He's blaming himself." I shake my head. "He does this, Jo. He's responding emotionally, and I don't know how to sort him out. I think he's hindering at this point, not helping. James has been amazing by the way—calm, efficient." The words jerk out quietly as we reach the cluster of people.

Fabian is sitting head in his hands, James behind him, lips pressed together as he stares at the screen on the desk in front of them.

"What's happening?" I'm surprised at how level my voice sounds.

"They're in the backup system. We can't keep everything running without it." Matt's voice is flat, his mouth pinched and white around the edges.

Jo gasps a horrified "No!" from behind me as "Oh shit!" tumbles out of my mouth. What an inadequate response. Icy fingers crawl up my spine.

James shifts out of the way, flinching, as Fabian jumps from his chair and kicks it with force, sending it flying back across the floor. He tips his head back to the ceiling, shouting, "Fuuuuucccck!"

"Dammit, Janus, I didn't work fast enough on this. We should have locked you down faster," Jo mumbles.

Our customers. Fuck.

"Have we got anything we can bargain with?" James says, hand flapping, and for the first time his steely calm appears rattled. "Who are these people? You know them, Fab. Is there anything we might be able to use on them?"

Fabian grinds his teeth. "They're a bunch of Russian hackers: I got into their system about six months ago; it was embarrassing for them. I didn't make it public, but I could have, and they knew it. They hate shit like that."

He runs his hands through his hair. "I need to offer myself up."

"*What?* Absolutely not. You've no idea what they might do," I say, staring at him. He glares back, jaw ticking.

"So, this is some kind of hacker war?" Jo says, interrupting our staring match.

Fabian sighs. "They're aggressive as shit; scary fuckers, too. The Russians have been into every system in the West, and at the time I thought it'd be fun to give them a taste of their own medicine."

"My God," Jo breathes, looking at him incredulously.

He's a lunatic all right.

My mind is working overtime. We need *them* running scared. Perhaps we could find some leverage if Fab could get in there again. I put my hand on Fab's shoulder.

"How did you get into their system last time? Could you do it again?"

He sinks into the office chair in silence for a couple of beats. "Well, maybe, but …"

Suddenly his face clears.

"Oh fuck, *of course!*" His hand comes down on the desk with a crack. "My God, I am an *idiot*." His hands start flying over the keyboard.

"What? Why?" I say.

"Best form of defense is attack," he says.

"They haven't locked you out? Reinstalled a backup?" Matt says.

"Yeah, undoubtedly they have." A careless smile is lighting up his face, and I almost laugh at his 180-degree turnarounds. "But I didn't just hack in once, so there's a chance they've installed an already compromised version of their software, and I always keep masses of information, including passwords. I've been working on some password AI, so maybe it's time to test it out. Let's see how clever you are, you bastards," he says, pulling up windows on his laptop as if his life depends on it.

"Jo," he mutters, nodding his head at the monitor next to him. "Get on that computer, I'm going to need a hand."

Fab works with no one. He trusts me, but he must think she's exceptional if he's happy for her to help him.

"We have to be stealthy," he says, turning his head to stare at her and narrowing his eyes.

"Okay," she says, and her curly head bends into his man-bun, conferring.

James turns to me and Matt. "Let's hope this works. I'm going to get on with the guys and shore up other parts of the system. Asia's more or less bulletproof now, by the way. We've used the work you and Jo did with the guys in Hong Kong and spread it around the network as fast as we can out there."

I nod at this. "I think Matt and I need to talk to some customers."

CHAPTER 48

Jo

The panic that I've messed up Janus's systems is slowly receding, leaving behind a queasy feeling that I've messed up something else. He's standing behind Matt, watching him on his phone; arms folded over a T-shirt that hugs his toned torso, biceps on full display. Goddammit. When I saw him standing in reception, all the tousled hair and the six o'clock shadow turned my heart over; he looked so worried and relieved all at once. Then he gave me a wobbly grin. Oh, God. I touch my lips, remembering his warm mouth on mine. How sweet that kiss was …

There's a growl from my right. "You concentrating?"

I blink over at Fabian, and he looks pointedly at Janus and then back at me.

"Stop ogling him and concentrate," he says.

I give him a weak smile in apology, and he mock-frowns as I drag my eyes back to my screen.

"You need to tell him how you feel," he says in a quiet rumble, and my eyes snap back to find he's stopped typing and is looking at me intently. His fake frown turns into a real one.

"He's been a mess these last two weeks, Jo. Don't throw him away."

Throw him away? "I'm not, really … I … What about Aubrey?"

He's still frowning. "What about her?"

"There was an article about her leaving her husband; she was in Janus's apartment. She came to a tech event with him. I thought—"

"I don't know about all that," he interrupts, tilting his head, "but I can tell you the only woman he's interested in is you. He doesn't do this often, Jo. He's pretty demanding in his life, of himself; he has to think something is worth it to go all in. I've only seen him like this about one other thing: his company."

His eyes roam my face for several pregnant seconds as his comments sink into my skin. Is that true?

Then he nods, growling, "Now quit staring at him and stop distracting me. Let's work this thing out."

CHAPTER 49

Janus

A loud shout echoes over the floor and my head jerks up to find Fabian hunched over the back of Jo's chair, watching her screen. A huge smile is splitting his face, and they're almost touching. Jo's sleepy face in his T-shirt blurs before my eyes and I clench my fists, muscles tightening. My feet carry me to where he's standing before I've even thought to move.

"Genius, woman," he says and high-fives her, before hurriedly sitting down. "Okay, we haven't got long before they realize. Let's put that code in there."

"You in?" I say, willing my body to relax. He's my best friend, and I'm being an asshole; they're sorting my system out for fuck's sake.

He nods, and I know better than to distract them further, standing behind their chairs as they work on the code. I'm being possessive, but I can't tamp it down. Jo's got some map of their servers around the world on the screen. My eyes flick to the software she's using to do it. How is she doing this so fast?

After about twenty minutes, she puts her hands in the air, waving them around.

"Oh yeah!" she says.

"Run it!" Fabian says, swinging toward her, and the gleam of excitement in his eyes is contagious.

"As soon as it starts, they'll know we're in there," Jo says, eyes fixed on him.

His eyes swing to me, then James, as he stands, looking over the screens. "James, how well protected are we elsewhere? Can they access other parts of the system?"

He shakes his head at him. "We've isolated all the bits we can," he says.

Fabian comes to stand with me behind Jo, and the code starts to run and spread through their network, infecting their servers one by one. This is fucking complicated; they're all over the world—*how* did they do this so fast? After about five minutes, my phone vibrates, and *blocked number* appears on the screen. Turning it around, I show it to Fabian, who nods at me. So I press the handset symbol, put it on speaker, and lay it down carefully on the desk between them.

A heavily accented voice growls through the line: "You need to stop what you are doing."

Out of the corner of my eye, I see Jo start some call-tracing software on her laptop.

"So do you." Fabian's face is a storm waiting to erupt, jaw tight. His voice vibrates, the earlier elation evaporated.

Some voices mutter in the background and then the voice says, "We will get you eventually, Fabian Adramovich. We will not forget." And the line goes dead.

Jo shakes her head. "I recorded it, but nothing else."

We all stare at each other. I run my hands through my hair. "Jesus. What now?" I say.

"Keep running the code, Jo," Fabian says, not taking his eyes off the monitor for a moment.

Minutes tick by as we watch code stream up the screen.

"Oh, here we go," James says, and we race around to his desk as his fingers fly over the keyboard. "The backup system is back."

"We'll need to run some checks—see how they got in, what they've been doing." Fabian views me apologetically. "I don't underestimate how hard that will be, Janus. The system is big, and it'll be like trying to find a needle in a haystack; they'll have covered their tracks."

"Whatever we need to do," I say.

"I'll work on it full-time," he says, voice dropping on a wince, eyebrows gathering like birds on a telephone line.

"We'll need to restore from another backup," Jo chips in, and as we all digest this I let my eyes wander all over her face because I think I can look at her like this now.

"Yeah," Fabian says.

One of the guys at the other desk groans. "Are you suggesting we throw all the work we've done away?"

Fabian and I are both nodding, as Jo says, "Should I stop this running?"

Fabian swings back toward James, who's still watching the screen, occasionally barking instructions to people to change the security or lock down various parts of the network.

"Dial it back gradually, Jo," Fabian says. "I've put loads of code in their system. But they'll probably restore a backup, too; maybe be more thorough about closing the holes in their system this time."

"How did you get in?" One of the guys pipes up.

"Modeling likely password combinations," Jo says.

Fabian sits heavily back down in the chair he's been in all day, waves an arm. "I had thousands of passwords from their system, hacking is an arms race." He runs his hands around the back of his neck. "I'm so fucking sorry, Janus."

I laugh and pat his back. "You've got to stop stressing about this. Problems happen all the time in companies, Fab. This is another one of those."

"Ha, ha, ha. Just an everyday problem? Really, man? One that you could have done without though, right? One you didn't create or ask for."

I shake my head at him and lean forward. "Stop it right now," I say, and I find myself right in his face, my limbs like noodles. I suck in a deep breath that gets stuck in my lungs.

He meets my eyes, and something passes between us, some old

understanding, some echo of me rescuing him, him saving me; and he subsides, sinking down in his chair, nodding.

"We've probably got to do at least a couple of hours just with the initial locking down," he mutters, turning back to the screen. "Don't close us out totally yet, Jo."

*

Jo yawns into her palm and scrubs her hand up her face into her hair for the third time in the last hour. I'm done watching how tired she is. I want to take her away from this mess, take her home with me, and sort out where we are. I pace over to where she and Fab are bent over a screen. My jealously from earlier has dissolved in the pleasure of watching them work together, seeing Fabian's lone wolf façade dissolve under Jo's warm smile.

I lean over her desk, placing my hand next to where she's clicking the mouse, remembering the conversation we had about my arms and hands, and my lips curve up as her gaze flickers toward my arm and her fingers falter on the keyboard. It makes something burn deep inside me, and the desire to bury my nose in her curls is nearly overwhelming.

"How are you doing?" I say, trying to swallow it all down.

She sighs and sits back, resting into me, and I freeze, eyes closing for a second. The red strands are soft against my chin, and I'm losing my head, watching in awe as she lifts her right hand from the mouse and places it on top of mine, threading her fingers through mine.

"I think my brain has shut down; I was running on adrenaline before. I'm worried I'm making a mess of this."

She nods toward her screen, and Fabian examines the pair of us, taking in where her hand is, his eyes meeting mine with a smirk.

"Take her home, Janus; we've got this," he says, nodding at James, who grins at the three of us over his monitor.

"Too right," James says. "The real men need to handle this now."

Jo stiffens under me, sitting up straighter and removing her hand from mine, and my chest tightens as I pinch the bridge of my nose and stare down at the fluff of her gray sweater.

"You—" she starts, pointing her finger over the screen toward James, and he's outright laughing now, waving his hand at her.

"You know I was joking, boss. Just go. We'll need fresh brains on this tomorrow. You guys go and get some rest, and you can take over come morning."

Before she can decide to stay or berate anyone else for making a sexist comment, I step back, pulling her to her feet. "Come."

She pulls her hair up into a messy bun on her head, securing it with a band. Her eyes search mine as she inclines her head before bending down to grab her bag from the floor. I give the guys a thumbs-up as we head to the elevator. I think I hear every clunk and grind of the gears taking us down to the basement. Jo stands on one side leaning against the wall, eyes closed.

My car is like an oasis of calm after the frenetic energy of the last few hours, and a long sigh slips out of me when I relax back into the leather seat. I catch Jo's blank expression as I back out of the space and turn right out of the entrance into the dark of a Manhattan night.

"Where are you taking me?" she says.

I risk a quick glance at her. A frown is hovering on her face.

"My place," I say, in a way that hopefully brooks no argument.

She stares out of the window of the car as we run through several sets of green lights.

"The apartment that Aubrey was photographed in?" she eventually says, and I peer over at her, narrowing my eyes. I can't quite place the tone in her voice.

"Yes. How did—"

"I saw the pictures in an interiors magazine on the plane."

I pull to a stop at some red traffic lights on an intersection and wonder what to say.

"*Why* did you mention that?"

She shrugs. Maybe she thinks something more is going on with Aubrey than there is? The idea is laughable, but my whole body goes tight.

"Those photographs were taken before I met you," I say.

"The article said she was separating from her husband."

I laugh at this—Aubrey and her bullshit marital drama. "Yeah sounds about right, she's always splitting up with him."

More silence.

"Has she lived with you?"

"*Lived* with me?" What is she talking about? "Well, she's stayed over once or twice." Then realizing how this sounds, I add, "Usually when her husband's chucked her out."

"*Of course,*" she says and my eyes swivel to her, pulse picking up at the slightly snipped tone. A tight laugh slips out as I swing my eyes back to the road. This is not the conversation I was expecting to have after she leaned into me in the office.

"What's up, Jo?"

She shakes her head.

"Jo, you can't seriously think—"

"I don't know what to think, Janus." She folds her arms over her chest, and my pulse takes off.

"Oh, no *way.*"

I pull the car into the side in a sudden swerve and brake to a stop, gazing out at the lights of the buildings. The car ticks quietly as I suck in air. I squint at the empty streets and run my hand over my jaw. Turning to face her, I find she's focused down on her hands. Does she think something is going on with *Aubrey*? She's *married* for God's sake, and she's manipulative and a terrible game player and … I would never go there.

"Jo, look at me."

But she doesn't turn, just keeps staring at where her fingers are playing with her worn coat cuff.

"Is *this* why you didn't get in touch with me? You thought something was going on with *Aubrey*?" My voice is rising now.

"I don't know what to think."

Some wildness starts to burn through me. *Fucking hell.* I'm scrabbling to hold on to whatever progress we've made in the last few hours like a drowning man. I am *not* losing her again over this. My chest caves in at the thought. The words bubble up in a rush falling over themselves to stumble out of my mouth.

"Jo, don't do this to us."

She focuses on me now with a small frown.

"She's with you at events, she's in your apartment, you are photographed all the time with beautiful women—"

"I've *never* been dishonest with you." The words come out in a low rush, and I wince at how sharp my voice sounds, but how can she be so uncertain about me, about us, when I feel so sure.

"Were you sleeping with other people while we ... in Hong Kong ..." She tails off.

What? "No! Of *course* not."

Does she think I'm even *capable* of lying to her? Everything inside rises up like a wave. I slam my hand on the wheel. "Damn it all to hell, Jo. I'm fucking *crazy* about you. Hong Kong meant everything to me. I've *told* you how it is; I thought you *trusted me.* I've never slept with Aubrey, and I've never wanted her or in fact any other woman—"

But before I can finish my sentence, she's climbing over me and grabbing my head, pressing her mouth to mine, and the rest of my words come mumbling out into her kiss.

"—the way I want you."

Her lips are soft and eager, tongue stealing out, and I groan as I lose it completely, burying my fingers into her silky hair, tightening into fists. I pull back, desperate to somehow get us back to where I thought we were earlier this evening.

"Please, Jo, I—"

"Shh," she says, pressing a warm finger over my lips.

"There's *nothing* going on with Aubrey," I mumble against it.

"Okay."

Her mouth is over mine again, and I can't shape my mind around any words. *Are we okay here?* But she's resting against me, and God help me my whole body goes wired. My hand sneaks beneath her thin T-shirt, and a loud groan vibrates up and out of my throat. She's not wearing a bra, and the knowledge she's been bare all day sends a shiver through me: Her secret nakedness is *mine.* She's soft and perfect under my hand, and her nipple hardens as I rub my thumb back and forth, so I bring my other hand around from right up the back of her top and cup both her breasts as she arches back. Her T-shirt is rucked up her torso, legs splayed over my lap, and I want nothing more than to trace the path of the freckles I can see on her stomach.

"Come back to my place," I whisper. "Let me drive you crazy all night."

She shifts forward to rest her forehead against mine, sucks in a shuddering breath. "I was going to come and see you the minute I got back. I read the *Wall Street Journal* article and thought it was such an amazing thing to do." She presses a shaky kiss to my lips. "But then I saw the interview with Aubrey on the plane coming back from Korea. She was in your apartment and I started to think I'd got it all wrong, that you'd had a thing with her for a long time and I'd been a distraction, but all along you'd wanted *her.* I thought perhaps both of you were playing games."

My mind blanks. Wait. *What?* She thought *what? A distraction?* I reach up to smooth her hair back from her face, trying to straighten in my seat and shaking my head at her; a knot forming in my stomach.

"No, Jo. No. I've never been that way with her. Print magazines have ridiculously long lead times, and that interview was done before I even met you. She's a friend, arguably a bit of a crazy one, but nothing more. I basically told that *Wall Street Journal* interviewer I was in love with you."

"You said, 'Every guy would love Jo Williams, but she's been the consummate professional with me.'"

"Yeah."

"I started to think you meant that in an 'every-guy-would-love-Jo' kind of way." Her voice drops to a whisper: "That the paper twisted what you said."

Oh, *God.* I lean back against my seat and close my eyes.

"I said, 'Every guy would *fall in love* with Jo Williams.' I was talking about falling in love with you." I open my eyes. "Aubrey's husband is an obsessive asshole, he's completely consumed her, her life. She plays games with him and she loves it. I think they both get off on it, I can't begin to understand their relationship." Her eyes are locked on mine, green irises flecked with brown. I blow out a long breath. "She's never held any interest for me. She really is a friend, Jo."

She nods at this, leaning in to lick my bottom lip, and my mouth chases hers when she tries to pull away. I slide my hand up into her hair, holding her still while my tongue wraps around hers, heat burning down my body. Eventually, she shifts on my knee, moving backwards.

"I'm sorry."

That wasn't what I was expecting her to say.

"What? Why?"

She opens her mouth, but the tension is seeping out of me now and the need to get my own apology out there rushes through me. "I'm sorry, too. Sorry for Aubrey. Sorry I was angry. You have no idea." I run a hand through my hair, and she stares at the top of my head with a dopey smile on her face. "The comment on that photograph *in The Gazette* didn't show you in a good light. It was sexist. You were totally right for wanting to keep this quiet."

Her eyes go wide, blinking back down to mine. "No I wasn't, Janus."

"What?"

She shifts on my lap and rubs her lips together.

"I hurt your feelings, and I'm not sure how soon I'll be able to forgive myself for that. You wanted to make us public, and I put my company and reputation before you. I'm the worst kind of person for being so self-absorbed that I—"

"I understand, Jo. Christ! You've worked hard all your life to get where you are." I run my palms up her thighs on either side of my hips. "I get it, I really do. I want you to be taken seriously."

"The *WSJ* interview was amazing. The things you said about me—"

"I didn't say anything you didn't deserve."

I may have got her some publicity, but she brings all her own talent to the work she does.

"We've got about ten hot prospects for business from one article. Samsung is *huge*."

"Glad to be of assistance," I say, laughing, lightness filling my chest with the idea that something I've done, in the hope of bringing her back to me, has had such a great outcome.

"Did you mean it?"

My hands tighten on her hips. I've as good as admitted it already tonight. I shouldn't have said it in public before I said it in private. I let my gaze wander over her clear eyes and the freckles forming an unending pattern over her nose and out across her cheeks. Does she feel the same? I suck in a deep breath.

"I meant it, Jo. I love you."

And her eyes soften, lips curling up like a slow-growing work of magic.

"You don't need to say it back," I say quickly. "Just don't push me away again, let me—"

But she interrupts in the quietest voice. "I love you, too."

"*What?*" My voice cracks, heat swarming up my neck. I rest my head against her forehead as I close my eyes. All this time and she's been so hesitant, so reluctant. *Jesus Christ.* Blood thunders in my ears. "You *love* me?"

My lips are inches from hers as her smile unwinds at the croak in my voice, and my answering grin splits my face. Her hands come up to cup my jaw, and she scratches through the scruff from the shave I didn't get a chance to have when I got the call from James. She leans forward lightly brushing her mouth across mine.

"*Yeah.*"

I draw back a bit so I can see her properly, lick my lips. "How, when—"

"I think I fell in love with you in the elevator the first time I met you; you were so cute and bashful and enjoying the game so much—"

She's describing it as a fond memory, whereas all I remember about that day was this gorgeous, unattainable woman who wrapped me around her little finger, and I couldn't read at all.

"*That* long ago?" I growl. "I've gone through all this worry and torture ..." I'm trying to act like I'm mad, but I know I'm failing when she grins at me.

"Oh my *God!*" I shout, tipping my head back to the velvet of the car ceiling, and she bursts out laughing.

I lean forward to kiss her. "I need to put my hands all over you *right now*." I skim my palm over her thigh, brushing between her legs, and she gives a little Jo hip wiggle. She does this when she's turned on and wants more, and it makes me feel like a king.

Winding her arms around my shoulders, she laughs as my knuckles rub over the seam of her jeans. Cool fingers invade my hair. She leans forward and nibbles my ear.

"I want to put my mouth all over you," she says.

Her hot breath against my neck sends shivers over my skin. I slide my hands to her bottom, pulling her down and grinding up into her, nibbling along her jaw. The reminder that she tortured me in Hong Kong, what she did and how she did it, causes the last vestiges of my restraint to fall away.

"I'm going to hold you to that."

I lift her up and over into her seat, putting the car into drive as she buckles up, and the tires squeal when I pull out into the empty street.

CHAPTER 50

Jo

We stumble into Janus's apartment hands grabbing, feet sliding on the shiny floor. He bumps into a side table and swears, steadying it with an outstretched hand as the other one slides under my T-shirt, tickling up my ribs. His thumb rubs slowly over my nipple, and shivers spread all the way down my spine and between my legs. His other hand laces through mine, trapping it against the wall by my shoulder. A low rumble gusts against my collarbone, and he mumbles something indistinct which sounds a lot like "mine." A sweet ache runs through me at the thought he might belong to me, too. I want to give him everything my body can do, every bit of pleasure. Is this what love is? This burning need to hand over as much as you possibly can to someone else? I've never been held like this, hand and hips pinned, and I push back as his mouth latches firmly on to my throat.

His head comes up, giving me a half smile as he keeps me stationary. "I want everyone to see this tomorrow." He bends his head and hovers, going back in to lick where he's sucked my skin so hard.

"I want to put marks all over you," he says.

But then he seems to change his mind, stepping back and letting go of my hand, folding his arms and looking me up and down. The move makes his pecs and biceps pop out, and all I want is his T-shirt off, so I can admire him properly.

As if reading my thoughts, he says, "Top off."

"So mark me," I say, peeling it over my head and leaning back against the wall.

He steps into me with his hands on the wall at either side of my head, gaze never wavering from my breasts, a pulse thrumming at the base of his throat as he stares at me like I'm his next meal.

I nod at his chest. "Yours, too."

The T-shirt I've been admiring all day is over his head in seconds. His skin is tight, muscles defined, and his half-naked torso is as shocking as the first time I saw it. I put my hands out, watching my fingers trail his smooth chest, stiff brown nipples, the curve where his biceps meet his shoulder. Is he mine now? I'm almost sure he's grinding his teeth.

Heat climbs in his cheeks, eyes closing for a beat, as his head comes forward, and he bumps my nipple with his nose before taking it into his mouth and hardening it under his tongue. When he moves to the other breast, I grab his hair to pull him up, leaning into him and rubbing myself against him. He groans bending to suck across my shoulder.

"I'm going to mark you all over, Jo."

This second statement comes out like a threat. I saw glimpses of this growly, demanding side of him in Hong Kong, when he wanted to give me every bit of pleasure he could as he ordered me around—as if I'd unleashed something inside. I want to give him permission.

"Just order me to do it," I whisper.

He pulls back, groaning, eyes meeting mine as he understands what I'm saying.

"I want you to enjoy it, too." His eyes flicker away, color high on his face.

"I do. I love it." And the admission slides out of me shakily as I press my face into his neck, slippery between my legs. I want to hand over all control to him.

"Is it a bad thing? I don't want to be a controlling asshole," he mumbles into my hair.

I stretch up to kiss his jaw, his cheek. "You have my permission to be a domineering asshole in bed with me." Running my hand down his arm, I capture his hand in mine. "Stop overthinking it, Janus. I love it."

"I want to pin you down," he growls out, and something about that idea has me reaching for the buttons of his jeans.

Before I can process what's happening, he slides two warm palms over my bottom and lifts me up, my legs dangling as he walks across the swirling rug and I try to get them around his waist, letting out a squeak as he dumps me on the couch. The pictures on the wall are illuminated by a few dim lights and Manhattan floats like a twinkling blanket outside the wide expanse of windows.

"Face the wall," he grunts, and I roll up onto my knees, facing into the soft cushions. There's a rustle as he shucks his clothes and I can't resist peering round, my breath coming out in a whoosh as I take in the toned abs, muscle-bound thighs, the outline of his erection in his boxers. He positions his legs between mine and presses in to kiss my lips, hand reaching around me to find my zipper and, for a too brief moment, the shape of him is hard against me. His mouth works my shoulder as he unfastens me.

"It's been too long since we did this," he murmurs. "I already have trouble lasting with you." He laughs through a half groan, and I lift each knee in turn, so he can peel the fabric down and off. His large palm and long fingers are on my ass and between my thighs, sliding through my wetness, teeth sinking into where my muscle meets the top of my arm and working his way across to the back of my neck, as my head bends forward. A small shift, and he straightens behind me, the faint rustle of boxers coming off, and I reach around with my hand, trying to get to touch his shaft before the rubber covers him up. When I grasp him, pre-come leaks over my hand and I dance my thumb all over him as he shifts closer.

"Jesus. Fuck, hold on." He gasps, resting his head on my back and looking down between us. Foil grazes my back as he tears the condom open with his teeth, and his length slips out of my hand as he moves to stroke the latex down.

Suddenly his weight comes right back into me as he leans forward, and I'm pinned to the cushions, breath leaving my body on a sharp exhale.

"Oh *yeah*, Jo." The hot words gusting over my ear send goose bumps all the way down my back. The soft hair of his stomach tickles as he places my palms on either side of us on the back of the couch, fingers winding through mine.

"So turned on right now," he mutters, and he pats my hands, telling me wordlessly to leave them where they are, before he eases back a little. Air rushes into my lungs as his hand snakes in at my waist, brushing over my mound, delving deeper. I widen my legs and his slide outward, opening me up, and I'm pushing back, desperate for the stretch I know is coming. His cock brushes over my folds, so I tilt my pelvis, and he dips to find my entrance as he guides the tip inside.

"Oh *fuck*. Fuck."

He powers me back against the sofa thrusting sharply as I lift my hips, hardly able to take the sudden invasion, lungs collapsing with the force of it. Pulling back, he does it again and the hard pressure of his hand on my mound pushing his forefingers into my clit makes me whimper. His other hand grips mine tightly on the back of the sofa, fingers digging in for purchase. Then he's pulling out and thumping back in, driving me forward every damn time, slamming into me over and over again, sweat and heat making his chest slide against my back.

"*Christ*."

His teeth sink sharp into my shoulder and I'm going to have marks later, and some dark part of me is awake and alive, thrilled at how he's let loose, and I cut free, arching back and letting my head thud back against his chest.

"Take it," he mumbles, fingers sliding messily over where I'm soaked and slippery and I'm gasping for air, unable to do anything except lean into where his hand is making everything tighten and pulse. In complete contrast to his thrusts, his touch is light and sloppy, and it tingles all the way down my legs as my toes curl against the back of his calves.

"You're so *fucking* tight. Fucking *mine*."

Caveman. Laughter bubbles up but I can hear the tremor in his words.

287

With anyone other than Janus, I'd think the guy was an asshole, but here I'm beyond myself, amazed at this rough sex, that I *like* it. The fast thudding of my heart almost too much for my small ribcage. I rub my head along his unshaven cheek, and his lips turn into my skin, letting out a long shuddering groan, as he brings our clasped hands up to my stomach, pressing me into him.

The pressure of his thighs on the inside of my legs shifts me further open, and I try to sink down into his hand and his cock, but I'm pinned in position, the muscles in his arms straining to keep me where he wants me. I'm so slick; my juices all over him and me. I lift my other arm, sliding it into his damp hair. The heel of his hand is pressing into my pubic bone, holding me still for him as he pounds into me. His finger exploring me gets more insistent and my orgasm hovers closer, but, God, riding this edge, I want it to go on and on.

"Dammit Jo, *get there*," he grits out.

I start to clamp down on his length, sensation rippling through my inner muscles.

"Fuck," he groans, "do that again." But I've got no control, no power here, and I rest my head back on his shoulder, nuzzling into his neck and tasting the wet of his sweat on my lips. He turns his head for a clumsy kiss. "You feel *fucking amazing*," he mutters.

He rubs me harder, and my mouth opens on a gasp against his skin as tightness rushes up and my limbs go rigid. His hips falter as I tip over the edge with a long shuddering wheeze.

"Oh my God, my God" comes fluttering out as Janus grunts loudly, and with a "fuck yeah," he starts to jerk inside me, collapsing us forward against the back of the couch.

CHAPTER 51

Janus

I wake slowly to find a tumble of red hair in my face, and for several seconds I'm back in Hong Kong. Then I remember the hack and Jo—and I groan out loud with the relief of it; it's too long since I shared a bed with this woman. Most of our mornings started this way and it was *bliss.* I breathe in the smell of her shampoo and bury my head farther in her hair to take in more of it. A part of me hopes she uses it forever. Fuck. I'm already wondering how soon I can tie her down to something more permanent, to *moving in.* I don't think I've ever done slow in my life, and I've been sure about Jo ever since I leaned over her in that meeting room and watched her draw detailed diagrams with colored pens, inhaling citrus and something indefinably Jo. My eyes drift over the covers flung all over the floor after round two and, *fuck,* the insanely hot sex on the sofa. The light is dim at the sides of the curtains, and the clock projecting the time on the ceiling says 5.30 a.m.: too early to get up yet. I close my eyes and curl into her, letting the feel of her small body seep into my skin.

My eyes blink open as someone feathers kisses down my chest and some bone-deep satisfaction settles over me.

"Will you wake me up every morning for the rest of our lives like this?" I ask, and her head jerks up, eyes wide and scared but, *fuck me*, the widest smile.

"Only if you keep this body as toned and gorgeous as it is now." She winks at me, before nibbling across my stomach and kissing the tip of my erection. The ache in my balls tells me without looking how hard I am but I want to watch, so I tilt my head up as she closes her mouth over me. The view of her doing this and the hot, wet heat makes the breath rush from my body, hips rising up off the bed.

"*Jo,*" I croak, head rolling back on my shoulders, trying to hold on. "Don't think I haven't noticed that you've dodged that question."

She stops, studying me, something working behind her eyes, and *then* she says, "The answer's yes."

I sit bolt upright and blink at her for a couple of beats. Hands shaking, I stretch forward to cup my hands around her chin.

"*What?*" Does she mean what I think she means? "Did you—are you—"

"I'm saying yes, in answer to your question." Her voice is an oasis of calm.

I grab hold of her arms, and she shrieks as I pull her upward, rolling her onto her back, chest to chest, settling my hips between her legs. Body rigid on top of hers, I stare down at her. Have I done the crappiest proposal in the history of proposals, or has she just said yes to the waking up for the rest of our lives? And isn't it kind of the same thing?

I stroke the hair out of her face. *The copper waves and the creamy skin.* Her lips quirk as she takes in whatever she can see in my face, probably pillow creases and crazy hair. But as I gaze at her the smile disappears and her eyes twitch, corners turning down. I need to do this right.

"Will you marry me, Jo?" I say, and her eyes widen, eyebrows shooting up to her hairline.

"*Janus.*" She gasps, hands coming up to grip my waist, mouth parting. "Janus, my *God …*"

That wasn't an immediate *yes,* was it? My gut drops through the bed. I narrow my eyes on her.

"You said yes to oral sex every morning for the rest of our lives."

"Yes, but I didn't agree who was giving it to whom." She's attempting to diffuse the intensity that's waiting there like a beast about to pounce.

I shake my head at her. She knows what she agreed, but I don't want to get into it right now. I've got a more important issue at stake here.

"You haven't answered my question," I say, trying to lighten things up by rolling my eyes. I'm incredibly hot and I shift my gaze to the window. Is the sun shining? Is the AC working?

Her hands come up and creep around my jaw, turning my face back to hers, fingers stroking in my stubble. She leans up and plants a tiny kiss at the corner of my mouth, feathering kisses across my lips slowly. It carries on for so long I'm suddenly not sure whether she's trying to distract me, and my muscles start to knot up one by one. I need to get off her. I can't lie here and—but then a soft "yes" is whispered against my skin, another one against the curve of my upper lip. My blood feels like it's thundering through my body like a freight train, and I pull back sharply, looking into her eyes.

"*Seriously*?" I say. Are we doing this?

"Did you ask it seriously?"

"Of course." My face is screwed up, I can tell by the amused cast of her mouth.

"Then the answer's *yes*."

I groan loudly and bury my head in her neck. My heart tumbles like an overexcited puppy, feet sliding on a polished floor.

"Oh my *God*, Jo." I think she's smiling at how thick my voice sounds. How is this possible …? *Jesus*. I roll off her and onto my back and the cool cotton bedsheet, and stare at the ceiling. I have no idea what's happening to my body, but if I wasn't supported by the mattress I'd float off.

My heads snaps sideways to look at her. "Seriously? You've said *yes*?"

She's full-on laughing at me now, and I lean in and kiss her lips, but *by God*, I have not done this up right, so I jump up—totally naked—rooting around for clothes, before remembering they're probably next to the sofa.

"What are you *doing*?" She's staring at me between the giggles, eyes tracking all over me. "Where are you going?"

"We need to buy a ring," I say, coming to a standstill, hands on hips. "I proposed to you without one. *Oh my God.*" I run my hands through my hair.

She shakes her head and sneaks her hand out to stroke my now flagging cock.

"We're doing something else first," she says.

Heat burns down my body to pool in my hardening length. "What's that?"

"The penalty you've imposed on me for the rest of my life."

"*Penalty?*"

"Oral sex," she says.

And I shake my head. "You don't have to do that. I didn't really mean—"

But she's shaking her head again. "I want to; I was enjoying myself. Come here."

I shift forward, and she pulls me kneeling onto the bed as her fingers feather over me a few times. When she bends down to take me into her mouth, I want to punch a hole in something.

"That feels incredible," I whisper.

She hums around my cock, and I thread my hands into the tumbling red curls.

"Jo, Jo. Jesus. Hang on."

But she takes me fully into her mouth and I stare up at the ceiling, looking for spiders, cracks, anything to calm my body down.

"That proposal was terrible, Jo. I wanted to make it amazing." I can hear how soft and strained my voice is.

She blinks up at me and pulls back, straightening up, moving closer, pressing right into my chest as she kisses me on the mouth. I pull her in tight, sliding my hand over her naked backside.

"It was amazing, Janus, especially the part when you leaped from the bed with no clothes on. It was a good reminder of what I'm signing up to."

But I'm not going to be distracted by her flippant tone. Maybe she isn't taking this seriously?

"No, you know, I want to take you somewhere special, go down on one knee, the whole romantic bit."

She laughs at this. "I'm sure most guys would think it was romantic that their cock was in my mouth."

And I'm abruptly doused in cold water. "Oh *fuck*."

"I tell you what, later on when I'm not giving you oral sex, I'll check if you still want to get married."

And oh! She's in real trouble now. I grab her waist, flip her over and collapse on top of her pinning her to the sheet with my weight and digging my fingers into her side. A loud shriek almost deafens me.

"Take that outrageous statement back."

"*Janus.*" She gasps, my cock hardening as she squirms under me. This is the best kind of foreplay.

"Oh no you don't, take it back. I was serious, Jo. I want to marry you."

"This is definitely the weirdest marriage proposal anyone has ever received," she wheezes.

And now, messing around aside, I don't feel good about this. I pull back on my knees before flopping onto the bed beside her, arm over my eyes, all thoughts of sex disappearing into the ether.

She turns her head toward me, then shifts, curling into me.

"What is it? What did I say?"

"It was a shit way to propose."

"*Don't*, Janus. I don't want to ruin this moment." She grabs my hand and squeezes it. "This was your proposal, and I don't want—"

"I don't want to be remembering a messed-up proposal for the rest of my life."

She strokes her hand down my chest and abs to my hardening length.

"It wasn't messed up, I loved it," she whispers, and I groan. "It was *you*, Janus. Crazy, unexpected, impetuous: That's why I loved it."

This girl. She likes the things about me that drive everyone else crazy. Her hand wraps around me, fingers playing, and with her thumb on the tip of my cock I can hardly concentrate on what she's saying. I move to stop her, but she grips me tighter, shifting over me.

"I want to do this," she says, jaw set. "I want to remember *this*."

And then her mouth is on me again, and I let her take over as my mind goes blank.

CHAPTER 52

Jo

I'm grinding beans and calling Fabian when Janus pads out of the bedroom, jeans slung low on his hips, hair a wild mess, naked chest. How could anyone resist this man? He's the sexiest thing alive. The map of muscle is …

"Hey, Jo," Fabian says, and I set the phone down on the countertop, pressing the button to put him on speaker. "You guys sort things out?"

I'm laughing because this is his first question, the thing he is most concerned about, but Janus leans over and says, "Be careful what you say here. You're talking to the future Mrs. Phillips."

Fabian emits a loud shout from the other end of the line, followed by some muffled noises, a thump, a far-flung *goddammit*, and a lot of cracking and rustling. Janus makes a funny face at me. Then Fabian's voice slides closer.

"I dropped my phone. *Fuck*." His voice goes distant again before he comes booming back, "Christ almighty, you guys—*for real?*"

We're both grinning at each other like idiots, and Janus leans in to kiss me, smooching my neck as he does.

"Yeah," he says softly.

"I'm the luckiest woman alive." My smile is so big.

"Uh-huh," Fabian says, "I'm sorry to say, Jo, that honor is for the woman who marries me."

"Fabian, if only I'd known you'd consider it, I'd have ditched this guy as soon as …" I tail off as Janus growls at me, but Fabian's loud hoot gusts over the line.

"I had to tie her down, Fab," Janus says into the speaker.

"Too right," says Fabian. "Did he have a ring and everything, Jo? Do it up right?"

Janus groans at this. "No."

"We're not talking about what I was doing while he proposed either," I say, my smile getting impossibly wider.

And Janus's eyes pop wide, and he makes an outraged face at me before screwing his face into a scowl. Fabian's laugh echoes around the kitchen.

"I can guess," he crows.

"Don't," Janus says loudly. "Anyhow, more importantly, how's it going?"

Fabian laughs again. "I'm glad you think the company is more important than getting married."

"I'm changing the subject here; I don't want her overthinking her answer. She's only marrying me for my money anyway," he says, and I shake my head at him and point at his cock. He gives me a knowing grin, reaching out and pressing my nose with this thumb and I snap my teeth trying to bite it, but he just laughs.

"I don't want to hear any more," Fabian says. "We're doing well actually. They seem to have backed off for now. I've come out of their systems, and hopefully we have enough information now for a boatload of ways in. Whether we can do that or not remains to be seen. The whole of Jo's team is in here, plus twenty of your tech guys, Janus, and they're working on reconfiguring your system and protecting it. We're not far off finished actually."

"*Wow.*"

"Yeah. James sorted it all out. He made the call that we needed more people on it, so he brought all your team in, Jo, and he got the Janus Industries CTO involved from your end, Janus. I mean there's a lot of long-term work to do, but short term we're good."

"Nice," Janus says. "Can I poach James to work for me?"

He's looking at me as he says this, and now I make an outraged face at him.

"In fact, Fab, how about *you* work for me?" he adds.

Fabian snorts. "You couldn't hack it, man. I'm a disrupter, not a team player."

Janus nods and smiles ruefully, staring unseeing at the bench as he leans over the phone. Why do I get the impression that this is a regular conversation?

"Anytime you want to change your mind, I'd have you in my business like a shot."

"Maybe in mine?" I say, smiling at Janus sweetly, and he frowns at me.

"Don't listen to her, Fab, there is no way you're allowed to help her if you won't work for me."

Fabian chuckles on the other end of the line. "It's nice to be wanted, you guys. I'll let you know if I ever need a job. Come in when you're ready." And the phone goes dead.

Janus raises his eyebrows at me. "He always hangs up like that."

I move into him, wanting to curl around him, and he grins down at me as I slide my hands around his waist, bending down to nuzzle my neck.

"You always smell amazing," he says. "Have you showered?"

"Yes, it's your shower gel."

He laughs. "You haven't changed your mind yet, have you?" he says.

I beam up at him, looking at the small frown marring his perfect features, his thick lashes, and brown eyes. "I'm never going to change my mind."

EPILOGUE:
TWO MONTHS LATER

I take in the sheeting rain and my blue velvet frock and wonder if it will survive this downpour. I don't want my first official pictures with Janus spoiled by the fact I resemble a drowned rat, or I unexpectedly discover my dress is see-through when wet. The driver of the limousine pulls up outside Janus's apartment block, and he dashes through the thunderstorm, umbrella tilting in the gusts of wind. I have seconds to register how outstanding he looks in a tux before he dives into the car, water sparkling all over him, but his smile disappears as he gets his first glimpse of what I'm wearing.

"Holy cow, Jo," he says, scanning the velvet material, "you look amazing." His hand lands on the split in the dress that goes up to the top of my thigh, and, as he leans over to kiss me, I instinctively pull back.

"Lipstick," I say, but he growls at me and keeps on coming, parting my lips with his tongue. My whole body heats up, and I've still not got used to this, how obsessed I am, how I want him all the time.

"I like this," he says, warm palm exploring my leg, and I put my hand over his, grinning. "But you still live in your apartment," he grumbles, pulling back a bit. I lean away from him, wiping my coral lipstick off his mouth with my thumb. He bites it.

"How come I didn't get to see you putting this on," he says, one hand still exploring under my dress, the other coming up to run a teasing finger around the scooped neck, "… See what underwear you're wearing," he mumbles into my throat, and I arch backward giving him better access, and he groans palming my breast.

"If you'd seen what's underneath, chances are we'd never have made it out," I say breathlessly as he tugs the fabric forward and looks down. I slap his hand away, but not before he's got a glimpse.

"Don't think I've ever seen you in blue lace underwear before." His grin is wicked.

I roll my eyes at him, but he's looking steadily at me. "Moving *in?*" he says patiently, sinking back into his seat and adjusting his trousers.

"We agreed after our official coming-out event," I say, smiling at his expression.

"It's ridiculous," he grumbles, looking out of the window at the shops and people speeding past, blurred by the rain.

This makes me laugh. He asks me about moving in every time he sees me.

"Mr. Impatient."

"We've got both PRs there, for the engagement announcement?" he says, and I nod at him, absorbing for once that his hair is only slightly messed up and his jaw is as smooth as silk. I can't decide whether I like this groomed look or the freshly fucked bed hair, scruff, and pillow creases I normally see instead. How lucky am I? I get to mess up him up. I lean in to kiss his shaven chin.

"I'll move in as soon as possible after tonight."

"Tomorrow?" he says hopefully. "We've got cats to introduce."

I laugh. "I've not given notice on my apartment yet."

This gets me a growl. Truth is, I was sure about Janus, about how I felt; but building something that would last? That felt different. I wanted to give it time. His impatience, my reticence; it all seemed like such a steep cliff. But here we are two months later. I wrap my arms around my body, mind stumbling over it all like water foaming down a cliff. We've got deeper and stronger, seen each other at our worst. We argue a lot, Janus is impatient, I'm a total buffoon; but we're both working around each other, relaxing into ourselves.

His gaze softens. "Nervous?" he says.

"Terrified."

He takes my face in his hands. "Jo, this is not falling apart, okay?"

"It's so public, Janus; it terrifies me."

He reaches down, pulling my arms from around my body and squeezing my hand. "Success, Jo. Success does that. You're getting more attention now, aren't you?"

It's true. Carly is now my full-time PR lady. Photos of Janus and me have surfaced out buying coffee and meals and going to meetings, and we had to confirm our relationship a while ago. I know we're lucky: We've avoided too much intrusion and I guess the interest in a pair of businesspeople is not like being a celebrity; we have some level of control.

"Yeah," I say, and I have to admit most of it has been good attention. I've had opportunities in the press that wouldn't have come my way if we hadn't been a couple. Janus beams at me and leans in for another kiss.

"Told you it'd all be good," he says, and I poke his side.

"Ouch! What was that for?" he says.

"Being smug."

"I love you, Jo," he murmurs, settling back into his seat and pulling me into his side, surveying the blur of traffic and rain whipping past.

"I love you, too," I say quietly, watching the lights from the buildings track across his face.

"I'd give it up in a heartbeat if anything I did caused a problem for you." And he's still looking out of the window when he says this, so I can't read him.

"Don't be daft. You wouldn't give up your company."

He turns around to study me. "I would." His face is steady, unsmiling as his gaze rests on my hair, my lips. "Well, hopefully, I'd sell it," he says, and I laugh. "But seriously, I'd do anything to make this work. You are the one: Whatever the problem is, I won't let anything get in the way."

Warmth floods through me, and I lean into his side and squeeze his hand. Despite all my initial resistance and worries, am I less worried now? It settles over me he's that important to me, too: We're together now.

"I feel the same," I say, resting my head on his shoulder, and he kisses the pile of red curls on my head.

"We're here, sir, ma'am." The driver's intercom buzzes as he pulls up to the curb.

I grip Janus's hand tightly, sitting up and gathering my wrap. I should have brought a waterproof. The announcement of our engagement is already out, a lot of press will be waiting.

Janus straightens his shirt. "Ready?" he says, taking my hand, and I nod at him and grin, leaning forward to give him a smooch. "I can't wait to get home and take that underwear off you," he mumbles into the kiss, and so it is I step out into the cameras with a broad smile on my face.

THE END.

THANKS AND
A SNEAK PEEK

Dear reader

My sincere thanks for reading *The Refusal*, the first book in my *Techboys* Series. I hope you enjoyed reading it as much as I did writing it!

By way of a small thank you, here's a sneak peek at the second book in the series, *The Outcast*.

Enjoy!
Eve M Riley

PROLOGUE

There's an unconscious man in front of me on the hospital stretcher, and a familiar sickness washing through my stomach. His long messy hair is tied up in a knot on his head, and sinewy muscles rope all over his body, long winding tattoos running down his arms and up his neck. Young. Rail-thin. *What's wrong with you?* The notes on my clipboard swim in front of my eyes: airway, breathing, circulation. No obvious signs of trauma. The form says: "found lying on a bench next to Prospect Park."

Breathe, Kate, breathe. You're all he's got. Above the oxygen mask strapped to his face, long dark lashes sweep down his cheeks. Will everything I've worked for go down the tubes if I don't lose this jitteriness that appears every time the doors to the emergency department swing open?

The new nurse, whose name I've forgotten, starts attaching him to monitoring. I pull out my stethoscope and listen to his lungs and the thump-thump of his heart. I check his pulse, lift his mask to check his airway and smell his breath for alcohol, and finally add to his notes. The nurse finishes placing the sensors on his chest, and the monitors spring to life. No arrhythmia. His blood pressure is low, but not unreasonably so. He's either incredibly fit or … I study the wiry muscles again. *Okay.*

"Sir, can you hear me? Sir?" I say, bending down and touching his hand. I'm sure the paramedic tried this. His tattoos are a blend of script, scenes, and birds that swirl into elaborate patterns.

The nurse glances at me as she moves around the bed.

"What blood tests do you want?" she asks, chin jutting as she checks the canula in his right arm.

Think, Kate. Think.

"Do a full set," I say, stalling for time, and she frowns.

"I guess he could be hypoglycemic?" She raises her eyebrows.

Of course. *Sugar. Diabetes.* I grab the glucose meter and test strips. "Yes. Did the EMT find anything in his pockets that might indicate anything about him? Diabetes or allergies? His name? We might be able to contact family."

"I think they searched him."

"No other belongings? Nothing at the scene?"

She shakes her head. "We should check him for drugs."

Jesus. Young guy … unconscious … of course! Where's my head? "Good idea," I say. "Let's take a urine sample."

I've never done this on an unconscious patient before, but she nods as if she understands, and I stare down at his translucent skin. *I'm sorry you got an intern.*

"How did he get here?" I say. What a stupid question. I wonder how long he's been unconscious.

She shrugs. "Someone called an ambulance. They couldn't find anything wrong with him, put an IV in his arm, put him on oxygen because they were concerned about his breathing, and monitored his vital signs. They wondered if he'd been hit by a car, but there's no bruising."

I look up as John Harvey sticks his head around the curtain.

"All right in here?" he says.

I purse my lips at him, and he comes through to stand beside me. As an attending physician, he's bailed me out on more than one occasion, so I give him a quick rundown of where we are and what I've done. He nods, bending over the patient.

"Pupils? Reflexes? Breathing pattern?" He leans forward and lifts the guy's eyelids. "Hmmm. Pinprick pupils," he says.

And my stomach drops. I didn't check those, and we've covered them time and again. I bite my lip. *That's so basic, Kate!* Every day I'm skipping over stuff like this. I nod at him slowly.

But John's gaze just flicks over the monitor and then scans his body. "Normal stats, no obvious trauma … hmmm."

He gives a long sigh, like this night has been too long already. "Well, you seem to have followed protocol." And he's being generous here, so I open my mouth to protest, but he carries on, "unless this is something unusual or he has an unknown preexisting condition, then I'd guess narcotics of some kind." He peers over my shoulder at the form. "Prospect Park? Drugs then. Sometimes people bring a bug or tropical disease back from abroad because New York is a travel hub, but given where he was found … He's stable, is he?"

His eyes flicker over the monitors again.

"So far," I say.

He nods. "Then follow the drugs angle, give him some naloxone, and let's see where that gets us."

I need to do a whole ton of research on drugs along with brushing up on basic protocols.

*

I open my eyes to a low beeping noise and blink up at round stains on square ceiling tiles. *Not my apartment.* The bedcovers are bathed in a dim green light. Unmistakably a hospital. *Fuck.* How did I get here? I was on the street next to the park. As I sit up, the room tips alarmingly, and I grab at the side rail, swallowing down the nausea. Something tugs on my chest, and I look down at pads and wires before ripping them off one by one as an angry beeping starts from the bank of machines by the bed. Examining the catheter going into my arm, I apply pressure and pull it out: I'm very comfortable with how to get things out of my veins.

Hurried footsteps echo down the corridor, and a nurse bursts through the door.

"Sir, what are you doing? You need to …"

A blonde woman in navy scrubs follows the nurse into the room, and my eyes land on rose-colored lips then drift across her porcelain skin up to a pair of sharp blue eyes: unfriendly eyes that are fixed on me. I stare back at her.

"Sir …" she starts.

I shake my head at her, and the room swims again. *Fuck.* I put my head in my hands, still trying to keep the pressure on my elbow where I've ripped the IV drip out.

"I need to get out of here." My voice is full of phlegm, and I cough in an attempt to clear my throat. "I can't stay here. No insurance."

She walks over to me, and small soft hands lock around my wrists as she moves them downward and looks into my eyes. A buzz runs right up my arm.

"Are you dizzy?"

She takes something out of her pocket before shining a light in my eyes, and I blink, turning my head away from the glare.

"Turn around."

Something about the way she says it, or perhaps because she's wearing blue scrubs, makes me shift around on the bed. The movement causes another wave of nausea, and I gag. A plastic tray is thrust into my hands as the doctor shifts my hospital gown and the cold of her stethoscope presses on my bare back.

"I can't stop you from leaving, but I wouldn't recommend it," she murmurs. "You're really in no state to go anywhere. What's your name?"

"Fabian," I say, "Fabian Adramovich." I understand they need to know, but then the beautiful doctor will look me up, discover my history, and become even more disapproving. I have to leave. "Where are my clothes?"

The nurse heads out of the room, but the lovely doctor ignores this. "Did you take something? Do you have a health condition?"

"Why do you want to know?" Medical professionals always ask these questions. It's my body, my lifestyle. But all my response garners is an impatient sigh behind me.

"You were brought in here unconscious."

I peer at her over my shoulder and narrow my eyes. I've never liked the idea that my records are on some hospital database: The less information people hold about me the better. She shifts my gown back together and moves back as I turn around to face her.

"Do you need a diagnosis for your files?" The last word comes out with a derisive snort.

"I'm curious," she says quietly.

I shrug, and she folds her arms.

"If you're going to be a dick and leave this place when you're in this state"— she waves her arm at me—"then at least give us the satisfaction of knowing what happened. We've spent time on you, and you've had us all worried."

I laugh. Well, she doesn't give a damn about her bedside manner, but fuck I like it, I like assertive women. Tests, though—how much money might that involve? My chest tightens. I've had to fight so many legal battles recently that my meager funds are all but wiped out, and I am not going to Janus for another bailout.

I sigh. "I took something," I mumble, not meeting her eyes.

"What did you take?"

I just shrug, and she tips her head back to look at the ceiling.

"Seriously?"

"It's none of your business," I say, starting to cough. As I lean forward, I retch into the plastic tray again.

"A recreational drug?"

"There are other kinds?" I say, trying to smile.

And her face softens as she laughs. "And you want to leave?" she murmurs, taking the tray and handing me another one as her eyes scan my face.

How am I going to survive a journey home? Fuck, I can't think like that. I nod.

She presses her lips together. "Let me find some medications to take with you and give you something for the nausea before you go. Do you think you could keep some tablets down?"

I look up at her and nod. I was expecting a lecture and form filling. Not this. She gives me one last glance before disappearing. Queasiness rolls down my throat, so I lie down again and close my eyes: I need to gather myself for heading out. In minutes she's back, clutching packets of drugs in her hands.

"Okay," she says. "This is for the nausea." She places everything on the locker by the bed and passes me a tablet and a glass of water. My hand shakes as I lift it to my mouth. This better get me home before I pass out again.

She purses her lips, before handing me a small packet. "Here's some more anti-sickness meds to take home. I'm not sure what the base of what you've taken might be. We gave you naloxone which would have helped if what you took was opioid based. Cocaine is more difficult, although, if it was a serious overdose, you'd probably be dead by now."

My eyes roam her creamy skin and blonde lashes, and a reluctant grin breaks free. "How come you know so much about illegal drugs?"

She straightens and squares her shoulders. "We have to learn about all the drugs that end up in the human body; they're pretty well known to the medical profession." She shrugs, then grins, looking a bit bashful and leans in like she's sharing state secrets. "We actually have a database called TOXBASE that tells you all about drug interactions and the effects on the body. There are chemists that make their own stuff, but that's very rare … and dangerous. You're not a chemist, are you?" I shake my head at her. "Many things are poisons in quantity. You'd have to be good to make your own."

Well, fuck me. I glance at her name badge: Dr. Thurman. A doctor who happily swears in front of a patient. And could I be any more of a cliché? I think I'm doing something alternative, but the truth is I'd know a lot more if I could have been bothered to study medicine or even chemistry. Turns out Janus was right: I *am* an idiot.

*

Something about this guy has loosened my mouth. And three things have become abundantly clear: He's a real worry, he's smart, and he's cute. Why do intelligent guys mess around like this? The analyst in me is watching every muscle twitch under his decorated skin, but all the doctor in me sees is red flashing lights. I've only been working in the ER for a couple of weeks, but I've had a few people walk out after treatment, and I understand the money thing.

The nurse, whose name I've now remembered—Melanie—comes back in with a set of scrubs and pieces of the patient's clothing. She raises her eyebrows at me.

"Ah, we had to cut off your clothes," I say.

He blinks at me, and then his lips turn up in a wolfish grin, gray eyes dancing between his thick lashes. My cheeks burn.

"Did *you* do that?"

I fold my arms and open my mouth, but he shakes his head and flaps a hand at me, taking the scrubs Melanie is offering.

"It's fine. It's fine."

I learned in my first week here that we can't stop people from leaving; they just need to sign the piece of paper that absolves us of all responsibility in case they expire on the way home. I don't think this guy is going to die but getting home might be a struggle.

"Where do you live?"

"Brooklyn."

A slight tremor is running through his hands, and his eyes go unfocused every now and again. He's also wincing from the nausea cramps in his stomach, but they seem to be growing farther apart as the meds kick in. He strips off his hospital gown, and although I've seen his body already, I look away. What am I doing? I'm a doctor! Amusement flickers through his eyes. And there's something about him—the sharp stare, long ropey muscles over a skinny frame: He's like a panther, all coiled strength and danger. But cold memories of another man, a disaster like this one, seep up in me. Melanie coughs, raises her eyebrows at me, and hands me a clipboard.

"I need your signature on this form to say you've checked yourself out against medical advice."

He nods, and the way he inclines his head and doesn't ask any questions makes me think he's done this before. He pulls on the pants, not in the least bit embarrassed, and his right bicep bunches as he takes the clipboard from me and scribbles on the form. He knew where to sign; there was no hesitation, no looking for the box. Have I missed something here? I scan his body. Maybe these tattoos are hiding other things, marks on his skin? Dammit, I need to check whether we've got any notes on him on the system.

"Be careful, okay?" I say. "You're likely to pass out if you try and move too quickly; go as slow as you can and rest often. Can you afford a cab home?" The thought of him going under the tracks on a subway line because he lost his balance doesn't bear thinking about.

He nods and waves his hand. "Yeah. And thanks. Thanks for everything. I probably seem ungrateful, but I'm not. I just hate hospitals."

"Why's that?"

He shakes his head. "I'm fine. You don't need to worry about me."

I narrow my eyes at him. "That's not how this works. You're my patient. Promise me you'll come back if your symptoms deteriorate." I give him my best doctor smile, but he just rolls his lips together. I glance down at his feet as he stands, the small, strange marks all over them. His chest is still bare. Close up, the tattoos are some combination of a script I don't recognize plus tiny words that look like they're in English. He coughs, and my eyes shoot up to find him smiling at me. I swallow.

He grabs the top from the bed and shrugs it on, swaying a little, and I grab his elbow to steady him. His skin is smooth and damp under my palm.

"What made you want to be a doctor?" he asks.

I laugh. "I'm not quite one yet. I'm still training."

He stares at me. "Seriously? Jesus, I'd have been more worried if I'd known." His face relaxes into that grin again, and he winks, leaning forward conspiratorially. "Are you sure you gave me the right stuff?"

I shake my head, laughing. This is not the usual way I engage with patients at all. Why am I finding it so hard to maintain my professional distance?

He presses a shaky hand to his chest. "Shit, I'm impressed—given you're still learning."

I'm not going to tell him how little I really understand about drugs or how proficient I've become at bullshit since I started in the ER.

THE TECHBOYS SERIES

THE REFUSAL

THE OUTCAST

All books available now, in paperback and for Kindle, from Amazon.

REVIEWS
AND MORE

I really hope you've enjoyed *The Refusal*, the first book in my *Techboys* series!

If you have, please consider leaving a review on either the book's Amazon page or any review sites that you frequent. Your feedback and support is greatly appreciated.

There are more books to come in the *Techboys* series and I'd be super-excited to share them with you. If you'd like to be the first to hear about the new releases, pre-orders, bonus chapters and special freebies, please join my VIP mailing list:

evemriley.com/signup

Thanks so much!

ACKNOWLEDGMENTS

As the old saying goes, it takes a village to raise a child, and every writer out there knows just how many people it has taken to help them on their journey to completing a novel. This overused cliché has never been truer this past year, and I couldn't be more grateful to all the people who helped get this book to publication during a very difficult time.

To every other independent author out there—the kindness you've shown is more than I could ever have asked for. Thank you for being a part of this journey. Barbara Kellyn, Devin Sloane, Garry Michaels, Izzy Matthews, J. D. Worth, Lisa Tony Fisher, Ruby Rana, Tanya Simons, and Tina Alicea, you have all been so supportive, both with my first forays on Instagram as I built an audience, and when I asked very obvious questions! I have learned so much from you all, and I hope I will be able to return the favor over time. To all the bloggers, influencers, and book fanatics who helped me spread the word about *The Refusal*, thank you. Alli, Alyssa, Amanda, Anne, Annie, Ashley, Ayana, C.G., Chloe, Chrissie, Ciarrah, Clare, Courtney, Danielle, Dodie, Emma, Erica, G.H., Jennie, Jessica, Kat, Lauren, Leigh, Lina, Linda, Lori, Taylor, Shannon, Shay, Vivian and Vivien—this story was able to get out there because of your support. This is for you.

Nicky Melville, you expand my writing horizons every week. Thank you for your patience. To the girls of my writing group: Clare, Eimear, Jan, Jill, Kirsty, and Moira—you have improved my writing, listened to me moan, been positive when the writing was dreadful, and are amazing, patient, tolerant, and all round wonderful people. I couldn't ask for a better group to spend my Friday mornings with, and I'm honored to call you my friends. A heartfelt thanks to Gavin Inglis whose writing classes were so much fun and who taught me how to structure a book.

To my earlier readers and wonderful editors: Sam Boyce, Alyssa Matessic, and Robert Tuesley Anderson. Not only have you been extremely patient with all my questions, this book has been immeasurably improved by your expert input. Thank you for helping me complete a story that I can be proud of. Sam, you were the first person to read this book in full, and without your enthusiasm for it, I don't think it would ever have seen the light of day. Lorna and Linda, you were my first proper audience and I am very grateful for all your positive and thoughtful feedback.

Mark Thomas, you produced a wonderful cover and eventually persuaded this nervous author to run with it! Thank you for all your hard work on the cover and the interiors of this book, and for always being flexible and cooperative.

To my family Rob, Grace, and Joe—thank you for your unfailing cheerfulness and conviction that I was writing a best seller! To my very own Techboy, Rob— thank you for supporting me through this hare-brained scheme to write. You have encouraged me at every point along the way, and there have been many extra meals made, and children sorted while I have been feverishly writing or editing. I appreciate everything you do for me, every day.

To Grace, my wonderful daughter and partner in crime in getting this novel to market. Your work on all the marketing for this book has been nothing short of amazing: I couldn't have done it without you.

To everyone who reads this book or recommends it to a friend—thank you from the bottom of my heart. All books are important, and authors put years of effort into them. It means so much to me that you've enjoyed reading a story as much as I have enjoyed writing it. I am looking forward to many more happy years working on Janus and Jo and their friend's stories.

ABOUT THE AUTHOR

Scottish-based author Eve Riley was born in Dunfermline, a small picturesque town in Fife. After graduating with a degree in Mathematics, she worked in advertising agencies for ten years before setting up her own market research company, which she ran successfully for twenty years. She then began working with technology startups, which spawned the ideas for *The Refusal*. Over the last eight years she has been pursuing her childhood dream of writing.

Her romance series The Techboys Series revolves around three young men, Janus, Fabian, and Adam, who by chance sit next to each other in their first computer science lecture at college. Their contrasting personalities result in them helping each other out, and, as they rescue one another from various scrapes, a deep bond develops. The books meet them years later in New York City as they struggle to get their lives on track.

Eve lives in Edinburgh with her husband and has two grown-up children.

Janus and Jo's story, *The Refusal*, is the first novel in The *Techboys* Series, and will be followed by a further seven novels exploring Fabian and Kate's, Liss's and Adam's unfolding stories.

Discover more about Eve via her website:
www.evemriley.com
You can also connect with her on social media:
www.instagram.com/evemriley
www.goodreads.com/author/show/21475584.Eve_M_Riley